MURDER IN THE MOUNTAINS

A Sheriff Elven Hallie Mystery

DREW STRICKLAND

www.drewstricklandbooks.com

For Sara,
my soulmate, my best friend, and my biggest supporter

JOIN MY READER'S LIST

Members of my Reader's List get free books and cool behind the scenes information to go along with them.

They're also always the first to hear about my new books and promotions going on.

To be a part of the Reader's List and get your free book, sign up at:

https://drewstricklandbooks.com/mail-list/

CHAPTER ONE

MONEY.

Just holding it made him feel better about himself. The way the paper felt against his fingertips as he pushed one bill past the other. The various conditions of the bills had some wrinkled and old, having seen many different hands over the years, while others were fairly crisp, probably less than a year old if he were to take a guess. Sometimes they felt so new, it was almost as if they were fake.

But he knew the difference between a real bill and a fake one.

Money made him feel bigger than he knew he was. But what was even more impressive was his ability to talk people out of it. To have them give it to him freely just because of the way he was able to say things. To make them feel about it.

The people who handed him the money weren't reluctant to do so, no, they were more than happy with their decision. They couldn't wait to open their wallets and throw as much of it as they could at him.

And the more money he got, the more powerful he became to get more money from people. It was a cycle that never ended.

And he loved it.

Spencer Caldwell sat in his chair behind a folding table. It was rickety and had seen some years, but he still hung onto it. It traveled well and a part of him felt like to change it out would be a disservice to the many years it had put in for him.

What could he say? Sometimes he was a little sentimental that way. And a little cheap.

But the table did its job. The grassy ground beneath his feet was soft, which was a nice change from their last place in Tennessee. Where they had set up shop there had been way too firm for him. Just walking on it had made his back hurt, no matter how cushioned his insoles were.

He set the cash down and stretched his arms out wide. He could graze both sides of the tent walls with his fingers when he did it. The fabric was heavy and rough, but that too had seen some time with him on his travels. It was a pain to set up and tear down, which was why he paid someone else to do it.

The thickness was necessary to keep the cold out, though in the other tent, the one that was big and held all the people who wanted to hear him speak, was a bit too much, holding onto the stench and heat from all the bodies, and making everyone sweat more than he would have liked.

Plus, the weight of the fabric made the bottom heap onto the forest floor, keeping all the animals and other creepy crawlies out. He shivered at the thought of something coming into his tent as he slept on his mattress in the corner.

The traveling life wasn't easy, but it was the best way he knew to make money. Though he truly hoped to find a more permanent place to set up shop now that he had his newer business ventures to attend to.

The opening to his tent flapped as if someone were knocking on it. It sounded like someone shaking out a parachute instead of a solid knock on wood.

"What is it?" Spencer asked, irritated he was being bothered so late.

The tent flap opened and in stepped Michaela. She was mousy, her skin pale. She always had that shy way about her, as if her head was trying to shrug into her shoulders like a turtle.

Spencer stared at her, impatiently waiting for her to spit it out.

She shifted her weight on her hips for a moment, trying to come up with the words. She could be a real pain in his ass sometimes. But she was his cousin, and because of that, he still felt the need to take care of her. Even if she didn't deserve any of it.

"What is it?" Spencer asked.

"S-S-S-Someone is here," she finally said.

"And? What do they want? Did you tell them we're closed for business?" He growled as he spoke. He hated his time being wasted with problems that had obvious solutions and didn't need his attention. "Both types of business," he added with a smirk.

She nodded. "H-H-He won't leave. S-Says he n-needs to see you."

"Oh, Jesus Christ," Spencer said, knowing that nobody who mattered was there to hear him take the Lord's name in vain. He knew when to keep up appearances. And when none of it mattered.

"S-S-Sorry," Michaela said.

He slammed his hands on the rickety table and stood. "Don't say *s-s-sorry* to me. What good are you anyway? I'll deal with it. You should find something useful to do, like bury the shit in the outhouse so the only thing to attract the flies around here is you."

Spencer pushed past his cousin and left her in whatever mental state she found herself in. Dumb, scared, completely blank. He didn't care. His words might be harsh, but to him, they were necessary. Sometimes an idiot had to be called out. They needed to know where they stood in life.

The night air was cold as he stepped out into it. As much as he might complain about the ground being too hard or too soft, or the smell of the outhouse, he actually liked being out in nature. There was a peace to not being surrounded by a bunch of strangers in buildings.

He passed from his small tent and into the large tent where they did their sermons and presentations. Even with having aired it out and not having a full house inside, it still clung on to the body heat from the afternoon. At least there was no foul stench of body odor to accompany it.

It was much different at night, the chairs now having been put away and stacked to the side on one large wall. It was just one big open room, lit by the battery-powered lanterns that hung from the wood posts driven into the ground.

A man stood at the opposite end of the tent, his back to Spencer with his arms crossed behind him. He was a larger man who held himself tall. It looked as if he was admiring the place where Spencer stood when he gave his sermons.

"This is a very nice set-up you have here," the man said, not turning around.

"Well, thank you for that, sir," Spencer said graciously, trying to size the man up.

It was obvious that whoever he was had a few decades on Spencer. And that he was a man to be respected. Spencer could tell that from the way he stood and spoke. Like he knew he was important.

"I like to give praise where I see fit, even if it isn't quite my thing," the older man said.

He turned around and Spencer tried to rack his brain for whether he had seen him before. He doubted it, at least just from the way this man seemed to be admiring the set-up. If he had been to one of Spencer's sermons, then it wouldn't be something to comment on now.

But Spencer wasn't familiar with that many people in the area. The county and town of Dupray was just another shithole of a place to travel to while he tried to find where he could best serve the community.

And make a lot of money doing it, of course.

The older man was much bigger than he was, so much so that

Spencer felt like he was being intimidated by just standing in front of him. The man had a beard on his chin that wasn't too long, but fairly cropped against his face. Spencer thought if he shaved his cheeks, he might look a little like Colonel Sanders himself, just with less white hair.

"I appreciate the comments, but I'm sorry to say we are currently closed right now," Spencer said congenially. "We'll be set up tomorrow morning and going into the late afternoon if you'd like to come by for a sermon."

The man smiled, his beard turning as he did. "No, I'm actually not here for that," he said. "Though I hear it is something to see."

Spencer furrowed his brow. "If you're looking for a more one-on-one style counseling session, I could squeeze you in. I don't mean to be so forward, but it is late, so I'll come right out and say that those sessions are more based on a donation for my time."

The man chuckled, looking Spencer up and down, like he was sizing him up. "I'm sure it is. And I don't doubt that you can really rake it in. Though Dupray is a bit of a black hole when it comes to money and faith."

Spencer was starting to grow more impatient than he already was when he'd had to leave his tent. Usually, he'd be on his best behavior, charming the shit out of this guy with his silver tongue. His gift of gab.

But this man seemed to want none of it, and he was being cryptic with his reason for being there. So Spencer decided being forward was the best approach.

"What is it you want then?" Spencer finally asked.

"I just wanted to stop in, see how things were going. See how the community was treating you. They seem to like you a lot. From the way they speak in town, wow, I'd say there was something special here. On top of that, Sunday services have grown thin down at the churches in town, let me tell you."

Spencer could tell where this was going and he wasn't going to have any of it.

"I mean, don't get me wrong," the man said. "Church attendance is always a bit sparse, the population being what it is. The disappointment in town being what it is. But there has been a noticeable difference since you showed up."

"I hate to say it, friend," Spencer began, "but if someone like me can roll through town and get people to come out and worship with me, then maybe they weren't truly your congregation to begin with. I mean, what kind of loyalty is that if they're so quick to leave?"

The man nodded, stepping closer to Spencer to bolster the intimidation factor. Except this time, Spencer knew that was his intention.

"I know there's something else going on here. I know what and who you are, so I'm giving you the chance right here and now," the man said. "Tomorrow is your last day here. Give the best presentation you can. I'm telling you, get crazy with it and go all out."

He pointed to the large open space where the front row would normally sit, the divots in the ground lined up from where the chair legs dug into the earth.

"Get ten people in wheelchairs right up front and throw them on the ground so they can walk right here in front of everyone. Get a blind man here, spit in his eyes and claim he can see. Hell, get an old woman with IBS to have her first solid shit in twenty years right in the front row for all I care."

It was the most animated the man had been since Spencer had started talking to him. It looked like he was having fun coming up with all the ways he could make fun of the revival.

When he was done, he returned to his position in front of Spencer, even closer so that Spencer could smell the tobacco on his breath.

"But you best be gone by the morning after tomorrow."

Spencer clenched his jaw, staring up at the man. He wanted so badly to pop him right in the jaw, and he wasn't even a fighter. But that wouldn't end well for him, and it wasn't his style of comebacks. He just didn't like being threatened.

"I can see you are quite the respected man around here," Spencer said, taking a step back, trying to get into his groove. "I can tell by the way you carry yourself. The way you speak to a man like me. And I appreciate your coming here to demonstrate, quite animatedly I might add, your lack of knowledge about what we do here.

"But we have permission from the governor himself to be out here. And that's not something that I'd want to mess with if I were you. No matter what your position may be locally."

The man nodded, seeming to appreciate Spencer's words. At least, enough to not lash out. "That is a funny thing," he said. "Strange that the governor, or the state I should say...I highly doubt the governor himself really had anything to do with it. But that they would give you permission during hunting season like this seems like it's an accident waiting to happen."

He walked by Spencer, making sure to brush his shoulder as he did.

Spencer spun around. "Thanks again for coming out. My invite still stands to come tomorrow."

The man didn't say another word as he exited the tent. Spencer's heart pounded in his chest, but he couldn't decide if it was from anger or fear.

CHAPTER TWO

ABOUT AN HOUR BEFORE BEARING WITNESS TO ONE OF THE MOST disgusting and foul-smelling scenes in his career, Sheriff Elven Hallie was in his Jeep, heading to the station.

The early mornings were always his favorite. Usually, he would sit out on his deck, watching the sun rise while in nothing more than his birthday suit. Except for socks. Sometimes the deck was a little too cold on his feet as the fall wore thin and winter started to shoulder its way in.

But today, he decided a leisurely drive to the station was in order. The road being as quiet as it was could be enough to clear his mind before his day started. The winding road that took him down from his house on the hill, the uneven dirt road taking him from the hill and to the main stretch of road that led him straight to Dupray Proper was sometimes all he needed.

Though that was usually if his ride was in silence.

But today did not go as planned. He knew he should have sat on his deck, letting the breeze flow over his skin, cold or not. At least he could have had some peace.

Instead, once he reached the main road to take him to town, his radio clicked on and he knew there would be no hope of peace.

"Elven, you up and out?" Meredith asked over a static laden channel.

He let out a long sigh and glanced out the window. The orange and brown leaves were becoming sparse and he knew that snow would arrive eventually. The radio clicked one more time, reminding him he still had a job to do.

He grabbed the radio from the console and held it in his hand, pushing the button down. He managed to keep the Jeep steady with his left hand, grateful that he had already made it off the hill. Otherwise he might have considered putting it in park.

"Yeah, Meredith, I'm up. Are you in the office already?" he asked.

Of course she was, he thought before she ever answered. Meredith was one of the hardest working and most loyal people he had ever known. It wasn't unusual for her to be manning the station this early—he just thought it was unusual that there would be much to do at this hour.

But as in past times, he was proven wrong.

"Just got a call from Frank Dority," Meredith said. Her voice was calm as usual with no note of panic. But then again, even in the worst situations, she was able to keep her composure.

"Over at the Dority farm?" Elven asked.

"You know another Frank Dority?"

He waited, knowing he didn't. She was straight to business this morning.

"Anyway, he was rantin' and ravin' about something on the phone. Kept saying it was a murder—no, a massacre."

"A massacre?" Elven repeated.

"His words, not mine. But Elven..."

"Yeah, Meredith?"

"I heard some gunshots in the background on the call. And then I heard two blasts of a shotgun, much closer than those in the background."

Elven bit his lip, trying to make sense of what could be going on at Dority's farm.

"You want me to send Tank? He says he's up for it," she said.

Elven knew Tank would be up for something like that. Or anything at all, considering he'd been kept to office duties since taking some buckshot on that Hawkins case. But Meredith had called him for a reason, and it wasn't because he would be there thirty minutes earlier than Tank could. Meredith's voice was steady and calm, but he could still tell she was worried.

"No, I'll head straight there," Elven said, clipping the receiver down on the console.

He spun his vehicle around in the opposite direction, slamming his foot on the gas, hoping he could get there before anything bad happened, if it hadn't already.

CHAPTER THREE

THE SCENE WAS CALM FROM ELVEN'S VANTAGE POINT AS HE pulled his Jeep onto the Dority property. The wood-paneled house sat at the front of the land, with muddy puddles speckling throughout the walkway up to the door. The white paint was worn on the wooden structure, but not peeling. Frank Dority took care of his property as best as someone could with very little money.

Elven opened the car door and stepped out, planting his boots onto the soft dirt underneath them. The first thing that hit him was the smell. He didn't make it a habit to visit Frank Dority's farm, but on the few occasions he had, he didn't remember it smelling so foul. It was a mixture of rotting death and something else. Something fecal.

But it wasn't the usual manure scent he would have figured. This was nearly unearthly. He quickly took to breathing through his mouth, but that ended quicker than it started when the taste of the air settled on the back of his tongue.

He hocked up something nasty and spit it out, carrying away the taste with it. He hated spitting, along with the regularity of the act that some people took to it. But desperate times...or something like that.

Elven thought about running up to the house and knocking on the door to check on Frank. But Meredith had given him so little to go on, other than shotgun blasts and background gunfire, it didn't seem like the type of situation to approach the front door as if he was asking to borrow a cup of a sugar.

He reached in the Jeep and pulled the rifle down from the mount on the partition behind the front seats. He wasn't much of a shot with the rifle, but it was better to be prepared and not need it than wish he had it. Being that Dority had a large field behind his home, Elven wasn't sure if he'd need something longer range than his pistol.

"Dority?" he called out from behind the Jeep.

There was no sense in sneaking around, trying to get the jump on something he didn't know about. It was more likely he'd get shot by the man himself. From the way Meredith had described, he was pretty wound up.

"Frank Dority," Elven called out again, this time louder.

There was no answer.

He let out a long sigh and stepped around his Jeep. A cool morning breeze brushed past the exposed skin where his shirt collar was open and he felt a shiver run up his spine. Along with the chill, it carried a stronger whiff of the foul stench, filling his nose again. He held back his breakfast from coming up.

At least the sun was peeking above the horizon enough that he could make out the details without needing any extra light.

He pounded his fist against the screen door, causing it to rattle against the frame.

"Dority, you in there?" he shouted.

"Sheriff?" a voice asked. But it wasn't coming from inside. It sounded further away, slightly muffled.

"Dority, that you?"

"I'm 'round the back," Frank Dority answered.

Elven grumbled, wondering what was going on. Frank didn't sound like he was in trouble. In fact, he sounded spry, like he was having fun.

As soon as he walked around the side, leaving the creaky wooden porch, a much stronger stench of that same fecal death invaded his very being. He quickly brought his forearm up to his nose, the scent of his worn, musky jacket thankfully taking over.

"Dority, is someone dead over there?" Elven asked, his mouth rushing full of saliva, letting him know he was only moments away from vomiting.

"Heh, no, ain't no person dead Sheriff. Not yet anyways," Frank Dority reassured.

Elven stepped around the house and found himself looking down the barrel of a double-gage shotgun. It was about two feet in front of his face. He quickly ducked and lunged forward, grabbing the barrel with his hands and shoving it to the sky.

"Christ, Elven, I ain't gonna shoot ya," Dority said, his raspy voice bordering on anger, as if Elven was the one in the wrong.

"You're lucky I didn't shoot you where you stood," Elven said, his heart still pounding in his chest.

He hesitantly let go of the barrel, making sure the old timer didn't point it back down at him. Once he was sure it was just a mistake, Elven took a look at the man.

Frank Dority was a peculiar one. He mostly kept to himself, but not in a hermit-like way. Everyone in town had nothing but good things to say about him. He was just old and didn't get out of his home much. His wife had died about four years back, and now it was just him and the animals.

About the only time anyone saw him in town was when he was getting a haircut or doing his every-other-month grocery supply run. Usually, they happened at the same time. Most people knew him as Frank, but Elven knew him as Dority. It was a holdover from when Elven was a kid. *Mr. Dority.* Elven had known him a long time and the best he could muster up was dropping the "mister" when he spoke to him, even though he'd been an adult longer than he'd been a child now.

Dority was closing in on eighty years and had a wardrobe to

match. But that was the way in Dupray, for most people anyway. He had mended the jeans he wore at least ten times over with random scraps of fabric. Elven wondered how long the old man could keep his fingers that nimble.

Dority put a hand on his back and stretched, shoving his pelvis forward. Two hard pops came and he stood much taller than the C shape he was in when Elven had been surprised by him.

"What am I doing here, Dority?" Elven asked. "Meredith said you were going on about a massacre. She said something about gunshots, too."

Dority grinned. "You betcha. It wasn't as dire as I first thought, but I ran 'em into the woods just now."

"Who?"

"The bastards that did this," Frank Dority said, hobbling his way toward the field in front of them. He motioned with his left hand for Elven to follow.

In the distance, Elven could see a small pen where he knew the pigs rolled around in the mud. He wondered if that's where the smell was coming from, but it was far to the left, and Dority was taking them to the chicken coops. The closer they got, the worse the smell became.

Elven was past trying to cover it up, swallowing constantly and trying to keep the upchuck at bay. He was mostly doing a good job with it.

The chicken coop wasn't some tiny backyard coop where a small family could raise a couple of chickens. Frank Dority had some land, passed down from a couple of generations, and it was all paid off. But he refused to sell it to make any *real* money. Instead, he tended to his animals and lived off of what he needed.

The coop was probably five times the size of what Elven would have expected to be in someone's backyard. Dority sold chickens at the market, or traded them with other farmers for whatever it was he needed. Parts of the coop looked to be made from solid wood, while other places had been mended with whatever scraps Dority could come up with. Chicken wire wrapped and encased the whole thing.

But it was when they walked around to the other side that Elven saw it and got a front row seat to what was causing the smell.

There was a huge hole in the backside of the fence. The wire was twisted and torn to create a jagged edge. Most of the chickens were still inside, unharmed. But there were about four dead chickens outside the coop, their necks flopped to the side. In the hole of the coop was one chicken, its neck caught in the mangled mesh. It hung loose, its feet barely grazing the ground. Blood was pooled underneath it, with the front of its white feathers stained red. When it got caught in the mesh, it looked like it panicked and sliced its own throat open wide.

"Ah my goodness, Dority," Elven said with a grimace.

Frank Dority looked at Elven as if he was now the peculiar one. Then he shook his head, turning back to the chickens.

"That ain't the worst of it," Dority said, pointing to the back.

He was right. It was bad, but that wasn't where the smell was coming from. The smell was further back, and in the front, and all over.

"I thought chicken coops were supposed to not stink so bad," Elven said.

"Maybe for them fancy city folk, working for the big names in the industry. Got them fancy fans and equipment to deal with circulation. It ain't supposed to be this bad though. Nobody's supposed to be running in here, smearing chicken shit all over the place," Dority said.

And that's what it was. Chicken excrement was scattered, or more like pasted, all over the place. It looked like something had gotten inside, dug around, and had themselves quite the time inside. Elven wasn't that familiar with chicken poop, but he was pretty sure it wasn't supposed to be like this.

Not only that, but it was a lot. It was like Dority hadn't cleaned it in quite some time, letting it pile up and up. Whatever had gotten inside had cracked whatever seal had formed over the top of the poop, reconstituting it with the mud and leftover puddles from the recent rains.

It was the worst thing Elven had ever smelled in his life. And that was saying something in Dupray.

And suddenly, a gust of wind picked up, throwing the stench right into his face. He bent over, dry heaving, just barely holding the vomit in. The last thing he wanted to do was taste his morning smoothie back the way it came.

"Not so used to this, eh?" Dority asked wryly.

"Not so much," Elven admitted. "That's a lot of chicken crap."

Dority shrugged. "Was gonna get to cleanin' it this weekend, but guess today's the day now."

"So that's it? What did this? You said you chased something into the woods?" Elven asked, looking into the forest that backed Dority's property.

Dority let out a raspy laugh. "Ain't something that did this. It was some*one*. A couple of 'em."

Elven stood tall, looking at the old man in front of him. "Did you kill them?"

Dority continued his raspy laugh, like everything Elven said was some comedy act.

"Sheriff, you sure do have an imagination. I ain't killed anybody. I told you no person was dead."

"So this is the massacre? The chickens?" Elven asked.

"You bet yer ass this is it. They might just be chickens to you, but they're how I make my living. Sellin' and eatin'."

Elven shook his head, wishing he had let Tank take this call instead of rushing to the scene to investigate this *massacre*.

"Alright, so you said you ran them off into the woods. Get a look at them?" Elven asked.

Dority grinned, spreading his wrinkled lips taut. "I did one better than that. Those boys out there ain't got no way to escape. The brush is too thick to exit on any end. They have to come back this way to get out. So they just been hiding out for now."

Elven looked into the trees as the sun lit up the forest. It was still too dark and too thick to see very far in.

"But I ain't going nowhere!" Dority shouted at the trees.

Just after he said it, the branches rustled in the thick forest. Elven stepped in front of Dority, gripping his rifle tightly in front of him. He didn't plan on pointing it at anything until he knew who he was up against. But to him, if they took off running away from an old man like Frank Dority, they weren't looking for a fight.

With one blink, Elven saw a figure dart out from the trees. It was a man, disheveled and muddy, sprinting as fast as he could to the side after he came out of the woods. He was not on the attack, but looked like a confused and scared man searching for an exit.

Elven loosened his grip on the rifle and started to step out, but Dority grabbed his arm from behind.

"Out of the way, Sheriff," Dority growled, putting his shoulder into Elven.

Dority was surprisingly forceful for his age. Elven stumbled to the side as he watched Dority raise his shotgun toward the fleeing man. Before Elven could stop him, he pulled the trigger.

The shotgun went off and Elven's ears rang as if a flash grenade went off near him. *What a great way to start the day*, he thought, before grabbing the shotgun from Dority before he could take another shot at the man trying to get away.

Dority frowned at Elven. "Give it back," he demanded.

"You just shot at a man who was running away from you," Elven shouted, still barely able to hear his own voice. "I might be taking you in for murder."

CHAPTER FOUR

DORITY LET OUT THAT LAUGH AGAIN. "AIN'T NOBODY DEAD. IT'S just birdshot."

Elven took one glance at Dority before running to the man who was now face down in the mud. Elven held both his rifle and Dority's shotgun as he ran. He had no intention of using either of them, but he didn't want Dority to get another bug up his rear and go off shooting again.

Elven reached the man, who was face down in the mud, moaning. He was wide-set, but nothing Elven couldn't handle. He rolled him to the side and the man screamed in agony. Elven took a good look at his bearded face, caked with mud, and realized it was Tony, the local drunk. He was filthy, covered in mud, and smelled a lot like the chicken coop. And, on top of that, he reeked of booze, with a touch of day-old vomit. Elven supposed that part was nothing new.

"Tony, what in Heaven's name are you doing here?" Elven asked.

"Oh Jesus, Elven. Fuck, it hurts so bad," Tony said, writhing on the ground. The bits of flesh Elven could see through the mud on Tony's face were red and blue, as if he was going to pass out at any moment.

"Where'd you get hit?" Elven asked.

Tony grabbed at his leg with both hands and Elven tried to see where he was injured. Tony rolled back onto his front, screaming as he did.

"Oh God, Elven! Help me. Oh shit, it hurts so bad!" Tony cried.

Elven looked at the back of Tony's thigh and saw where the shotgun blast had hit him. Even thought it was birdshot, Elven knew that at the right range or scattering, it could still kill a man. But where Tony's leg had taken the hit was nothing like that.

In fact, it looked like there was only one small pellet that had pierced Tony's leg. The rest of it had missed him completely. If Elven hadn't seen it himself, he would have thought Tony was shot with a BB gun.

Elven rolled his eyes. "Tony, I'm no expert here, but I'd say you're gonna live."

"It ain't that," Tony said with a clenched jaw. "When I took a dive down, I got my pecker all twisted up in my underwear. Oh Jesus, I think my testicles are on top."

Elven pushed Tony back onto his back. He couldn't tell where his shirt ended and the mud began with how filthy the man was.

"Sit up," Elven commanded.

Tony tried to lift himself, but was having issues, grabbing at his crotch. He was a complete mess, with the mud, excrement, and most likely still being drunk from the night before. Elven shook his head, letting the man figure himself out.

"Sheriff, there's more of them out there and they got guns," Dority said, trying to meet up with Elven. His running ability was a combination of skips and hobbles.

Elven turned to the woods and stuck his fingers in his mouth, letting out a loud whistle.

"Anyone out there who doesn't want to get shot, come on out with your hands and guns in the air! This is the sheriff speaking!" Elven yelled.

A few branches cracked before five men came walking out of the woods. They were of varying heights, but all looked dirty and muddy. It looked like they'd been out in the elements for quite some time, but given the dense foliage behind Dority's property, Elven imagined just a few hours could make them look like that.

They each held a rifle above their heads, in a non-threatening way. Tony was the only one who appeared to not have a weapon. Elven wondered if he had left it in the woods or if he didn't have one at all.

"These friends of yours, Tony?" Elven asked.

Tony looked to the four men and gave a small nod, still grimacing in pain.

"He gonna live?" the tallest man asked.

"He'll be fine. Might need to get a pellet dug out of him, and maybe one stitch," Elven said, then frowned at him. "Who are you and what are you doing out here? Hunting season is starting up, but not on private property."

The man in front motioned with his hands and rifle, wanting to put them down. Elven nodded, making sure he did it slowly.

The five rifles were put down on the ground slow. It satisfied Elven enough to motion to them to put their hands down.

"I'm Herb, this is Dan, that there is Tim, and Scotty and Brandon in the back," Herb said. Herb was lanky, with a beard that reached the center of his chest. Dan was a miniature version of Herb, by about a two-foot difference. And Tim was completely clean-shaven, but had a beer belly the size of West Virginia itself. Scotty was shy and kept his eyes down, as did Brandon.

Elven couldn't help but chuckle. "Five of you, plus Tony makes six. Ain't nobody gonna say that you can't handle your business, Dority."

Dority spit at the side with a nod, proud as ever.

"Alright, Herb, I'm Sheriff Elven Hallie. I know who Tony is, but I don't recognize the five of you. Not sure how this all happened, but looks like there's been some property damage here."

"We didn't do that," Dan protested, his voice strained.

"Bullshit," Dority said.

Herb put a hand out to Dan and turned back to Elven. "It's true. We met Tony here at the bar last night. We like to go shooting vermin. A lot of coyotes, too. We ain't game hunters. Ain't no good at that, but people pay us for the small stuff if we bring it in sometimes.

"Tony told us a good place to find some critters. Came out here, went shooting some animals, and then he went all batshit on the farm here, saying something about he was a chicken and he was gonna get in his house. I tell ya, I ain't never seen anything like it. I thought he lost his damn mind."

Elven looked at Tony, who slumped his shoulders in shame. "That true, Tony?"

Tony shrugged. "I don't remember much. Had a lot to drink at the bar, then brought out a bottle of JD with us."

Elven looked over by the chicken coop and saw a completely empty bottle of whiskey. He shook his head.

"I mean it, Sheriff. Me and my boys can put it away, but I ain't never seen anyone drink like that fella there," Herb said.

That did sound like the Tony Elven knew. "That's why you smell like chicken poop?" Elven asked Tony.

Tony nodded, still hanging his head in shame. "I may have shit in the coop, too. Think I got it on myself. It's hard to tell what's what."

Elven sighed and looked to Dority. "You wanna press charges?"

Dority did not look happy. "I want my chicken coop fixed. They killed my chickens, too."

"We had nothing to do with that," Herb reiterated. "It was all Tony, I swear. He started clucking like them when he was in the coop and—"

Elven raised his hand. "I think we get it. You didn't do this."

He turned to Dority. "Look, Dority, I can take Tony in for the damages, but you won't get your chickens back or your coop fixed. You and I both know that taking Tony to court will just waste a lot of time and money, and neither one of you's got any of that to spare. These other boys were trespassing, but that's about it. If you let it go,

I'm sure Tony will come out, fix your coop, and tend to anything else you might have that needs fixing."

Dority snarled his lip, like he wasn't sure about any of it. But Elven could tell by the look on his face that he thought Elven was right, even if he didn't like it.

"Isn't that right, Tony?" Elven asked.

Tony groaned what sounded like a yes.

"Once he gets his pecker situation resolved, that is," Elven said, then headed back to his Jeep.

CHAPTER FIVE

THE AIR WAS COOL, MUCH COOLER THAN SHE WAS USED TO. Having lived in Arizona most of her life, the chill of the fall in Dupray was worse than the worst days of winter in Mesa. She dreaded the upcoming weather shift in the coming weeks. Snow was great for a visit, but she had never lived through a real winter.

It was going to take a lot of getting used to.

She zipped her jacket the last inch to her collar, knowing she was twice as bundled up as everyone else in Dupray. But they could all fuck off for all she cared. She didn't have a lot of love for anyone in the county, mostly because she barely knew anyone.

And those she did know, she either despised or had betrayed.

She took a deep breath as she approached the doors to the station. She didn't see Elven's Jeep out front, which was unusual. He was the type who was first in, last out. Unless he was called away early in the morning.

And being Dupray, it was probably to birth a cow or maybe help some old guy get the hinges off the door to his trailer so he could get his junkie daughter out of the bathroom. She wouldn't say she hated

Dupray, but she hadn't had a ton of good experiences in the town so far.

Though she wasn't one to talk. Being who she was, being related to who she was, and running from her previous life, she was part of the problem.

Before she could reach the door, she heard the footsteps behind her. No words, but she put her hand on her gun and was ready to spin around.

"Deputy, don't think you'll be needing that," Hollis said in his usual fatherly tone.

But he was far from a father to her. Or maybe he was. One that manipulated and abused his kids, making them feel like they were worthy of his praise as long as they did what he asked of them.

How her mom had tolerated him at all was a mystery to her. But then again, maybe it was why she got out of town all those years ago.

"Hollis, what the hell are you doing here? What if someone sees?" she asked, her voice low in case anyone could hear.

Hollis smiled wide, his face wrinkling as he did, yet giving off a calming feel. If she didn't know what he was capable of, she would have been won over by it. It's how he was able to gain his status in the town.

"What do you mean? Sees what? A concerned citizen making a report to the deputy sheriff in this fine county," he said.

She paused to look at him. He presented himself well. His jeans and plaid shirt were worn. He still looked like he belonged in Dupray, among the others who lived in the holler. But he dressed it up nicely. He could easily afford better than what he wore. She knew that everything he did was about presentation.

She put her head down, like she was trying to keep a low profile, even though anyone who saw her would know exactly who she was. The Dupray Sheriff's Department emblem on her jacket sealed that deal.

She approached Hollis cautiously. "Look, I don't feel great about any of this, okay? Elven is a good guy and what I'm doing with you, it just doesn't seem right."

She met Hollis's eyes and could see the understanding in them. Maybe she had gotten him wrong. Sure, she knew he was capable of a lot of things, but he was still a man. And he was family. At least, that's what he kept telling her.

"I understand your turmoil," Hollis said. "And you are absolutely right. Elven is a good man. Hell, he might be the best man I've ever met. On the right day, depending on the weather, if asked, I might admit that this county doesn't deserve him at all.

"But Maddison, I don't care if it don't feel right. Hell, none of it is, but then you and I both know that. But you came to me. You're the one who needs help. Running out here with your crocodile tears, no place to go. If you want, you can run on back home to the hot Arizona desert you came from. I'm sure your husband will be thrilled to see you."

Maddison swallowed hard. Just the mention of her husband, not even by name, was enough to get through to her. The last thing she wanted was to go back to that nightmare. And being Hollis's snitch and spy, doing his dirty work, was better than that alternative.

"What do you want?" she asked.

He grinned. "I knew you'd see it my way. Why don't I buy you something to eat later for my appreciation?"

She didn't respond. She would do what he asked, but she didn't have to play nice, either.

"I suppose you're right. Straight to business, then. I need you to keep an eye on some things for me," he said.

She shrugged. "Yeah, isn't that what I'm already doing?"

"Smart girl," he said. "This is a bit specific. Let's say I'm running some business ventures I want Elven to stay out of, alright?"

"Okay, yeah. Why now? Was he already looking into it? Or is it something new you're dealing with?" she asked. The more information she had, the faster she could understand how to keep Elven out of it.

Hollis shrugged. "I don't want to get too detailed with my involvement."

"Thank God," she said, not able to help herself.

He took it in stride and kept the conversation moving. "My customer base seems to be thinning. Now I'd know if people in the county were dying at the rate I'm losing them—hell, I think everyone would notice that. But I thought maybe Elven had been sniffing around, picking up some of my customers lately."

She looked at him, fishing for more information. But he wasn't giving it up so easily.

"What business might that be?" she asked.

"Just keep an eye on it," he said. "If you pick up a lot of people lately, you be sure to tell me, alright?"

She threw a hand in the air. "And how the hell am I supposed to know what I'm looking for if you don't give me any sort of idea who these customers of yours are?"

The roar of an engine filled the air and she looked over her shoulder. Elven's Jeep pulled up to the front of the station, mere feet away from their cozy conversation.

Shit.

There was no way he wasn't seeing her standing with Hollis right then and there. She felt her face go flush, the blood escaping from it just as fast as she wished she could escape from the situation she found herself in. The same words kept running through her head.

He's going to know. He's going to know.

And if he knew, then what did that mean for her? She'd be fired for sure, but then Elven would investigate her, and maybe he'd find evidence that she tampered with his investigation. If that happened, then she'd go to jail.

But most of all, she found herself dreading the disappointment she would feel from him. And that shocked her the most.

When she'd accepted Hollis's offer, she hadn't known Elven from the next guy. It was easy when she'd first thought of him as some idiot sheriff that didn't know anything, or maybe even someone that was cruel, who lorded his position over those less fortunate than he. Someone like her ex.

But when she'd met him and worked closely with him, she came to find that this wasn't the case at all. And that didn't make things easier for her. She wished he was the asshole that she'd built him up to be. Then she wouldn't give two fucks about what he thought.

Now she cared more about what Elven thought than what Hollis thought.

She watched the Jeep idle for a moment and saw Elven's eyes on her. He climbed out, but his face wasn't accusatory. It was of concern. He was a kind man, and handsome at that. His jaw was square and his hair just the right amount of sand-speckled color.

Elven immediately shifted toward anger as his gaze went to Hollis.

She watched Elven clench his jaw and make his way to the both of them. She took a much-needed step backward, releasing just a small amount of the claustrophobia from being under Hollis's thumb.

"What's going on here?" Elven asked, keeping his eyes locked on Hollis. "Are you okay, Madds?"

"She's fine," Hollis said in his jovial tone that Madds had come to learn was so rehearsed he could flip the switch whenever he wanted.

"I was talking to my deputy," Elven said.

"I'm fine, Elven."

"She was just helping me with some concerns I had," Hollis continued.

"Concerns?" Elven asked. "About what?"

Hollis shrugged. "Hunting season, I suppose. I hear those woods ain't just filled with animals these days."

"And you came to tell my deputy that?" Elven asked, lifting an eyebrow.

"Would have told you, but you weren't in. I know you don't think much of me, but I don't want to spend my day sitting around waiting just to talk to you. I figured a report is a report, and it can get to you through her."

Elven nodded, looking Hollis up and down. "Didn't think you were much of a hunter? Least not anymore."

Hollis chuckled. "On and off, I suppose. Just not in the typical way you might think." Hollis rubbed his leg that Madds had seen him limp on since the day she met him. She knew there was a story there, but it was nothing she was curious enough about to ask.

"If that's all, then I'll make a note of your *concerns*," Elven said.

Hollis spun around, making his way back to his rusty truck at the end of the parking lot. The one he most definitely didn't need to be using, but did anyway. Always about the appearances.

Madds swallowed hard. It wasn't just about what she was going to make up and tell Elven, though Hollis had mostly covered that for her. But it was about what Hollis had asked of her. To keep an eye on whatever business venture he might have going on. And knowing that whatever it was, it was no good.

CHAPTER SIX

WHAT A WAY TO START HIS MORNING, ELVEN THOUGHT. FIRST, there was a detour to Dority's farm, having to deal with the asinine crime from the six idiots breaking into Frank Dority's chicken coop. And now having to deal with Hollis Starcher before ever stepping into the station.

Elven wished he had taken the time to sit out on his porch, sipping on his smoothie instead of opting for a quiet drive into town. Without his moments to commune with himself, he felt thrown into the chaos of the day with no plan. Actually, he didn't just feel that way—it was that way.

He'd get over it. He always did. If he wanted a peaceful life, he wouldn't have picked such a demanding job. In the end, it was all for the better of the town and the county.

As soon as he and Madds walked into the station, she turned around, her brunette hair brushing over her shoulder. She quickly pulled it back with a hair tie, tossing it into a quick, but messy bun.

"Elven—"

"Are you okay?" Elven asked, not waiting for her to finish.

She looked at him, as if she didn't understand what he was asking. "Me? Am I okay?"

"Yeah, I know how Hollis can be. If he doesn't get what he wants...well, he can get nasty," he said, truly hoping she hadn't met the Hollis he knew.

"Fine. What would he not have gotten?" she asked.

"To speak with me," Elven said. "No offense, but he's not the type to settle on speaking to a deputy, no matter how good they are at the job."

"Oh, right," she said, letting the tension out of her shoulders.

Elven could tell that it had shaken Madds up a bit. He was glad to be of slight relief.

"Good," he said. "Kind of strange for him to come by just to bring up hunting season, so I'm sure that wasn't all he wanted. He's always got his hand in something. Best not to get too close to him though. He seems friendly enough, until you get to know him."

"Don't have to tell me twice," Madds remarked.

"That goes for all the Starchers, come to think of it," Elven added, even though he knew that Lyman and Penny might be different. But his distaste for that family could sometimes have a very broad reach and make him forget the details.

Madds didn't reply, which was good. He didn't want to get into any details about the Starchers, though from the previous case involving them, he'd hoped she could figure it out herself, more or less. Even if they hadn't ended up behind bars as Elven would have liked.

Elven held the door for his deputy, catching a slight whiff of her body wash as she walked by. It wasn't obtrusive, like a perfume overpowering his senses. But it was crisp and clean, allowing anyone that did smell it to form their own opinion of the person. For Elven, it was a pleasant one.

And Elven couldn't help but appreciate the fact that Madds seemed simple when it came down to her routine. He'd known many women who would have woken up an hour earlier to make themselves *presentable*, whatever that meant. Trying too hard to look like they didn't try too hard was more like it. With Madds, though, he was confident that she didn't.

Inside the station, whatever scent Madds carried was quickly overtaken by the cheap carpet smell from decades ago. No matter how many vacuums or shampooers ran over the threads, there was no getting the smell of the seventies out of it. And that was alright with Elven. To him, it was familiar and comforting.

It was much busier than he had planned on it being when he first left his house that morning. Then again, he never planned to make the detour to Dority's farm and have to crack the big case of a broken coop and dead chickens. He let out a long exhale as he took off his hat.

Everyone was in house today. Tank hadn't healed up completely since taking a scattering of buckshot to the side, but he hadn't let that stop him and eagerly jumped back into work as soon as Elven allowed it. It was nice having him back to pick up a lot of the slack, though Elven was still hesitant on letting him take on too much work. Tank was mostly locked down to small tasks in the office. The last thing Elven needed was to get him out on the town, ripping his stitches open.

He was sure Sandra, Tank's wife, wouldn't be too pleased with him either if that happened.

"How'd it go at Dority's?" Meredith asked.

Elven knew she knew the answer. He'd radioed back to her when he was on his way, giving her the broad strokes of what went down. He looked up at her, catching the slight slip of a smirk on her ruby-red lips.

"Everything worked out fine," Elven said.

"Didn't bring anyone in?"

"Be glad I didn't. The smell alone would make you want to take a sick day," he said.

"And today would be the worst day for it," Meredith said,

standing up from the desk, cutting Elven off before he could make his way back to his office.

She handed him a slip of paper, notes scribbled all over it that ignored the fact that there were even lines across the yellow background.

"What's this?" Elven asked.

"Complaints," Meredith said.

Elven breathed in deep as he looked down at the page. Meredith's perfume flooded into his nose, but cut off sharply when she plopped back down in her seat.

"Meredith, just give me the highlights," Elven said, setting the paper down. He knew she'd taken the time to write the notes, but it would be faster if she just gave him the lowdown instead of his having to decipher what each complaint was about.

She sighed, shaking her head as she took the paper from him.

"Maybe you should think about getting glasses," Meredith said, slipping her own pair on.

"Don't need them," Elven said, though now he was beginning to question if that's why he sometimes had trouble deciphering handwritten notes.

"You had four phone calls—"

"This morning?" Elven asked.

She nodded. That was really something, considering the sun had barely made an appearance, he thought.

"About what?"

"If you'd let me finish, then you'd have all that information," Meredith said, bordering on impatient.

Elven kept his mouth shut.

"All hunters. The Johnson brothers, then there's Billy, Del Rochester, and that Henson fella," she said.

Elven looked at her, waiting for the rest of the memo. She smiled, seeing that he was letting her speak.

"They aren't too happy about that church out in the woods," she said.

He waited again, but this time, Meredith stared back, having nothing more to say.

"That's it?" he asked. "A church in the woods?"

Meredith nodded.

"Why would there be a church in the woods?" he asked.

Meredith once again let out a long sigh. "You got a notice from the state that they were going to be setting up shop. I gave it to you and you said—and I quote—'Why would I care about some people singing praises to the trees?'"

Elven bit his lip. It did sound like something he would say, but he couldn't remember specifically. "Alright," he said. "And what are the complaints about?"

"They say—"

Before Meredith could finish, the door opened and two men rushed in.

Their appearance was the first thing that Elven noticed. They both wore camouflage jackets that were mostly covered in mud. Each of them looked like they hadn't shaved in weeks, though Elven wasn't sure if they'd intended to shave later or not. They were both dark-haired and had blue eyes. They looked to be brothers, maybe five years apart.

When the bigger and older brother stepped to the side, Elven caught the details on the younger brother. His jacket and neck were covered in blood.

Elven stepped up to them, ready to help out however he could. As soon as he got close, he could smell both of them. If it had been weeks since they'd shaved, then it was months since they'd showered. And there was a hint of something else that extended past body odor. It reminded him of the fecal smell back at Dority's farm.

"Are you hurt?" Elven asked, ignoring the smell. He caught Meredith out of the corner of his eye. She was already on the phone, calling Doc Driscoll no doubt, and wheeling her chair back a few feet to avoid the smell.

"What? Oh, no, I'm fine," the younger of the two said after noticing Elven's interest in him specifically.

"The blood?"

He chuckled nervously. "Caught a deer. Had to carry it on my shoulders back to the truck. Dumb shit here ain't no help though." The younger brother kicked at his older sibling in the rear end.

"Shit, you made that mess yourself, you can carry it on your shoulders. I ain't gonna smell that way, too. Numbnuts over here shot the deer and missed the heart. Had to follow him for nearly a day until we caught up. Must've nicked its bowels cause that shit is nasty," the older brother said.

Elven couldn't help but feel bad for the deer. He knew in Dupray, hunters were gonna hunt. There was no avoiding that. But to hear about a creature having to go through so much pain for so long was never easy for him.

"Isn't that gonna spoil the meat?" Johnny asked, coming in from the hallway.

The oldest brother shrugged. "I'm sure there'll be plenty to keep."

Elven stared at them both. He'd seen them around, but didn't know them by name. Dupray may be small to most people, but in actuality it was a big spread of a county. Elven couldn't get everyone's name and remember them when he saw them.

"What can I do for you boys, then?" Elven asked. "There's no taxidermist in here, though I think maybe Johnny has a cousin that dabbles in it."

Elven winked back at Johnny, who had a stupid grin on his face. He thought he was making a joke, but Elven was pretty sure that the wonky-eyed heads in the pawnshop were the work of that idiot cousin of his.

"No, Sheriff, it ain't about that. We found someone in the woods. He looked to be in real bad shape," the elder brother said.

"Is he out in your truck?" Elven asked, beginning to head past them. But the men didn't move.

"No, Sheriff, he's still out in the woods. I can take you to him though," the man said.

Elven bit his lip. "How bad of shape is he in? You couldn't move him?"

"Wasn't in that bad of shape. Just really sick or something. But we had the deer, and there was no way we could take him at the same time," the younger brother said.

"What are your names and where are you from?" Elven asked.

"I'm Walt and this is my brother Rod. We live out in Birchwood," the younger man said.

Elven nodded. "Alright, Walt and Rod, so you came to tell me that there's a man that is in bad shape out in the woods. And that you left him there because you decided to carry the deer that you gut shot instead?"

Walt widened his eyes. He looked at his brother as if he was in trouble and needed to be bailed out.

"We came straight here though. Didn't stop to drop the deer off or nothin'," his brother said, coming to his rescue.

"How commendable," Elven said.

"Hey, we couldn't just leave the deer out there. Some animal would've come along and taken him. We tracked him all day. That was our kill. Ain't like we could kill another one, unless we wanted to get fined for two bucks on one license," the younger brother said.

They had a point about the legality of killing a second deer. And Elven knew how it was in Dupray. Hunting was a big part of life, and to some people it wasn't just *big*, it was all there was. So was being an idiot, apparently. But he didn't have time to debate it any further.

"You can take us out there? How far in?" Elven asked.

"Ten miles at least," the oldest brother said. "We can drive a big chunk of the way, but then on foot for a while."

"Johnny, wanna come with?" Elven asked his portly deputy, who had a donut half-stuffed in his mouth. It was covered in powdered sugar, and when he was called to attention, Johnny coughed, peppering himself with the white substance.

"Jeez, Elven, ten mile hike in the woods? I don't know if I can handle that right now," Johnny said with a half-full mouth of donut. Elven wasn't even going to try to debate with him that they could drive through most of it and it wouldn't be ten miles of actual hiking.

Elven rolled his eyes. Johnny might be lazy, but he also wasn't lying. His eyes darted to Tank, who looked like a puppy ready to go for a walk, his eyes big and a grin slapped on his face at the thought of seeing a case, but Elven thought better of it with his condition.

"Madds, you're up," Elven said, watching Tank's hopeful expression immediately drop.

CHAPTER SEVEN

THE AIR WAS COLD AS IT FILLED HIS LUNGS. WINTER WOULD BE here soon enough, and trips out in the hills through the forest would not be so pleasant. As it was right now, he was chilly enough. His jacket was good for now, but come time for snow, he was gonna need something heavier.

He caught a glimpse of Madds out of the corner of his eye. She seemed like she needed more than what she wore, even though she was bundled twice as much as he was. Her arms wrapped around herself as she put one foot in front of the other. He could see it in her eyes, the focus on the ground. He knew that look. It was the one that concentrated on just getting the task at hand done, and try not to think about the cold, or heat, or pain, or whatever it was that was making you miserable.

The pine needles on the forest floor were still damp from the recent rains, creating a soft bed that kept the leaves from the oak trees from reaching the mud beneath them, causing them to dry out and leave them to be crunched beneath their boots.

Elven let Walt and Rod lead the way for a bit and hung back, waiting for Madds to catch up to him. He could see her breath, clouding at a heavy rate while she hiked. Soon enough, she would create enough friction and body heat so she wouldn't be so cold. At least, that's what he hoped.

He'd never been to the desert, so he didn't know what she was used to. There'd been plenty of warm places in his travels, but they were usually full of thick, humid air. It was natural for him to feel like he constantly had water lingering in his lungs.

He met Madds's eyes and could tell it was just the opposite for her. And maybe that's why she also looked like she was ready to tear someone's head off.

"You doing alright?" he asked.

She glared. That's when he realized that maybe she wasn't ready to tear *someone's* head off, but *his* head.

"We can just take it easy," he said, hoping he was heading in the right direction and not digging himself deeper, whatever his transgressions against her were.

She panted as they walked. It was probably twenty seconds of silence before she finally let it out.

"What the fuck was that about?" she asked.

In his past conversations with the many women he'd come across, he knew that such a loaded question about something so incredibly vague was nothing but bad news. The last thing he needed to do was assume it was one thing, only to have it be something else. Then again, if he asked, that could make it even worse, as if he had no idea what he did was so wrong.

But it was the truth.

"What—"

"I should have known," she spat. "You don't think you did anything wrong, do you?"

He chuckled. He couldn't help it—she read him very well. He could easily put this to bed by pulling the *I'm your boss* card out. But she wasn't being disrespectful, just angry. There was no harm in that.

Besides, he liked that she was pissed. It meant she cared enough about the job to be pissed, even if it was at him.

"Back at the station. Why did you not immediately ask me to come out here?" she asked.

"Oh," he said, finally realizing.

"You went for Johnny first? I mean, I love Johnny, I do, but c'mon, really? And then I saw it in your eyes, you were going to ask Tank. If he wasn't half Swiss cheese right now I'm sure you would have."

Elven nodded, letting her finish her rant. When he was satisfied that she was done, he spoke up.

"Johnny knows hunters. I thought maybe it would be better to have him come out here. This wasn't something I needed backup for. We're just finding someone that needs help and bringing them to it. And you are darn tootin' that I would have brought Tank out here if he wasn't, what was it, Swiss cheese?"

"Tank is a big guy. I don't know Tweedle Dee and Tweedle Dum up there, but I do know that they decided they couldn't take this fella down the hill with their deer at the same time. Tank and I could have carried him."

"So you don't think I'm strong enough?" Madds asked.

Elven smirked. "Now you're just trying to trip me up."

He watched her face change composure. She was still pretty angry, but maybe not so much directly at him. Or maybe that was just wishful thinking on his part. She didn't seem happy, but then again, she was hiking in the cold, which she didn't seem to take too well.

"I also didn't know how well you'd do on a hike in the woods in the cold. Or what you think is cold anyway," he said with a knowing smile.

"I'm freezing my tits off," she said, wrapping her arms around her tighter. He wished there was a smile accompanying it, but he didn't get what he wanted.

"Well, we wouldn't want that, now, would we?" Elven said. "After this, we should get you a warmer coat, especially once the real cold gets here."

"Oh, fuck. Remind me why I took this job again?" she asked.

He smiled as they walked up the hill together. "I believe you stated, 'I'd like to keep my reasons my own.'"

CHAPTER EIGHT

"It's up here," Rod said, pointing.

Elven brought his speed up to a jog, careful not to put too much distance between himself and Madds, but also wanting to get to the man who was apparently in bad shape.

He hoped they could offer some help. The brothers weren't very descriptive about what was wrong with the fella, so Elven needed to expect the worst.

The pine trees were dense in this part of the forest. There were points that Elven had to turn sideways to get between two trees without scratching his shoulders against the bark. It was even more noticeably wet on the forest floor. Elven stole a glance upward and saw that the branches and leaves intertwined above their heads, letting little sunlight through and leaving the vegetation without a fair shot at drying out.

Elven breathed in the moist air and felt it settle on the back of his tongue. It was an earthy taste, not far from the smell of the wet ground itself. The bark on the trees, the ground, and the dead leaves and pine needles all seemed so brown and dark to him. Not a hint of color outside of their own clothing, and even that clothing blended in with the earthy tones.

The brothers looked back at Elven as he finally made his way to where they stood. Below them was the man in question.

He was pale and his eyes were closed. He had a film of sweat all over him. That, or it was the morning dew. Either way, Elven wondered if that man was dead, because he sure looked it. The only places he had any color was underneath his eyes, which held a jaundice yellow hue.

"This him?" Madds asked, panting for breath.

"I'd venture a guess that it is," Elven said, crouching down.

Elven reached a hand out and touched the man's forehead. It was cold, and Elven didn't have a good feeling about it. He placed his fingers under his jaw at the neck, checking for a pulse.

"Has he moved from when you first saw him?" Elven asked.

"No, Sheriff. He was just like this when we found him," Walt said.

"Did you check his pulse when you found him?" Elven asked, irritated to know that they could have walked up on a dead body, which may not have been so dead when the brothers first found him.

The brothers looked at each other, but said nothing.

"Didn't even give him a shake? Maybe just call out and ask if he was alright?" Elven asked, receiving zero answers. His irritation bordered on contempt.

"Is he dead?" the younger brother asked.

Beneath Elven's fingers, there was the faintest thud against the tips. The man was alive, but barely.

"Nope. Not yet, at least," Elven said. He knelt closer to the man. "Sir, can you hear me?"

The man remained silent. Elven pulled up the man's eyelids and saw the whites were webbed with red lines. He moved his hand and opened his jaw. There was nothing in his mouth, but his tongue was swollen and white, as though he was massively dehydrated.

Elven couldn't tell if any of the sour and overwhelming scents he smelled were coming from the man, the forest, or the brothers next to him. Either way, it didn't matter. The man needed help, and they didn't have much time.

"Let's get him up," Elven said, lifting the man's arm. The jacket slid off his shoulder and exposed his arm, revealing the track marks and bruises in the crook of his elbow. It wasn't just the dehydration and elements that put him here. He was a drug user.

The older brother grabbed at the man's other arm and, together, they lifted him off the ground. The man's head flopped to the side. A low groan came out of him.

"Oh, shit," Walt said.

"I told you he wasn't dead. What did you expect?" Elven asked sharply, losing his patience.

"Wh-wha—" the man muttered as his head rolled on his shoulders again.

"Sir, can you hear me?" Elven asked again, leaning him against the tree. He turned to Madds. "You got any signal?"

Madds looked at her phone and shook her head. "Nothing."

"We'll have to take him to Driscoll's ourselves then. Was hoping he could meet us here," Elven said, wishing he'd had told Meredith their location when they got to the trail. At the very least, she'd phoned him earlier so he was expecting them to arrive.

Elven looked at the man, pushing his head back against the tree so his head stopped rolling. He pulled his eyelid open again as Rod held him firm. The eyeball underneath, still bloodshot, rolled around suddenly alert.

"Arggh!" the man yelled out.

Rod jumped back. Elven was caught off guard as well. Moments ago, he thought he was dealing with a dead body, and now this guy was very alert.

The man, still looking near death, pushed against Elven and Rod with a strength that was unexplainable.

"Who the fuck are you?" he yelled, pushing his back against the tree he was found sitting against earlier. He looked like a cornered animal, ready to bolt. He swayed back and forth slightly, as if he could topple at any second.

"Sir, I'm Sheriff Elven Hallie. These two men found you and brought me here, and they tell me you're in bad shape," Elven said, keeping his hand out to try to keep the man calm.

The man's bloodshot eyes darted from person to person, never settling on one spot. "I feel like shit."

"I think you're dehydrated," Elven explained. "What's your name?"

Finally, the man stared at Elven, about as solidly as he could expect.

"A-Adam," he sputtered, reminding Elven of a scared rabbit. His messy hair was soaked in sweat and dew, and it flopped to the side as he twisted his head to look around.

"Alright, Adam. How'd you get out here?"

Adam looked at Elven for a moment. Then swiveled his head around, seeing the other people watching him. His face twisted in confusion, then he fell against the tree again.

"I don't feel so good," he said. "Wh-where's Charlie?" His voice was light and drifting into the air when he spoke. He looked to be losing consciousness again.

Elven squatted next to him. "Let's get him back up, we need to hurry," he said to the brothers. "Adam, who's Charlie? How'd you find yourself here?"

"I was, I—the light," Adam said, smiling and lifting his eyes up, like he was reliving a pleasant memory.

"Oh, Jesus Christ," Rod grumbled, grabbing onto him.

"What?" Madds asked.

"It was beautiful," Adam said. He looked around, confusion on his face. "I don't know how I ended up here, but the journey led me to this place. And I still don't feel so good."

"Let's go," Elven said, lifting him with Rod's help. "Adam, we're gonna get you out of here, alright? Just one foot in front of the other, as best as you can."

Adam seemed to understand and nodded, but his face twisted in pain and disgust. He quickly doubled over, pulling free from Rod's grip, and vomited at his feet. It was thick and chunky, with almost no liquid at all. It came out like a bulky caterpillar made of carrots, rice, and what Elven could only describe as what smelled like powdered cheese mix from stale nachos at the gas station.

Elven didn't think he'd be eating any time soon. This morning was full of some awful scents.

"Fuckin' A," Rod said. He scooted back, but was in no danger of splash with how concentrated the puke was.

Madds was far enough away that she didn't need to worry. She started to circle around, taking a look at the foliage and stopped in her tracks. "I think I found Charlie."

Elven looked at Walt, who took his place at holding Adam. Elven didn't want to have to lift Adam from the ground again. They were already wasting too much time with this game they were playing, but he needed to see what Madds was talking about.

When he reached her, only feet away, he saw. There was a small drop in the forest floor, about four feet down. Below it, a body laid crumpled in a twisted position, like a bizarre pretzel. Only this body had no chance of survival.

It wasn't the elements or even drugs that had killed him. It was the massive hole in the back of his head. The front of it had exploded out, leaving a mass of brain spatter against the pile of rocks three feet away. And if there wasn't enough at the scene to explain what happened, a small revolver laid at the feet of the dead man.

"Looks like Johnny's gonna have to make the hike up here after all," Elven said.

"What about him?" Madds asked, motioning toward Adam who looked more confused than ever.

"Can't interview him if he's dead or passed out. Gonna have to get him to Driscoll's," Elven said. "Adam, we need to get you down the hill and to the doc. Think you can manage?" He really didn't want to have to carry him.

Between heaves, Adam managed a nod.

Thank God for small favors.

CHAPTER NINE

ELVEN HAD MADE IT BACK TO THE JEEP WITH MADDS, ROD, Walt, and Adam. They got Adam all loaded in the backseat and Elven said a little prayer that Adam didn't have anything left in his stomach to make its way all over his upholstery. It wasn't that he wanted to keep it pristine, he just didn't want to have to deal with the smell for the rest of the vehicle's life.

And Elven intended on keeping that Jeep for a long, long time.

Adam had made the trek with a little help from Rod and Walt, but managed to stay on his feet until he was put in the backseat. After that, he passed out completely. Elven hoped it was just from exhaustion, but they needed to get him to Driscoll's as soon as possible. Adam was in bad shape physically, and there were a lot of questions Elven needed to ask him.

But first, he had to attend to the crime scene.

Madds had protested a little, saying she wanted to stay and help, but he needed her to take Adam to Driscoll's. He would wait for Johnny and Tank while she took care of that. He'd given Walt and Rod a very stern talk, telling them that they needed to follow Madds to the doc's place. They didn't give him any pushback when he gave them orders.

And Madds did as she was told.

Johnny and Tank showed up quickly enough and the three of them headed back to the crime scene. Elven was worried about Tank making it out to the spot. He didn't want him to rip any stitches, but Tank was a trooper. More than that, he seemed a lot happier being out in the field, so to speak. It was Johnny that he should have been worried about.

The trek to the spot wasn't too difficult, but it wasn't the easiest hike either. When Elven had to turn sideways to go between the trees that were close together, Johnny had to make complete detours around the thick vegetation due to his size. Tank went with him on most occasions, due to his healing wounds and the fact that his upper body was nearly the size of a barn. On top of that, Johnny was dripping sweat and out of breath by the time they made it to the body.

Elven let Johnny take a much-needed water break and catch his breath for a moment while he and Tank looked at the body.

They both took a look at the crumpled mess of the man. Four feet down wasn't very far to fall, but they already knew it wasn't the fall that killed him. Elven wondered if he had fallen after being shot, or if he was down there already when he was killed. It probably didn't matter either way.

Elven scaled down the drop with ease, lending a hand to Tank so he didn't have to exert himself too much. Though it did seem like Tank was doing fine. If Elven wasn't paying attention, he'd have missed the very small glimpse of a wince that crossed Tank's face, only to vanish a split second later. The man really wanted to work, and being torn up by some shotgun pellets wasn't going to stop him.

The body that lay in front of them hadn't been weathered too badly yet. Which meant that he was probably killed the night before, though Elven was no expert. He figured there was no reason for Driscoll to come out and take a look unless they found something out of the ordinary. He had Adam to attend to, which was more important than any medical evidence they may come across at the scene.

The man had long hair that was wet from the morning dew and the previous day's rain. Just as it had been in other parts of the forest this deep, there was little sunlight to make its way through the branches and leaves, entangling above them to create a natural shade. There was a slight smell emanating from the body, which was easily explained by the wet, brown stain on the seat of his jeans.

The shirt and jacket he wore were stained up from mud and other mysterious substances. It was very possible that they hadn't been washed in years by the looks of it. And then there were the blood and brain chunks, most of which had ended up on the nearby rocks.

Tank crouched next to the gun that lay on the forest floor next to the untied boots of the body. He picked it up with a pen and slid it into a bag.

"What do you think?" he asked Elven. "Any chance that this wasn't the guy's buddy?"

Elven sighed. "The weapon being left here, and the friend still alive with no gunshot wound himself? I'm sure a GSR test would tell us for sure, but I think it's safe to say we have the suspect in custody."

Tank nodded, standing up. "I'll get Johnny and we'll take some pictures before loading the body up to take down the hill."

Elven took the man's arm and slid the jacket sleeve down. After his interaction with Adam, he was curious. And just as he had thought, the man's bare arm had needle marks in the crook of his elbow, just like Adam's. This one had a lot of them, like literal railroad tracks, surrounded by a large bruise.

They had the murder solved, more or less, but that wasn't what was bothering Elven. What bothered him the most was why they were out there in the first place. Most people shooting up didn't decide to go for a hike in the woods. There had to be some other reason they were out here, and Elven intended to find out.

CHAPTER TEN

"YOU WERE RIGHT ABOUT HIM BEING DEHYDRATED," PHIL Driscoll said, washing his hands at the sink.

The basement of the funeral home, which doubled as a medical office and many other things, was unusually cold that day. Elven had been inside the building more times than he could count. It was one of the biggest buildings in Dupray, mostly because of how many hats Phil wore in the county, but also because his was the only funeral home in town.

No matter where you were in the world, no matter how rich or poor, dying was always in business. As long as there were people, there would be customers. Phil wasn't one to flaunt money, but Elven knew he had to have a stash socked away.

And good for him. He treated everyone like they were family to him. Mostly because over the years, he had become a part of everyone's family when treating illnesses or standing by as loved ones passed. And he was more than accommodating in the empathy department.

"Is he gonna be alright?" Elven asked, knowing that the brothers were outside, probably close to wetting their pants after hiking back down to the vehicles. Elven had told them bluntly that if anything happened to Adam, he was gonna hold them accountable as they'd decided the deer they shot was more important than helping the man out.

Phil took his glasses off, his eyes becoming beadier without the magnification from the lenses, and wiped them on his shirt. He lifted the side of his mouth in a smile, as if he knew exactly what Elven had told those hunters when they'd brought him in. The bright halogen bulbs in the room made his skin look paler than he really was, and his face looked almost skeletal as he smiled.

"I'd say he'll live another day," Phil said.

Elven turned to Madds, who sat in the corner, seeming disinterested. "Go ahead and let them know they're off the hook," he told her.

She got up and made her way to the stairs that led up from the basement and to the front door.

"But let them know that if they see someone who needs help again, I don't give two shakes about their buck. They bring the man down first."

"Two shakes, is it?" she asked without a smile before exiting.

Phil gave Elven a sideways glance.

Elven shrugged. "She's not the happiest with me at the moment. I may have stepped into it with a gender-biased comment. Unintentionally, that is."

Phil chuckled. "I do not envy the kids these days. As everything becomes more advanced, things just seem to get more complicated because of it."

"It's a brand new world out there," Elven said. A chill suddenly ran up him and he shook it off. "Phil, it is colder than Madds's shoulder right now."

Phil chuckled again. "I figured you'd know the drill by now. Gotta keep it cold when I got a cold one here."

Elven nodded, closing his eyes. Of course, he thought. "Anyone other than the body we found?"

"Tobias Utt," Phil said.

"Really?" Elven asked. "Darn shame, he was a decent man. What happened?"

Phil shrugged, his shoulders covering up what little bit of neck he actually had. "When a man weighs as much as he did, sometimes the ticker just gives it up. Makes it work too hard. His wife rolled over in the morning, and he was gone."

"If you see her before I do, give her my condolences," Elven said.

"Will do," Phil said.

The two men stood in silence for a moment too long and Elven cleared his throat. He wanted more information about Adam, but didn't want to just push on with questions after hearing the news about Tobias.

"Right, so your man, Adam. I've got him on an IV drip to replenish his fluids," Phil said.

"Do we need to take him down to the general?" Elven asked.

Phil shook his head. "Nah, he'll be alright. You can if you want, but it would just cost him money he probably doesn't have, so then it would cost the hospital the supplies and time that they're already so sparse on."

"Fair enough," Elven said, knowing it was all true. He could probably count on one hand the amount of people who had health insurance. It was a big change from when his parents still had the mines running. Check another box for the reasons people had to hate his family.

"He was muttering some things before he passed out again," Phil said. "Not sure if it's of any use to you, but it was something about a church that put him on the path?"

Elven leaned against the counter, putting himself closer to Phil. He felt like hopping up on the counter, but maybe that would have been too comfortable of him.

"He mentioned something about a beautiful journey that led him there. In his condition, I just figured he was so out of it. You know, visions and whatnot from malnourishment."

"Hallucinating is definitely a symptom of that. But there's something else, too. Without running tests on what it was, it's pretty clear he was on drugs. I'm sure you noticed his arm."

Elven nodded in agreement, having seen the bloodshot eyes, and the way Adam immediately vomited after awakening. It was bizarre. Then again, when the body was in survival or shutdown mode, it could react different ways.

"Any guess what he might have been on?" Elven asked.

Phil shrugged. "Could be a number of things. Heroin, meth—hell, even Oxy. Coupled with being out in the woods for days, kind of hard to put a finger on it. By now, if it were any of those, he'd have pissed it all out and it wouldn't show up on a blood test. You want me to give the best guess I got? By the looks of him, I'd say it's methamphetamine."

Elven sighed. Drug use wasn't unheard of in Dupray, but Elven was doing his best to make it less and less common. But when Elven normally found junkies in his county, they were in a rundown, derelict building. Maybe in a back alley. The fact that Adam was ten miles into the woods was strange. He hadn't been out there hunting.

"Did he say anything about this church?" Elven asked.

Phil shook his head. "What I told you is all I heard. Want me to send one of his hairs to the lab? Confirm my guess of drugs?"

Elven thought about it, but knew it would be too long to get results of anything. And in the end, it wasn't like it would do any good to arrest Adam for having something in his system at an undeterminable point in time.

"Nah, thanks though. I doubt I'd get anything out of him at this point, even if he was awake."

Phil nodded.

"I'll send Johnny to come pick him up when he's awake. Send him home, see if there's anything he can get from him," Elven said, but he knew there would be nothing to gain from Adam. That's why he was going to put Johnny on it.

"What are you going to do next?" Phil asked.

"Time to get right with God, I suppose," Elven said.

CHAPTER ELEVEN

"So you are telling me that you think this druggie came from the church out in the woods? The one that Meredith has been getting complaints about?" Madds asked as Elven drove his Jeep back toward the woods where they'd found Adam.

He'd had to radio Meredith to get the information about where the church in the woods was. After being scolded for about five minutes for not listening to her the first time, brushing it off, not having enough respect for the job she did, and being too cocky for his own good, Meredith had finally given him the location.

Elven made a mental note to buy Meredith something nice at the end of the month for a job well done. And he hoped she wouldn't see right through what he was trying to do when he gave it to her. Even if she did, maybe it would still help smooth things over.

He couldn't remember her acting that way toward Lester when he was the sheriff.

Madds had been quiet during the tongue-lashing that Elven took, though he could sense a certain satisfaction radiating from her as she sat listening to the whole thing. Stealing a glance her way after setting the receiver down, he caught a slight smirk on her face to solidify his feeling.

The location of the church was about twenty miles from where they had found Adam. That seemed like a very far distance for him to have traveled from. But in Dupray, twenty miles was a lot shorter than it might seem.

"Elven," Madds said. "Why wouldn't he have come from the road? Or any other location, for that matter?"

He looked at her, seeing the emerald green in her eyes. He lifted the corner of his mouth, recognizing that even when she was irritated with him, she could still make him smile.

"Are you just gonna be irritated all day with me?" he asked.

She closed her mouth and cocked her head. The loose strands of hair poked out from her sloppy bun. "What?"

"I obviously offended you," he said. "About my asking Johnny to come with, then considering Tank. And while I still think I wasn't necessarily wrong as Tank is a very strong man, I want to know if you're still mad."

She stared at him in disbelief. "First of all, it seems like you don't want me to be irritated with you. So instead of apologizing for offending me, you state how you offended me, followed by the fact that you don't think you were wrong?"

Elven blinked twice while staring at her. He could already tell this wasn't going the way he had wanted.

"Yes," was all he said.

"Jesus tits, Elven. You need a lesson in how this all works. You can't just flash a smile, maybe swipe your hair to the side, drop your sunglasses, and it becomes alright."

"Is that what you think of me?" he asked.

"It isn't what I think of you, it is who you are. And that's fine, believe me, you're a good guy. But you're also sometimes too cocky for your own good."

Elven didn't say anything but, "Hmm."

"And for the record, yes, Tank is a very strong man. And maybe

Johnny would have been able to help, though he did state that a ten-mile hike wasn't for him."

"So what is it then? It's not that I don't think you're capable of the job. Believe me, I am one hundred percent on board with women doing the same job as men."

"Christ, Elven. It's not even that. I just thought that I was sort of on your team, you know?"

"My team?" Elven asked, not following.

She shrugged and leaned away, toward the window. "Never mind, I guess I was wrong."

"I'm gonna say this once, then from here on out, you'll know. If you tell me never mind, that you were wrong, I'll leave it at that. If you don't want to tell me what's wrong, then so be it. But don't expect me to dig and play your game of getting me to try to figure you out."

She sat upright. "Fair enough. I know you're my boss, but after the last case, I figured when everyone was available, I'd be the first pick. I have the experience and we worked so well together. No offense, but Johnny—"

"Is Johnny," Elven said, acknowledging that fact. It didn't make Johnny any less of his deputy, but there were some jobs that were just not meant for him.

"Right. So that's it," she said. "Maybe it's stupid, but I said it."

Elven nodded, thinking about it. It had come out of nowhere for him, but then again, he didn't know Madds as well as any of the others. She was still new in town, and probably didn't feel too comfortable yet as a resident. But maybe she did feel comfortable with Elven, seeing as how their last case went, and she was clinging on to that.

He could understand that.

"Alright," Elven said. "I'm sorry." His words came out jarred and forced, but he meant every word.

She chuckled knowingly. "Don't say that too often, do you?"

"It's how you feel, so I recognize it. And I appreciate it. But let's skip the attitude and hostility next time, and maybe just tell me when

I messed up, okay? I may be incredibly smart, charming, maybe the most handsome guy you've ever met, but I'm still human."

Madds rolled her eyes, but a smile lingered on her face. And that was exactly what Elven wanted. He knew he was being over-the-top, though most of what he said he knew to be true, but it worked for him. It worked for her, too.

They sat in silence for a moment, the mood clearing up.

"So Meredith really let you have it there," Madds finally said with a smirk.

CHAPTER TWELVE

WHAT HAD BEEN A USUALLY EMPTY LOT AT THE MOUTH OF A hiking trail was now full of cars. Elven hadn't been out to this part of the hills in over a year, but he knew it hadn't been this busy for some time. Really, not many places in Dupray were this busy anymore.

Most of the vehicles were as would be expected in Dupray, in various states of needing repair, but still working. They were much older models of trucks and cars that had been handed down multiple times, possibly sold for a few hundred dollars here or there, and ended up being owned by the next person who couldn't afford more than a quart of oil, not to mention the many repairs it desperately needed.

"There is no way this many people decided it was a good time to go on a hike," Elven remarked as he maneuvered his Jeep, shiny and completely out of place compared to the rest of the vehicles.

"And I doubt they're all hunters," Madds added.

"This church really pulls this many people out here?" Elven asked.

He caught Madds's shrug out of the corner of his eye as he pulled the Jeep up along the edge of the trees after not being able to find a decent place to park. He threw the Jeep into neutral and pulled the brake up.

"Good enough, I suppose," he said, climbing out.

It was a much different place than where they had found Adam, lost and seemingly out of his mind. The trees in this area weren't clustered as tight together, and the air felt thinner, less claustrophobic. The sun could reach between the branches, drying out the fallen vegetation below.

"Are we gonna have to hike out there?" Madds asked. "Who the hell thought it would be a good idea to put a church out in the middle of the woods?"

Elven was thinking the same thing. There were plenty of places that could house whatever church it was—though, as he thought of it more, there was little to no cost for setting up shop on national forest land. Except, of course, special permission from the governor. It seemed like a lot of trouble to go through.

"Meredith says it's not that far. Just a few miles in," Elven said.

"A few miles?"

"Hey, you said you wanted to be the one to come. And here you are. You want to hand it off to Johnny or Tank?"

Madds grumbled to herself, but didn't say a word to Elven. He smiled as she trudged forward onto the dirt path.

MOST OF THE trek was actually peaceful. Elven spotted a few birds that made him smile, knowing he had a friend who would have loved to take the time and draw a picture of them. Being in nature had its own way of calming him down, making him introspective at times.

It was why he liked to sit on his deck and watch the sunrise most mornings. Rather that than pull a gun on someone for some asinine reason like breaking into a chicken coop.

Even Madds seemed to be in a better mood from the fresh air. It was possible that the sun being out also helped, shining down on her skin to thaw her out. He chuckled when he thought about how miserable she would be in another month or two. Best let her find that one out on her own.

After about twenty minutes on the trail, the quiet turned to murmurs in the woods, like someone out in the unknown conversing with themselves. Eventually, the murmurs turned louder, until they became hoots and hollers.

"Gotta say," Madds said. "That doesn't sound like any church I've gone to."

Elven watched her push on, glad that she wasn't out of breath like Johnny certainly would have been by now. And she was right. There was a very loud, audible voice saying things that he couldn't quite make out. After a few moments, it would be followed by what seemed like cheers.

"What kind of churches have you been to?" Elven asked, slightly joking and slightly curious.

She shrugged. "You know, the normal types, I guess."

"Normal...that could mean anything to anyone," Elven said. "I'm sure my normal is a lot different than yours."

"Not quite a mega church, but close to it," Madds said. "There's guitar-playing and rock music. The pastor is usually pretty good, not too boring, I mean, as far as church goes anyway."

Elven couldn't help but laugh. "I'm pretty sure you just described a typical white suburban area church. For younger Christians, that is."

Madds shrugged. "Isn't that normal? What type of church is your normal?"

Elven smiled, thinking about the many places he had been to and seen. Some right there in Dupray, others through the nation and the world. So many different places to describe, but none of them truly *normal* unless you grew up in the area.

But as soon as he opened his mouth, the trail broke away into an opening in the forest. The trees parted and the sun shone down on top of a large, brown tent. It looked heavy, like something from a retired military camp. Elven imagined there would have been rickety, metal beds underneath it at one point in time.

Instead, at the top of the tent was a large cross that someone had nailed to the front post. The horizontal part of the cross had a slight sag to it, like it was trying so hard to be an *x* instead of a *t*. The dusty flap below it hung loose, like someone with a slack jaw snoring in their sleep.

Inside was where the commotion was coming from. It sounded like everyone was having the time of their lives. Cheering, clapping, a few shouts of *praise Him!* and *Amen!* could be heard above the rest. It seemed like the party was happening on the other side of the burlap fabric.

But Elven wasn't interested in stepping in just yet. He walked around the large tent, Madds following his lead. Off to the side of the clearing he saw a scattering of ATVs alongside a couple of wagons and trailers. It must have been how they had brought everything into the woods, seeing as how there was no way a truck could make it up the tight path. Not even Elven's Jeep would have fit on that trail.

He heard a thud and Madds let out a curse. He spun around and saw her stumbling forward. He held out a hand, but she caught herself before needing his help. She looked back at the ground where her foot caught. A stake in the ground had popped halfway up, the dirt too soft to hold the tension of the one stake. It looked like the others were picking up the slack of the one, as the tent hadn't sunk inward.

The ropes that were attached to the various stakes in the ground looked as if they had seen some wear over the years. Most likely from being bundled up and thrown about, moving to the next place. Elven had a feeling he knew what this church was about just from the looks of everything. And he was already forming a sour opinion.

As they walked around, there were a handful of smaller tents behind the large one. They were all made from the same, rough-looking material as the one that housed the worshippers. Next to one of the smaller tents, two men sat. They ate from bowls around a small fire in the ground that created very little smoke.

One of the men had a gray mustache and bald head, and he never even looked up from his stew at Madds and Elven's approach. Or maybe it was chili. Whatever it was, it smelled awful. Like the meat had gone off a few days beforehand, but they were hoping the seasoning would cover up the taste. One more reason for Elven to be grateful he didn't eat beef.

The other man, his shirt filthy and torn at the sleeve, did look up at Madds and Elven. There was no smile or friendly greeting as he did. He chewed his food with his mouth open, steam lifting from it. Elven could see he was missing his front two teeth, and sported a severe underbite when he closed his mouth.

When the man swallowed his mouthful of food, he finally spoke.

"Employees only back this way. You wanna be inside," he said, holding a finger pointed toward the tent.

"Is that what you are?" Elven asked, unzipping his jacket. "Employees?"

The man shrugged. "Get paid to keep an eye out, set up, and tear down as needed," he said, staring at Elven's badge pinned to his shirt. Though the way they were dressed, the word *sheriff* embroidered all over their clothes, should have been enough proof.

"You live in Dupray County?"

The man shook his head. "No, sir. Got hired in Mississippi," he said, the word coming out like *Missipi.* "They liked us so much they asked if we wanted to come along, so we helped 'em through Tennessee, Kentucky, and now here we are."

"I see," Elven said. "That's a long ways to go."

The man shrugged. "I ain't have nothing to keep me there, and they pay me well and on time. Can't say I'm used to that."

Elven smiled. For someone who wasn't from Dupray, the man sounded a lot like he knew what life could be like for someone here.

"What's your name?" Elven asked.

"Wayne," he answered. "This is Sammie."

Sammie still didn't look their way, which was fine with Elven.

"Thank you, Wayne. Maybe we'll head on inside now," Elven said. "You don't go inside and listen?"

The man shook his head, letting out a little laugh. "They're honest folk and pay me well. I like to keep it at that. I heard everything they're saying along the way. I ain't got no need for that anymore than I need a stick in my eye. My daddy beat Jesus into me over the years so much that I don't reckon I'll ever have a need to look at a cross again."

Sammie, who hadn't yet said a word, got up and walked away from the fire. There was a small, rickety wooden structure ahead of him. It looked like it could only fit one person at a time. He went inside and slammed it shut, the walls shaking as he did. Elven could guess what was inside from the way the flies hovered around it. He decided not to get any closer unless he wanted to confirm it by scent.

"Guess he feels the same way," Elven said.

He turned to head back to the front of the tent, wanting to double back instead of passing by the makeshift outhouse, but just before he did, a woman came from around the tent. She was young, probably no older than twenty, and she wore a plain dress, off-white, with dirty flats on her feet. She was pretty, though a little plain for Elven's taste, but he also knew that for every Eve there was an Adam out there.

No relation to the Adam he found in the woods earlier, of course.

"Thanks, Michaela," Wayne said with sincerity. "You make the best darn lunches I ever had."

Elven's stomach churned at the smell again, wondering what Wayne was used to eating if the sour-smelling stew was the best he'd ever eaten. Maybe he was being polite to the girl, but by the way he was scarfing it down, Elven didn't think so.

Michaela stole a glance at Elven, offering a shy smile. He tipped his Stetson hat at the girl and spun back around.

It was time to see what the church was all about.

CHAPTER THIRTEEN

"AND I SAID: 'WOE IS ME! FOR I AM LOST; FOR I AM A MAN OF unclean lips, and I dwell in the midst of a people of unclean lips; for my eyes have seen the King, the Lord of hosts!' Isaiah six five," the preacher at the front of the tent announced.

As soon as he set eyes on the preacher, heard him speak, and saw the energy in the tent, Elven knew exactly then and there that it wasn't just a church. It was a revival.

The place sat what seemed to be around forty people. And by that, it literally only had forty chairs. Most of them were metal folding chairs, though a couple were plastic rickety things that looked as if they had been scooped up off the side of the road after a rough storm.

There wasn't a soul actually sitting in the chairs either. Every person stood, and those who didn't have a chair behind them stood against the edges of the tent, pushing their backs into the thick fabric, not seeming to mind the rough texture against them.

They were too busy watching the show up front.

Elven was disgusted.

It wasn't just the thick, stale air, like he'd stepped into a teenage boys' locker room after having run the mile. The sweat hung in the air and settled on the back of his tongue as he breathed. Even though it was cool outside, the amount of bodies inside made the air unbearable.

Even Madds unzipped her jacket and pulled it off. She loosened her shirt at the top, revealing her undershirt at the collar. Elven followed her lead, though he lacked the undershirt. The thick coat draped over his left arm was less than ideal, but he was hoping he wouldn't need to draw his pistol on this trek. It was a church after all. Or something like it.

But no, Elven was disgusted because he knew exactly what type of church revival this was. The flamboyant, over-exaggerated, and enthusiastic preacher at the front could spin a good tale, maybe rope them in to believing whatever he was spouting off about, but in the end, it was all about one thing. Separating people from their hard-earned cash.

Elven supposed the same could be said about all churches depending on how one looked at it, but all the other churches he knew didn't perform scams they called miracles. That was where he drew the line.

There was no music playing, but the preacher had a singsong tone to his voice, encouraging people to clap to a secret beat that he'd made up, but seemed to let everyone in the tent know about. Elven was a little impressed at the rhythm of the claps. They were mostly even.

Madds leaned in, cutting through the thick air with her body wash. It was a much welcome scent to Elven's nostrils.

"Jesus, I've never seen a place so lively," she said. "Is this how church goes in Appalachia?"

Elven shook his head. "Not at all."

He watched the preacher at the front of the tent as he paced back and forth, his white button-up shirt soaked in a deep U shape under his collar. His pits had formed large dark circles underneath them, too. He had beads of sweat dripping from his forehead.

Elven had to give this guy credit. He was truly working for his money.

The man was around Elven's age, possibly a little younger. Mid-thirties was a good guess. He had short-cropped brown hair on his head, which was longer in the front. A strand dangled in front of his eyes as he spoke. He shook his head, flinging his hair backward along with sweat. His face was smooth, but what seemed to be even smoother were his words.

He was handsome, that was for sure, but Elven figured that the man was able to talk a woman out of her panties before she could get a single word in. Maybe the face was the opener, but his tongue was the closer.

Possibly in more ways than one.

Elven was familiar enough with the Bible, but he could probably count on one hand the amount of verses he could recite from memory. The preacher, however, didn't even need a Bible to say the words. He only needed a Bible so he could wave it around as he spoke, adding emphasis to his words by shaking it from time to time.

Everything sounded as if it would be found between the pages of the black book he held, but Elven couldn't be completely sure. There may have been a few liberties taken on some of the words, most likely twisting them to make for a better cause. Which meant whatever the preacher was trying to get at.

At some point, the preacher slowed down and stopped speaking. Elven watched as he lifted his hands in the air, placing the Bible underneath his sweaty armpit, spine first so as not to dampen the pages.

"We're gonna come to a point now where I'm asking you to look deep inside yourself. Look deep inside," the preacher said, closing his eyes and hanging his head.

"Amen!" someone shouted.

"Blessed is the Lord!" someone added.

"Amen to that," the preacher said. "With everything you have been through in these trying times, your hearts were heavy when you came here today. I could feel them. I could feel the weight as you came through that very entrance."

The preacher pointed to the opening of the tent, right where Elven and Madds stood. Elven locked eyes with the man, and for one brief second, Elven thought he saw the man stumble. It was more of a swallow, a quick pause, but he was sure he had seen it.

And just as soon as he saw it, the preacher was right back on script.

"Those heavy feelings you came in with, I have no doubt in my mind that they have been lifted from you. That your heart no longer bears the weight you can no longer handle. That the Lord Himself has taken that burden upon Himself, for you."

Tons of cheers erupted along with a number of shouted *Amens*. Elven watched as a woman in the front row dropped to her knees in front of the preacher, as if she lost the ability to walk. The man quickly helped her up, touching her forehead as he sat her in her chair. She cried and held onto his hands for as long as she could until he broke away from her.

"So I ask you now, look deep in yourself and ask Him what He would like you to do," the preacher said. "The Lord is calling upon us to give of ourselves, because He knows that we can. Because He has taken that burden off your shoulders, knowing that now you can give so much more without the weight upon yourself."

And with that, the preacher ducked out the back of the tent. He was completely out of sight. *Where was the call?* Elven thought.

But then, a woman stepped into the spot where the preacher once stood. She looked very similar to the man, with her brown hair and that same fair skin.

Madds leaned in again with her whisper. "Girlfriend or relative?"

Elven smirked. "What makes you think it's not both?"

Madds snorted, stifling a full-blown laugh. But the woman at the front of the tent still noticed. She narrowed her eyes at them before she spoke.

"Hey, ya'll. We're gonna pass around the offering plate now, asking you to help however you can. However you feel the Lord is asking you. Be as generous as He would expect you to be," she said. She passed a small satchel to the front of the line and Elven watched as the people dropped various amounts of money inside.

Even with over forty people in the tent, he doubted they'd break two hundred dollars. But sometimes people could surprise him. After all, he did miss the miracle portion of the presentation.

"What do you think?" Madds asked.

Elven shrugged. "I say we hang around till everyone disperses and we can talk to the man himself."

"God?" Madds asked, with a smirk.

He couldn't help but chuckle and feel glad she didn't seem angry with him anymore.

CHAPTER FOURTEEN

Elven and Madds had a long wait for the service to be over. It wasn't really the service itself that took so long, but the amount of people who wanted face time with the preacher. After the collection—which was less than thrilling, given the look on the woman's face—Wayne wheeled in a small organ. The preacher played the organ as did the woman, who, as he later learned, was named Betsy, led a song.

Elven had to admit that she had a very nice voice as she sang *How Great Thou Art*. When she was done, the preacher stood up, thanked Betsy, and closed the service in a prayer. Elven was already holding his hat, but he hung his head, joining in out of respect. Just because the place may be a scam didn't mean that the people gathering weren't there for the right reasons. He glanced at Madds, whose eyes wandered over everyone, not joining in the prayer herself.

Elven didn't focus on what the preacher was saying, though he was sure he could make up the gist from all of the many prayers he'd heard in his life. Plus the preacher's own special spin on giving that little extra that you might have clanging around in your pocket. It made Elven crawl in his skin.

Once the service was over, the people dispersed. And then came the line to speak to the preacher one on one. Elven gave the man credit though—he sat through every handshake and every little bit of face time that people wanted to have with him, as if he were some celebrity they were lining up to get an autograph and picture with.

A large man with a wooden cane made his way down the aisle toward Elven, after saying whatever he had to tell to the preacher at the front of the tent. He limped every time his left leg had to support his weight. The suspenders he wore on his pants looked as if they were as tight as they could go, extending over the man's belly.

Elven smiled because he knew him. It was Dale Croft, straight from Dupray Proper. The funny thing was, Elven had known Dale to volunteer many Sundays in the youth Sunday School program at Dupray Methodist, mostly with the elementary kids. Dale was harmless, and even more so, he was quite the jovial fellow and great with kids.

"Oh, Sheriff Hallie, funny seeing you here," Dale said as if he'd been caught with his hand in the cookie jar.

"I could say the same thing. I thought you still went to church down at Dupray Methodist with Pastor Magner."

Dale shifted his weight, sweating more than even the stuffy tent called for. "Oh, sure do. Sundays. Today's Thursday, though. Figured I'd come out and see what this place was like. Everybody was talking about that young preacher, Spencer Caldwell. Said he had the gift of gab when it came to the Lord."

Elven nodded, not having any disagreement in that. Though he figured it extended past the Lord. "I'd say they're right, wouldn't you?"

"I'd say so," Dale said, a lift of excitement in his voice. He leaned in. "Say, do me a favor and maybe don't mention this to Pastor Magner."

Elven smiled and placed a hand on the old man's shoulder. "I doubt it would come up," Elven said, not giving a straight answer. But he watched the relief settle in Dale's face all the same.

"Mighty kind of you, Sheriff," Dale said, pushing past him and making his way out of the tent.

"I take it he's not supposed to be here?" Madds asked after Dale had left.

Elven shrugged. "I suppose not, though he's entitled to his freedom. Just strange to see someone who has spent over thirty years—that I can remember anyway—in the same church come out to a place like this. In fact, I see quite a few familiar faces around."

It was true. There were a number of people Elven had seen at one time or another down at a church in Dupray. Not just from the Methodist church either. There were various places of worship in the county, mostly Christian, just varying denominations. And while Elven hadn't had a chance to step inside them all, he'd seen more than a few open their doors on Sunday afternoons for their mass exit.

Maybe it was just that it wasn't Sunday. Maybe people were just curious. Word did travel fast in Dupray, after all. But he felt for Pastor Magner. He'd been doing his thing, as honest as he could, for as far back as Elven could remember. Was a flashy young kid out in the woods really going to pull his congregation away?

After what seemed like a solid two hours, the last of the audience was on their way out of the tent. Elven had exchanged plenty of glances with people from the town, most of whom seemed embarrassed and ashamed at being caught. In all honesty, he didn't know why he cared so much. Maybe it was because he hated to see people in his community get scammed. This pop-up operation didn't care about them like Pastor Magner did back in town.

Spencer Caldwell, the charismatic preacher with the sweat-laden shirt, unbuttoned his top button and started fanning himself with his hand. Betsy squeezed his shoulder as she passed by him and gave him a quick smile, which he returned.

"I'm putting money on girlfriend or wife," Madds said as the two made their way down the aisle toward him.

"I still stand by my statement about that from earlier," Elven said with a grin.

"Disgusting," Madds whispered.

Wayne and Sammie entered from the back of the tent. Wayne kept his mouth shut, his bottom lip overlapping his top so much that it made him look like a bizarre Muppet. Sammie had what looked like a second bowl of that stew, except most of it had made its way onto his shirt. They started folding the chairs up without even being asked.

"Thank you, boys," Spencer told them. "It was a great turnout today."

Nobody spoke back to him, which seemed to be fine with Spencer. He was happy with his own statement and company. He finally noticed Elven and Madds heading his way.

"Oh, Sheriff," Spencer said in greeting. "Were you able to catch the whole sermon?"

Elven noticed Spencer wring his hands like he was tired and ready to bow out. The tent still held most of the stuffy, sweaty stench from the audience. Yet, the closer he got to Spencer, the more he wondered if he was the main cause of the body heat.

"Can't say I did," Elven said. "We popped in a little late."

"That's a shame. We'll be set up again tomorrow about the same time if you're interested."

"Is that when you do the snake handling? Or do you start with healing the cripples first?" Elven asked.

Spencer stood, a grin frozen on his face. His eyes went between Elven and Madds as he decided what to say next.

Madds broke the ice first.

"How long have you been traveling around? I heard you picked up Wayne and Sammie in Mississippi," she offered.

Elven didn't mind the silence, awkward as it was. But he was also confident in the fact that he wasn't a lying scumbag like Spencer. Just looking at him, Elven knew he could size the man up.

But Spencer took Elven's words in stride, and turned his attention to Madds as he wiped his forehead clean of sweat with his sleeve, leaving a translucent smear on his forearm.

"We did pass through there," Spencer said. "But Betsy and I are from further south."

Elven noted that he didn't specifically mention where *further south* was. And Elven didn't care much where he'd come from. He just wanted to know why he was there in the first place, and how long he intended to stay.

"Didn't have anyone willing to travel with you from your own hometown?" Elven asked. "I'd figure a likable guy like you would have plenty of people you could count on."

Spencer grinned at Elven, who did not return the smile. "Plenty of people would have, but we like to bring those we think we can help out in the long run. Make a difference in some lives. Wayne and Sammie there have been a great help, and I hope we can help them on their own journey with the Big Man himself."

Elven did everything he could to avoid snorting out a laugh. Already, Spencer was caught in a lie. Wayne had made it very clear he was there just to get paid and fed. He wanted nothing to do with what they were actually selling.

"I'm sorry," Spencer said. "Maybe we got off on the wrong foot somewhere, though I'm not sure how."

"Why do you say that?" Madds asked.

Spencer took in a deep breath and let it out in a sigh. "It seems your boss here isn't a big fan of me, or maybe it is what I'm preaching?"

"That obvious, am I?" Elven asked, standing tall.

"I'm not sure what I did to offend you, Sheriff."

Elven stared down at Spencer, deciding what to say next.

"It's what you do," he finally said.

"Preach?"

Elven chuckled. "We both know it's more than that."

"And what is it I do then?" Spencer asked. "You seem to know more about me than I do."

"You take advantage of those who need help," Elven said.

Spencer kept his cool, though Elven could see there were cracks forming under the façade.

"I'm not sure why you say that. You've barely just met me. I never even told you my name, though I'm sure you picked it up from the crowd. And I just know you by Sheriff."

"Elven Hallie," Elven said. "Sheriff Elven Hallie."

"Well, Sheriff Elven Hallie, I'm here to prove you wrong. I'm not sure what happened when you were a young'un, but we ain't that type of church here. We take care of those who seek redemption. We teach the Word of God, and we don't diddle little boys so they grow up to hate those who are trying to do good in the world."

Elven lifted an eyebrow. There wasn't a lot that set him off, but Spencer was toeing that line with his bold words. He stepped forward, but Madds quickly jumped between them.

"Alright, maybe we all need to cool down here," she said. She placed a hand on Elven's chest and looked at him, her eyes pleading for him to tone it down. Then she turned to Spencer, who returned his grin to his face and lifted his hands as if he had done no wrong.

"My apologies, Sheriff Elven Hallie, I'm so good at talking that sometimes I don't know when to stop. My daddy always said that God forgot to put my jaw hinge on straight so it was always flapping. Forgive me."

Elven cleared his throat, but he let it go for Madds.

"So why are you out here? Dupray, West Virginia does seem a little odd for a stopping place, doesn't it?" Madds asked, leading the conversation back to its intention.

"Wherever there are people, there will be a need for God. No matter how small or big, we all need the Word," Spencer said.

"And your wife—"

"Sister," Spencer corrected.

Madds let out a *Mmm,* and Elven couldn't help but feel a smug sense of satisfaction that he was right despite joking around.

"Your sister, then. You just travel around? How long until you're on to the next stop?" Madds asked.

"We're hoping to find our forever home for our little church here. Dupray might just be that fit," he said.

"Why set up out in the hills? The trees? Seems a little off when the people who need help are in town. Seems all you're doing is making enemies with the hunters in these parts," Elven said.

"Oh, it's nothing new to preach out in God's forest. Hell, if the Mormons can do it, why can't we? What better way to connect with God than to be surrounded by that which He created?"

"The hunters don't bother you?" Madds asked.

Spencer shrugged. "We've had an empty threat or two, but when I hear that, all it tells me is that they have something deeper going on inside of them." Spencer tapped his chest as he said it. "And that maybe, they will come to me in that time of need."

Elven rolled his eyes.

"We're all signed off by the state to be out here, so if there are any issues, you'll have to speak to someone in the governor's office," Spencer said with a smug hint to his voice.

"Won't be necessary," Elven said. "Though we did pick someone up a few miles away. Said he came here and saw the light."

"Those exact words?" Spencer asked, lifting a brow.

"More or less."

Spencer smiled. "Doesn't surprise me. God is working amazing things through me."

"He was also higher than the top of those pine trees out there. Dehydrated, lost, and completely doped up. You wouldn't happen to know anything about that, would you?" Elven asked.

Spencer never dropped the smile. "Sheriff, I hate to admit it, but doing what we do, helping the lost and hopeless, sometimes they have turned to physical vices to elevate them to what they think they need, when all they truly need is the Lord Himself. So, yes, we do have some drug users who come here. But it's our hope that we can save them, too."

Elven nodded. Spencer may be a smug con artist, but what he said wasn't completely unbelievable. He just really didn't like the

preacher and what he was doing. Nothing about him and his operation seemed honest to Elven.

"Oh, and he wasn't alone. He was there with his friend. Except
his friend had the back of his skull blown out from a gunshot."

"That's terrible," Spencer said, shaking his head. "His friend have
anything to do with it?"

Elven shrugged. "He's too out of it to know for sure right now."

"I'll make sure and say a prayer for the man and his friend."

"So you wouldn't happen to know where they procured the drugs
then?" Elven asked.

Spencer shook his head. "As much as I might be able to help them
out, where they attain such dreadful items is beyond me."

Elven was growing tired of talking to Spencer, though there was
no reason to believe he had anything to do with the drugs themselves.
It was just another way Elven could put pressure on the man, mostly
due to his dislike of him.

Betsy came up behind Spencer, rubbing his shoulder again as she
did. Her hand seemed to linger just a split second longer than seemed
appropriate. Elven and Madds exchanged knowing glances. Maybe
his joke wasn't too far off from the truth.

"Is there anything I can help you with Sheriff?" Betsy asked, her
voice upbeat, but forced, like a customer-service employee who hated
her job but had to keep it. "Spencer is doing his best to help you out, I
can see, but he's also exhausted. With his schedule, he's gonna need
to get some rest and time to pray."

Spencer smiled at his sister. "Thank you, Betsy. Is there anything
else I can help you with then?"

Elven didn't think there was any point in staying longer. Spencer
and Betsy had done nothing illegal, so far as he could tell. And giving
people hope while encouraging them to empty their wallets might be
morally wrong, but it also wasn't within his job description to
monitor.

Michaela, the pretty yet slightly plain girl from outside who had
attended to Wayne and Sammie's meal, entered the tent. She carried

a large case, but as she walked, her foot caught the edge of a chair. She sprawled forward, the case opened, and papers scattered all over the floor.

Both Betsy and Spencer spun around at the commotion. Elven was quick on his feet, and was already down at her level, offering her his hand. She took it and he lifted her up. He was met with a shy, yet welcoming smile. She brushed her hair behind her ear.

"Oh, hell, Michaela! Can't you do nothing right?" Betsy snapped, stomping her way over to Elven and the girl.

Michaela's smile quickly disappeared as she started to pick up the papers. Squatting down, then standing again, only to repeat it at each loose paper on the ground.

"Sorry, Sheriff, but our cousin doesn't quite understand how to do things the way we ask them to be done. Somehow she manages to mess up even the smallest of tasks," Betsy said.

"Ain't that the truth," Spencer added. "But family is family, so we do what we can to help."

"She's related to the two of you?" Madds asked, joining in to help pick up the papers, which Elven noticed that neither Betsy nor Spencer did. They were both more concerned with scolding Michaela.

"Our cousin, on our mother's side," Betsy said. "How she ended up the way she did, I'll never know."

Elven watched Michaela's response to Betsy's stinging words. She looked as if she were going to cry, but held it in. It also looked as if this was a normal day for her. She never spoke out in protest.

"We all make mistakes," Elven said, grabbing a stack of papers and handing them to Michaela. She smiled at him again as she took the papers. "And a smile like that goes a long way to making up for them."

She blushed, but not a word was said.

"You don't need to be so kind, Sheriff. She's a bit dumb and don't talk much," Betsy said.

"And you don't need to be so harsh," Elven returned. "Like you said, family is family, and someone who's trying to help should be appreciated. Not ridiculed."

Betsy made no reply.

"Sheriff, is there anything else?" Spencer asked, his patience obviously wearing thin.

"Can't say there is...yet," Elven said. "Though with the complaints I've gotten from hunters, and what I see going on here, I do hope that you find your forever home. Just not here."

And with that, Elven left the tent, with Madds following behind. He'd seen enough to know that something was off with the preacher and his cohorts. Maybe it wasn't completely illegal, but it didn't mean he wasn't going to keep an eye on them and do some more digging.

CHAPTER FIFTEEN

"What was that about?" Madds asked.

"Which part?" Elven asked.

"The part where you accused them of drugging up a man and setting him loose in the woods," Madds said dryly.

He shot a glance at her as he drove. The hike back to the Jeep had been a quiet one. Mostly because Elven was still inwardly fuming about Spencer and his sister. At least Madds could pick up on that and realized it wasn't the best time to talk. Either that, or she was trying to keep up as he rushed down the trail back to the Jeep.

The lot of cars was nearly empty, the audience from the show already having left to go back to their lives in town. No doubt they'd be back, which made Elven even angrier.

"I said no such thing," he said. "I'm not sure what conversation you were in."

"You didn't have to. I can read between the lines, and I think Spencer could, too."

"Good," Elven said with a hint of satisfaction. "Not sure if you couldn't tell, but I do not like that man."

She laughed. "You could have fooled me."

"I have a job to do, Madds. And that job is to investigate the complaints of the hunters in the county and to protect the citizens."

"Bullshit, you wanted nothing to do with the church in the woods," she said. "Not even Meredith could persuade you into looking into it."

"That was before I knew what it was. *That* is no church. That is a place for people to empty their pockets. It's no better than a drug dealer. Selling a bunch of bull hockey just to get people to believe something that's false."

"That's how you see church? And God?"

Elven grimaced. "Of course not. It's how I see a man like him in a place like that. He knows all the right things to say, but he has no real belief or understanding behind it. It's all about the money for him."

"What's all this have to do with the murder? You think there's more to the murder than one drug addict killing another?"

"Doubtful. But I intend to find out where those drugs came from."

Madds was quiet for a moment. "So what now? You gonna keep twisting the screws on them, even though we have no evidence against them? I wouldn't even know what you'd charge them for. They have permission from the state to be out there."

Elven nodded. And he had no idea what it was he was going to do about it, but he wasn't going to just let it happen. He wanted them out of his county, so he was going to make sure that everything they did was under a microscope.

CHAPTER SIXTEEN

"The point of being here is?" Madds asked, letting her words linger in the air, waiting for his reply.

Elven sat in his Jeep with the engine still running as he looked at the building in front of them. The drive to get here wasn't too far off the beaten path, but it was still tucked away from most people's everyday trek. In a way, he thought that most people in Dupray would rather not be reminded on a daily basis about the old and dying.

It was easier to pretend they were already dead, as if they were a memory to cherish, instead of facing the truth about the end of their actual lives.

The sign out front read DUPRAY ASSISTED LIVING.

It wasn't exactly the most creative name, but then again, it was still a jump from how most people thought of what life inside must be like.

"There's only one person who has a big handle on meth out in Dupray. Other than an idiot or two who might try to cook up in their own RV for themselves, which most likely ends with them blown to bits. David Malick is the guy we want to talk to," Elven replied, climbing out of his Jeep.

The building was one story and had a V shape when walking up to it. He knew that inside, one section shot off to those who still had a little pep to keep them going, until they needed to be in the other section of the building. That section housed those who were practically knocking on death's door—hospice care for the terminally ill.

From the outside, the building looked old, but it was kept up well. Elven was sure they received enough money from the government to keep up with maintenance. And if they didn't maintain, then they surely would no longer receive that money from the government.

Once inside, though, it was obvious they made sure to meet the *minimum* requirements. There were no bells and whistles. There was only one piece of wall art in view, and that was only upon entry. Maybe it was to make those dropping off their parents feel better, or maybe because the receptionist was sick of looking at a long faded wall.

Elven was sure that the painting, a red boat in a blue lake with a little man sitting on it, had either been found in a back alley or donated to them. There was no way that the man who ran the place, Hector Snyder, would have spent an extra penny on anything that wasn't required.

"This place seems charming," Madds said in a low whisper as the receptionist returned to her desk from somewhere in the bowels of the nursing home.

"And this is the nice part," Elven whispered back, lifting his eyebrows.

The receptionist was young and had a friendly smile on her face, something that may have been forced due to Elven's uniform. He couldn't blame her if it was. He had to give anyone credit who could work in a place like this.

"Can I help you?" she asked, her voice teetering on the point of offering help, though not wanting to deal with any of it.

He noticed her hair was tightly pulled back behind her head, almost to the point that it lifted up her eyebrows. He could imagine the amount of times that someone got a grip of her loose strands when fighting, not wanting to eat their peas.

"We need to speak to David Malick," Elven said, tracing his finger along the edge of his hat as he held it in front of him.

The receptionist handed him a clipboard, which he and Madds quickly signed. She led them down the dimly lit hallway, the cheap linoleum floor squeaking underneath their boots. They passed by a handful of open doors, their televisions on at high volumes. Most of the people watched *The Price is Right*, while others stared catatonically at some talk show on a different station. It might have been the only two channels they could get a clear picture on.

Everyone he was able to see had the same blank look as they watched their shows. Some were hooked up to oxygen, and others to machines that he didn't recognize. It gave him the chills to think about spending his last days in a place like this. He'd never liked to flaunt his family money in front of others, but it was one time that he felt comforted by the idea that he could afford someplace better for himself.

"He's right here," the young lady said. "Doesn't get many visitors, though I'm sure he'd rather that than you two showing up."

"Yeah?" Madds asked.

The receptionist nodded, lifting her eyebrows. "He's not big on authority. Just telling him to roll over so the orderly can change his sheets is a nightmare. I don't really want to stick around to see what happens when the sheriff shows up."

Elven nodded his thanks and she quickly went back to her desk, her tennis shoes squeaking all the way down the hallway until they faded into nothing.

"So the meth dealer of Dupray lives in a place like this?" Madds asked.

"We always knew what he was up to, but never caught him in the act. Lester, the sheriff back then, found it a waste of time to try to pursue him. Most people he sold to were long-time drug abusers.

Malick never tried to get kids started on it, so we sort of left it alone. The junkies stayed where they knew it was safe and mostly out of the public places, so we didn't have many problems."

"Sounds like a wholesome guy," she said sarcastically.

"Hey, things are different in a small town. I don't like drugs in my county any more than the next sheriff, but Lester might have been right about this. If it wasn't hurting anyone, our time was better served elsewhere. As you can see, it's not like we have a large supply of resources or manpower."

"So what now? Now you want to get to the bottom of drugs in Dupray?" Madds asked.

"Now that I've got someone murdered, I sure do. And the same time as this revival coming into town...it just doesn't sit well with me."

Elven knocked on the open door and stepped into the room slowly. It was lit only by the half-open blinds. Most of the sunlight filled one corner of the room. In the other corner was the bed that faced a small television, one of those CRT models that looked straight from the fifties, bolted in the upper corner of the ceiling.

"Is that ol' Lester Fenech, sheriff of Dupray himself?" a voice asked from behind the door.

Elven quickly spun around and saw a faux-leather brown armchair. The footrest was outstretched, with the door knocking against it. A pair of feet stretched out, covered in blue socks that had an anti-slip rubber design on the bottom. The socked feet belonged to David Malick, who was wearing grey sweatpants and a white T-shirt spotted with orange grease stains.

Elven closed the door, letting Malick get a full view of him and Madds. Elven's eyes adjusted to the dim lighting and he saw a sour expression on Malick's face as Malick saw he wasn't Lester. The sparse, spiky whiskers on his face poked into his nostrils as he did.

"Who the hell are you?" Malick asked. He turned the television down with his remote and Elven could hear the oxygen puffing every so often.

Malick sat up straight and started coughing. He doubled over as he did and reached his hand down on the other side of the chair.

"Hands," Madds said, putting her hand on her gun.

Malick didn't comply, but he didn't bring his hands out either. Elven quickly grabbed Madds's hand, worried she'd pull her gun in the nursing home.

Malick laughed, but it started to come out in long wheezes. "Haven't felt my heart race like that in some time," he said. "Now can I put my oxygen on, or are you gonna shoot me?"

Malick slowly brought his hand up, showing it held only the plastic tube that was hooked up to the scratched silver tank. He lifted his salt and pepper eyebrows, still wheezing.

Madds lifted her hand off her gun, following Elven's own release. "Sorry, just—"

"Oh don't go apologizing now," he said. "Made my blood pump for once. Made me feel alive. Gave me my first stiffy in two years. C'mon and check it out."

Malick lifted his hips up from his chair, his sweatpants pitching a lame attempt at a tent. There'd be no way to sleep under that thing at a campground.

"Maybe later you can make my heart beat even faster," Malick said, smacking his lips together.

"You sure I can't shoot him?" Madds asked Elven.

Elven grinned and cocked his head. "Don't know how we'd explain that one."

"Too bad," she said.

Malick looked back to Elven. "What do you want? Lester can't come out here himself, he's gotta send his rich lackey?"

Elven let it roll off his back. He'd been called far worse by people far better than Malick. "Lester's retired," Elven said.

"No shit?" Malick asked, looking truly surprised.

Elven nodded, not wanting to get into the details of Lester's retirement.

"Well, damn," Malick said. "He was a good one, that sheriff. Never bothered me, and I stayed out of his business."

"I'm pretty sure the business of cooking meth and dealing it is sheriff business," Elven said.

Malick snorted. "There's a fine line there," he said. "Lester and I both knew where it began and ended."

Elven knew it to be true. He had told Madds that very thing just moments ago.

"I know the line very well," Elven said.

"But you're here knocking on my door," he said. "Hey, wait a second, does that mean you're the sheriff now?"

"I am," Elven said.

"Oh, Jesus, what has this county become?" Malick grumbled to himself. "Didn't think this county could line your coffers any more than they already were. When the hell was this election?"

"Couple months ago," Elven said, ignoring his accusations.

"I swear, this place is a hellhole. Not telling me when the election is, confiscating all my *Penthouse* magazines, only lettin' me have one cup of Jell-O at dinner. It ain't right."

"Didn't take you for the voting type," Elven said.

"Never voted a day in my life, but maybe I would have started. Ain't got nothing else to do around here," Malick said, putting his hand down his sweatpants for an adjustment. He was shameless.

"Not to break up this reunion, or whatever the hell it is, but we came here for some information," Madds said, her voice thinning from impatience.

Malick began to cough again, but this time was able to contain himself.

"I didn't even know you was sheriff. What the hell kind of information you think I got to give you?" he asked

"Who's dealing these days?" Elven asked.

Malick stared at Elven for a moment, like he was trying to translate the words in his head. Then he laughed. "You came here to find out who is dealing? Shit, rich boy, what makes you think I would tell you that? Maybe Lester, but not you.".

"Lester shot you through the kidneys seven years ago," Elven said. "You think he had any respect for you?"

"That's because I toed the line. And he stopped that shit then and there. I deserved what I got, and after that, I knew the rules," Malick said, appreciation lining his eyes.

Elven kicked the footrest down and into the chair, springing Malick upward.

"Oh, hell," Malick said, grimacing.

Elven leaned down into Malick's face where he could smell the sweetness of his breath. Most likely from diabetes that wasn't being well-managed.

"I know you aren't in the game much anymore these days, not since you got put in here. Too much breathing the junk you cooked ruined your lungs. Your one good kidney ain't so good anymore, and I'd be surprised if you didn't lose a foot in a year or two. Who did you hand the operation off to?" Elven said.

Malick scoffed, but that was the extent of his fight. The years had not been kind to him. "Tried passing it off to my son a couple years back, but that didn't go so well," Malick said.

"Why?" Madds asked.

"Went and got himself blowed up. After that, I had nothing. Nobody to hand off the business to. Didn't much care about any of it after losing my boy, so I just let it go." Malick raised his arms. "This is all I have now. Fucking Drew Carey on *The Price is Right,* though I prefer the Bob Barker reruns."

Elven shook his head. "That's it? You just let it go? And now you don't know who might be trying to take over because you're not in the business?"

Malick nodded. "Dupray has been without the crystal for some time now," he said. Then he lifted his lip into a smirk. "Unless, that is, they haven't. And you just don't know shit about who's been dealing for the past few years. Cause it ain't been me."

Malick started another one of his coughing fits and Elven stood up. He hated to admit it, but Malick was right. Did he really think that meth hadn't been in Dupray since Malick had given it up? No, he'd always thought Malick was still involved in some capacity. But if what he was saying was the truth, then it meant that someone had been dealing under the radar for quite some time.

CHAPTER SEVENTEEN

"WHAT ARE WE EVEN DOING HERE?" MADDS ASKED.

She looked at Elven's face, his mouth a straight line. On the ride over, he had been adamant about finding out who had been dealing meth in Dupray. But it was more than that. It was like he knew exactly where he wanted to go.

And that's when she figured it out. That's when she saw they were headed straight to Hollis Starcher's house.

Elven pounded on the door forcefully, like he was half expecting someone to pull the door open and come at him swinging. He was angry and Madds wouldn't have wanted to step between him and whoever opened the door.

But she also knew what that meant for her. She had been to Hollis Starcher's house a number of times since moving to Dupray. Of course, Elven only knew of a handful of those times, mostly because he had also been there for them. What she did in her time off, he never really asked about, which was good for her, considering Hollis was her uncle.

Of course, nobody but Hollis and the rest of the family knew who

Madds really was. And nobody but Hollis and the rest of the family knew what she was up to.

So when she found herself on the doorstep of the large, old house, she was less than thrilled. In fact, she was horrified. She was supposed to be keeping Elven out of Hollis's business.

And now she was doing the exact opposite.

The last time, Hollis had given her a few words when she'd helped Elven arrest Corbin. After finding out what Hollis was capable of when she did that *errand* for him, she wondered how many times she could screw up before it became more than just a stern talking-to.

She swallowed hard at the thought.

Elven pounded on the door again three times. He grumbled something as he waited, then pounded it again.

This time, he didn't wait.

"Get out here right now," Elven demanded. "I know you're in there, Hollis. Open up."

There was still no answer, which made Madds feel a little relieved. But the relief didn't last for very long. Not with Elven in the mood he was.

Elven stomped his way around the house, his boots crunching in the loose dirt that surrounded the walls of the building. He pressed his face against the first window he came upon, cupping his hands around his eyes as he peered in. His breath fogged up the glass as he exhaled. He ran his hand over it quickly so he could see. Madds peered over his shoulder, noticing that the house was dark inside.

"Elven, what are we doing here?" Madds asked again.

She was getting tired of his silence toward her. She had been angry with him earlier for trying to take Johnny or Tank on this case. Sure, maybe a little of that anger was sparked because Hollis needed her to keep tabs on Elven. But a part of her anger was genuine. At her core, she was still a cop doing her job.

And being overlooked by her boss to the other men who she knew were not as capable as she was really fired her up. And now, here she was, being ignored by that same man.

She watched Elven continue back around the house to the back, where more windows were. There were no fences on Hollis's property to signify where the backyard started and ended. It just opened up to another side of the property.

The sun was getting low. And doing anything in Dupray seemed to take at least twice as long due to the distance between everything in the county. It had been a long day, between finding the addict and taking him to Driscoll's, finding the body, visiting the revival, and talking to the meth dealer in a nursing home.

And now they were at Hollis Starcher's house without any reason she could uncover. At least one that Elven was sharing with her.

"Elven, stop."

Finally, Elven turned to her, his eyes lit with anger. His face was stony, his lips still sealed tight. But she could match the best of whatever he gave her. She crossed her arms and shifted her weight, staring right back at him.

Neither of them said a word.

But Madds wasn't budging. She solidified her resolve and narrowed her eyes at him, tiny slits so fine that a razor blade couldn't get in.

Finally, he shook his head. The crow's feet spread from his eyes as he softened them.

"Fine, you're right. I keep forgetting you're still new in town. I don't know what you think of Hollis Starcher, but I thought I'd made it very clear about who he is as a person. And that person is somebody you do not want to get to know," Elven said.

Madds looked around at the dusty patch of concrete in the ground that they stood near. The siding on the house had been well taken care of. Most of Dupray had old fading paint, mostly half peeled off. But Hollis Starcher's house was different. It was obvious he took care of it. It was a very old home, most likely passed down to him from his parents. But there was an obvious pride in ownership. Nothing frivolous or flaunting, but still noticeable.

"It's more than me being new here. I'm well aware of how you feel about Hollis. Hell, I'm well aware of how you feel about all the Starchers. I witnessed that the last time you and I worked on a case together. There was no love for Corbin, Wade, or Hollis. Though I'm still confused about Penny and Lyman," Madds said with a shrug.

"I'm not here because I don't like the Starchers," Elven argued.

"Are you sure? Could've fooled me. Because what it looks like is you hate Hollis so much that you're trying to place blame on him, or any of his kids for dealing meth. Or is it for the murder of that junkie? The one that we already have a suspect in custody for," Madds pointed out.

Elven grimaced. "You don't know them like I do."

Madds threw her hands up in the air. "Then tell me. You keep saying this, but there's no proof. You have zero proof that Hollis, Corbin, or Wade did anything related to this case. And all you do is tell me to not get to know them. Don't talk to them. Maybe there's something you know that I don't. Maybe if you could just tell me what happened in your past to make you feel this way, I could understand. Because, Elven, for a town that seems to know everything, you are the only one that tries to blame Hollis. Tank and Johnny aren't out here trying to pin a murder on them. It's only you."

Madds waited and watched Elven mull over her words in his head. She'd said her peace. And you know what? She meant it. Elven had a big hard-on to pin anything on Hollis Starcher.

Sometimes it felt like there were two people inside of her. One who worked for Elven, and one who worked for Hollis. But both of them saw no evidence here to pin on the Starchers.

In a way, she didn't blame Hollis for bringing her in to keep tabs on Elven. The way he was acting toward Hollis and his clan could be called harassment.

"I have my reasons. I'd like to keep them my own," Elven said.

What an asshole. It was the very statement she'd told him when

MURDER IN THE MOUNTAINS

she was asked why she wanted to leave Arizona and take the job in Dupray.

Maybe it was better that she didn't know. After all, she had put herself in bed with Hollis Starcher, though she would much rather use a different phrase than that when referring to her uncle. She'd had a glance of who he was. Though he had his minor crimes like selling moonshine, she knew he was capable of so much worse. Like murder.

Was there more to find out about the man? And if she found out who he really was, or what he really did, would she rethink her position in his network? And if she ended up doing that, how vindictive would Hollis be? What did that mean for her relationship with Elven? Would she lose the protection that Hollis provided?

Just thinking about going back home, or anyone knowing where she was, frightened her more than anything.

Before she could answer any of those questions for herself, Elven continued around to the east side of the house. They were nearly completing a circle around the building at this point. She scurried up toward him, trying to keep up with his fast pace. But she could tell that he was already back to his mission of trying to pin everything on Hollis Starcher.

CHAPTER EIGHTEEN

ELVEN MADE HIS WAY AROUND THE STARCHER RESIDENCE AND into the side yard. Without the fence, it was all too big of a piece of land to be called a *yard*, but it was on the side of the house, so it fit. The temperature in the air was dropping along with the sun, a breeze picking up the loose dirt into the air. The property behind the house was vast, which was different from when one looked at it from the front of the residence.

Elven knew the Starchers had money. He just couldn't prove where they had gotten most of it. Hollis Starcher liked to keep up appearances in all aspects of his life.

On paper, the money he earned looked proportionate to the jobs he held in town. The house he lived in looked only slightly better than the rest of the community. But there was more underneath the façade.

There was a large shed around the side of the house. It was a large wooden structure in the distance, which was still all Starcher property. It looked like a rickety thing, but he knew that on the inside, it was well-supported. He had been inside that structure once before.

Elven's boots crunched over the pebbles in the dirt lot that was

Hollis's yard. Madds tailed behind him. He didn't blame her for wanting an answer. In fact, when she'd spoken to him, it did seem like he was a little crazy. There was no proof against any of the Starchers that they had anything to do with the meth dealing, the murder, or even any piece of the revival in the forest that Spencer was running. Maybe Elven was way off on this one.

But his distaste for the Starchers and everything Hollis stood for kept driving him.

"Are you in there, Hollis?" Elven asked.

There was no answer.

Elven continued on. "Come on out right now!"

This time, the rickety-looking door to the shed swung open. But it wasn't Hollis who stepped outside. It was Corbin Starcher.

Hollis's oldest son, and Elven's least favorite of Hollis's offspring.

Corbin was just as large as his dad, but with Hollis's age also came frailty. It wasn't that Hollis was weak by any means—no, it was just that he had a demeanor about him that wasn't always threatening.

Corbin did not have that.

Corbin was slightly older than Elven. He had large shoulders and a broad chest, but he also held a lot of weight in his gut. His hair was buzzed so close to his head that Elven wondered why he didn't just shave it all off.

"Shit, Elven is that you?" Corbin asked. He pulled out a cigarette from a pack in his hand just after smacking it in his palm. He slid it between his lips, cupping his hands around it as he lit it.

"Where is Hollis?" Elven asked.

Corbin chuckled as he let out a puff of smoke, breaking it up into tiny clouds as he laughed. "How the hell should I know? You know he might be my daddy, but we ain't got a relationship like that. I don't know where he is at all times and he don't know where I am at all times. Funny how that works when you work for your money. Speaking of, how's your daddy?" Corbin taunted.

Elven looked behind Corbin toward the door to the shed that was swinging in the breeze. Inside, he saw all the metal equipment that the Starchers used to make their moonshine. There were a few copper pieces and a couple of pots. Elven didn't know all the ins and outs of the machinery, but he certainly knew what the end result was.

Before Elven could say anything, Corbin drew his eyes toward Madds behind Elvin.

"What is this about? It's one thing for you to come snooping around our home by yourself, but now you're bringing this bitch with you?"

"You already know my deputy," Elven responded.

Corbin chuckled. "Sure do, but you sure you want to be bringing her around here? I don't think you have any basis being on my property right now." Corbin looked at Madds. "I know he's your boss, but you ready to go to jail for trespassing along with him?"

"I wouldn't be talking about trespassing when you're making hooch out in the open like this. I'm sure if I take a few steps backward off your property, I can see straight into that shed and what you're doing," Elven said.

Corbin scoffed. He blew a long cloud of smoke out into Elven's face. "You and I both know you ain't gonna do nothing."

"If that's the case, then you and I both know that *you* ain't gonna do nothing," Elven mimicked.

"Two names in this town can do whatever they want, so long as they don't try to get in each other's way," Corbin said threateningly.

"Who is that?" Madds asked.

Corbin grinned. "Starchers and the Hallies." He flung the cigarette butt into the open field they stood in. It caught a patch of dry grass, seemingly ready to catch fire, but instead it smoldered and went out. "That's why you can come in here like you do. Why you can demand what you want. Because your name and title. But as much as you might want to, you know it also means you can't take me in. You do that, and I'll be out in the morning. And then, you'll have stepped into something you really don't want to be in. Didn't you learn that last time?"

"Able to do whatever it is I want? You mean like running a car off the road wearing a bunch of ski masks? Is that the sort of thing you mean?" Elven asked.

Corbin shrugged. "I got no idea what you're talking about, Sheriff. But if that happened to you or one of yours, maybe you don't have as much of a handle on this town as you think you do."

Elven stared Corbin down, watching him lick his chapped lips.

Madds stepped in. "You have no idea where Hollis might be right now?"

Corbin thought about it, then smiled. "No I don't. But maybe you should ask that game warden who came knocking at my door earlier today. He seemed really interested to know the same thing."

"Game warden?" Elven asked. Why would there be a game warden in Dupray right now? And if there was one, then why didn't they come into the station first?

"Holy shit," Corbin said. He laughed like he had heard the funniest joke in the world. "You really don't have any idea about what's happening, do you? You know, earlier I was just busting your balls about not having a handle on the town, but from where I stand, I'm starting to really believe you aren't as good as you think you are."

Elven bit his tongue, wanting to say more than he knew would be right. The inquiry into where Hollis was would have to wait.

He turned around and headed off the Starcher property and back to his Jeep without another word to Corbin. Madds lingered for a second and as he turned, he thought he saw a hint of something in her eye.

Something she knew and that he didn't. But he was probably just being paranoid, being angry and fired up about the Starchers. And the last person he needed to take it out on was the only person who was backing him up.

CHAPTER NINETEEN

ELVEN WANTED TO INVESTIGATE MORE. HE WANTED TO BE outside, putting his feet to the pavement (or dirt path, in Dupray's case), trying to get to the bottom of what was happening in his county. Drugs, murders, random preachers scamming people, and now some game warden who was asking questions without checking in with him first? There were so many questions that he didn't know where to start.

But he also hadn't eaten since the morning.

He knew that whatever was happening right now, whether it was all related to the same case or not, was going to take time to figure out. And that meant he was going to need to clear his head and think.

Which was why he found himself in his kitchen, making dinner over a hot stove.

He liked to think cooking was always a great way for him to do that. He could let his hands do some work while his mind could straighten out his thoughts. He picked a dish he made often. His hands were taking over, the muscle memory going on autopilot, which meant he didn't have to spend too much time thinking about the food.

MURDER IN THE MOUNTAINS

He sautéed some vegetables in the stainless steel pan and sprinkled some seasoning over the top. He lifted the pan and jostled it back and forth. The scent of the sugars being released from the onions filled his nose with each shake of the pan. He glanced to the side and saw Yeti, his white fluffy Great Pyrenees dog that he'd inherited from Carolina, who'd inherited him from Lester, staring at him, hoping to catch a rogue vegetable that made its way to the floor.

"You're not gonna want to eat this," Elven said to the dog. "There's no meat here."

The dog whined as if he understood Elven, but Elven knew that if a vegetable somehow made its way to the floor, Yeti would only sniff at it, lick it once, and then turn around with disinterest. He smiled at his dog. He'd never had one before Yeti.

Growing up, his parents had never allowed animals in the house. His father never had time for such nonsense and his mother worried too much about a dog being too dirty for the upholstery, or whatever items she could complain about. So living with an animal wasn't what he was used to, and he never got one once he moved back to Dupray and took the job as deputy. But he had to admit, taking Yeti in had been one of the best decisions he'd ever made. He loved that big white floof of a dog.

"Is this your usual dinner conversation?" Madds asked.

Elven set the pan down on the stove, turning the heat to low as he smiled at her. She sat behind the kitchen island on a stool and leaned on the counter. He had given her a moment to let her eyes wander all over the home, which he understood someone new to Dupray would find completely out of place.

"Most nights," he said with a nod. "But some nights we do have chicken, which is Yeti's favorite meal. He's not so keen on fish though."

"And you just eat all the steak yourself, not sharing? Poor dog."

"I don't eat beef," Elven said. "Have we not discussed this? I've looked a cow in the eye and saw her soul. Haven't eaten it since."

Madds laughed. "I'm pretty sure I'd remember that conversation.

Let's hope you don't make eye contact with a chicken, or else Yeti is going to have some disappointing dinners to look forward to."

Elven scoffed. "Chicken is different."

Madds shook her head. "I'm not sure which to bring up first. Should we talk about the house and how giant it is? I mean, have you seen the rest of the town? I feel like half of it could fit in here alone."

Elven chuckled, but inside, her comment didn't make him very happy. He didn't like to know that people in his community were suffering and struggling to get by. But it would do no good for him to abandon his home and live somewhere else just because it was big. It wasn't like anyone was looking to cash in on real estate where his house was anyway.

No he wasn't flaunting his money by living in that house. He was tucked away out of sight, not looming over the town at all times as if he was pressing his thumb down on them. But he wasn't ashamed of it either. No, he felt like he was working for the county. He felt like he was doing the community a service. He felt like he was trying to make the Hallie name something more than what his parents had done to it.

"And what would the other topic be?" Elven asked.

"How about why you invited me over for dinner in the first place?" Madds asked. She leaned over the counter, eyeballing the contents of the pan, scrunching her face as she did. "So no chicken or beef. We're eating vegetarian tonight?"

Elven went to the fridge and pulled out two bottles of beer, the necks cold against his fingers. He held it up so Madds could see the label, and she nodded. He popped the bottle cap off the first one on the edge of the counter, the release of carbonation spritzing in the air. He slid it over the granite counter to her. He popped the cap off his and took a swig.

"Technically, that was two questions you just asked," Elven said.

"Why don't you take your pick and answer one?" Madds said. She continued to drink her beer, the air bubbles forcefully making their way into the bottle.

"First of all, this dish could easily be made non-vegetarian if you would like, but I urge you to try it as is," Elven said.

Madds held up her hand, as if she was letting him win that one.

"As for why I invited you over?" Elven asked. "Why not?"

"I haven't exactly been the most pleasant person to you today," Madds admitted.

Elven shrugged. "Wouldn't be the first time someone was angry with me." He pointed to her and cocked his head. "Through no fault of my own, I might add."

Madds rolled her eyes, but he thought he caught a hint of a smile at the edge of her lips.

"I do hope we can put it behind us," Elven said.

Madds narrowed her eyes at him. "So you're just gonna cook for me and nitpick at me to get over it?"

"I was kind of hoping that." Elven flashed the best smile he could muster up.

It may not have worked as he'd planned, but it still had an effect on Madds. She let a little laugh escape from her lips. He knew he was hard to stay mad at for long. It was all part of his charm.

"I'm sorry," he said. "You're a good cop, and I'm not opposed to being partners. Or something like that anyway. But I'm still the sheriff, and I may need Tank and Johnny to do things from time to time. You can't be the only one I ask do things."

Elven walked across his large kitchen and opened a rustic-looking cupboard, pulling out two white square plates and placing them side-by-side next to the stove. He spooned half of the pan onto one plate and the other half onto the other plate. He scooted one plate in front of Madds.

Madds smiled and stabbed at the vegetables on her plate, piercing one of the vibrant orange carrots. She took a large bite, keeping her mouth open and letting the steam rise out.

She started talking before chewing and swallowing. "Fair enough. So what's the plan now? Are you still going to hunt Hollis down? Because Elven, I don't mean to push buttons, but there's no evidence pointing toward him. He might be an asshole, or a bad guy as you'd say, but you're shaking trees when there's no fruit in them."

Elven relented. He understood what she was saying, and she wasn't wrong. He just had a bad feeling about Hollis. But truthfully, when did he not?

"You're right. Maybe we need to sleep on it and regroup in the morning."

Madds smiled as she chewed. "This is delicious by the way, but in all of this huge house, do you not have a dining room table for us to sit at?"

Elven laughed and shook his head. "I might have a table somewhere in the house but it's a little too formal for me. Wasn't aware I was having dinner with someone so fancy." He winked at her.

CHAPTER TWENTY

ELVEN WAS HAPPY THAT HE HAD MADE DINNER FOR MADDS THE night before. Not only did it take his mind off the new troubles that were plaguing Dupray, but it also gave him the chance to make amends with her. He liked her, and didn't want there to be any animosity between them. No matter how trivial it might be.

It enabled him to do his job better, not having to worry that the person he was working most closely with might have some grudge against him. And he figured it gave her more of a clear head, instead of seeing red whenever Elven told her to do something. Instead, she could think about the delicious dinner and the fantastic conversation he was capable of.

There were a number of things he didn't understand about yesterday, that was for sure. But the night's rest gave him the chance to think about it with a fresh mind. And he was going to need that if he was to deal with all the seemingly random bits of news he had gathered the day before.

He walked in the station with a smile on his face. He'd taken a bit more time that morning to get himself ready, to get himself in the zone, so to say. It would be a big day of piecing things together, so he allowed himself some extra morning meditation.

"Good morning," Elven said to Meredith, who sipped on coffee. He could smell the hot brew as he passed by her desk. It smelled great, but he had already made his green juice smoothie that morning and didn't need anything else, especially a stimulant. Maybe that would change as the day went on, but for the time being he was content.

Johnny and Tank stood by the back wall in front of the table where the coffee pot sat next to a box of donuts. Half of the box was gone already. Johnny shoved a long john covered with powdered sugar into his mouth. Remnants of jelly and chocolate frosting sat at the corner of his mouth, telling Elven that the long john wasn't his first pastry of the day.

Tank and Johnny seemed excited about something. Tank was actually smiling and poking Johnny on the shoulder, like they were gossiping schoolgirls in the hallway. Johnny laughed out his nose, snorting a gust of powdered sugar all over himself. He looked down at himself with a frown. He looked like a human beignet.

Elven couldn't help but laugh at the sight. "What's going on?" he asked, his curiosity getting the better of him.

Both of the men turned to him, excitement filling their eyes. Johnny turned his frown back to a smile, like he was a kid with big news to tell his daddy.

"Did you hear there's a game warden in town?" Johnny asked, chewing the last of his donut.

"I did," Elven said. It was good to hear that they knew about the warden. He had finally made himself known.

"Pretty cool, right?" Tank said. "You know, I'd thought about being a warden when I got back from the service. Settled into this job instead though."

Johnny looked at Tank with a grin. "Oh man, you would have made a great warden. What a job that would be. Being out in the wilderness all the time." Johnny had a dreamy look on his face.

Elven rolled his eyes. "Johnny, you can barely hike out there when we get called. How do you think you'd fare having to hike out there full-time?"

Johnny shrugged. "I can dream, can't I?"

Elven placed his hand on Johnny's soft shoulder. "Yes, you can, Johnny. I'm sorry."

Johnny smiled, like he'd forgotten all about it.

"So who is it? Last warden in this area was Reggie Arneson. Figured that old coot would be retired by now." Elven asked, "Is he waiting for me? Or did he leave his information?"

Tank and Johnny exchanged glances. Tank finally spoke.

"No, we haven't actually met him. We just heard he was in town," Tank said.

"And who told you he was in town?" Elven asked.

"I heard it down at Hank's diner this morning," Johnny said.

"I picked up a case of beer when I was in Jolo last night. The girl that checked me out told me," Tank said.

Elven couldn't believe what he was hearing. Everyone in town... actually, everyone in the county knew about this game warden in Dupray. And the warden still hadn't been in the station.

Elven was not happy. "Are you kidding me?" he finally asked.

Both of the men dropped their smiles.

"He comes into my county. My town. And starts asking questions, but doesn't even make introductions with the sheriff? I'm ending this now," Elven said.

Elven was getting fed up with not knowing things happening in his own county and hearing about them secondhand. He had someone dealing meth, possibly for some time before even taking over as sheriff, that he didn't know about. There was a scammer revival church in his woods, and now there was some warden asking questions on Elven's territory without even the professional courtesy of saying hello.

Elven was going to deal with it.

CHAPTER TWENTY-ONE

"WHERE IS HE?" ELVEN DEMANDED WHEN HE WALKED INTO THE lobby of the motel.

Moe Olsen sat behind the counter and looked at Elven, scrunching his face in confusion. It was obvious he had no idea what Elven was going on about. His feet were kicked up on the counter and a magazine lay open on his lap. In the background, a television played a fuzzy picture of some talk show, the volume on low. Elven could smell the breakfast that Moe had nuked in the microwave earlier.

The white tile was old and scratched to the point that it looked gray. The walls were bare, except for the one fake plant in the corner that had years' worth of dust layered on the leaves.

"What?" Moe asked. He sat up, his eyes narrowing down on the sheriff. He had a fine layer of sweat covering his forehead that extended further up to his receding hairline.

"The game warden. Everyone else knows about him, don't tell me you don't. I know he's gotta be here," Elven said.

There were very few motels in the area, and if he wanted to be as close to the action as possible, then Moe's motel was the place to be, even though it was on the outskirts of town. That is, unless he had someone he knew personally to stay with, of course. Airbnb was pretty nonexistent in Dupray after all.

"I can't just tell you my guests—"

"Cut it," Elven demanded. "You can, and you will."

"Room three," Moe said, pointing down the way. At least Moe was no dummy when it came to reading the room.

"Thanks," Elven said, making his way outside.

He'd been to that motel plenty of times in the past. In fact, there was one specific time he could remember that he wished he couldn't. But that's how life was sometimes. Just gotta let it roll off and move on. He couldn't control the decisions of others, so it was best to let it go.

But this time was different. This time, someone was in his town, asking questions about something Elven was investigating, and wasn't even going to fill the sheriff in on it. There was no way that would have flown with Reggie Arneson and Lester.

Apparently, times were different.

Elven found room three, the number that used to be affixed to the door was long gone, leaving only a faded imprint in the paint from the years of sun it had seen. It still served its purpose even after being long gone. It was a lot more than most people could hope for in their short time on earth.

He pounded on the door with his fist. It rattled so much that he was worried it would break down just from the force of his anger. He waited a moment, but there was no answer.

This time, he pounded again, taking care to hit it at its center instead of at the edge, just in case the hinges couldn't support any more abuse.

"Open up, Warden," Elven said, his words creating a slight fog in front of him. Elven's mood had made him so hot that he'd lost awareness of the chill outside.

He heard a loud groan from inside, the bed springs creaking as they sprung back up from what he assumed were hours of heavy stress on them. There was a shuffle, a couple of thuds, footsteps toward the door, but no answer.

It was shocking how thin the walls were at Moe's, to be able to hear all of that from the outside. He glanced around, checking the parking lot. A couple of trucks he didn't recognize, with Moe's Camry and Elven's Jeep parked close to the building. The rest of the lot was empty.

Elven's attention was pulled back to the door when he heard a familiar click. The click was unmistakable. It was the hammer being pulled back on a revolver.

Elven widened his eyes and spun to the side, putting his back flat against the wall next to the door. He heard what sounded like metal sliding against itself, the security chain on the door. He spotted the handle turning shortly after.

The door flung open, and the first thing Elven saw was the glint of a handgun. The silver barrel stuck out, but straight out toward the open air. Before the man behind the door could turn and check the side, where Elven was, Elven grabbed at the gun with his left hand.

He slammed it against the doorframe, then gripped the man's wrist firmly. Elven worked his eyes up the man, who wore nothing more than boxer briefs. He had a decent build to him, with a bit softer midsection than himself, but nothing that Elven would consider an extreme gut. He had a red goatee covering his chin that wrapped around his upper lip.

The man struggled, but Elven slammed his hand against the door again, planting it there firmly. His finger was no longer on the trigger. The man pulled his free fist back, his lip snarled. But Elven wasn't in the mood. The man was armed, he was dangerous, and he didn't know what his intentions were.

Elven wasn't even sure if he had the right guy.

Before there could be any more of a fight, Elven pulled his .357 Magnum from the holster on his hip and placed it in the man's face. The long barrel pointing right at the man's left eye.

The fist froze, still pulled back, and the man's eyes went from narrowed to surprised.

"Let's not do this," Elven said. "Drop the gun."

The man growled and took a deep breath. Elven felt the man release his grip on his own revolver and it clattered on the floor next to them.

"You the warden?" Elven asked.

"Depends on who's asking. You gonna pull that trigger if I say yes?" he asked, his voice low. But there was no fear and no pleading. It was defiance to the end.

"Take a look down with your eyes," Elven said. "Slowly."

Elven still held his gun only a few inches from the man's face as he watched his gaze lower slowly. He wasn't going to give him the chance to get the jump on him, no matter who he was. He just hoped he didn't actually have to pull the trigger.

As soon as the man's eyes settled on the badge on Elven's shirt, he felt the tension leave from his shoulders.

"Christ Almighty," the man said. His shoulders slumped and he let out a loud breath. "Mind taking the gun out of my face now?"

Elven smiled. "Does that mean you're the warden?"

"Fuck yes, it means I'm the warden," he said.

Elven wasn't taking any chances. Having a gun pulled on him put him in a deep focus. "Got any identification?"

"Yeah, in my pants," he said, motioning with his chin behind him.

Elven let the man's wrist go and motioned with his head toward the pile of clothes at the side of the bed. He then scooted the man's revolver to the side with his foot, just outside of the door where he couldn't reach it if he tried.

Elven watched the room and saw a woman roll over in bed. Her top was off, revealing her large, saggy breasts. Elven averted his eyes upward, thinking her face looked familiar. But half of it was covered in a sheet, so he couldn't place her.

The man pulled something from a pocket and held it up slowly. It was a small black item, like a wallet or badge holder. He walked to

Elven, holding it open. Elven took it from him and dropped his eyes to the ID inside.

JESSE PARSONS

WEST VIRGINIA NATIONAL RESOURCES POLICE OFFICER

It was followed by a picture of him that looked about fifteen years younger, though the red beard was unmistakable. He had a dopey smile on his face and was a bit more clothed than his current status, but it was still him. It all seemed on the up and up to Elven.

Elven tossed the badge back to Jesse. It landed against the mixture of red and white hairs on his chest as Jesse caught it.

Elven cleared his throat and motioned to the woman in bed, her breasts still splayed out for all to see.

Jesse kicked the bed, rocking her to the side. She opened her eyes and turned her head. Her makeup was smeared to the side and she had the imprints of the wadded-up bedding in her skin. Again, she was familiar, but he wasn't sure from where.

"Get up, sheriff's here," Jesse said to her.

"Oh, shit," she said, scurrying off to the back, not taking the time to cover herself up. Elven caught a glimpse of her backside, which surprisingly didn't sag as much as her front. Then she disappeared into the bathroom.

Elven bent down and picked up the revolver from the ground. It was hefty, and not much unlike his own. Except Jesse's was a S&W Magnum. Jesse snatched it from him, setting it down on the dresser.

Elven finally holstered his own.

"That a Colt Python?" Jesse asked, referring to Elven's revolver.

"It is," Elven said, waiting for Jesse to put some clothes on.

"Didn't think they made them anymore."

"They don't. Not like they used to anyhow," Elven said.

Jesse pulled his pants on, but didn't bother with a shirt.

"Those things are worth a pretty penny, ain't they? Sure, take it out every once in a while, but as a daily driver?" Jesse whistled.

"The Colt hasn't let me down since I started with it. Don't see a reason to change. And I don't much care for an increase in value. It was a gift," Elven said, not wanting to elaborate more. He honestly didn't care much about firearms other than if they did the job or not. It wasn't his favorite part of being sheriff.

Elven still wasn't happy. In fact, he was downright angry with Jesse for coming into Dupray unannounced. But after their tussle with the guns, the only thing he was feeling now was pure adrenaline and focus.

"You know, you could have avoided this whole thing if you'd just announced who you were at the door," Jesse said.

Elven smirked. "Oh, yeah?"

"Yeah," Jesse echoed. "Seems a little unprofessional to come to a man's room without announcing yourself."

"I guess now you know how it feels," Elven said.

Jesse cocked his head. "I get the impression that you aren't just pissed about me pulling out a gun."

"You know, I have to admit, you're not as dumb as you look, Warden Parsons," Elven said. He couldn't resist pushing buttons. Nobody came into his town unannounced and got away with it.

Jesse clenched his jaw. "Are you looking to get your ass beat?"

Elven chuckled. "I'm pretty sure we just caught a preview of how that would go down. But no, I'm not looking for a fight. What I'm here for is to find out why a game warden comes into my county, starts asking questions to the community, and never once does he make himself known to the sheriff. What do you know about that?"

Jesse grimaced, then released the tension in his face. He let out a hearty laugh that rivaled Santa himself.

"Oh, hell, that's what this is about?" Jesse asked.

Elven tipped the front of his head down so slightly that if he wasn't wearing his Stetson, no one would have noticed.

"Shit, Sheriff, I humbly apologize," Jesse said.

Elven wasn't buying it.

"I can tell you ain't buyin' it," Jesse said, as if reading his thoughts. "But it's the truth. I'm known to get ahead of myself and forget things."

"Kind of a big thing to forget," Elven said, unimpressed.

Jesse shrugged. "I didn't mean nothing by it. Got into town, wanted to get a few errands out of the way before I got settled in at the motel. I should have gone in to see you, but my one-track mind sometimes gets ahead of myself."

Elven raised an eyebrow, considering the man for a moment. He truly didn't seem like he was joking or trying to make a fool of Elven.

"Reggie Arneson would never have pulled something like this. In fact, he and my predecessor had a pretty good working relationship," Elven said.

Jesse chuckled. "You knew Reggie? Oh, man, that old guy was somethin' else, wasn't he? He'd probably still be assigned to this region if he hadn't taken a bullet from a piece-of-shit poacher."

"He's dead?" Elven asked.

"Nah, just lost all movement in his left hand because of it. Took to early retirement," Jesse said.

"That's a shame. He was someone I could respect," Elven said pointedly.

"Truly, sheriff. I apologize. Won't happen again." Jesse approached Elven, holding his hand out.

Elven hesitated, but took it into his own and shook the man's hand. It was firm and surprisingly dry for having just had a gun shoved in his face.

"Elven Hallie," Elven finally said.

They broke the handshake and Jesse chuckled. "Man, they told me the guy you took over for used to be a hard-ass. If this is how you deal with someone coming into your territory, I'd have hated to see how he'd have dealt with it."

"You don't wanna know," Elven said. "What brings you out here then?"

Jesse yawned and rubbed his face. "That church group up in them hills. I heard they're causing quite the stir."

"That they are," Elven said. "Tell you what, why don't you get a shirt on, eat some breakfast, and head into the station once you're ready. We can go over it together."

Jesse nodded. "I would much appreciate that. Can't really function before my morning dump, you know what I mean? It might be the only reason you got the jump on me."

"Wonderful," Elven said. "Just head on in. I'll be around. If not, Meredith will get me on the radio and I'll come around. Then we can put our heads together on this thing."

CHAPTER TWENTY-TWO

Elven sat in his Jeep at the end of the parking lot. He was less than encouraged after meeting Jesse. The man seemed like a sleazy—and dangerous—version of Johnny.

And something just didn't seem right about the guy. He believed he meant most of what he told him in the room, especially about not meaning anything by his forgetting to head to the sheriff's station. But maybe he wasn't really there for the reasons he alluded to.

Elven didn't plan on staying there all day, but something was rubbing him the wrong way about the warden and he wanted to find out if he was right about it. So he let the engine run, keeping the heater on as he waited.

He spent a few minutes running through his thoughts, taking some deep breaths, calming himself down after the little altercation he'd had with Jesse. His heart rate slowed down and he was back to normal in just a few moments. He could think straight and not be on autopilot, letting his hands take over.

And as he waited, exactly what he thought was going to happen, happened.

The once-green door to the motel room opened up and the

woman with the saggy breasts exited the room. She was fully clothed this time. She looked around before walking away from the room. There was no goodbye exchanged, no kiss at the door, it was only her with no Jesse even remotely around. Though, Elven knew he was still inside. She slid something in her purse, which Elven assumed was money now that he recognized her.

It was Lorraine Whitcomb. He hadn't recognized her from the sheet covering her and not having her face loaded with makeup. Or, at least, put together and not smeared all over.

He would have thought of her job description as a lady of the night, but it was mid-morning at this point, and most of her work, as far as he knew, took place in the daytime. She and a few other girls worked on the outskirts of Birther Hollow, having joined together so no man could run them around. Most of the county knowing exactly where to go if they needed her expertise. It was just a couple of trailers set up, run under the guise of a legal business.

There was no shortage of what they were offering around the county, such as Yolanda and her *healing massage* business in Starcher Hollow. But while Yolanda was more selective and, what some might call *upscale,* at least for Dupray, Lorraine was more down-to-earth with her services. Not everyone wanted steak for dinner when a fat, juicy burger would suffice.

Of course, there was no proof that it was a house of ill repute—or houses plural. And there was mostly nothing to bust in the way of danger. The most Elven could think of was when a certain city official had gotten rowdy and had been *encouraged* to leave by Lorraine's paid help...and had complained to Lester about it when he was sheriff.

Elven smiled, thinking about Lester's response.

"If I go in there to bust them for assault, it'll end with a fine and then they'll be back for you. Next time, I suggest you pay the lady for her time. Then go find a blowjob that's free."

The city official had scoffed, but turned away and walked straight out. Nothing ever came from his complaint, and as far as Elven was concerned, Lester had saved that man from a severe beatdown. The operation didn't cause any problems, but they would definitely solve their own if one arose. Lorraine was a strong and smart woman, and had more than the means to pay for protection.

Elven watched Lorraine walk off, squeezed tight into her halter top that seemed about a size and a half too small for her. He could see the tiger claw marks at the side of her muffin top as it bulged between the skirt and top she wore.

Elven wasn't aware of an outcall service that she provided, but that was one thing that he would have to keep an eye on. Setting up shop in the outskirts of town was one thing, but going out in the open where the good people of Dupray could see was another.

But what it did confirm for him was the type of man Jesse Parsons was. A man with a badge, coming into town unannounced and paying for a hooker.

It was just one more line on the growing list of things that Elven didn't like about the man.

CHAPTER TWENTY-THREE

"METH? ARE YOU FUCKING KIDDING ME RIGHT NOW, HOLLIS?" Madds demanded as she stormed into the Starcher residence through the back door. The screen flapped against the frame as it swung shut behind her. The inner wooden door was propped open by a small statue of a turtle that looked like it was made of solid concrete. The entire house was a few degrees warmer than outside, but still leaving Madds glad she wore her coat.

"And hello to you too, Deputy," Hollis said as he sat in his recliner, a spread of biscuits and gravy in front of him on a wooden TV tray. *Dr. Phil* played on the television in the living room across from his chair.

"Oh, cut the shit. I'm alone," Madds said as she paced toward him.

Hollis didn't respond. Instead, he looked at the TV and shoveled a steaming bit of what looked like borderline excrement into his mouth. He chewed, not bothering to keep his mouth closed as he did, and swallowed it down.

"You hungry? Penny made a big ol' batch of this," Hollis said as he cut into the soggy biscuit with the side of his fork. The gravy looked like it was supposed to be white, but was a light brown, with dark brown bits of sausage poking up from it.

"Her mother used to make the best biscuits and gravy, but I gotta say, Penny really perfected the recipe. The secret is to load it with Tabasco. It sure don't look too appetizing, but it tastes divine. Come on, get yourself a plate," Hollis insisted.

"I think I'll pass on the self-induced diarrhea, but thanks," Madds said, her voice dripping with sarcasm.

Hollis cleared his throat. "I must say, Maddie, that wasn't very nice."

Something on Dr. Phil caused a big *Ooohhhh* from the audience and Hollis laughed.

"Oh, I love this guy. He tells this girl that she can't go smacking her mother around and wearing shorts that leaves her ass hanging out while she is living under her mother's roof. I tell ya, kids these days got no respect. If that was my daughter, I'd—"

Madds grabbed the remote from the armchair, her thumb smearing the drop of gravy that landed on the side. She pushed the power button and the TV blacked out.

Hollis looked down at his plate and sighed.

"I don't give a shit about Dr. Phil, or your damn biscuits and gravy, or how your boys are the biggest dipshits in the county, or that your daughter fucked the football team after a state championship—"

Hollis growled and his eyes flashed for a brief moment. "That's your cousin, and I will not have you talking about family that way."

Madds watched Hollis sit up and shove his tray to the side, nearly toppling the plate of gravy to the floor as he did. He stood to his feet, wobbling a bit on his bad leg and stepped forward, planting himself firmly. Madds regretted going off like she did, but she was still in the dark as to what she was even doing. And as much as Hollis talked about family, she didn't know these people at all.

She hadn't spent summers in Dupray with her cousins and uncle. The only time she had ever met them was when Hollis's wife had died. Her mom and dad had taken them to West Virginia for the funeral and spent one night there. That was the first, and only, time she had met her extended family. Until recently, of course. She didn't remember it much since she was younger, but she could count on one hand the amount of words she had spoken to any of them.

Her father had left Dupray a long time ago and had said he never wanted to go back. Her mother had expressed the same feeling after that one visit.

Madds could see why.

"I didn't mean anything by it. I'm sorry. Won't happen again," Madds said, backtracking before Hollis could do worse.

He grumbled and nodded, accepting her apology.

"But I need to know. Elven is on the hunt right now for a meth dealer. Is that what I'm supposed to be keeping an eye on for you?" she asked. "Are you mixed up in dealing drugs?"

Hollis brought a smile back to his face. The one that, on the surface, seemed inviting and like a man without a care. But she was beginning to understand who he was underneath.

"I appreciate the tip," he said. "But don't stress out so much about these things."

"Jesus, Hollis," Madds said. "You know that not giving an answer is pretty much giving me an answer."

Hollis shrugged and took the few steps over to his chair. He grabbed the glass of brown liquid, most likely sweet tea, from the table and pulled a swig from it. A ring of water remained on the wooden top where the glass once sat. He smacked his lips when he finished.

"It's good you're keeping tabs. That's exactly what you're supposed to do. As far as the meth? Things are complicated right now and I don't want to get into any specifics."

"So that's a yes, then? Cause the specifics are yes or no."

"Things aren't as cut and dry as you make them out to be," Hollis said. "But I will not have you come into my home and demand information from me like this. Your job is to do as you're told and keep Elven out of things."

Another answer Madds hated. How the hell was she supposed to keep Elven away from Hollis's business when she didn't know for sure what Hollis's business even was. And at the same time, Elven kept trying to put every crime on Hollis?

"There's also a game warden in town. We found two methheads out in the woods, with one dead. If you've got your hand into dealings out there, then Elven isn't your only problem," Madds offered.

Hollis smiled. "Jesse Parsons? Don't you worry about him. He's no threat to us." Hollis gave a wink like he was giving her some inside knowledge that she was supposed to know about. But it was just more confusion for her.

"You know him?" she asked.

"About as well as one can truly know someone," Hollis said. "Had drinks with the man last night. Fun guy, that one."

Madds clenched her teeth. She understood Elven's frustration with the warden not making himself known. She felt like she was dealing with the same thing, just on the opposite end.

"Don't worry too much," Hollis said again. "I'm sure Elven will have his hands full in no time with something else." Hollis clicked the remote, powering the TV back on before sitting down again.

Madds left it at that, knowing that Hollis had plans he wasn't telling her. And while the less she knew the better it was when lying to Elven, she also wondered how bad it could be when it all backfired on her.

CHAPTER TWENTY-FOUR

Elven drove his Jeep back from the motel. The stretch of road from the outskirts of Dupray Proper back to the station was long and quiet. There wasn't a single car he passed on his drive back. But he was used to long, lonely roads in his line of work.

Along the way, a building stuck out to him. It was one that he passed almost daily, but he found himself rarely visiting.

It was a small building that to the untrained eye would seem like any other vacant, or near-vacant, storefront. Except it wasn't a store at all. Sure, in Elven's years around the globe, he could make a solid case for the idea of them actually selling something. But the government didn't tax them for it, so he wouldn't dive into the ins and outs of it.

It was the Dupray Methodist Church.

Usually, Elven would just keep driving. Maybe say a little prayer to himself or perhaps give it no thought at all. Growing up, he hadn't been too involved in the church, with his parents mostly commenting on how the church only wanted their money for donations. Elven let their reasons for not going be their own, just like he came to make up his own mind about how to live his life. Though he had been known to visit the church from time to time.

But today, something tugged at him. It wasn't any sort of higher power, but his own curiosity.

He pulled into the small parking lot that wrapped around to the back of the building. There was only one other car in the parking lot, seeing as how it wasn't Sunday. But that was good. It meant it was just the pastor inside, and that's who he wanted to see.

He walked by the small flower bed that lined the wall leading up to the door of the wooden building. It was dotted with flowers, though he could barely see them. It mostly contained hostas and English ivy now, the green leafy bushes growing so that it covered what previously existed of the flowers and spilled out onto the walkway.

He pulled the door open and was suddenly hit with memories of his childhood. He may not have attended church as a kid, but that didn't mean he hadn't been to the building often enough back then. Most of the school fundraisers were hosted by the Methodist Church, seeing that it was the most central church in Dupray.

The smell was what hit him first. It filled his nose with the scent of stale crackers and old glue. The carpet he walked on was the same dark brown from when he was a child, except the spots near the windows were sun-bleached and faded from the long afternoons when it saw most of the warm rays.

The building was small from the outside, and was no different on the inside. There was a stretch of walkway down the center of pews on each side. But it was hardly anything Elven would describe as deep.

The man across the way looked up from his podium, glasses resting on his nose. His skin was pale, almost yellow, and he was balding on top. He looked deep into work, but smiled anyway at the distraction.

It was Luke Magner, the longtime pastor of the church. He had been there as long as Elven could remember, and longer. He was now in his sixties, and while Elven didn't have memories of his sermons, he had plenty that involved conversations with a kind man.

"Elven Hallie?" Luke asked, narrowing his eyes in recognition.

"Pastor Magner," Elven said, returning the smile.

"Oh, go ahead and call me Luke. You're an adult and now the sheriff, so I suppose it's only fair you start acting like we're both adults," Luke said. He walked out from behind his podium and stepped off the platform that was only one step up from the ground.

"You know, service is Sunday morning, though I suppose that's not why you're here," Luke said.

Elven smiled. It seemed whenever someone spoke of church, or was a pastor of one, they always tried to finagle their way into getting you to attend. Luke had apparently dropped the finessing and went straight for the ask.

It wasn't that Elven had anything against religion, or God. In fact, he wouldn't say that he was a non-believer. He just had his own reasons for not wanting to attend regularly, and being confronted with his own flaws and mortality every week wasn't his idea of a good time.

And sometimes, it just came down to not knowing.

After college, he'd spent a lot of time backpacking the world and there were many different viewpoints and religions he had encountered. He'd spent time talking with Buddhist monks in their temples, discussing life and religion.

Most people would try to give him answers about why they were the right religion to be a part of, but he'd always liked the Buddhists. They straight up told him that they didn't know when they didn't have an answer.

It wasn't enough to convert him, but he had a high respect for them for that reason.

Luke Magner was a man that he respected, too. But for different reasons. As a kid, Luke had never treated him any differently from the others. It didn't matter that Elven came from money. If Elven needed help, Luke would give it to him. But on the flip side, if another child needed help, then Elven would get no extra attention than was necessary. He was treated just like the rest of them.

It was the main reason Elven had wondered if his parents were ever right about their decision on where the church stood on people with money. That they were just after their wallets. Elven found it to be the opposite of the truth.

"No," Elven said, watching the old man make his way to the center of the aisle. "But I appreciate the info."

Luke smiled, causing the wrinkles to create even deeper caverns on his face. "You know I gotta try."

"And I don't fault you for it," Elven said.

Luke offered a hand toward the closest pew and sat himself. Elven sat at the one across the aisle, facing the old man.

"My joints these days," he said. "After the knee surgery, I don't like to stand so often anymore."

Elven glanced to the podium. It wasn't quite a pulpit, what with there not being steps leading up to a large enclosure, but it was fairly wide.

Luke winked. "I keep a stool behind it when I'm working on the sermon. When I'm giving the sermon, I tend to lean back and take breaks."

Elven chuckled. "Seems a little over-the-top to hide a stool. Aging is a part of life. I'd think anyone would understand."

Luke blew out through his lips like he wholeheartedly agreed. "This is an old-fashioned church, Elven. These people don't want a young pastor with gelled hair, or a guitar with their music, and they do not want to see their pastor on a stool. Sometimes, I feel like a little change could be a good thing though."

"Does that mean you haven't seen your numbers dwindle with Spencer Caldwell setting up shop out in the hills?" Elven asked, figuring it was the perfect time to segue.

Luke grinned. "Spencer Caldwell, is it? The name alone sounds like he's one of those fly-by-night pastors, doesn't it?"

Elven winked and shrugged.

"I suppose we've had a few people here and there be conveniently absent from a Sunday or two. But most of the people have been here for years."

Elven hated doing it, but he had the examples and needed to get some information, so he decided to throw Dale under the bus. It's also why he didn't give him a straight answer the other day. Not committing to one didn't make him a liar. "What about Dale Croft?"

Luke leaned back and chuckled. "You've been doing some home-work, haven't you? You wouldn't be attending a church that wasn't mine, would you?"

Elven grinned.

"Though I do have to say, if you were, it would make me smile knowing you were getting right with God, even if it wasn't from my sermons."

"Just doing my job," Elven said.

"Dale Croft comes and goes. He's here and he's not. Just the way things shake out, I guess. But to tell you the truth, if he's after some-thing flashy and entertaining, well, I guess that makes sense. It's prob-ably why he's been stepping out on his wife with a little tartlet. Always wanting the new and fun thing."

"Pastor Magner," Elven said, somewhat shocked.

Luke crossed his legs and waved a hand. "Oh hell, half the town knows what he's been up to. I'm sure his wife does, too. It's probably her favorite time of the week, getting to hang out with her girlfriends playing rummy without that nuisance of a husband."

Elven couldn't help but laugh. "So the revival out there doesn't bother you?"

Luke shrugged. "Sometimes the Word can be a bit dry. If someone wants to punch it up in their own way, still following the teachings, of course, I don't see why that's a bad thing. But if it's more than that, then sure. Jazzing it up is one thing, but scamming people is another."

"You and I agree on that," Elven said.

"But I'm fine here," Luke said. "Nothing to get my nose out of joint over. Though I have heard that Abnel Foster over in Glover Hollow is having more of a problem."

"That so? How?"

"I don't want to be the one to say anything ill—"

"Like about a man stepping out with some tartlet?" Elven asked teasingly.

"Alright, alright. Abnel was never the best at connecting with people. He's got his own way of doing things that, well, frankly, is boring as the dickens. But he'd had lots of community outreach, so I figured that's why he had the flock he did. But now that this Spencer Caldwell is in town, a lot of that flock seems to be going there."

Elven nodded, trying to put it together. "And is that bad? I get it might be a pride thing, but like you said, isn't following God the overall goal?"

"Elven, I hate to put it this way, but it's the truth. And maybe something you don't have to worry about, being in your situation. But donations are what pays the bills. Without the tithe, there's nothing to keep the doors open. It's a shame."

"What's that?"

"That even with religion, a lot of it boils down to money."

CHAPTER TWENTY-FIVE

Spencer sat in the front row of his own version of a traveling circus. And why wouldn't it be considered that? That sheriff had shared some strong feelings about it, most of them derogatory and full of ill will. And those who wanted to be there, who wanted to see what all the hubbub was all about, they wanted a show.

And who better to give it than the ringleader?

No, he didn't think the same way that Sheriff Hallie did. But he could see the reasoning behind it. Spencer held a wadded-up bundle of cash that had been collected from the day's event. It was moist and wrinkled, dropped in the collection plate from various sweaty palms, but it all spent the same.

Money was a lot like the people who showed up to his church in need of something. It didn't matter what shape they were in. At the end of the day, they still served their purpose and were welcome in his house.

But it wasn't the daily presentations that brought in the serious money. That was the other thing he had learned about acceptance. Those that came by, needing something more than an ear to bend or a performance to be entertained with, they needed to have their own way of being satisfied. Satiated.

And one way or another, someone would eventually do it.

So why shouldn't it be him?

"You don't have to help us out," Wayne said at the other end of the tent.

Spencer glanced up and saw Michaela grab two chairs, one in each arm. She carried them to the stack that the men were building against the side of the tent.

"I don't mind," she said, her voice timid but friendly.

Spencer rolled his eyes. His cousin was a nuisance, but she might as well put herself to use. If helping the guys out with their tasks was what she wanted, then so be it. As long as she was out of his hair.

"Thank you kindly," Sammie said, placing four chairs on one arm, and another four in the other.

Spencer sighed. Even the most menial of tasks she couldn't do more than half-assed.

"Say, you know what would be great tonight? Those little hand pies you make. Think we could get some of them later this evening?" Wayne asked.

Michaela blushed and nodded quickly, tucking her hair shyly behind her ear.

"Mmmm. I think we got a can of apples. You could use them for the pies. I don't know if it'll be as good as the peach ones you made, but hot damn, my mouth is watering at the thought," Wayne said with a smile, revealing the gaping void where his teeth were missing.

Spencer watched in amusement. He wasn't sure if Wayne was just that hungry or if he was flirting with Michaela. He wasn't one to judge, he thought, but Wayne didn't come off as so desperate when Spencer first met him. His cousin was wrong in every way, even for a man like Wayne.

"I can try," she said.

"That'd be amazing," Wayne said.

Michaela spun around and, as always, wasn't watching where she was going. She bumped straight into Sammie, his arms full of another load of folding chairs. He dropped them and she fell backward, landing on her backside in the dirt.

The chairs clattered against each other and Sammie let out a groan as he took a knee to stabilize himself.

Spencer closed his eyes tight, his head pounding at the sound of the chairs and the overall commotion. "Are you kidding me right now?" he yelled.

Wayne, Sammie, and Michaela tensed up, turning their attention to Spencer. He stood and made his way over to them.

"Michaela, don't you have something you can do that isn't getting in the way of the men I'm paying? You have to fuck everything up, don't you?"

"Mr. Caldwell—"

Spencer held up a hand, cutting Wayne off. "Wayne, I appreciate you trying to include someone like Michaela in things. Make her feel like she ain't the stepping stone that she finds herself to be in life, but just because you humor her doesn't make it any less true."

Wayne closed his mouth, but helped Michaela to her feet.

"Maybe you can go bother Betsy for a while. Or maybe you could find something a little less important to interrupt and make a mess of, at least," Spencer said to Michaela. "Or do like Wayne asked and cook up some dinner that won't tear up my insides."

Michaela nodded and disappeared from sight. He was sure she was crying, with the way her shoulders hunched and how she hid her face, but he couldn't have cared less. She needed to understand her position in life.

Spencer looked at the two men who slowly gathered the chairs. Neither of them looked at him. Spencer smiled, satisfied that everyone was back to work and he could return to counting his cash.

"You know, you shouldn't be so mean to that girl," a voice said. At first, Spencer was ready to go off, thinking it was Wayne or even

Sammie from underneath his bushy mustache. But the voice didn't match and it sounded a hell of a lot more confident than either of those men.

Spencer tensed up and turned around. He snarled as he saw the man who stood before him.

CHAPTER TWENTY-SIX

"AND WHAT THE FUCK DO YOU CARE ABOUT IT?" SPENCER asked, dropping the preacher routine when it was obvious the newest visitor wasn't there for a sermon.

The man in front of him curled a lip in a smile. His red mustache tickled the edge of his nostril as he did. Spencer looked down and saw he was wearing a uniform similar to the sheriff, though not exactly the same. This one had a badge, but it meant jack shit to Spencer.

"Department of Natural Resources?" Spencer asked. "What the hell is that supposed to mean?"

"It means I'm the law out here," the man said.

He chuckled and Spencer once again realized how different this man was from the sheriff. They were built completely different. Sure, this man looked like he had strength to him, but he also looked like he went heavy on the cake and beer. His midsection pushed the limits of the shirt he wore.

"I don't know about that. If you're here to shake me down, I'll have you know—"

"I know, I know," the man said. "You've got permission. That's why I'm out here, actually."

"Does that mean you're gonna tell me your name and what the fuck you are? Cause I gotta say, your title doesn't really strike authority to me."

"Jesse Parsons," he said. "I guess the short term for what I do is game warden."

Spencer nodded, and glanced at Wayne and Sammie. They worked slowly, not making eye contact, but Spencer could tell they were trying to hear everything spoken.

"Why don't you boys take a break. Maybe Michaela will have dinner started and you can hover around," Spencer said to them.

The men didn't have to be asked twice. They found the nearest open flap of the tent and disappeared.

"You closing up shop for the day already?" Jesse asked.

"Hold most of the services in the day, though we are open to smaller sessions and sit downs with individuals. You in need of that, warden? My time is valuable, but I'm willing to offer a discount for a man of the law like yourself," Spencer added.

Jesse shook his head. "Don't worry about me. Me and the big guy upstairs have a sort of agreement."

"Oh yeah? And how's that?" Spencer asked, mildly curious.

"He doesn't fuck with me and I stay out of his business," Jesse said.

Spencer couldn't help but laugh. "Oh really? I'm sure that goes over real well. What is it you're into? Drugs? Too much booze? Power? Hookers?"

Jesse eyed Spencer when he landed on the last one.

"Ah, the ladies, is it? I'm sure there's some power involved with that though. Having them attend to everything you need and want. Like you are the one in control. If only you didn't have to shell out cash for the interaction, right?"

Jesse licked his lips, and Spencer could tell he was pushing some nerves, maybe a little too hard, so he let up. It wouldn't be the first time his mouth got him in trouble, but he'd rather not get a beating from someone the size of Jesse.

Spencer was a lot of things. Manipulator might be the best description. He was definitely not a fighter.

"So, warden, what can I do for you?" Spencer finally asked.

"I heard you were having some trouble lately. Threats and all that. How's that going for you?" Jesse asked.

Spencer shrugged. "Nothing I can't handle. Just ruffling some feathers in town, I suppose. It's bound to happen when competition rolls in."

"Competition?" Jesse asked.

"You know, other churches. Some might say we are stealing their flock."

Jesse chuckled. "You Jesus boys throw down after seminary then? Man, who would have thought. I was more concerned about the hunters and their feathers. Doing any ruffling there?"

"Guess that's bound to happen, too, being where we are during hunting season. But there's miles and miles of forest. We are just one small spot. Does one cut off the blemish of their face when the rest of it is in perfect condition? Or do they wait for it to be gone on its own?"

Jesse cocked his head. "I don't suppose I know that one. Who is that? Peter?"

Spencer smiled. "That's all my own. No scripture. Maybe just a little inspiration."

"Thought it sounded like some straight horse shit," Jesse said. "But those hunters may not want to wait for that blemish to clear up, depending on how long said blemish is gonna last. If you catch my drift."

Spencer nodded.

"Can't say I don't blame them either. They ain't too happy. Some of them hunt these grounds every year. A sort of tradition, and you being smack dab in the middle of it...well, you're impeding on tradition."

"So you're here to ask me to leave?" Spencer asked. "Or is it more than ask?"

"Of course not. I guess I'm saying that with me here, maybe I could deter them from acting on those impatient impulses. Maybe I could even get them to take a year off from the tradition. Find themselves a better hunting spot."

"I tell you, I'm not sure you have as much sway as you think. The actual law, the sheriff, was here—"

"Oh, fuck that guy. He's too busy looking like he stepped out of an underwear ad to be doing any real work. I'm a man of the people, and because of that, people love me."

Spencer frowned. "What is it you're asking for?"

Jesse shrugged. "Just something to keep in mind, I suppose. Not asking for anything, really, but I guess if you felt the need to entice my efforts, I wouldn't be opposed. I've been rethinking my position on lots of things lately."

"Is that so?"

"Maybe we could help each other. Wouldn't you want a warden around, protecting your affairs instead of meddling in them? I'm sure there's a little more under the surface than just preaching the Word. Am I right?" Jesse asked with a wink.

Spencer grew hot under the collar. Did this man really know anything about his business? Or was he just fishing?

"How much are we talking?" Spencer asked.

Jesse laughed, and Spencer felt annoyed at the sound. "Can't put a price on peace of mind. That's something for you to decide. I'll be around. You give it some thought."

And with that, Jesse left the tent. Spencer clenched his jaw, wondering how much Jesse really knew and how much he was going to dig to find out.

CHAPTER TWENTY-SEVEN

ELVEN STARED AT THE CLOCK ON THE WALL AS HE SAT BEHIND his desk. Most of the day, he'd just clicked around on his phone, wasting time as he ran his thoughts over the case. He hadn't figured anything out.

And now he was thinking about Jesse Parsons.

How did any of the things connect? Did they even relate at all?

Was he spending too much time worrying about something that wasn't even a case? The murder was cut and dry. The two methheads had gotten into an argument, or something like that, and one man ended up dead. Whether or not the man meant for it to happen was another question that didn't matter much. Drugs could do that to a person.

So now, Elven was digging. And for what? Because someone was dealing meth in Dupray. If he was honest with himself, it wasn't like it was anything new. So what if it wasn't Malick dealing any more? And so what if the drugs started to show up a little more frequently around the county?

It was all part of the job. He would make arrests, he would follow the clues and leads, and eventually, whoever was dealing would end up in his jail.

So why was he stressing out so much about it?

Because something didn't feel right. It was more than just someone dealing drugs in his county. It felt like something bigger was happening. Something underneath the surface. And he felt like he was being made a fool of because of it.

And now, it was late. He'd been in the station for quite a while that day.

Jesse Parsons never showed.

Elven wasn't surprised. Well, in a way he was. He'd waited, and was obviously stood up. But he had extended professional courtesy and faith to the man who didn't deserve it. And now he was left high and dry with a man who apparently had zero respect for Elven or his office.

But now, he knew for sure where Jesse Parsons stood.

As if he didn't have enough things on his mind.

He stood up from the desk, stretching his back. Sitting in the chair for most of the afternoon had stiffened his muscles, which only added to his frustration.

He headed out of his office and down the hall. He passed Tank and Johnny's office, both of them at their desks, acting as if they were working. Tank, maybe, though he wasn't sure how much office work the man could get done anymore. The poor guy had become a glori-fied secretary after taking the buckshot to his gut. Elven would have to give him some light fieldwork sooner rather than later.

Johnny, however, was most likely playing solitaire on that old computer on his desk. Elven was sure that if he wanted, he could walk around to the front of the monitor and witness it in action. But what work was there to do right now? Elven was the one putting the pieces together in his head. Nobody else could help with that.

He entered the main lobby, where Meredith was putting her sweater on. Her purse was on her seat.

"Leaving already?" Elven asked.

"It's already dark out, Elven. How much longer did you want me to stay?" she asked.

Elven shook his head. "It's not like that. Just irritated is all. Not with you."

"That game warden?" she asked.

Madds walked in, the door letting a burst of cold air flow into the lobby. She stopped when she saw Elven. He thought she looked as if she had just been caught doing something she wasn't supposed to. What that was, he didn't know. But it was most likely because of his own anger at Jesse that was making everyone look suspicious to him.

"Where were you?" he asked.

She cleared her throat and took off her jacket, holding it over her arm. "Out patrolling. Just seeing if anything looked strange out there."

Elven nodded. "And did it?"

"What?" Madds asked.

"Did anything look strange?" Elven asked.

"Oh, no. Not that I could tell," she said.

Elven turned back to Meredith. "Don't suppose that the warden came by or called to leave a message?"

"You know I'd have told you right away if he had," Meredith said.

"Right, of course," Elven said, his anger building. Was he supposed to hang outside his motel room, waiting for him to show up and put him in his place again? That apparently didn't do much the last time.

"Did you say you were looking for the game warden?" Madds asked.

Elven met her eyes and, once again, something in them seemed off. The suspicion rose in him a little, but he pushed it off, knowing he was overwhelmed with his feelings toward Jesse.

"You know something?" he asked.

She swallowed. "I heard he was at the bar the other night."

"Doesn't surprise me," Elven said.

"With Hollis Starcher," Madds added.

He clenched his jaw. That son-of-a— "Where did you hear this?"

"Around. Some people mentioned it," she said, her eyes shifting to the side. "Wouldn't surprise me if he was gonna have another beer with him tonight. You know how Hollis is."

He nodded, grinning. But his grin wasn't a happy one. It was one that knew exactly how Hollis was. If someone of questionable integrity like Jesse Parsons came around, he knew Hollis would be trying to get the man into his pocket any way he could.

"Thanks, Madds." Elven strode toward the door. "Have a good night, Meredith."

"You want me to come with you?" Madds asked.

"No, I'll handle this on my own," Elven said. He left the station without seeing the fear fill Madds's face. The expression that would have made him most definitely think that she knew more than she was letting on.

And that it was eating her from the inside.

CHAPTER TWENTY-EIGHT

MEREDITH LEFT RIGHT AFTER ELVEN HAD RUSHED OUT OF THE station. Madds felt guilty about giving that little tidbit of information to Elven, but then again, she needed time to think. The main question running through her mind was if she felt guilty due to throwing Hollis under the bus or because of what she was doing to Elven?

With Meredith gone, that left Johnny, Tank, and herself in the station. It was a slow night, so she figured they wouldn't really miss her there. Besides, had Elven ever drawn up a set schedule for them to work? It seemed to her that Johnny mostly took the slowest nights and days whenever Elven asked him to.

It made her wonder again what sort of life Johnny had outside of work. But not enough to actually ask him. At least, not when she had her own problems to deal with.

And Tank was looking for any sort of action he could get, so he lingered around the station hoping for any morsel to come across his desk that required him to leave the station. His injury still really held him back.

If he only knew what was actually going on in the county. Hell, if *she* only knew what was going on. She was spying on Elven and selling him out, and she still wasn't fully aware for what.

She shouted to Johnny and Tank that she was leaving the station about five minutes after Meredith had left. The lobby was empty and the men were in their offices, so she didn't expect an answer. And she didn't expect to be missed.

Right then, she had to get out and get what was in her mind out in the open. At least, the best way she knew how.

She was still getting used to the county in general, but had pulled up on her phone the route to a Catholic church. It seemed a little ridiculous now, but growing up, she was raised Catholic. She didn't much practice that religion anymore, but when times were tough and trying, she still found herself falling back into the old habits that her parents had ingrained in her.

Sometimes it wasn't a great thing, but other times, it comforted her. Even if it was nothing more than a familiar tradition to give her stability, it was something.

So she'd taken the twists and turns that the map led her on. At one point, she noticed her phone dropped all bars and started searching. She was glad she'd decided to screenshot the map and could follow along that way, otherwise she'd never have figured out how to get there on her own. And she wasn't going to stop to ask for directions.

The road ran up the hills then down, like a rollercoaster at times. There were so many things that were different about West Virginia than where she'd grown up in Arizona. Not even considering the weather and dialect, but where she was from was referred to as *The Valley,* and Mesa, specifically, was exactly as its Spanish translation. It was flat, like a table.

It was just a reminder of all the things she still wasn't used to. And all the things she was running from. If it were up to her, she never would have left. And, to be honest, she missed Arizona. This line of work, the type she was doing for Hollis, wasn't for her.

But she had no other choice. She couldn't go back, and she couldn't just go anywhere. Not if she wanted to stay under the radar.

A rural road came up with a number on it. It turned to the left and she looked down the long stretch of dirt road. According to her screenshot map, it was the turn to take, though it looked a little less urbanized than she had hoped.

She didn't expect much, maybe just a building sticking out somewhere, like a gas station. But there was nothing at all. Just one road connecting to another, without a single soul in sight.

She turned her car down the path and continued on, hoping for the best. And that's all she could do about anything it seemed.

Hope for the best.

After some time of driving, she was beginning to feel like she had made a wrong turn, but pushed on. She knew what was behind her, and unless she wanted to double back just to get lost somewhere else, she figured it was best to see the road through.

Her headlights lit up the road that had no streetlights ever since she'd pulled off the main highway and onto the rural road. Dust kicked up behind her, and in front of her was nothing but pitch black.

The road curved around and her heart sank more. Where the hell was she?

After a long curve, she saw a light in the distance and felt immediate relief. There was at least someone or something out there, and she wasn't completely lost. She wasn't big on directions, but as soon as she got to whatever that light was, she planned on finally asking around.

She drove toward the light and what was one light, became many lights. In fact, it was like a strip mall on the side of the road. The buildings were all adjoined, with their fronts lit up.

Her face felt hot, as if she had been holding back her fear and once she was able to release it, it all came out and her body couldn't handle it all at once. She laughed at how stupid she felt now.

It was one more thing that made her miss the suburbs.

Across the road from the strip center was the remains of a building. It looked like it had been fairly large, and possibly tall, but half of it was burned down. The back wall stood untouched and connected to a completely charred wall. A bit of the roof remained and sloped upward, but besides that, it was nothing but charcoal and ash.

On further inspection, she realized that some of the ash and remains of the inside of the building were church pews. The very church she was trying to get to.

"Are you fucking kidding me?" she asked.

She slumped her shoulders and looked to her right where the strip center stood. None of the stores looked open, as the lights were all off inside. She couldn't even tell what sort of shops they were or if they were even occupied, since there were no signs above the doors or on the windows.

The only lights were those that lined the small street, and one building at the end.

She drove her car down the street and pulled off onto the side of the road where it opened up to a dirt lot. She put the vehicle in park and let the engine idle for a while, staring into the black void of nothingness that surrounded the building. If there weren't lights around the building, she would never have thought anything existed at all where she now found herself.

She looked at the building, the brown bricks crumbling at points underneath the lights. The lone shop at the end was the only place open. And then she noticed that it wasn't a store at all. It looked like it might have been an old butcher shop by the way the door looked. An old imprint of what looked like a cleaver was in the center of the wooden door, just under the window at the top. But on the window, backlit from the inside, a cross hung.

The way the cross illuminated, beaming like an aura, made her think it was a beacon, calling her to enter.

She stepped out of the car and exhaled, her breath creating a cloud in front of her. She wrapped her coat more tightly around her body and looked at the surrounding area. The lot was empty, except for one other vehicle. The rest of the building was vacant. And she couldn't see anything past a few feet in the darkness. Not a soul in sight.

She almost didn't enter the building, but she had driven the whole way to get there. It was stupid not to go inside. Something felt off about the place though. She couldn't quite put a finger on it, but maybe it was just the location. Being across the street from a burned-down church was an odd place to be.

If the cross on the door was a beacon, she was getting mixed signals from the darkness that surrounded it. Like a warning begging her to stay away.

She swallowed hard and crossed the empty lot, pushing her way into the building.

CHAPTER TWENTY-NINE

ELVEN'S PREFERRED WATERING HOLE HAD ALWAYS BEEN Martin's Bar. Being downtown in Dupray Proper, it was easiest to get to after work. His acquaintanceship with Martin had grown over the years, so there was little reason to go anywhere else. Martin's Bar was also probably the liveliest place in town. He'd been going there for a long time...even before he was technically of age to drink.

Being the son of the richest and most well-connected family in town had its perks.

Elven had made his way through his younger years the best he could, like any other kid or teenager. But as he got older, he felt as though he was gaining a different perspective of the world than the one that his parents wanted him to have. He was able to mold himself into the man he was now, and that included his privileged past. But through it all, he still had Martin's Bar to go back to.

But this time, he wasn't at Martin's Bar.

Instead, he found himself at The Thirsty Toad, and he didn't like it at all.

Martin's Bar wasn't anything special. No fancy beers on tap, other than a local brew from the other side of the state. But it was almost a second home to him. The worn bar stools and countertop had charm and a way of making him feel he was welcome. Martin himself seemed to like having Elven around as well.

But at The Thirsty Toad, he was an outsider.

It was well known that Hollis Starcher was a regular at The Thirsty Toad. It being down in Starcher Hollow had a lot to do with it. The other reason was that Hollis was a silent partner in the bar. When the original owner, Lee Simons, had fallen on hard times, Hollis was quick to step in and lend a hand.

But that hand wasn't what Lee had hoped for. Gone were his decisions to do as he pleased, and so Lee had found himself becoming an employee instead of his own boss. Which was the whole reason he had opened the bar in the first place—to get away from doing what someone else told him to do.

But that's the way that life was. Especially when getting into bed with Hollis Starcher. Elven felt sorry for Lee, but at the same time, there wasn't anything he could do about it.

Elven had been to The Thirsty Toad back when it had been solely owned by Lee. And to put it bluntly, it had been a crapfest hole in the wall. But Elven could see why the locals might often find themselves there.

Now, when Elven stood inside and looked around, he wondered what had happened to the bar. What was once small, quaint, and cozy, was now filthy and dark. The charm of the local dive was gone, and instead, it had been replaced with a wannabe corporate setting, yet full of clutter. It was as if someone had come in, taken everything that made it unique, piled it against the wall, and then never finished getting rid of it. Like he had walked into an old shell of the former bar. In fact, that's exactly what he had done.

Half the lights were burned out. Some of the booths in the back weren't even open, but were full of boxes of miscellaneous junk that should be in the dumpster instead of prime customer seating. A radio played in the background, but it wasn't loud and sometimes cut out with white noise in the middle of whatever song played.

There were hardly any customers to speak of. Before Hollis had put his money into it, Elven remembered there being at least twice as many people in the bar. He would have asked how it ever stayed afloat, but he knew the answer.

Hollis sold hooch on the side. And he knew there was probably a few other businesses he was into that were less than legal. And whatever they were, they needed to be run through a legit business so the IRS didn't wonder where that money came from.

Of course, Elven had absolutely no proof of any of that. And there was no way he would be able to find any if it came down to him searching. That wouldn't be the way he was going to take down Hollis, whenever that day came.

Unfortunately, that day wasn't today.

But at the very least, he knew where Hollis would be drinking his beer—if he was meeting with Jesse again, that is.

Elven looked to the bar top where a defeated-looking and much older Lee stood behind it. He poured a beer from the tap, with the label on the handle being long worn off from being the most popular choice. Most likely Hollis's favorite, and most likely tasting something akin to what sat at the bottom of the porcelain bowl.

Lee looked toward the door where Elven stood, his facial expression curious, most likely from the idea of someone actually wanting to spend time at the Toad. Though, maybe lately with Jesse in town, that seal had already been broken.

But as soon as Lee realized who was standing in his doorway, his eyes widened. It was no longer curiosity, but fear. The beer began to overflow over the glass, far more than just the intended head.

"Hey, you're wasting the product," Hollis shouted at Lee, snapping him out of it.

"Oh, uh, right," Lee said, pushing the handle back upright. He swallowed hard and nodded to Elven.

Elven returned the nod, then followed Lee's gaze through his long, oily hair. Hollis sat at the center of the bar, just as Elven had figured. But what was even better was that Madds's tip was right— Jesse Parsons sat right next to Hollis, that emblem on his shoulder mocking Elven right to his face.

Elven clenched his jaw as he watched Lee lean in and whisper something to Hollis.

Hollis laughed and then turned to the door, seeing Elven standing at the entrance.

"Well, shit. Sheriff Hallie, how is it you find yourself in my bar?" Hollis asked, stepping down from his stool.

Elven noticed the use of the word *my* and Lee's visceral reaction to it. Lee reminded Elven of a beaten dog, the fight no longer in him and just taking more abuse while whimpering in the corner.

Hollis was his usual larger-than-life character that he liked to present himself as. A man of the people, yet still above them all. The last thing he'd want was for anyone to mistake him as an equal.

Elven scoffed as Hollis hobbled his way over, as if his leg had fallen asleep. It was that same bum knee getting the better of him, and maybe the only weakness Hollis would ever let show.

"I'm not here for you, Hollis," Elven said.

Hollis grinned. "I gotta be honest, Elven. The beer tastes like warm piss here. Nothing like the imported stuff you're used to, I'm sure. But we're happy to have you anyway. Martin's place full up right now?"

Elven looked over Hollis's shoulder and set his eyes on Jesse Parsons. Jesse spun on his stool and smiled at Elven. His seated position made his gut more pronounced against his lap, like an extra bag. His beard clung to tiny droplets of beer and his mustache was lined with foam.

"You," Elven said, brushing past Hollis.

Jesse looked confused, but stood. He was bigger than Elven, and this time fully clothed. But Elven didn't intend to get into a fistfight with him. He intended to give him a right and proper reaming.

"Sheriff, what—"

"Where were you today?" Elven asked. "I waited for you to show up at my office and you didn't."

Jesse chuckled. "I'm sorry about that, Sheriff, but I'm a busy guy. I don't have time to babysit a man in his own county."

"Babysit? Are we really going to have this conversation again? If I remember correctly, you got yours handed to you this morning. Does that need to happen again for you to understand?" Elven asked, stepping into Jesse's personal space so he could smell the man's sour beer breath.

Jesse dropped the smile and stepped right up to Elven, his gut pushing firm against Elven's body.

"I'd like to see you try," Jesse said. "I ain't gonna be surprised this time though."

"Whoa there, fellas," Hollis said, placing his hand on Elven's shoulder. Elven allowed himself to be gently pulled back.

Surprisingly, Hollis was breaking up the fight. Why was that? Then Elven reminded himself that he was in the man's bar and it would cost him money if anything was broken. Though, by the looks of things, that might add to the decor.

"Why don't we sit and have a drink? Maybe we can iron this whole thing out," Hollis said smoothly.

"Very diplomatic of you, Hollis. But I don't feel like drinking with swine like you," Elven said. "I'm here to know why this man is here in my town and doesn't want to meet with me."

"About the revival up in them mountains?" Jesse asked. "Shit, why the hell would I need to involve you in any of that? I can deal with hunters in the woods. I don't need a sheriff to police my terrain."

"It's called professional courtesy," Elven said.

Jesse shrugged. "I did need help, actually. So I sought out someone who seemed to have some real pull in the town. And I gotta say, he's a lot nicer than the asshole I see barking at me right now."

"Hollis? You think he cares at all about the people here? He's just hoping to get someone in your line of work in his back pocket," Elven said.

"Whoa, Elven. You know, I will not be insulted in my own bar. Even if I consider you one of my own," Hollis said.

Elven rolled his eyes in disgust. "You can forget thinking of me that way starting right now," Elven spat at Hollis.

"Even after the favors I done for you?" Hollis said with a sly grin.

Elven stared at Hollis. His fight wasn't with him right now, but it really seemed like he was trying to step into it. No, he was angry at Jesse. Actually, he was angry at the whole situation. He was in the dark about everything.

"You know, I know you think this is your town, your county," Jesse began, "but it's my district, too. You don't have sole rights to it. If that's the case, then you can think of them woods out there as mine, and any time you enter them, you should be checking in with me."

Elven shook his head. Jesse was definitely something else. "You may not know how things work around here," Elven said. "So I'm gonna give you fair warning right now. You do not want to get into it with me. Hollis here may be able to get away here or there on some minor things, but even he knows the game just like I do."

"And what game is that?"

"You don't mess with the Hallies."

"I can see that you two might have more to talk about than I do," Hollis said. "I'll leave you to it."

Hollis turned to leave, but Elven stopped him. "No. You stay. I'm leaving."

Elven turned to leave, but Jesse shouted at him. "There's been some reports come into our offices about some hunters not happy about that church out there. That's the only reason I'm here. Nothing more."

"You gonna do something about it then?" Elven asked.

Jesse shook his head. "I'm here to make sure nothing happens to anyone. Hunters can be quite the animals when they don't get what they want. But those people have permission. Not sure why they got special permission, but I hear that preacher of theirs has quite the ability to talk people into things."

"So that's it?" Elven asked.

"Don't like it much, but sure. I suppose that's it," Jesse said. "Buy you a drink?"

"No," Elven said, then turned and left the bar without another word.

CHAPTER THIRTY

Inside, the heat was more than welcoming to calm her nerves about being there. The interior was well-lit, a stark contrast from the dark night outside. Madds had all but forgotten any of her initial reservations once she entered the church. She even unzipped her coat as she stepped inside.

There were rows of folding chairs that filled the building. One aisle on the side was left open so anyone could walk down it. It was a small space, but it looked like they utilized it the best they could.

In the front row sat two men. One wore a long robe, and the other looked as if he had just come out of a year-long isolation. Both of them drew their attention to her when she entered.

Neither of them smiled.

She did though. The man in the robe turned back to the other and said something to him. They both stood and the robed man looked at her. The other man, the one with the dirty clothes and holes in his flannel shirt, walked toward her. She smiled to him, but he did not return the smile. Instead, he grimaced as he tried to push past her. His teeth were discolored and chipped. When he brushed past her, she smelled stale urine and BO.

He was out the door before she could get another look at him.

The man in the robe then approached her. He was a larger gentleman, with a well-trimmed beard. He smiled at her and the corners of his eyes wrinkled into crow's feet. His hair was turning gray, but there was still a large amount of brown in it.

"I'm sorry, we are actually closing right now," the preacher said in greeting.

"Oh, I—Uh, I'm sorry. I didn't realize you closed. Is this the Catholic Church?" she asked, looking around. She saw a cross on the wall, so it was in the same realm of religion she was looking for, but there was no Jesus on the cross.

"That old place was across the street, and burned down to smoke and ash years ago," he said.

"And this?" she asked.

"Episcopalian," he said.

"I see," she said.

He smiled, and did not offer any other words. She looked at him, hoping he would open up so she could say something, confess something. But, as he said, they were closing.

"If you'd like to come by tomorrow," he said.

She nodded and let out a long breath. She looked back to the door and back to the preacher. Or was it pastor? She didn't know how those things worked in Episcopal churches.

"Funny, I didn't see any other cars out. That man, does he live around here?" she found herself asking. Such a bizarre question, she thought. Dupray was not the cleanest of places, and the people weren't the most well-off. So what if he smelled like piss? He had every right to be there, just like she did.

But she was a cop. And she liked to ask questions.

The preacher cleared his throat. "We get a few people here who aren't in the best position in life. We do an outreach program and I'm here to help them if need be."

"I see," she said.

He glanced to the door then back to her. It was obvious he was in a hurry to leave. He didn't wear a ring on his finger, so there was no home-cooked dinner waiting for him, she assumed.

"You seem a little distressed," he said. "If you can't wait till tomorrow, maybe I can squeeze in a quick talk?"

"I am distressed," she said, plopping down on the folding chair in the front row, though not the same one that the foul-smelling man had been sitting on. "And that's why I came all the way out here. I was hoping for some sort of confessional, but apparently, even that had to be ruined in this shit town."

She locked eyes with the minister and grimaced. "Sorry."

She was beyond frustrated. With more than just one thing. It was Hollis, it was Elven, it was being in Dupray, and so much more. With practically everything in her life at the moment, really. But she realized it wasn't fair to take it out on the preacher. He had his own life that he was trying to manage. She'd just hoped he could have helped her.

He exhaled and placed two fingers on his eyebrows, like he was trying to get rid of a headache. He took a deep breath and exhaled again, sitting in the chair next to her as he did. He adjusted his robe, making sure it didn't get caught in the chair hinges.

"Well, I don't really have a confessional booth," he said, smiling at Madds.

She looked at him and saw his eyes had softened. "I'm sorry, I didn't mean to insult you or anything."

"It's alright," he said, taking her hand in his. He was older than her, and she felt nothing more than the comfort of a fatherly figure when he did it. She was grateful for even the slightest gesture.

"I had thought about building a small booth just to appease those Catholics who found themselves here," he said. "I don't think God would have minded if I blurred the line on denomination here or there, do you?"

She laughed. "I don't know much about that, but I suppose not."

"Anyway, we're all going to the same place, right? I just didn't have the space for one. So what's on your mind...?"

"Madds," she said.

"Nice to meet you, Madds. I'm Abnel Foster," he said.

"You don't have somewhere to be?" she asked.

"Well, I do, and the more you ask about it, the less time we have here. I don't mean to be rude, but let's just get to it," he said. He wasn't sharp with his words, just matter-of-fact.

"What do you do when you find yourself in a situation that was necessary to get into, just to get yourself out of a worse one? But then, you realize that the situation you traded yourself for wasn't really that much better. Just different?"

She found herself trying to be as vague as possible. She couldn't just blab that she had left a life behind where she had come from that was dangerous and would most likely have ended in her death, and now found herself doing the dirty work of her uncle whom nobody knew she was related to, and was now doing some very illegal things. Even if it was confidential and between her and the priest, she couldn't have said it.

He considered her for a moment. For a while, she thought he wasn't going to have an answer at all. Probably quote scripture and leave it at that. That was the last thing she needed.

"To be honest, I'm not sure. Was the situation you were in worth staying in?" he asked.

She shook her head, not even needing to think about it. If she'd stayed there, she knew it would have only ended badly. If she hadn't ended up dead, then it would have meant either someone else would have or she would be in a world of torture. And both of those situations would have been worse than death for her.

"Then maybe you made the right decision," he said.

"And what about where I find myself now? How do I get out of what I've dug myself into?" she asked. She was bordering on letting a stranger in on hints of her life, which she didn't like. But she was desperate.

He bit his lip. "Sometimes, we have to do things that aren't good. To protect ourselves and others we care about, we need to make tough decisions and take that pain onto ourselves. And after all that, we can reflect, repent, and try to do better going forward. Sometimes there is no avoiding it."

She leaned back and looked at the man in front of her. She smiled. Maybe he was right. She had to make those decisions, and going forward, she would just try to do better. Easier said than done, of course, but it was something.

Maybe she could still dig herself out. Maybe she could just slowly, day by day, find herself in a better situation. It would take work, but maybe she didn't have to keep digging herself deeper.

"Now if you'll excuse me, I really need to get going," he said, standing up. He un-Velcroed the back of his robe and slipped it off, revealing a button-up shirt tucked into a pair of slacks. The robe had covered up much of his girth before, as she hadn't realized he was so big.

"Thank you. I was hoping that maybe we could have—"

"I'm really sorry," he said. "But this time I really do have to go. Maybe we can continue this tomorrow."

And with that, he rushed out of the building, leaving her alone in the building. It was very odd to her, and maybe they left the building unlocked at all times for people to come and pray. But she felt out of place sitting there alone, with nobody to keep an eye on the place. Was there some unwritten rule in Dupray that made people leave churches alone? Or did the minister really trust the community to that extent?

Maybe she was reading into the situation too much.

She heard an engine rev up outside and then take off down the street.

What could have possibly been so important for him to leave so quickly?

CHAPTER THIRTY-ONE

"I DON'T WANT TO FIND THIS ANYWHERE NEAR MY TENT OR MY congregation, you understand me?" Spencer asked.

The man in front of him nodded. He was unkempt and smelled of stale sweat. His hair was greasier than the teenage kid who worked the deep fryer at the chicken shack in the next holler over.

Spencer watched as the man held his hand out with a sweaty wad of cash in it. Spencer looked around and made sure nobody was watching.

Wayne and Sammie were the only other ones in the tent. Spencer paid them well enough that they weren't going to say shit to anyone. They'd already seen enough and knew what was good for them. They knew the score and what was on either side of that coin if they decided to flip it.

Spencer took the wad of moist bills from the man. He set it in the cubby of the podium next to him. He pulled out the baggie that was stashed in there. He would count the cash later, but he wasn't worried about being shorted. If that ever happened, it was far worse for the man who tried to pull one over on him.

Spencer held the bag in his hand, squeezing it and feeling the rocks grind against each other inside of the plastic.

The man held his hand out, waiting for Spencer to hand it over.

Spencer held on for a bit longer, watching the man's arm shake as he held it out. The marks up his arm said a lot about his life to that point. How many drugs he'd gone through, maybe a life's worth until he'd settled on what Spencer was doling out. But Spencer didn't care. He was giving him what he wanted.

That man might need Jesus, but what Spencer was going to give him would make him feel like he was a god.

"I mean it. You make sure and find yourself somewhere far away from here when using this. That place ain't out in those woods."

The man scratched at his neck as he waited impatiently. He could hardly keep eye contact with Spencer, he was so twitchy. "I ain't gonna—"

Spencer didn't let him finish. "Maybe find a hole to hide in somewhere in town, maybe get a video game going or something else to occupy yourself. Just stay the fuck out of trouble. You get caught, I don't think I need to say what happens if you tell where you got it from, do I?"

The man shook his head, eyes wandering around.

"And don't come crawling back out until you're ready for more, you got me?" Spencer asked.

"Y-yes," the man said.

Spencer cocked his head and stared him down.

"Y-yes, sir, I mean," he said.

Spencer smiled and passed the bag to the man. The man stared down at the bag, squeezing it as if he'd been expecting more. He looked at Spencer, perplexed.

Spencer shrugged. "Take it or leave it. You know it's better than anything you'll get out there."

"Where's the rest?" he asked.

"Prices are up. I've got a lot of characters sniffing around here after some asshole found himself dead in them woods. And I ain't gonna risk it all for any less."

The man considered Spencer, then looked back at the bag in his hand. Spencer smiled as the man came to the conclusion that there was no way he was going to give back what he held. That was the beauty of addicts. They just couldn't see past immediate gratification.

The man turned around and headed to the entrance of the tent, ready to leave and hopefully take Spencer's advice of finding a place to hunker down while he tended to his needs.

"What the fuck are you doing in here?" Betsy shouted from behind Spencer.

He turned to see Betsy raising a hand toward Michaela. His sister could really put the fear of God into their cousin sometimes. As much as he was often annoyed with Michaela, he sometimes felt a twinge of guilt when Betsy rained hell down on her. Of course, not enough to do anything about it.

In the end, Betsy was right. Michaela was mostly a waste of space, and if it wasn't for their blood connection, he would have left her behind years ago. But being a Caldwell meant that family was to be taken care of. Even if he didn't think they deserved to be.

Michaela scurried her pale self off somewhere behind the wooden wall that stood behind the podium, which added additional support to the massive tent. Behind it was where Spencer liked to enter from when doing his sermons, and behind that was the exit to the tent so he didn't have to slide by all the sweaty assholes wanting to shake his hand. He only did that when he knew it would end up with a full collection plate.

"That fucking cousin of ours," Betsy said, coming toward Spencer. The curls of her hair bounced with each stomp of her foot.

He chuckled. "Don't I know it."

"How'd we do tonight?" Betsy asked.

"Won't know until I count it up, but I'd say it wasn't too bad. Not many people have money here, but there sure are people willing to spend what little they do have just for a chance to be close to God, and those that want to *feel* close to God. I could see us planting roots here."

"What about the competition?" Betsy asked.

Spencer shrugged. "Nothing to worry about. As long as we stay away from the Oxy, I'd say there's room for expansion."

"Never did like that hillbilly heroin anyway," Betsy added. "Can't believe there ain't nothing established here."

"We might be stepping on some local toes, but it's all games. Nobody has the market yet."

And Spencer meant all of what he said. Dupray wasn't well off, but there were a lot of people wanting to forget that fact, and to do that, they were willing to spend everything they had. If it weren't for those two idiots the other day in the forest, he'd say they were easily getting away with it.

And even with the dead junkie, all it meant was that a sheriff who didn't like him was trying to pin something on him that he had no proof of. He could deal with that.

"We're closed tonight," Betsy said to someone who entered the tent. "Unless you're here for a one-on-one that is."

Spencer looked up to see who'd entered. And he didn't like what he saw.

"I suppose you could say that is why I'm here, little lady," the man said.

He was big, but that hadn't changed since the last time that Spencer had seen him. What had changed was his clothes. He was no longer dressed in his more than identifiable style, but this time, wore a raggedy flannel shirt and a hat to match. It was like he was a hunter who had just stumbled into the tent by accident.

But Spencer knew it was no accident.

"What are you doing here?" Spencer asked. He was no longer in the power position he'd held with the addict. The large man towered over him as he drew closer. But he wasn't going to let this man come into his house and threaten him either.

The man smirked, his beard twisting. Spencer watched him slap his midsection and his gut rumbled underneath the flannel.

"I figured I'd come in and see if there were any new updates," the man said.

Spencer smiled and shook his head. "As if I'd tell you any of that. You here to shake me down, like you said?"

The man looked around like he was casing the place. Spencer watched him look at Wayne and Sammie, who stopped loading the chairs as they noticed what was happening. They stood firm, staring him down. Then he looked at Betsy and Spencer.

"Not quite what I thought this was going to be, but so be it," the man said.

Behind the large man, a number of men stepped into the tent from the main entrance. They were wiry and dirty. They looked like hunters, and all held rifles.

"If you think you're gonna come into my tent and threaten me, then you're in for a rude awakening, my friend," Spencer said, approaching the large man in front of him.

"No, I'm not here to threaten you," he said, pulling out a large revolver.

Spencer stopped in his tracks as he found himself staring down the barrel of the gun. He clenched his teeth and sneered. Spencer was ready to kill this man. For so many things. But nobody stuck a gun in his face and got away with it.

The problem was, this man was going to get away with it.

And the man was right. He wasn't there to threaten Spencer.

Spencer discovered that when he watched the man pull the trigger and the cylinder rotated in front of his own eyes.

After that, there was an explosion. But Spencer didn't have to worry about anything else that came next. The lights were out and his worries were gone forever.

Because Spencer Caldwell was dead.

CHAPTER THIRTY-TWO

THE BULLET FIRED AND MICHAELA WATCHED HER COUSIN'S head explode in the middle of the tent. From where she stood, she saw the back of Spencer's head explode out the back, splattering a rain of red and gray all over Betsy.

The man who'd towered over Spencer now stood alone in the center of the tent as Spencer's body crumpled to the dirt floor.

The motion in the tent seemed to slow down. The ringing in Michaela's ears overpowered anything else. Nobody moved for what seemed like an eternity. Wayne and Sammie stared at the spot where Spencer had once stood, no longer the strong men they presented themselves to be. Betsy stared in disbelief, her brother's brain matter and blood running down her face in streaks and globs. A wad of hair and bit of skull rested on her shoulder. Eventually, it slowly slid down and slopped onto her arm.

Betsy slowly lifted her hand, seeing the bit of skull riding down her arm like a miniature rollercoaster car from hell. She stared at it, still in shock.

The ringing faded in Michaela's ears to a low frequency in the background.

A split second later, Betsy screamed.

That's when time started again.

She continued to scream, but it didn't matter. Nobody was around to hear her, at least, not anybody who could do anything about it. And even if they could, they'd never get there in time to stop what had already happened. And was still happening.

But it wasn't the large man in the center who did much of anything. After killing Spencer, he just stood, watching the other men behind him do his will.

Wayne and Sammie went for the pistols on their hips. Michaela had sometimes seen them out shooting when they were on their lunch breaks. They'd even taken her out and let her try her hand at it. Of course, they all promised not to tell Spencer or Betsy. It had been fun, and the last thing she wanted was for her cousins to catch wind of her having fun. She'd be scolded and berated for the tiniest of joys.

But one thing she had noticed when out shooting with them was that they weren't great at aiming. They were fine, sometimes shattering an old vodka bottle after a few tries. But if it came down to an actual firefight, she figured they would be fairly useless.

And unfortunately for her, she was right.

Before Sammie could even lift his pistol, he had taken two rifle blows to the chest. The bullets knocked him back into the stack of folding chairs. They clattered against each other as they sprawled out over the dirt floor, pushing against the edge of the tent fabric. Sammie did not get back up.

Wayne, however, opted to not draw his gun. Instead, he sidestepped and locked eyes with Michaela from across the tent. She was so scared, and felt that he could see it in her eyes. God bless him, he came running for her instead of trying to save himself.

He yelped when he caught a bullet in his arm, but he was better off than Sammie. He rushed toward her, and on his way to her, Betsy stood screaming still.

The barrage of bullets came at them both. Maybe they were intended for Wayne specifically, or maybe they were for both Wayne and Betsy, but either way, Betsy caught most of them. Her body convulsed as if she was shaking off a horde of ants.

Wayne made it to Michaela as she stood frozen against the side of the wooden wall, peering around, watching everything unfold in front of her. She was safe from gunfire for the moment, but it would only take two seconds for that to change.

"Michaela, get your ass moving," Wayne growled.

She did as she was told, and he pushed her around. They ran further behind the wooden wall and toward the exit. Wayne pulled his gun out and she thought he was going to try to take out some of the men, but she was wrong.

Instead, he reached around her and placed the gun in her hand, pushing her out the exit.

"No, I can't. Why are you giving me this?" Michaela found her timid voice ask.

"Just go, I'm right behind ya. Find a place to hide," Wayne said.

She kept running out the tent and then heard the bullets. She turned around. He smiled at her, revealing his toothless grin, the kindest man who had come into her life, and then his smile dropped and he grabbed at his neck. Blood started to pour out from underneath his hand and he turned around.

She cried, but the words he had said to her stayed in her head.

Find a place to hide.

So she did just that. She spun around and ran. She didn't listen anymore to the bullets that had come and killed her friend. His last moment on earth was spent helping her, that made sure she lived for just a few more seconds.

Now she had to honor his sacrifice and turn those seconds into something much longer.

In front of her were two options. The forest, the trees thick and ever expanding. But she wasn't familiar with the woods around here. She could get lost and die out there alone. Or she could be found immediately. If those men were local, or just lucky, she'd be dead before she knew what hit her. She was scared and tired. She couldn't run for long.

The other option was the outhouse. The flies buzzed around the rickety structure and she could smell it from where she stood.

"I swear, someone was with this asshole. I think it was a girl," a man's voice said from inside the tent.

She only had a second before he would step outside and find her. Her choice had been made for her.

She grabbed the door to the shaky outhouse and tucked herself in. The stench was overwhelming, but she didn't care. She closed the door behind her and peered out the crack at the hinge. It was a place to hide, and that was it. If they decided to open that door, she'd be found.

And worse, if they decided to just unload their weapons, the thin wood would offer no protection at all.

She watched as a man with long hair stepped over Wayne's body. He looked around, but Michaela knew he couldn't see her.

Wayne groaned from the ground and grabbed the man's ankle. Her poor friend was still alive, even after all the bullets he had taken.

"Holy shit, this fucker's still kicking," the man said.

A blast came from inside the tent, then another one. It didn't sound like the rifles the men had been shooting, but instead, sounded like the loud bang that had come from the revolver when Spencer had been killed.

The man with the long hair and the rifle pointed the barrel at Wayne's head as he lay on the ground, grasping at air.

"Go find the girl, if you're so sure there is one," the man with the revolver said.

The man with the long hair left Wayne on the ground, and another one of the dirty rifle-holding men came from around the front of the tent to meet him.

"Nobody around there," he said. "Just that asshole who came here to buy, but he's down for the count. Took this off him."

He held up the baggie that Spencer had given him earlier.

The revolver went off again, and Wayne was down for good. Michaela let out a whimper as she watched her friend's head splatter in the dirt.

The two men with rifles turned to the outhouse.

"You hear that?" the first one asked.

The other one shrugged. "That goddamned pistol has my ears ringing. I ain't hear nothing that I ain't imagining."

The first man stepped closer to the outhouse. Michaela held up the pistol, knowing she could shoot the man and most likely kill him. But it would end at that. The other men would easily kill her after that.

And maybe taking one of them down was enough. Her life hadn't been great as it was. But again, Wayne's words stayed with her and she knew she had to try to live.

She turned and looked at the toilet seat. It was just a long board with a hole in it. She lifted up the board and looked down. It was a long drop down, and it was dark. The smell alone was enough to make her gag.

When they had set up camp, she had helped the men dig the hole for the waste. So she knew how deep it was. Spencer had wanted to make it as deep as possible, considering how long he intended to stay there. It was deeper than any grave she had seen. She just hoped it wouldn't be hers.

She heard the footsteps just outside the door.

There was no time to waste.

She held her nose and slid down into the hole just as the door to the outhouse rattled. She felt herself hit resistance and slowly sink into the muck like it was some sort of sick quicksand. She gasped as she felt the fecal matter slide over her sandals and between her toes.

The gasp was enough to cause her to upheave and she tasted the bile in her throat. It splashed out of her mouth and into the shit she found herself in. She wiped at her mouth and felt something smear against her cheek.

She didn't care to think about it. Eventually, her feet hit the bottom of the trench, and she was waist-deep in the soft muck of human waste. The smell was awful, and she tried to breathe through her mouth after the little fit of vomit she had just had.

The taste settled in on the back of her tongue, combining with the bitter taste of bile that was already there. There was no way to avoid any of it. She was just going to have to sit still until it was all over.

The door finally ripped open and she heard the man above her. She pushed herself against the wall of the trench and gripped the pistol in front of her face. She was ready to shoot anyone that wanted to get a closer look.

"Holy shit, it fucking reeks in here," one of the men said.

"What the fuck did you think it was gonna smell like? Roses and candy?"

"Ain't nobody in here," he said. He shuffled to the board and stared down it.

Michaela shifted as much as she could so he couldn't see her. She felt every bit of the muck creep into every crevice available for it to find on her body. She froze as soon as she saw the whites of the man's eyes.

But instead of shouting or saying a word, he spit into the pit. It landed in front of her in a white glob. It was too dark for him to see her down there. She was covered by the shadows.

Then she heard the distinct sound of a zipper. Then the sound of the man shuffling his jeans down his waist. A couple of grunts came, and then the trickle started.

The warm stream of urine rained down on her, but she didn't say a word. She was frozen, her mouth open, breathing. The salty urine splashed on her face and she was pretty sure it landed in her mouth. Either that, or she was just imagining the taste that vividly. She closed her eyes, tears managing to squeeze through the little slits as she waited for it to be over. The moment or her life, she wasn't sure.

Wood slammed against itself, then the small amount of light from the hole above eclipsed and she started to panic. What if she couldn't get out of there? Were they going to cover up the hole so she couldn't climb out?

Before any of her questions could be answered, one man yelled to the other.

"What the hell you doin' in there?" one asked.

"I'm in the shitbox. What you think I'm doing?" the man above Michaela said.

"I thought you said someone was in there."

"Ain't nobody in here but me now," he said. "Give me a minute while I pinch one off."

"Are you fuckin' stupid? Get the hell outta there now. Go take your shit somewhere else far from here. We don't want to be anywhere near this place now."

"Goddammit," the man above her said, and then he must have stood up because the small amount of light came through the hole above her again.

She thanked God that nothing more came down the hole as she tried to take short breaths only as needed.

The door opened and the man yelled out in pain. "Hey, what the fuck was that for?" he asked.

"Someone could stumble on this place any minute. We gotta get the fuck outta here. You're lucky we didn't just leave ya here."

"Fine," the man said, his belt jangling as he pulled his pants up.

She heard a few more words, but they trailed off in the distance as the men walked away. Michaela's heart pounded in her chest and she shook as if she was freezing, even though she couldn't feel anything at the moment. It was all just numb fear.

She didn't hear anyone else the rest of the night, but she clutched the gun in her hand, ready to take the first shot at the next face she saw look down at her. It was the only thing she could do.

No more tears came. She was paralyzed to that spot until daylight. And even then, as much as she wished the warm rays of the sun would shine down on top of the outhouse, she wasn't so sure she would ever be able to get herself out.

CHAPTER THIRTY-THREE

"THANKS FOR THE TIP LAST NIGHT," ELVEN SAID TO MADDS.

She sat at her desk, still not fully settled in to her space. She had a mishmash of items on her desk, like she was deciding the best way to set it up. She'd been there for only a short period of time and had come from such a different place. Her organizational skills would come with time, he hoped. Worst case, he could give her a few pointers. After all, he had cleaned up Lester's mess, and that was years' worth of case files.

There were a few boxes that needed unpacking and a stack of papers at the corner of her desk. It was a cakewalk compared to what he had done with Lester's office.

"What?" Madds asked, looking up at him.

"You told me Jesse had been at the bar with Hollis the other night. He was there again. I had a few words."

"Oh," she said, her eyes going vacant.

"So I was saying thanks," Elven said, shifting his weight back and forth. Madds seemed a little off.

"Yeah, of course," she said.

"Everything okay?" Elven asked.

"Of course, why wouldn't it be?"

He shrugged. "Just checking. You seem a bit off."

"Guess I had a bit of a long night," she said.

"Fair enough," he said.

"You know, you're a good boss," Madds said. "Sorry if I was whatever before, I mean."

He cocked his head and watched her carefully. "Whatever before? You mean, angry with me and letting me know?"

"Yup."

"No problem. Oh, and I know I am a good boss." He smiled wide and winked at her. She did not return the smile. "You sure you're okay?"

Madds bit her lip, like she was contemplating something. "You ever feel like you're not in the right place?"

Elven considered the question and leaned against the doorway. "There's lots of times I feel that way. But when I do, I usually try to carve myself a spot to call my own. Is something on your mind?"

Madds looked like she was about to say something. Something in her eyes told him that not everything was alright with her. But then Meredith called out to him from the lobby.

"Elven, someone's here to see you," she said.

Elven turned and looked down the hall, then back to Madds. "Hold that thought, will you?"

Madds smiled and nodded. "Go ahead."

Elven walked down the hall, wondering what was going on with Madds. Maybe she was still beating herself up for how things had ended with the Sophia case. It was she who had been on duty, and he knew he would have blamed himself if it had ended the way it did for her, no matter how many times someone had said it wasn't his fault.

But he'd have to find out later. When he set foot in the lobby, he saw that Jesse Parsons stood in front of Meredith's desk in full uniform.

"Wow. To what do I owe the pleasure?" Elven asked.

"You told me to come by, didn't you?" Jesse asked.

"I'd say you're a few days late. But I suppose a guy like you doesn't understand timing, just like he doesn't understand courtesy."

"Look, I'm here 'cause there's been a development," Jesse said.

Elven looked at the man. He wasn't being defiant or intimidating. In fact, he almost seemed humble. If he had a hat, he might have had it in his hand, by the look of him.

"And why would I want to help you with a development? Didn't you want important people to help you? I'm sure you can find Hollis Starcher around—"

"There's been a murder in the mountains," Jesse said.

Elven stopped his chiding. "Where at?"

"The revival."

"Who was killed?" Elven asked.

"Everyone."

CHAPTER THIRTY-FOUR

JESSE WAS RIGHT. EVERYONE WAS DEAD.

Elven and Jesse had hiked up the trail after parking in the empty dirt lot Elven had been at just a few days earlier. Madds and Johnny were on their way, moments behind them. Jesse had explained to him that someone had gone to seek counsel from Spencer Caldwell, and when they got there, all he found was death. According to Jesse, it was just dumb luck that the man had found Jesse and not gone to Elven first.

Elven had asked Jesse who the man was, but Jesse said he didn't know. Of course, when pushed to see if he had given a statement, Jesse said no.

Elven had already formed an opinion of Jesse, so it was no surprise to him when a few key elements and procedures appeared to not have been followed through. But he had to take Jesse's word on it and maybe they could find this mystery man who had, according to Jesse, been on his way to find Elven when he bumped into Jesse, completely a mess of himself.

Jesse, being the super-nice guy he was, told the man that he would take it upon himself to report it to the sheriff and the man could go home and relax, knowing he had done a good thing and wouldn't need to stress any more about it.

Elven was beginning to form even newer opinions of Jesse Parsons, and they stretched beyond his character and ability to do the job. These opinions were more about what he truly was doing in Dupray and how much he was concealing from Elven.

Once they set foot on the clearing on which stood Spencer Caldwell's church, Elven immediately felt the difference.

The air was cold, but thick. It was the feeling of death. Like the blood had infiltrated the air, weighing it down. And it was more than a murder. It was a massacre.

Elven and Jesse both approached the scene carefully. Each man drew his revolver, having no idea if anyone was still at the scene or if they were just watching from afar. Either way, they didn't know what they were in store for.

The first body they saw was at the front of the tent, right outside the entrance. Elven didn't recognize him, but he didn't look well. And that was before the being dead part.

His hair was greasy and in his face. Elven moved the hair away from the man's face and saw he had pockmarks on his face. His mouth hung open and revealed teeth that had been ground down and chipped. He had a giant hole in his head from a bullet and various smaller bullet wounds on his body.

Elven moved the man's arm and saw a small glass pipe fall from his shirt pocket. It was no secret that the man was a drug addict, but what he was doing there was the question. Was what Spencer said true? Did junkies go see him for counsel or when they were troubled? Elven had a feeling there was something more to it than that.

Elven and Jesse both entered the tent, stepping around the dead drug addict in front of the opening. What they saw inside the tent was much worse.

Elven didn't even vocalize it. It was Jesse who said the first words.

"Jesus Christ," Jesse said. Elven couldn't help but find it a little more than inappropriate to say, considering where they were.

But Jesse was right in his reaction. The first body they saw was that of Spencer Caldwell. He was a crumpled mess in the center of the tent. No chairs were around, but if they were, he'd have been in the center aisle between them all.

Behind Spencer was a long trail of blood and brain splatter that went all the way to his sister, Betsy. Spencer was different from the man outside and Betsy. There was only the one gun shot, and Elven was no spatter analyst, but from his experience, mostly walking in on the aftermath of suicides, it looked like Spencer had taken a bullet near point-blank.

Betsy was riddled with bullet wounds just like the man outside. The smaller wounds were all over her body, but there was a larger hole in her head. The spatter was on the ground extending from behind her head, so it looked like she had been shot dead after lying down.

Sammie, the mustached man who had sat silently with Wayne when Elven had spoken to them only days before, was sprawled out over the mess of chairs on the side of the large tent. Another body covered with bullet wounds and a single hole in the head.

"This is strange," Jesse said. "It's like they were executed."

Elven nodded, having no disagreement with Jesse's observation. Elven walked around the wooden wall that served as Spencer's entrance to the tent as he'd seen on his previous visit. Behind it he saw a man's arm lying on the ground at the tent opening.

Elven pushed the flap and saw Wayne, dead on the ground. His mouth hung loose, with his tongue sliding out where his teeth were missing. He was another body, slaughtered by smaller bullets with one large bullet hole in his head. Blood spattered like a spider's legs from his head. Elven noticed that the holster on Wayne's hip was empty. He looked around in the dirt, but saw no gun.

It didn't mean much, other than the person who'd killed him had either stolen it or they'd find it in one of the other tents somewhere.

"Oh my God, Elven, what happened here?" Madds asked, walking around the outside of the tent. She was pale, and he didn't blame her. This was a slaughter. There was no other way to describe it.

Elven looked at the outhouse that stood in front of him. The door was ajar and he could see through the small opening that nobody was in it. He figured it would be the worst place for someone to hide if they were to ambush anyone. He could smell it from where he stood.

"You and Johnny are gonna need to canvass around. Check the nearby trees just to make sure nobody is hiding out at the perimeter," Elven said. Then he looked at Madds. "I don't mean that as busywork. I need your help on this one."

"Got it," Madds said.

"Oh, maybe you can keep Jesse busy for a moment, too?" Elven asked.

"Busy?"

"I want to go digging at something and don't need him looking over my shoulder the whole time. Between you and me, I don't really trust him."

Madds smiled. "I'm pretty sure that's no secret."

Elven shrugged. He was done playing nice after the bull Jesse had pulled. It was time he figured things out without giving any more information to those he didn't trust.

"I can do that though," Madds said.

"Thanks," Elven said.

He turned and set his sights on the tent across the clearing. It was the biggest tent, other than where the sermons happened, of course. So that meant it must be Spencer's quarters.

Which also meant that if there was anything to be found, it would be there.

CHAPTER THIRTY-FIVE

THERE WERE A FEW TENTS IN VARIOUS PLACES, HELD UP BY large poles in the dirt and spiked into the ground at the edge of the flaps, like the other tents. Except they were much smaller, and some of them were torn.

Elven could see where someone had taken a knife to them and cut large slits in the side, as if the entrance was just too cumbersome to figure out so they had to make a new one that they could understand. The canvas material was thick, so the knife used had to be sharp, like one a hunter might carry. It was obvious that each tent had been tossed, the belongings and thin mattresses peeking out from under the heavy fabric that folded to the side from where it had been sliced open.

But Spencer's tent was different. There were no slits or holes cut into the heavy material. The main flap for the entrance was open, the corner of the opening tucked and rolled to the side. Elven could see straight inside to the desk that sat in the center on the dirt floor.

He set foot inside and looked around. The room was no different than the other'. Every drawer in the desk was on the ground, not in a neat pile. The drawers had been thrown to the side, their contents having spilled out. The various items, mostly pens and papers, had not been what whoever was in there last was looking for.

The mattress and small cot to the side of the tent had been flipped over. A large knife slit started at one end and continued to the other, the stuffing sticking half out. It was no spring mattress, but instead, a thin cot that one might find at a summer camp.

Elven had been in various parts of the world. He had seen and experienced different ways of sleeping, but he had to admit to himself that nothing beat an expensive, thick memory-foam mattress. It was one of the things he wouldn't want to trade in his life.

But Spencer had put up with that cot, and according to him, it was all for preaching the Word. Elven still didn't buy it. And whoever was in there last must not have, either.

Elven recognized the shells on the ground as rifle casings. And at first glance, he might have assumed it was the work of some rogue hunters. Or at least, it was a possibility.

But the fact that they tossed the rooms pointed to something else. They were looking for something that had nothing to do with Spencer being in their prime hunting spot.

But what was it?

He kicked one of the drawers to the side and saw a small lockbox. It was thin gray metal, which was laughable. The only thing the box was going to keep out was an animal. Anyone who truly wanted to steal from it would have no problem smashing the lock.

Which is exactly what had happened. There was no money inside, other than a few coins that Elven kicked up in the dirt with his boot.

Was that all this was for? Someone killed all those people just to rob the collection plate?

Elven knew it wasn't a far-fetched idea, but at the same time, he knew that there was no way they could have accumulated that much money. It couldn't have been more than a thousand dollars.

He exhaled, knowing that a thousand dollars in Dupray could be exactly what someone was willing to kill over if they were desperate enough. Or if they needed the money for drugs.

As he dragged his boot across the dirt, he saw a line underneath the wooden desk. The desk looked like it was square to the tent, as if it were exactly where it should be if Spencer were to sit at it. But in the dirt was a small half-circle that curved outward from the leg, like it had been dragged into place.

Elven holstered his weapon, grabbed the side of the desk, and shoved it, pivoting it on one side so it followed along the curve in the dirt as if it was a large compass. He stopped when there was no more drag mark in the dirt going in the opposite direction.

He walked around to the front of the desk and looked at the ground. He kicked at where the leg of the desk was and felt something firm against his toe. It was hard, like wood. He crouched down and brushed at the dirt, uncovering something underneath.

He felt around until he felt the surface of a wooden object. He uncovered it, like a layman's archeologist, using his hands. It was about a square foot in size. He wedged his fingers around and was able to pull it up, but instead of the box being lifted out of the ground, just the top opened up and hinged at the back.

It was a lid to a box.

Inside the box, though, was exactly what whoever had been in here last had been looking for.

Elven stared down at the number of bags crammed into the box. It held a lot more than he thought it could, but it must have been fairly deep, because as Elven began to pull out the bags that were inside, more and more bags lay underneath.

The bags were full of small, nearly clear, crystals.

It was meth. And a lot of it.

Elven looked down, still holding one of the bags and rustling it in his hand. The rocks inside were grinding against each other like they were bits of candy. He clenched his jaw as he thought about how he had been there a few days ago and Spencer had looked him in the eye, knowing everything that was going on.

He hated someone coming into his county and trying to pull one over on him. And apparently, so did someone else.

He thought about anyone who could have done this, but that just led him back to thinking about how he didn't know who might be dealing in his county since Malick was no longer in the business. It was definitely no hunter feeling angry about their favorite spot being occupied. Someone else knew what Spencer was up to.

Elven heard boots crunching in the sand, heading his way. He threw the bags back into the box and slammed the lid shut. He pulled the mattress over the box before whoever was out there could see. It wasn't that he wanted to keep anything from his deputies. He wanted to keep it from Jesse.

Jesse stuck his head in the tent and looked around. Elven stood, putting his foot on top of the mattress and leaned against the desk. His heart was beating a tick faster and he felt like he was being too obvious with trying to keep a secret.

But Jesse didn't seem to notice. The game warden whistled and shook his head. "Hot damn, what the hell were they looking for?"

Elven shrugged, then kicked the broken lockbox into view. "Collection plate robbery, I suppose."

Jesse looked at the box, then up at Elven. He scrunched his brow. "That little thing? What's it hold? Five grand in all hundreds maybe?"

"I've heard of a lot worse for a lot less," Elven said.

"Ain't that the truth," Jesse said.

"What's up? Where's Madds?" Elven asked.

"That little tart of a deputy you got? I tell you what, she was chatting my ear off a bit. I mean, I'm all for being a shoulder and an ear, but damn, usually there's a payoff between the sheets later. Didn't think that'd be happening, so I told her, honey, this ain't no date, then came to find you."

"I'm sure she loved that," Elven said, laughing inwardly at what Madds was probably thinking about Jesse at the moment.

"Ain't no thing," Jesse said. "But I wanna show you something."

Jesse waved his hand and ducked back out of the tent. Elven stared down at the mattress that covered the meth. He'd have to come back and get it out without Jesse knowing about it. He'd probably have Johnny do it while he kept the game warden distracted.

He'd also have to canvass a bigger area in the woods. If he were a betting man, he'd put money on a set-up out there that was for cooking the drugs. What better area than in the thick of the woods to cook them up. But first, he had to get Jesse out of the area. He had a few reasons why, but mostly, his gut was pulling him a strong direction to keep that bit of information away from Jesse.

"You coming?" Jesse shouted.

Elven relented and left the meth in the ground.

CHAPTER THIRTY-SIX

"I DON'T LIKE THIS AT ALL," JOHNNY SAID.

He shuddered, but Madds knew it had nothing to do with the weather. Johnny wasn't the brightest guy Madds had known, but he was definitely the kindest. What he lacked in intelligence and foresight, he made up tenfold in generosity and heart.

That's why he didn't want to be up there. Someone with the amount of care that Johnny had for his fellowman shouldn't have to see the kind of murder that had taken place in that clearing.

It was part of the job, but Madds still felt for him.

"Tank should be the one up here. He's made for this sort of work, not me. I should be the one pushing papers and answering phone calls," Johnny continued.

"It's okay, Johnny. I'm sure Tank would rather be here, too. But you're still doing great up here," Madds said. "I know I feel better with you here."

Johnny laughed. "Yeah? What for? Didn't think you were the type that needed taking care of."

That made Madds laugh. And no, she definitely wasn't that type, and if she didn't care about hurting Johnny's feelings, she would have said that he wasn't able to take care of anyone. At least, not in the sense that he meant.

"You're right about that. I can take care of myself. But I also like knowing there's some heart up here with me. One that's not afraid to admit it."

Johnny grinned wide and she hugged him. He squeezed her tight, not in any way more than a brother who hadn't seen his sister in a few days. She couldn't help but think the hug felt really nice. Like family.

He squeezed tighter and she pulled away. "Oh, sorry," he said.

"No, you squeeze any tighter and I'll pee my pants," she said, laughing. She shuffled on her feet, only now realizing she'd been holding it for a while.

Johnny chuckled and pointed out to the trees the lined the clearing. "I just went and watered those bushes over there a few minutes ago."

"And you washed your hands?" she asked.

He shook his head. "No, why? Ain't nowhere to wash up out here."

She twisted her face, feeling the damp spots on her jacket from where he had been hugging. She tried not to think about why his hands had been wet.

"Maybe I'll try the outhouse," she said.

"Good luck on that," Johnny said. "It stinks to high heaven over there."

"Is Elven rubbing off on you now?" she asked. She approached the rickety outhouse and immediately gagged. "Cause I tell you what, if that's what heaven smells like, I don't want anything to do with it."

"I am tellin' you, just go squat in those bushes," Johnny said again.

Madds looked to the bushes again, really disinterested in going anywhere closer to the outhouse that looked like it had been set up in a hurry. On top of the smell, it looked like it could collapse in on her at any moment, and then she'd be in a really shitty situation, quite literally.

But the bushes were in plain sight. The trees didn't cover anything, and maybe she could squat low behind one, but she knew she'd be seen. And the last thing she wanted was for that disgusting game warden to get any ideas of peeping in on her.

She shook her head. "I don't know, that game warden creeps me out. His eyes lingered a little too long when I was in there talking to him earlier. He's probably waiting to catch a show."

"I'll stand by and keep watch," Johnny said, a stupid grin on his face, but she knew he didn't mean anything by it.

The idea of Johnny standing close enough to hear her was enough to push her.

"Thanks," she said. "I think I'll manage in there."

She held her breath and swung the door open to the outhouse. She gave Johnny one more glance before stepping in. He scrunched his nose, like he was more disgusted with that than the dead bodies all over the place.

CHAPTER THIRTY-SEVEN

Jesse squatted down, hovering over Betsy Caldwell's body back in the largest tent. He looked her over and pointed at the hole in her head.

"This hole is bigger than all the other wounds she got," Jesse said.

Elven stood, not squatting down with him. He didn't need to get that close to her to know what Jesse said was the truth. Every other body was the same way, except for Spencer's, of course. He only had the one bullet hole in his head.

"I got that," Elven said. "What's your point?"

Jesse pointed to Spencer. "I think he got it first. That someone stood in front of him and shot him square between the eyes." He tapped his forehead when he said it. "He obviously wasn't expecting it."

"Obviously."

"Then whoever shot up the place did it to just distract and maybe help out. But they weren't professionals," Jesse said, finally standing up. Elven could hear the pop in the man's knees when he came up.

"You mean, professionals like hitmen?"

Jesse shook his head. "Nope, I mean hunters."

Elven couldn't help but sour his face. "I thought this was supposed to be the work of hunters. That's why you're out here, right?" Elven knew it was more, but by offering that up, he'd show his hand that he knew there was more to it.

"It is," Jesse said. "But look at what they used."

Elven looked at the body again, but shrugged. He had no idea what Jesse was talking about.

"You grew up here?" Jesse asked.

"I did."

"And you're familiar with hunting, right?"

Elven nodded. "Yeah, I guess so."

"But you ain't a hunter yourself, are ya?"

Elven shook his head. He kept his reasons to himself, as he knew they would probably be a mocking point for Jesse, not that Elven minded. He held a high belief in life, and if someone was going to make fun of him for that, well, they had a bigger set of issues themselves.

"Figures, pretty boy like you. Doesn't want to get his hands dirty," Jesse more than grumbled.

"You gonna tell me what this is about, or are you going to just check me out and compliment my butt some more?" Elven asked.

Jesse clenched his jaw and Elven knew he'd hit a nerve. Apparently a big man like Jesse didn't like being poked fun at about commenting on a man's looks. Big surprise.

"The bullets they used, they ain't for taking down big game like a buck." Jesse bent over and picked up one of the spent shells, holding it out to Elven. It looked like a rifle shell, but he wasn't well-versed in hunting ammunition, like Jesse had been all-too-quick to point out.

"What am I looking at?" Elven finally asked.

"Those are Ruger .204. You can also tell by the entry point in the bodies."

"Just tell me what you're getting at."

"Jesus, you really don't know shit, do you? .204 Ruger is smaller and faster, meant for smaller animals."

"Not big game?" Elven asked. "It's buck season right now."

"So what experienced hunter would be up here, shooting bullets that couldn't take down that animal?" Jesse asked. "My guess is that they weren't experienced, and maybe just used whatever they had. And that's why someone came through with a Magnum and finished them off. Again, nobody's out here hunting big game with a handgun."

Elven nodded, finally understanding where Jesse was coming from. He wasn't surprised at Jesse's knowledge, but more surprised that he was actually proving useful.

"So who would use the .204 bullets?" Elven asked.

Jesse shrugged. "It's mostly just for vermin. Can take out a coyote pretty good, too."

Elven nodded, knowing he'd recently run into a few coyote hunters and would need to pay them a visit.

"This whole thing seems odd, don't it? If not about hunters, then what?" Jesse asked.

Elven knew exactly what, but he wasn't going to share that with Jesse. Not until he really got to the bottom of things.

CHAPTER THIRTY-EIGHT

Madds slid the metal slide lock across, and it slammed against the edge of the door. She put her weight into the door to get it to line up correctly, then shoved the metal piece an inch further, finally getting it to latch. The walls shook when she took her weight off the door.

She took a deep breath and almost threw up right there. To say it was foul would have been an understatement. She'd been to camp-grounds with permanent outhouses that smelled better than this one. There had been no intention of cleaning this literal shithole out.

It was dark inside, but small rays of light made it through the cracks where the walls and ceiling were supposed to line up. The guys who had put it together had obviously little care about anyone commenting on their workmanship. They probably didn't even care about having walls in the first place, but with Betsy and Michaela there, she figured that part was non-negotiable.

The seat of the toilet was just a board that sat across on top of another board. And then there was a hole in the ground. She peered down it, but it was too dark to see. It went pretty deep.

"Disgusting," Madds said.

They would have been better off with a bucket that they threw out after every use. Why wouldn't they have done that instead?

It didn't matter. Her bladder was warning her, pushing her, that if she didn't go now, worrying about the decisions of Spencer Caldwell's outhouse set-up would be far from her mind.

She unbuckled her belt and slid her pants down. She was ready to just plop down on the board, but it was so dark in the hole that her fear of the unknown kicked in. She didn't really care to see the amount of fecal matter at the bottom, but she did have a very real want of not having anything crawl up on her. It was somewhat irrational, she knew, but she rarely had to run into a situation where it came into play.

Of course, now was one of those situations.

The thoughts ran through her mind. There could be anything down there. Snakes, or some random animal. Hell, what if it looked so dark that the shit was piled all the way to the top and it splashed back on her? She gagged at the thought.

There were so many different scenarios, so she grabbed her flashlight off her belt and penguin waddled the two steps to the hole, her pants still around her ankles.

She would take a look, just to make sure. The last thing she wanted was to sit down and get a black-widow bite on her ass.

She clicked her Maglite on, just a small little tube that was easily handled with two fingers. She peered down the hole, seeing the dirt walls of the trench. At some point in its time being there, it seemed like someone either had some serious IBS or ate something that didn't agree with them, because the splatter as high as it was, well, it would have been worrying if it had been her.

She peered deeper, just to make sure there were no creepy crawlies around. Even if she was satisfied, she was sure she would have to maneuver her ass so it hovered just above the hole and not make contact with the board.

The flashlight beam passed over a lot of brown muck at the

bottom, and then something else. It seemed foreign, but she couldn't quite figure it out.

Then, deep in the brown muck, she saw two white eyes open up and stare at her.

"Oh, Jesus Christ," Madds said with a gasp.

And then she saw the barrel of a gun point up at her.

CHAPTER THIRTY-NINE

BANG.

It was unmistakable. A gun had fired nearby.

Elven was still in the main gathering tent with Jesse. Both of them stopped looking at the bodies, stopped bantering back and forth about who didn't know what about their job, and took to foot.

They both ran out of the tent and stopped.

Johnny stood dumbfounded, staring at the outhouse. Madds was nowhere in sight. There were no more gunshots. The trees in the distance swayed in the slight breeze.

"Johnny, what happened?" Elven asked.

Johnny stared at the outhouse and pointed. "I, uh, I—I don't know."

Then a scream came out. It was Madds. It had to be. It came from the outhouse. The walls shook like someone had pushed their body weight into one of the walls.

Elven ran to the door and pulled, but it was locked.

"Madds! Madds are you okay?" Elven yelled.

He pulled on the door, but it still wouldn't budge. And Madds wasn't answering.

"Get out of the way," Jesse said.

Elven turned around and saw Jesse coming right at him. Elven's first reaction was to reach for his gun, but he slid out of Jesse's path.

Jesse rushed to the door and lifted his foot, kicking the door hard. The shanty building shook so much Elven was worried the whole thing would collapse in on itself. But it managed to stay standing, and even better, the door splintered at the slide lock and swung inward.

Jesse had his revolver pulled, and Elven did the same. But Jesse stopped and immediately grinned. Elven stepped up to him, turning to see what he was staring at.

Immediately, Elven was met with Madds's bare ass staring back at him. Her pants and panties were around her ankles, resting on her boots. He could feel his cheeks flush as he saw her milky white flesh sticking up at him. He glanced at Jesse, noticing Jesse's shit-eating grin on his face.

"What the hell?!" Madds asked, looking behind her. She reached behind and pulled her pants up as best as she could, though it was an awkward angle with her on her knees and looking down into the hole of the toilet.

"We heard a gunshot, and you didn't answer, we thought—"

"Turn the fuck around and give me a bit of privacy, would ya?!"

Elven spun around and shoved Jesse, who was reluctant to give her what she asked for. He started giggling like a schoolboy who had seen his first set of breasts.

Elven took a quick glance and saw Madds pull her pants up all the way.

"What is going on?" Elven asked her.

"You can turn around now," Madds said. She was back down on her knees, but this time she was fully covered. Her belt and gun were on the ground, as was her phone.

"Madds what—"

"Just be quiet and give me a second, would ya?" Madds asked.

Elven shut up and watched her. She had removed the board and had her hand down in the hole.

"It's okay," Madds said. "We're the police, okay? Nobody here is gonna hurt you. I'm gonna help you, you understand? Okay, good."

Elven watched curiously. He wasn't exactly sure what was going on until she pulled her hand out and a gun, covered in what looked like human excrement, was held in it.

She set the gun on the dirt, away from her things.

"Okay, that's good. Thank you," Madds said. "Can you grab my hand and come out of there? I'll pull you up."

Madds looked back and Elven came closer. She was talking to someone down there, but he had no idea who it could be, but whoever it was, he did not envy them one bit. The smell alone was enough to make him rethink his lunch plans.

"Johnny, go get me some blankets, you hear me?" Madds yelled.

Elven took a look at Johnny, who seemed to unfreeze at her command. He nodded, even though she couldn't see him, and ran toward the path that led to the parking lot. But Elven knew it would be too long for that.

"Check the tent over there," Elven said. "There's blankets on the beds, just take those."

"Got it," Johnny said, spinning around and running to the tents.

Elven turned back to Madds and set foot in the outhouse with her.

"This is my friend, Elven," Madds said.

Elven glanced over Madds's shoulder and saw what looked like a girl down in the hole. If it wasn't for her white eyes, he wouldn't have been able to tell there was a person down there. He could just barely make out the shape of her. She was covered in excrement, like she was taking a horrific mud bath.

"You wanna give me a hand?" Madds asked to Elven.

Elven nodded, knowing what she was planning on doing, and once again, didn't envy her either.

"We're gonna help you out of there, okay?" Madds asked. "I'm gonna come down and help, so don't get scared, alright? We're all here to help you."

Madds seemed satisfied enough, and having the gun out of the girl's hand was probably the main reason why. She held her hand to Elven and he took hold of it. She slowly lowered herself into the hole, clenching her jaw as she did. He could tell it was taking everything she had not to throw up.

"Oh, God," Madds groaned, settling into the muck. She was waist-deep in it and Elven couldn't even imagine how she was able to get over the mental hurdle of it. But she was helping someone, so maybe that was all it took.

"Okay, I know you're scared, but we're gonna do this all together, okay?"

Elven watched the girl nod as she looked at Madds. She didn't say a word, though.

"Good. Let's raise your hand and Elven up there is going to grab it. He'll pull you and I'll help lift you up, alright?"

Again with the nod and no words.

Madds helped the girl lift her arm. It was like she had no strength left of her own to do anything and Madds had to be the puppeteer. But the girl let Madds help her.

Elven grabbed the girl's hand, slick with things Elven didn't want to think about. But he pulled and Madds lifted. And then the girl was pulled out of the muck with a loud *thwack* sound.

And just like that, Johnny appeared in the doorway with a blanket. Elven grabbed it and wrapped the girl in it. Johnny held her as Elven held out a hand to Madds, who was lifted out much easier, as she was only covered with the muck up to her waist.

Johnny wiped the girl's face with the blanket, and Elven saw it was Michaela Caldwell. Spencer's cousin. She was paler than usual, which was definitely saying something. Elven was sure if someone had found her in the woods, they would have sworn she was a spirit. The girl that had been berated and treated poorly, and had survived the night in that hellhole.

"You okay?" Elven asked Madds, noticing that she had a large cut on her face. It dripped blood down her cheek.

"Yeah, just cut myself when I fell backward," she said. "I got pretty lucky."

Elven looked at the bullet hole in the top of the ceiling, letting more light in through the hole. She was right. She got very lucky.

"What the hell happened?" Elven asked.

Madds shrugged. "I had to pee. Was met with a bullet. Don't worry, I went when I was in the hole. Figured nobody would be able to tell."

Elven scoffed and raised his eyebrows. She wasn't kidding, but she was right about nobody being able to notice. He worried that the smell would never come out.

"So, whose car are we taking to Doc's?" Madds asked.

"Wanna ride with Jesse?" Elven asked with a grin.

CHAPTER FORTY

"WHAT THE HELL HAPPENED TO HER?" PHIL DRISCOLL ASKED.

Elven had radioed Meredith to call the doc and tell him they were on the way to his place. He gave a quick rundown of everything, but skipped over some major details, just saying they had found someone alive and that they may or may not be injured. In truth, it was all Elven really knew.

So when Doc had asked, Elven gave him no answer. He was in almost as much of the dark as the doc was.

Before getting Michaela into the Jeep, they had tried to wipe her clean enough so that she wasn't dripping all over. He couldn't have said he wasn't concerned with his Jeep getting messy, but it wasn't his biggest concern. Getting the girl safe and clean took highest priority.

She wasn't covered in the fecal mess head to toe, but getting it completely off her was impossible with just blankets at their disposal. Her clothes and skin were soaked in it. She didn't smell any better, but nobody had commented about it. Madds cared more about getting the girl clean and comfortable than she did about herself.

And that impressed Elven.

Madds had put the girl before herself. He was sure someone like

Johnny would have done the same, except that Madds had been able to act on it. Johnny had frozen. And someone like Jesse would never have jumped down in that hole. In fact, he was more concerned with seeing some skin than any concern for what was happening.

They went straight through the lobby of Driscoll's with Michaela and slowly down the steps to the basement. They had to coax the exhausted and frightened Michaela into each step. The things she had seen must have been traumatizing.

But they were also the things that Elven needed to know.

What she had witnessed could solve the whole case and put everything to bed. The meth, the murders, and any other inkling Elven might have, like the one about Jesse Parsons.

But she wasn't talking. And Elven would need to talk to Doc about that. Maybe he would have some ideas of how to get her to open up.

Jesse followed behind them. As much as Elven tried getting the game warden to stand outside and wait for them, he refused. He just kept saying it was as much his case as it was Elven's, as it had taken place in his woods. Elven didn't have enough of a fight in him to argue, not while they had to get Michaela seen by the doc.

Thankfully, Jesse stayed mostly quiet when he entered Driscoll's funeral home.

"Just have her sit down here," Driscoll said, wheeling a chair around. It was just a stool on wheels, but it was the best he had to offer, unless he expected the girl to get up on one of the tables. Which, thankfully, he didn't.

Elven and Madds got Michaela to sit down on the chair, her legs trembling, and Madds crouched down. Michaela looked down at Madds, a blank stare on her face.

"This is Phil Driscoll. Sometimes people call him Doc. Either way, he's good people, and he's just going to look you over to make sure you're not hurt. Is that okay?" Madds asked.

Michaela looked up at Doc Driscoll who had a stethoscope at the ready in his ears. She looked back to Madds and grabbed her hand.

"I'm not leaving, I'll be right here, okay?" Madds said.

Michaela let go and nodded.

Driscoll stepped up, his stethoscope out. He pushed it against her chest and listened. He brought his wrist to his nose and opened his mouth, like he was trying to avoid the smell.

"Jesus, what did they find you in?" Driscoll asked.

"You don't wanna know," Elven said.

Jesse laughed as he stared at the various instruments and pills in the glass cabinets along the wall. "Ain't that the truth," Jesse said.

Doc narrowed his eyes and nodded, not pushing the question again. He seemed satisfied with whatever he heard in her chest and put the stethoscope around his neck. If he had a white coat on, he'd look like a doctor in a hospital. Instead, it was just a flannel shirt.

"Anything that is hurt? Injuries or physical pain?" Doc asked Michaela.

She just stared at him, no answer given.

"She's not saying anything," Elven said.

"I see that."

"Anything we can do to change that?" Elven asked.

Madds stood up, but Michaela grabbed her hand, preventing her from straying too far from her. "Are you fucking kidding me right now?" Madds asked. "This girl has seen some terrible things, and had to survive all night in that shit. And now you're pushing to get her to talk, and worse, acting like she's not sitting right here to hear you talk about her."

Elven opened his mouth, then shut it. Madds was right. It had been a little insensitive of him. He was so concerned with the case and trying to figure out what was going on in his county that he'd ignored the trauma Michaela had been through.

"Maybe we can get a shower going, clean you up?" Doc asked Michaela.

She looked at Madds, with a look that was little more than blank. But something that seemed like she was interested, accompanied with a nod.

"Good, I have a separate shower down here that you can use," Driscoll said. He turned to Elven. "You know, that meth addict you brought in here the other day woke up."

"Really? When did this happen?" Elven asked.

Driscoll shrugged. "Hospital called earlier and told me. That's all I know."

"Why don't you go and do your investigation? Ask the questions you need to ask and figure it all out. I'll take care of her," Madds said. "I'm sure we'll need some time."

Elven looked at Madds, who also looked like she was wanting a shower herself. And she was right. Getting Michaela comfortable and cleaned up was just the first step. Who knew how long it would take for her to open up, and it seemed like the only person she wanted around was Madds. So maybe she'd have better luck alone.

"You sure? Just want to make sure you didn't want to partner on this one—"

"Oh just go," Madds said, a hint of irritation in her voice. "Besides, looks like you've got a partner already."

Elven looked over his shoulder and saw Jesse looking at the narcotics in the cabinets. He rolled his eyes and let out a long sigh, hating that Madds was right.

CHAPTER FORTY-ONE

Dupray County Hospital had seen some better days, but it was the only place they had around that could handle things that Doc Driscoll couldn't take care of himself. And that was quite a long list. The ongoing joke was that people went to Dupray County to die. And in Elven's history of knowing it, that wasn't a far-off assessment.

Sure, plenty of people lived, but it did seem like they weren't able to give the best care. Then again, when they had to deal with people unable to pay bills, taxes from people who lived off disability draws of their dead relatives and just plain low population, they didn't have the greatest advantage.

As much as Elven would hate to admit, if something happened to him, he'd rather be taken out of the county than to be at the mercy of the doctor's knowledge and expertise in Dupray.

Usually, someone who was a murder suspect, or really, more than a suspect, would have had a deputy appointed to sit outside the door until the person was able to be taken back to jail. But this was Dupray, and deputies were scarce. Instead, Elven had asked the hospital security to have someone monitor him and keep him cuffed to the bed.

The addict was no mastermind and stayed put in bed after he'd woken up.

The hospital room was typical. A television in the corner, except it looked like it was straight from the eighties. A tray with a half-eaten sandwich and an empty pudding cup was tucked against the wall. And most notable of all was that it wasn't even a room where the patient had privacy. It was shared with another patient.

A curtain was pulled between the beds, and Elven peeked over to the other side where an old man lay, connected to some machines. He had tubes coming out of his nose and mouth, and looked like he wouldn't be waking up for quite some time. If at all.

"You know, I had to come here a while back when my grand-mother was here. Dialysis and some shit. Was here a month, and then she left in a hearse," Jesse said.

Elven nodded, not interested in knowing about Jesse's family history.

"I don't like being in hospitals, especially this one," Jesse said.

"If you wanna wait outside, I can do this on my own," Elven answered.

Jesse chuckled. "No chance, Sheriff."

The patient, Adam Grolsch, as it said on the chart in front of him, lay napping. Apparently, no one had told him they were coming to ask him questions, or they had and he just didn't seem to care.

Elven cleared his throat loudly, but Adam was out. Elven did it again and, still, nothing.

Jesse shook his head. "Hey, asshole, wake up!" he shouted.

The man didn't move. Jesse rolled his eyes, went to the bedside, and shook the bed. Then he grabbed the IV bag that was attached to the needle in Adam's arm. He gave it a squeeze.

That did the trick. Adam rolled over with a yelp.

"Jesus Christ, what the hell are ya'll doin'?" he called out.

"Oh, looks like someone's awake now," Jesse said with a smile.

Elven didn't like Jesse's methods, even if they were proving to be effective. Torturing or roughing someone up just to get answers was never the way. He was smarter than that. And ultimately, he was better than that.

Adam looked around at Jesse and then Elven. His hair was long and greasy, looking like nobody had bothered to clean him up much while he was in the hospital. His skin was pock-marked and when he opened his mouth, Elven could see the black teeth in the back of his mouth.

"Shit, what's going on?" Adam asked.

"As if you don't know," Jesse said.

"We found you in the woods the other day," Elven said. "Do you remember me?"

Adam narrowed his eyes and shook his head. "I don't know, maybe. You're the sheriff, right? That's what it says on your shirt anyway."

"Smart guy," Jesse said.

He looked at Jesse, a confused expression on his face. "Who the hell are you?"

"Doesn't matter who he is. He's here to help figure things out with me," Elven said.

"Whatever it is, I ain't gonna help you," Adam said.

Elven nodded. "All I wanna know is who you bought your drugs from. The doc says its meth that was in your system. Not that we couldn't tell from the looks of you. So where'd you get it?"

Adam scoffed. "Like I said, I ain't telling you shit. You think I'll just snitch 'cause you asked?"

"If you want out of this, yeah," Elven said.

"They'll kill me if I talk," Adam said.

Elven saw a smirk on Jesse's face, but he wasn't sure what that meant. Jesse seemed to like a fight, or assert his power. At least, in the little bit of time he'd known the man. But something else pulled at Elven that he couldn't just push from his mind. Like Jesse knew something that he wasn't saying.

"Fine. Right now, though, you're on the hook for murder."

"Murder?" Adam asked.

"Your friend you were with in the woods? He didn't exactly make it out alive. And by the looks of it, you must have been higher than the tops of those pine trees 'cause you don't seem like you remember any of it."

"Craig is dead?" Adam asked. "How?"

"Probably the gunshot to the head you dealt him. Not sure what went down, but drugs can mess with a person's mind, from my understanding."

"You're full of shit," Adam spat. He watched Elven, who didn't take back anything. Adam's face twisted in realization. "I killed him?" he asked. He truly looked upset, like he really didn't know he had anything to do with it. Or that his friend was even dead. Elven felt a little for him, but he also knew Adam had made his own bed.

"The thing is, you tell us where you got your drugs, and we'll have a much better time saying it wasn't your fault. And that the real culprit was whoever was dealing," Elven said.

Adam thought a moment, his head hanging low as he looked at his handcuffed wrist. He looked up again, less defiant and sadder.

Adam looked like he didn't want to say anything, but with the threat of prison over his head, he seemed to understand. "The church. I buy from the church. They said they'd take care of me. That I had nothing to worry about anymore. They had me covered. But I guess, I mean, I shouldn't have tried—"

"Too bad for you," Jesse said, cutting him off. "Everyone at the church is dead. Gunned down, in fact. Can't really pin a murder on a dead guy when you're sitting right here having pulled the trigger, now can we? And what's more, we're looking for who might have done all that killing, too."

Adam looked to Elven, like he was in need of saving. "I ain't got nothing to do with any of that. I was here the whole time."

"Yeah, I know that," Elven said.

"When can I get outta here?" Adam asked.

"When you can tell me who else is dealing around here. Otherwise, when they do release you, you'll go straight to county lock-up."

Adam sat up taller. "I told you, it was the church. That's who was selling. That's who I get it from normally."

Elven turned around, Jesse following behind him. "When you can give me anything else, I'll listen," Elven said. He was going to let him sweat it out.

CHAPTER FORTY-TWO

THE FLOORING IN THE HALLWAY WAS CHEAP AND FADED. IT WAS in desperate need of replacing, but once again, money being brought into the equation was the problem. Elven walked across the worn linoleum to the vending machine that hummed lightly in the corner.

He slid a dollar in and pushed the button for a bottle of water. Jesse ran up to him, looking at the selection.

"Got a spare dollar?" Jesse asked.

Elven looked at him, then pulled another dollar out of his wallet. He handed it over and pulled his water bottle out of the dispenser. Jesse ran the dollar over the edge of the machine, smoothing it out, before sliding it in the machine. He bought himself a diet root beer. Not even name brand. Some generic stuff Elven hadn't even seen at the grocery store.

To each his own.

Elven looked down the hall at the small window at the end. The sun was getting low and an orange glow started to fill the building.

"What's this methhead about?" Jesse asked, taking a swig from his root beer.

"Found him in the hills along with his dead friend, about ten miles from Spencer Caldwell's set-up. It's the closest place to where we found them," Elven said.

"So you think Spencer was dealing?" Jesse asked. "Seems a bit of a stretch. A preacher selling drugs? Why'd you follow that lead?"

"Does it? Seemed to make the most sense to me. And it looks like I was right. He says he bought from the church. And now, everyone there is dead. Wouldn't you think those things are all linked?"

Jesse nodded. "Makes sense now. But the word of a methhead doesn't count for much with me."

"And the murders?"

Jesse shrugged. "Could be anything. I thought it was a robbery for the money, but you think it was for drugs? Find anything at the scene?"

Elven took a swig of his water and shook his head. He knew he would be better at lying if he didn't have to vocalize it. Jesse nodded in response.

"Just going off a hunch," Elven said. "Usually, I'm right about things like this."

It wasn't a complete lie, other than the head shake maybe. His hunch had been right about the meth though. Finding it at Spencer Caldwell's place was the proof. Adam's confession was going to have to be enough for Jesse, until Elven knew if he could trust him or not.

"Fair enough. So what now?" Jesse asked.

Elven shrugged. "I'm not really sure. If we know Spencer Caldwell was dealing drugs, or at least, someone at the revival was, then it makes me think it was a turf war or something like that."

"Shit, like in the movies. What is this, Detroit? I never been there before," Jesse said.

"Something like that, I guess. Does seem a little bit more than Dupray is used to seeing, but times are changing. The old guard is leaving, and that makes people think they can take the place at whatever cost," Elven said.

"Any ideas who?"

"I was thinking about what you said in the tent, about the ammunition used," Elven said.

"You mean the .204 Ruger? The type that no big game hunter would use?"

"That's the one. You said it would be used for coyotes?" Elven asked.

Jesse tipped his head back and chugged the diet root beer back down his throat. Elven watched the bottle glug down, air bubbles filling the bottle until there was no soda left. Jesse let out a loud belch when he was done.

"Yeah, it could definitely take one out," Jesse said. "Why?"

Jesse tossed the bottle at the trash can next to the vending machine. It hit the lip of the receptacle then bounced off the other edge and fell to the floor. He made no attempt to pick it up.

"I've got another hunch," Elven said, picking the bottle up and placing it into the trash.

"Great, I'll come with, partner."

Elven didn't want to bring Jesse along, but then again, he knew he wouldn't be able to lose him. For someone so intent on avoiding him when he rolled into town, Jesse really seemed interested in what Elven was doing now. Elven found it difficult to not think it was suspicious. He didn't like thinking that way about another man of the law, but then again, his hunches were often right.

CHAPTER FORTY-THREE

Madds was glad to have the men out of the room. Doc Driscoll had been kind enough to let Madds and Michaela use his downstairs facilities while he went back upstairs to do something else. She was sure he had work to do in the basement, but was being kind enough to let them have some privacy.

It was obvious that Michaela wasn't going to open up to anyone except Madds, and that wouldn't go any easier if someone else was around.

The bathroom was small, but more than enough to give them some privacy and exactly what they needed. It was just a small room with a tub/shower combination. The toilet sat next to the shower and there was a sliding glass door above the tub instead of a curtain. A single sink was in line with the toilet, and then the door.

Madds ran the water hot, holding her hand underneath until she was satisfied. She turned to see Michaela standing, shaking in front of her.

"It's gonna be okay," Madds reassured. "I'm gonna let you get undressed and I'll be right outside."

Michaela shook her head, her body shaking double-time along with it.

Madds sighed. "Do you want me to help you?"

Michaela nodded, her lip trembling.

"Okay, come on," Madds said.

She walked around behind Michaela. There was a small zipper at the back of her neck on the dress she wore that was stained brown. There were polka dots at the neckline, and had it not been covered and stained by the literal shit, Madds would have thought it was cute. She pulled the zipper down.

"Can you step out of it, or do you want me to pull it over your head?" Madds asked, unable to see Michaela's answer.

Madds directed Michaela's arms down and she worked the dress down her body. It was still damp in some areas and crusty in others, making it difficult to get off. But she managed. Michaela stood in front of her in her bra and panties, both stained brown from the ordeal.

The thing that caught Madds's attention were the marks on Michaela's back. They weren't from the slaughter at the revival the night before. No, these were old scars. Long marks that raised up into gnarly patterns from where it looked like she had been carved with a knife. Maybe even beaten and whipped.

Michaela stood there, still trembling. Madds wanted to say something about it. She wanted to reassure her that everything was going to be alright. But more than anything, she felt sorry for the girl. Someone in her life had done this to her, most likely multiple times over the years. Whether it was Spencer, Betsy, or someone else, she had to live through it and continue to take it.

With how Madds had witnessed the treatment Michaela received from Betsy and Spencer, if it wasn't them, things had shifted from physical abuse to mental abuse. And Madds could feel the tears welling up in her own eyes.

It made her think that the girl who stood before her could have been her if she had stayed in the life she used to have before moving to Dupray.

"I'm so sorry," Madds whispered.

Michaela didn't say anything. She didn't respond physically either. She just stood there, like she was a specimen on display. Madds continued to help her out of the rest of her clothes and held Michaela's hand as she stepped into the shower.

Michaela had gripped Madds's hand firmly, but as soon as Michaela felt the hot water wash over her, Madds felt the tension release from her grip. Then she let go of her hand completely.

Madds had promised she wouldn't leave, so she sat on the toilet, still wearing her own crusty pants that she couldn't wait to get out of herself. But first, she wanted to make sure Michaela was taken care of.

She sat and waited, listening to the water run over the girl. Madds ran over all the bodies she'd seen that day in her head. Both of Michaela's cousins, the men that were hired to set up, and the one addict outside that Madds didn't know. Michaela had witnessed most, if not all of it, and then had to hide in the most disgusting place to survive.

That poor girl.

Now everyone wanted to know who did it. Why they did it. And Michaela had to know all those answers. But they were so quick to just pressure her for answers. Madds was angry, and she wanted to know, too.

She wanted to know who put those marks on Michaela's body. She wanted to know who murdered those people, and she wanted to know who had caused Michaela so much trauma. But she didn't want to push her.

The water turned off, the last remaining drips hitting the tub and falling from Michaela. Madds quickly stood and grabbed a towel from the counter. She opened it up and turned her head, trying to give Michaela a chance at a little bit of dignity.

Michaela climbed from the tub and Madds wrapped the towel

around her. Instead of pulling away, though, Michaela wrapped her arms around Madds. The girl started crying into Madds's shoulder like everything had finally come out at once.

Madds hugged her back and whispered into her ear, "It's all gonna be okay, now."

And then Madds started to cry herself. She didn't know who needed it more, but she knew that Michaela giving her the hug and opportunity to cry herself was exactly what she needed.

CHAPTER FORTY-FOUR

"So wait, you're telling me that this guy gets drunk in town, meets up with some random assholes, and gets on this guy's property and kills his chickens?" Jesse asked.

Elven nodded. "Apparently he was clucking like one, too."

"Shit, man. I've seen some drunk-ass people, but that's a bit much," Jesse said.

"Tony's mostly harmless, but just not the best at decisions I suppose," Elven commented.

"Apparently not."

Elven had parked the Jeep onto Frank Dority's property and parked it next to the house. It looked the same as it did the last time he was out, but hoped that when he walked around back, the chicken coop and other property damage was going to be mostly taken care of.

Jesse's truck was parked next to him, pointing in the opposite direction. Elven still hadn't thought of a way to get him off his tail since the murders, and maybe that was alright. By keeping Jesse with him, he could get a better gauge on whether his hunch had anything to it or not.

He'd phoned ahead and Frank had let him know that Tony was

still working to make things right, and, actually, to Elven's surprise, was doing good work. That was great to hear, but Elven was mostly interested in Tony being there so he could ask him some questions.

Elven walked up to the porch and knocked on the door. This time, Frank yelled out through the door.

"Who's there?"

"Frank, it's Sheriff Hallie," Elven said.

"Sheriff?"

"Yeah, I called earlier. You said Tony was here doing work."

"Right, right," he said. "Give me a sec."

Jesse snorted a wad of mucus from his nose and into his mouth. Elven watched him swish it around before launching it across the dirt drive, landing right next to Elven's front tire. Classy.

The front door opened and Frank Dority stood with the shotgun in his hand.

"Pete's sake, Frank, it's me," Elven said, sidestepping out of line of the barrel.

"Can't be too careful," Frank said. The old man looked over to Jesse. "Who's this you brought wicha?"

"Jesse Parsons. He's a game warden," Elven said.

"West Virginia Natural Resources Police Officer," Jesse corrected.

Elven rolled his eyes.

"Oh, fancy. What's a— uh, what'd you call it?" Frank asked.

"Natural Resources Police Officer," Jesse said.

"Right, so what're you doing out here? All this for my murdered chickens the other day? 'Cause Tony's making it right, I tell ya. He's doing so good I might just offer to pay him to come back out for some other work around the farm," Frank said.

That was a shock. Tony doing something more useful than emptying a bottle was unheard of. Elven was actually impressed. He liked Tony, even though he was mostly a screw-up around town.

"Good for him," Elven said. "But no, we just wanted to talk to Tony about something."

"Hopefully nothing bad. Like I says, he's been real good here."

Elven shook his head. "Where is he?"

"Round back," Frank said. "C'mon, I'll take you to him."

Frank rested the shotgun inside the doorway against the wall and closed the door behind him. Elven was relieved the old guy didn't feel it was necessary to bring the shotgun with him. Especially after the last time he'd seen him in action with it.

Around the back of the house, Tony was out in the field next to the chicken coop. He was extending the chicken wire out and looked like he was nailing it to the wood. Except, the coop looked much bigger than it had originally.

Tony wore a thick flannel shirt and jeans. And to Elven's surprise, he seemed completely sober. Of course, he had seen him sober before, but it was nice to see him getting some work done.

"Sheriff, come out to make sure I'm good on my word?" Tony asked.

Elven shook his head. "No, I had no doubt that you'd keep it. You're a good man when it comes to things like that."

Tony smiled, and looked like he stood a little taller when Elven said it. A little compliment could sometimes go a long way, and Elven would have to remember that more often.

"Sheriff and the Natural Resource policeman here—"

"A what?" Tony asked.

"Game warden," Elven said.

"Ah," Tony said, understanding.

"They want to ask you some questions. Don't worry, it's got nothing to do with what you done the other day. I told 'em you done real good work for me."

"Thanks, Frank. I went ahead and extended the coop like we talked about. Just like you said you'd wanted," Tony said, another hint of pride in his voice.

Elven saw Frank Dority smile and thought how crazy it was that a drunken event that had happened could put those two men together and they'd get along so well. And it was good for them both.

Tony was taking pride in his work, and Frank had someone to help him since he couldn't get around so easy.

"So what can I do for you?" Tony asked.

"It's about the men, from the other night. The ones who came out with you when you did this," Elven said.

Tony nodded. "Yeah, I was a little too far gone when I did all that. Lots of blackouts, you know?"

Jesse chuckled. "Been there plenty myself."

Elven gave him a side glance up and down, and couldn't help but vocalize his thought. "I'm sure you have."

Jesse matched his glance back to him, obviously unhappy about the comment, but he didn't push the issue.

"What about them?" Tony asked, wiping his forehead with the back of his sleeve. Even with the chill out, he'd worked up a sweat.

"Don't suppose you know where they're at? Maybe exchange numbers?" Elven asked.

"Nah, nothing like that. Maybe they got my number in their phone, most likely under drunk idiot," Tony said, biting his cheek. Elven heard a hint of shame in his voice.

"Know where they're staying? Where they'll be?"

Tony shook his head. "Sorry, Elven, but I got no idea. I met them at the Wolf Tavern the other night. If they're still in town, you might check there. They seemed to like the place."

Elven nodded. That was about the best they were gonna get. And with Tony, he might be a screw-up and a drunk, but he was known for nothing less than honesty with him.

"Thanks Tony," Elven said. "And Tony, hard work looks good on you. Maybe try more of it instead of the bottle."

Tony smiled and gave Elven a nod. "I think I might, Sheriff. Thanks."

"Time to wrap it up anyway," Frank said. "Sun's just about snuffed out for the day."

Elven left Frank and Tony to finish whatever had to be finished.

"So what do you make of all that?" Jesse asked as they walked back to their vehicles.

"About what I expected, I guess. Tony's telling the truth, so if they're even in town, not much to go off of on finding them," Elven said.

"Alright, so we go hit this Wolf Tavern?" Jesse asked. He looked in the distance. "Seems about drinking time."

Elven laughed. "Around here, anytime is drinking time, but I suppose you're right."

"Lead the way," Jesse said.

Elven opened the door to his Jeep and paused for a moment, coming up with a different idea. He wanted to know what was going on, and if he thought there was something off about Jesse, he wouldn't get the answers he wanted. Not with Jesse over his shoulder the whole time.

"You know what, I think I'm gonna swing by my place, throw on a change of clothes. The stench of the outhouse is still on me."

"I was wondering how long you'd go before getting sick of it," Jesse said. "But what the hell am I supposed to do?"

"Head to the station. Talk to Tank, he's my deputy. Good guy. He's friends with the bartender at Wolf Tavern. He'll point you in the right direction and be able to open up a conversation easier than me. I'll catch up with you."

"Whatever you say," Jesse said, slamming the door of his truck.

Elven knew how long it took to drive back to the station and then to Wolf Tavern. He'd have plenty of time to check the bar out himself by the time Jesse figured anything out. It would probably piss him off, but when Elven thought about it, he couldn't help but smile.

CHAPTER FORTY-FIVE

A LOUD CRASH WOKE HER IN THE MIDDLE OF THE NIGHT.

Madds sprung upward, her hand going straight to her gun on the table next to the bed. The darkness seemed to engulf her so much that not even the moonlight could penetrate in the room. There was a light hum in the background, the only noise in the dead silent building.

Phil Driscoll had insisted that Michaela stay the night at the funeral home. It wasn't just the funeral home, but also Phil's residence. It was extremely large, not just because it doubled as Phil's home, but because Phil had no family, at least family that lived with him. He had plenty of room to spare. And of course, since Michaela was so upset at the idea of Madds leaving her, he invited Madds to stay the night as well.

They could have stayed in separate rooms, but Madds knew Michaela would never get to sleep alone. The room held two twin beds, and Madds was closest to the door. Michaela was sound asleep in the bed next to hers. For someone who had been shocked into silence, the girl seemed to have no problem sleeping in the pitch-black of night. Then again, the poor thing was probably exhausted to the point of having no choice but to pass out.

Madds listened, and still heard nothing.

Had she imagined the noise?

She pulled the comforter off of herself and already regretted her decision. It was freezing inside the house and her body wanted nothing more than to crawl back underneath the warmth of the covers. But her mind pulled her, needing to know everything was okay.

She set her feet on the cold wooden flooring beneath her. Even with socks on, the soles of her feet protested. She held the gun firmly in her grip and went to the closed bedroom door, placing her ear against it.

Only the slight hum of the refrigeration in the background, the bit of white noise to keep the house at ease.

She let out a long, slow breath, trying to hear anything that might be movement in the house. She didn't know anything about Phil Driscoll's sleeping habits. Even if there was movement in the house, that didn't mean there was anything sinister afoot. The old guy might be looking for a snack in the kitchen, or be on the verge of pissing himself and rushing to the bathroom.

She looked back over her shoulder and made sure that Michaela was sound asleep, which she still was. Good for her. She needed it, and Madds hoped that nothing would wake her the rest of the night.

Still, Madds felt the urge to check the house.

Her legs were cold, not having brought any pajamas with her. Driscoll had an old, oversized flannel shirt that he let her use as a nightshirt. It fit loosely on her, half of it hanging off her shoulder. She hoped to God that it was truly just an old shirt that had belonged to him, and not some stiff who had made his way through the doc's doors.

Her socks only made it halfway up her calves, the exposed flesh above them riddled with goosebumps from the cold.

She twisted the doorknob as slowly and quietly as possible, her gun in her hand by her waist. She slid out into the hallway and pushed the door back, not latching it. She'd be back soon enough to close it all the way and get right back under the covers.

She walked cautiously down the hall, keeping her gun low. She hoped it was her imagination, but on the chance she ran into a half-asleep Driscoll, she didn't want to give him a scare. Especially if she ran into him before he had a chance to make it to the bathroom.

She looked down at herself and thought that maybe she should have put pants on. Hers were currently in the wash, but she didn't even check any of the drawers to see if she could scrounge up a pair of jeans. If she didn't scare him with her gun, she'd give him a good rile-up in her current attire. Her panties were barely covered by the length of the shirt.

She smiled, considering the hilarity of running into the man in the hallway.

Her smile quickly dropped when she heard a thud come from somewhere in the house. This time, it was much closer as she made her way toward the center of the large building.

She pressed herself back against the wall, debating on making herself known or not. It would calm her nerves to know that Driscoll was putzing around, and would quell her investigation immediately.

But on the off-chance it was something else...well, she decided to keep quiet.

She picked up and put her feet down as soft as she could, heading down the stairs to the lobby. There was no light in the building, except through the windows of the house letting in the moonlight. Her eyes were as adjusted as they could get. She peeked around the wall and into the room.

What she saw in the lobby disturbed her.

A beam of light passed over the room, illuminating the couch and chairs that Driscoll had set up for people to wait as they were either consoled or in shock, she assumed.

And then the light passed over the floor and she saw a body on the floor. But it wasn't just any body—it was the body of a short, little man. It was Phil Driscoll.

She swallowed hard and brought her gun up. All thoughts of the cold flushed from her mind, though the thought of putting pants on first had lingered a little while longer. Too late now.

The flashlight spun around and she saw the silhouette of a man. He wasn't very large—tall, yes, but little more than a skeleton when it came to girth. The flashlight, followed by the silhouette, made its way to the stairs that led down to the basement. After a few moments, it disappeared.

Madds quickly rushed over to Phil Driscoll. She slid on her socks when she got to the body and knelt down. Blood pooled around his head, though not as much as a gunshot wound or even a more serious head injury would cause. She shoved two fingers against his neck, feeling for a pulse.

It was strong enough that she knew he wasn't in any danger. He was still alive, just knocked out.

Relief would have to wait. There was still someone in the house, and they were capable of violence. What exactly their goal was, she didn't know. She would find out when she arrested him.

She took soft steps to the stairs that led to the basement, setting her first foot on the step leading down.

"You think she knows we're here? That was a pretty loud crash," a man's voice whispered from behind Madds.

She spun around and saw not one, but two flashlight beams jostling across the floor from the other room. Only a few seconds and they'd be in the lobby. Madds debated for a brief moment and decided heading downstairs to confront the one man was too risky. Even if she incapacitated him, there were still two more.

And she still didn't know what the end goal was.

"Maybe if you hadn't broken that fucking window I would say no, but with this old guy coming out, shit, I'm sure she heard," another voice whispered.

Madds shuffled quickly to the stairs leading back up to her room where Michaela slept, her socks never leaving the floor, like she was her own puck in a game of air hockey.

She dipped behind the wall, keeping her back against it, her gun ready for anything.

Footsteps started coming up from the basement, the beam of light popping up every step.

"Would you assholes keep it down up here?" the man from the basement whispered, though it sounded like he was struggling not to shout.

"I was just askin' if anyone could hear us," another one of them said.

"With you whispering so loud up here, I'm sure the whole fucking county can hear us," the basement man snapped.

"I was just—"

"Shut it. They ain't down there."

"And they ain't here either," the third man said.

Madds knew where the conversation was headed and she wasn't waiting to hear it. It was either try to stop the three men right then and there, exchanging bullets until all three men, or just she, caught one. Or get Michaela and get out of there.

She was confident in her marksmanship, but with there being three of them, and not knowing whether there was anyone else in the house, the odds were against her.

She took the steps two at a time, thankful she had decided not to put shoes on before venturing out in the house. The socks had really come in handy when keeping her movements stealthy.

The door to the room was just as she'd left it, with only a crack of an opening. No sign that anyone had been up there.

She rushed into the room, closing the door behind her. Michaela was still sound asleep under the comforter in the bed against the far wall. Her stomach rose up, then back down with each breath, as if nothing were wrong and there weren't three or more men in the house looking for her.

She hated to startle the girl after everything she'd been through, but she also needed to keep her quiet. Madds placed her hand over Michaela's mouth, her breath warm against her palm before clamping her fingers shut.

Michaela's eyes went wide and Michaela screamed, which came out less than muffled due to Madds's hand.

She lifted a finger to her lips. "It's me, it's Madds. Can you calm down?"

Michaela seemed to understand and nodded. Madds slid her hand off the girl's mouth.

"There are men in the house and they're looking for you. We have to get up and move," Madds whispered.

She pulled the covers off the girl and helped her out of bed. She wore a similar outfit to Madds, an old frayed flannel shirt, except she wore a set of gym shorts that were tied in a double knot at the waist. Her clothes were so bad that they hadn't even been worth washing. Michaela went to grab her shoes, but Madds stopped her.

"No time," she whispered.

Madds went to the second-story window and unlatched it. She tried pulling up, but it wouldn't budge, most likely not having been opened in a decade or more.

They were going to have to hide in the house.

Michaela's hand was visibly trembling. Madds grabbed it, feeling her squeeze tight, and led her to the door. It was only a matter of time before the intruders would be in the hallway and be able to see them if they left.

But nobody was there yet. She could hear the whispers and footsteps echoing down the hallway, finding their way up the stairs.

Whoever was after Michaela wasn't being too sneaky. Their boots were loud enough for Madds to know they had only a few seconds.

She ran into the hallway, both of the girls keeping their feet light. Madds tugged Michaela and headed in the opposite direction from the stairs. She passed by a few different rooms with their doors closed. Driscoll had said something about closing doors to rooms kept the heat in better and kept bills low.

At least, for the time being, he'd be able to see another utility bill.

She pulled Michaela into the bathroom at the end of the hallway. This one was bigger than the basement bathroom. There were two sinks that led to a single shower, which then had an adjoining door that led to a single toilet.

Madds closed the door, but not all the way. She peeked her eye through the slit of an opening and watched the men walk into the hallway.

The first man stared right at her, seeming to look right into her eye. She thought for sure she was boned. But then he looked away.

The hallway was too dark to see her.

The three men gathered, whispering loudly as they had been downstairs. It made Madds wonder where they came from. The way they spoke, it really didn't seem like this was their normal gig.

But that didn't mean they weren't still dangerous.

"Check this room first," the man with the long hair who had been in the basement said. "We'll go down the hall and check each room."

Madds watched as one of them slowly opened the door and crept inside. They all turned their flashlights off, leaving the hallway in complete darkness. The silhouettes of the other men headed to each closed door that lined the hallway.

She thought she saw something other than a flashlight in their hands, but couldn't make it out. She had to assume it was a weapon.

It didn't matter. She had to figure something out before they searched the rest of the house once they realized that Michaela wasn't there. But even if they made it out of the house unnoticed, Madds didn't have a car. And she didn't know where the doc kept his keys.

They were too far away from any other homes, the funeral home being fairly isolated.

No, she would have to figure something else out.

And that most likely involved fighting.

CHAPTER FORTY-SIX

IT WAS TOO DARK OUT, AND TOO COLD, FOR HIS LIKING.

Jesse wasn't a fan of the sheriff, but there were things he needed him for. And right now, Elven Hallie was the one that knew about the town and those that lived in it. He also had some information on men that might lead him to the end of this whole mess.

So as much as he didn't want to, he'd have to partner up with the pretty boy for the time being.

He entered the station, just as Elven had told him to do. The priss needed to change his clothes, he'd said, apparently too good to be a little dirty. Jesse found that laughable.

As a game warden, there were times that he had to be out in the wild for weeks at a time. Going without a shower or change of clothes the whole time. The fancy sheriff gets a little shit on himself and he needs to stop an entire investigation to get a clean pair of trousers.

Jesse chuckled. Trousers. He's sure that Sheriff Hallie would use a term like that. And maybe hold a pinky up as he drank some tea.

The station was quiet, that old lady receptionist being absent from behind the desk. It looked so pathetic.

Then again, in his line of work, he didn't even have an office or a station. Just a house where people would come visit him if they had problems. And then get sent to various places in the county by the state.

Maybe a part of him wished he could have a home base and some people to count on along with it.

And just like that, one of the sheriff's deputies came out from the hallway.

It was the muscular one who hadn't been at the crime scene. He'd heard the man had taken some buckshot to the gut a while back, so he was on limited duty. Sucked to be him.

"Help you?" the deputy asked before seeing the emblem on Jesse's shirt.

"Yeah, Sheriff Hallie sent me here to find you, I'm pretty sure."

"Oh, right. Don't think we've actually met yet. I'm Tank," Tank said, holding a hand out.

Jesse smiled and grabbed his hand. It was a firm shake and Jesse could tell that there was a respect from the man. He'd probably served in the military at some point.

"Jesse Parsons. Nat—"

"Natural Resources Police, I know," Tank said, a stupid grin on his face.

"That's right," Jesse said, impressed that he didn't call him a *game warden* like most people. It wasn't that the term was necessarily wrong. It was part of the job, but it just wasn't the whole job, and in West Virginia, Jesse took pride in knowing that he was an officer of the law as it stated on his badge.

"You know, I used to want to do that. Be a warden, I mean."

Jesse nodded. "It's a pretty great job, you know."

"Oh, I do," Tank said.

"What stopped you from trying?"

Tank shrugged. "After the service, I came to Dupray. Lester, the old sheriff, saw something in me and said I should come down to apply for a job as one of his deputies. I did, and then life happened, you know? Settled down, had a couple kids, all that."

"Kids, huh?" Jesse asked, not really interested. He liked not being tethered down to a woman and rugrats. The woman part he had down, though it was entirely possible he had a few little swimmers out in the world, depending on if the eight hundred bucks he gave Marcy Bentworth and Suzie Weiland went to what it had been intended for.

But nobody came knocking on his door looking for him or any more money, so he was probably in the clear.

"Yeah, so now it's dinners at night with the family instead of long treks in the woods, hunting down poachers and murderers."

Jesse laughed. Like that was any part of his job, until now, of course.

"Oh, yeah, I tell you, sometimes it can be a real thrill," Jesse said. What could he say? He liked the attention.

"Gotta say, I'm a little jealous of the freedom you guys get," Tank said.

"It's pretty great. And you know, the women love a man in uniform," Jesse said. "Though, I'm sure you know all about that, right?" He winked at Tank.

Tank twisted his face. "I said I was married, right?"

"Oh, sure did. But I know how it is. Nothing wrong with a little on the side. After all, the job is stressful. Gotta let off some steam where you can," Jesse said, not noticing that Tank was no longer impressed with him.

"And you know, you get all the free ammo you can use, and then some," Jesse said. "If cash is a little tight, you just sell the bullets on the side. Can make more than a month's rent just from that."

"That sounds, uh, well—"

Jesse laughed and slapped Tank on the shoulder. "Yeah, I could always put a good word in for you if you were still interested."

"What did you say Elven told you to swing by here for?" Tank asked, changing the subject.

"Gotta go see if some assholes are down at that Wolf Tavern bar," Jesse said.

Tank lifted his eyebrows. "Don't think you'll have trouble finding an asshole, or group of them, there. But anyone in particular?"

Jesse chuckled. "Not sure about the name, just some guy that broke into some farm."

"How do you know who you're looking for?" Tank asked.

Huh. Jesse hadn't thought about that. Elven knew what the guys looked like and Tank didn't. So how was he supposed to know who it was?

"Elven said he'd meet us down there," Jesse said, only half-believing it himself. "Said you can show me the way."

Tank shrugged. "Sure can, though not real familiar. That place is a dive by Dupray's standards, and in Dupray, the best you can hope for is a dive by outsider standards. That place attracts a real iffy crowd sometimes."

"And you're friends with the bartender there? Kind of odd."

Tank cocked his head to the side. "Not sure where you got that, but I ain't friends with nobody from Wolf Tavern."

Jesse knit his brows together.

"Maybe you got confused. Sure, I can take you, everyone knows where it's at. I can definitely see how all that meth Elven found was tied to someone at that shithole."

Jesse no longer smiled. He knew something was off with that sheriff.

"Meth he found?" Jesse asked.

CHAPTER FORTY-SEVEN

THE WOLF TAVERN WAS ABOUT AS LIVELY AS EVER.

Elven spied the motorcycles lined up along the front of the building. He had no qualms with bikers, but sometimes a group of drunks filled with testosterone could give a place a certain reputation.

He'd been called out to a bar fight getting out of hand more times than he could count. The ones that the bar itself couldn't handle with their own muscle.

Two men were outside, the one with a gray beard sitting on the first bike closest to the door. They each looked at Elven with a scowl.

"Gentlemen," Elven said, tipping his hat.

He was met with a loogie at his feet.

At least it didn't land on his boots. Then he'd have to do something about it.

And he had plans that needed to be done within a certain time limit. Otherwise he'd have to involve Jesse, and he didn't want to be put in a position of trusting him yet. If ever.

The bouncer was a man in his sixties with biceps the size of a muffler. He sat on a stool outside the front door, though Elven wasn't sure what his job was outside. It wasn't like there was a dress code or that the bar actually limited who could walk in.

But Elven didn't criticize him. He'd seen him on numerous trips and was met with nothing but respect from the man, even if he didn't know his name.

He gave him a tip of his hat and the bouncer nodded back at him.

The music inside was exactly as loud as he would have expected, given the volume he could hear from the parking lot. He took two steps, the door just closing behind him, before someone ran right into him.

The leather-clad man tumbled backward, holding a pitcher of beer, spilling it all over himself. Elven caught the guy from behind and stood him up. Thankfully, the man was big enough to take all the beer that spilled and not a drop landed on Elven.

"What the fuck is—" The man started, but then set eyes on the badge on Elven's chest.

"Just move along," Elven said.

The drunk, heavyset man paused, thinking over his options for a moment. Elven let him catch up, resting his hand on the butt of the pistol that sat on his hip. His elbow was cocked behind him, ready to draw if needed, though it was mostly for show.

The man considered, his front dripping with half the pitcher. And it seemed like he was still on the fence. It wasn't until one of his more clear-headed friends came by, grabbing him by the leather jacket, that he made his decision.

"Sheriff," his friend said.

"Have a safe night, gentlemen," Elven said, making his way through the crowded bar.

The cigarette smoke in the drab building was thick and nauseating. But Elven powered through, hoping to get done and out of there before he would have to worry about any long-lasting effects.

Elven smiled, setting eyes on one of the men from the farm the other day. He was easy to spot. He was one of the few people there who wasn't wearing a leather jacket, vest, pants, or anything really that was made out of animal skin. He was also the only one drinking alone, looking like he was a sad mess staring down at the bottom of his glass.

Elven saddled up next to him, taking the stool to his left.

"Where're your friends?" Elven asked.

The man's face moved faster than his eyes, a side effect of the alcohol. By the time his eyes caught up, he realized who he was looking at and started to cry.

Elven looked around, thinking this situation went completely different from what he was expecting. For one, he didn't think there would be a man crying in a bar filled with bikers.

It wasn't the leader of the group that he sat with. He didn't know names, but it was one of the guys who had kept his mouth shut and stayed quiet in the back at Dority's farm, letting his long-haired friend do most of the talking. Fine with Elven, as long as he got the answers he needed. Even if there were beer tears.

"What's going on?" Elven asked, a little confused.

The man just shook his head. "You're here for me, ain't ya? I don't even know how it happened...I swear, Sheriff." Snot bubbled from his nose as he sputtered the words.

"Why don't you tell me about it, then? I'm sure this can go easier if you do," Elven said. Seriously. Was he just going to get a confession right there in the bar?

"I thought we was just up there to scare people. I swear on my momma's grave. I didn't know—I mean, I didn't want to. Oh my God, those people," he said.

Elven watched him pick up his glass and throw it back, but it was already empty. All he got was one drop, not that it seemed to matter to him.

"What's your name?" Elven asked.

"S—Scotty."

"Alright, Scotty. So you're telling me you know what happened at that church in the hills, right?"

He nodded.

"And that you were up there with your buddies and gunned those people down?"

"I didn't know we was up there to murder anyone. But then that big guy just pulled a pistol out and shot that preacher man in the head with no warning. Then everyone drew, and what were we supposed to do?"

A man stumbled between them, his back hitting against the bar. He was even drunker than the man who had spilled his beer when Elven entered. He put his hand on the bar and Scotty's glass slid off the bar top, shattering on the floor beneath it. He leaned into Scotty, his face inches from his own.

"What you crying about, little girl?" he asked menacingly, his words slurring.

Elven grabbed the drunk by the collar and stood up. "Private conversation, friend." Elven shoved him off.

Elven glared when the man spun around, his fist clenched. The second moment of clarity Elven witnessed while being in the bar. He really didn't want to wait for the next drunk to run into him.

Elven shoved his way through the room toward the jukebox that sat in against the wall. He leaned over and pulled the plug, the Buckcherry song coming to an immediate halt.

"Hey, what the fuck?" someone yelled out.

Elven stood tall, hand on his revolver again, feeling the mental boost.

"I'm having a conversation with my friend over here, you all got that?" Elven asked. "I do not want to be interrupted again. Feel free to drink and have a great time. But if one more of you yokels comes around, getting your drunk face in my way, I won't even give you the chance to decide if you wanna take a swing. Got it?"

Elven felt all the eyes on him. He had all the confidence in the world to win a fight, but this wouldn't be a fight. There were at least twenty men he was addressing, and none of them seemed friendly. If they wanted, they could hand Elven's butt to him.

But luck was on his side, or maybe it was more than that, as the man who had pulled the first drunk off Elven stuck his fingers in his mouth and let out a whistle.

"Everyone hear the sheriff? Anyone doesn't do what he asks, I'll be the one to take you outta here. After that, if the sheriff wants to have a crack, he can do as he pleases."

Elven swallowed hard. He'd never interacted with these men, as far as he knew, but there was an obvious hierarchy. And a respect toward that man.

The man nodded at the sheriff and everyone went back to their drinks. Elven tipped his hat, then plugged the jukebox back in.

Elven plopped back down on the stool next to Scotty. He hadn't moved.

"Why'd you do it?" Elven asked.

Scotty shrugged. "Supposed to get paid. Thought we was just muscle to threaten though."

"Who paid you?" Elven asked.

"The big guy. I didn't catch his name."

"How did you find him?" Elven asked.

"I don't know. It was all Herb that set it up. He does most of that stuff. We just follow what he tells us."

Elven nodded. The problem with talking to the lackey was that he didn't get all the information. "Can you describe him? Did he talk at all?"

"Didn't say much that I could hear. Just a big dude. A bit older, had a kind of beard, trimmed."

Well, that didn't do much. Half of Dupray fit that description, even some women.

"Your friend, the one who set it up, where is he now?" Elven asked.

Scotty shook his head. "Not here. Said there was another job, but I just—after the last one. Not me. Not anymore."

"Another job? What was it?"

"Something about some girl. That big dude says we missed someone. I guess some girl or something. I don't know. I ain't got the stomach to kill anyone else."

Some girl? Elven slid off his stool, making his way through the crowd and back outside to his Jeep. If they were after Michaela, then he had no time to waste.

As soon as he set foot outside, he was met with a scowling Jesse. If Elven wasn't in such a rush to get to Driscoll's, he would have savored getting one over on the man. But that wasn't the case now.

"What the hell do you think—"

"No time," Elven said cutting Jesse off.

Tank stood behind Jesse and Elven grabbed him by the shoulder.

"Grab the guy at the bar and put him in a cell immediately," Elven said.

"Which guy? The place is packed."

"He'll be the one with more tears in his glass than booze," Elven said. "Jesse, you're with me."

"I ain't just gonna follow orders after the stunt you pulled, if—"

"Frankly, I don't care if you come or not. But I'm going, so if you want to come, then shut up," Elven said, continuing for his Jeep.

Jesse stood in the parking lot alone for a moment as Tank headed into the bar and Elven toward his Jeep. Finally, he picked his feet up and jogged toward his truck, firing it up before Elven left the lot.

CHAPTER FORTY-EIGHT

Madds watched from the slit in the bathroom door, Michaela shivering behind her, gripping her arm so hard that Madds thought she was drawing blood where her nails dug into her flesh. The men slid into the rooms and Madds knew there were only two options.

Run or fight.

If they ran, they'd have to move quickly down the hallway where the men stood just inside the doorway. They were there for Michaela, and if they were the ones who had been at the revival in the woods, it was no secret what they were capable of.

The hallway stretched down into the darkness, like a never-ending abyss where anything could happen if they ever reached the end of it.

Madds didn't have faith that they would, though.

All it would take was one of them to hear a weighted footstep, a creak in the floorboard, or just the fearful exhale as they ran by. Then they'd be dead before they reached the stairs.

Madds opened the door as slowly as she could, praying that there would be no squeal from the hinge. It opened just enough that she could slide through sideways. She wasn't willing to risk opening it further.

She began to work her way into the hallway, but Michaela tugged on her arm. She turned to the girl, her eyes glazed with tears, still too shocked and frightened to speak. She convulsed where she stood, her head shaking an inch each way, demanding Madds stay with her.

Madds took her free hand and placed it over Michaela's fingers where they dug into her arm. She squeezed her hand, then brought her hand up to her face. She stroked her cheek gently, trying to reassure her that everything would be alright without actually saying it, lest she risk alerting the attackers.

She was grateful that she couldn't say the words, otherwise it would be obvious that she was lying. Madds wasn't sure of anything right then.

She lifted her finger to her own lips and pursed them, even though it was obvious Michaela wasn't capable of being anything more than silent.

Michaela let go and Madds drifted into the hallway. Michaela backed away into the bathroom, engulfed by the shadows, but Madds still felt the girl's eyes on her. It made her feel tethered to the reality of the situation, but she knew that she was going to need to step into the other room. The one where Michaela's tether wouldn't reach.

The closest room was a spare bedroom that Phil Driscoll had at the top of the stairs. He'd said it housed most of his late wife's things, which is why he didn't normally offer it to anyone. He claimed it was a mess, but Madds was sure there were more sentimental reasons to it.

She raised her pistol, ready to take out anyone who set foot in the hallway. But she knew if it came down to firing her weapon, there would be no more element of surprise. She'd have to find shelter and then it would be a fire fight. Bullets exchanged for more bullets. And those men had more firepower on their side.

Her heart pounded in her chest and she began to have second thoughts. Maybe it wasn't too late to run. If everyone was upstairs, all she had to do was sneak by and make it downstairs. After that, they could run as fast as their feet could take them. She could just hold her hand out toward the bathroom, and Michaela could slip her fingers against her own and the two of them could leave together.

But as soon as she'd imagined it, that dream came shattering down.

"I think I got her here, boys!" the man yelled from the room she and Michaela had left before they came upstairs.

And then the gun went off. A rifle fired and then another shot followed it. Madds assumed it was at the two beds where both she and Michaela had been sleeping in only moments ago. In her haste to leave, she had still managed to plump up the blankets with pillows to give the illusion that someone was underneath them.

They didn't even check the beds. Had Madds not heard the break-in...that might have been it for them.

No time to think that way.

"Dan, shit, hold your fire!" the man from the middle room yelled.

Madds knew they'd all be out in the hallway in no time. She pushed into the room in front of her before the middle room could open up. The man who had entered the room stood with his back to her. He held a long rifle, the barrel pointing off to the side.

She began to raise her weapon, ready to tell him to drop it. Ready to announce that she was a cop. Ready to do so many things.

But she didn't have the chance.

He turned around too fast. It was like he could sense she was behind him.

And she was not ready for it. But neither was he.

It happened like it was in slow motion. She wanted to raise her pistol, but she saw what would happen if she did. He would raise his rifle at the same time and they would both fire. Whoever had their sites first would win, or they both would, or neither. But whichever way happened, it would be the end because all of his buddies would come rushing into the room.

And even if she still stood, she wouldn't be able to hold them all off.

Instead, while he lifted the rifle, she ran at him full force. She shoved into him with all her body weight. Her hands, sweaty yet steel, wrapped around the barrel of the rifle. He grunted as she pulled, losing control, his finger slipping away from the trigger.

He reaffirmed his grip, but his hands were not where they needed to be. He had a tight bond to the stock of the rifle, but not anywhere near the trigger. Madds pulled, but he kept his grip. That was when she realized it was a useless tug-of-war that she would never win.

More shots were fired from down the hall. Her mind immediately went to Michaela. Had she done her wrong by leaving her in the bathroom?

Then a yell, but from a very masculine voice.

"Goddammit, you can't go shooting right next to my ear, you asshole!" he yelled. "I ain't gonna hear nothin' now. My ears'll be ringing for days."

Madds's attention was pulled back to the fight she found herself in. Her opponent groaned loudly again, this time muttering something unintelligible. He was moments away from yelling out, alerting his buddies to come help him. Madds couldn't risk it.

She could feel her advantage of surprise slipping away from her. He was confused and caught off guard, but he was also a lot stronger than she was. She squared her eyes to him and saw his scowl through the darkness.

He was against the wall, his feet wide trying to stabilize himself from toppling over, which with his height, put him in her direct eye line. She reared her head back and threw it forward, landing a blow right against his face.

Her forehead took the brunt of the blow. It wasn't her ideal maneuver, but it was all she could think of at the time. Her head throbbed and a blip of blackness overtook her vision, immediately coming back like it had never happened. Though by the reverberating headache, she knew that wasn't true.

The man hollered out and dropped the rifle. It clattered to the floor by her feet.

She felt warm, slick wetness on her head, smearing down her face.

Was she injured?

One look at her opponent told her all she needed to know. She landed her headbutt square on his nose and it had exploded in a bloody mess. She remembered what her training officer had told her if she was ever to get in close quarters combat.

"The nose is like the testicles of the face. If you can't hit them down below, hit them right in the center," he said.

At the time, she had wondered what would happen if she was ever in close quarters combat, but now was very grateful for the tip.

Her opponent brought his hands to his nose and buckled over. For a brief moment, it was like he forgot that she was still there, holding a gun and that he was supposed to be there to kill her and Michaela.

She raised her pistol. "On the ground. Sheriff's department," she managed to say out in the loudest whisper she could muster, not wanting to give away her position to the others.

But he didn't listen. Either that, or he couldn't hear her. She wasn't sure which, but it didn't matter. He rose up in the darkness, which she could see. What she couldn't see was his hand swatting at her pistol.

He connected and once again, she suppressed her urge to pull the trigger. It might have been stupid. She probably should have just ended it there, letting him take a bullet where it landed and dealing with his accomplices as they came. But she wanted to do this her way.

Her arm went wide and he grabbed at her wrist, trying to wrestle the piece from her grip. That wasn't happening, though, no matter how much he tried.

What was happening, though, was he was giving her the advantage. He held her arm and struggled as she kept holding onto the gun.

He shifted his weight and pulled her in, while at the same time twisting around so his back was facing her.

She wrapped her free arm around the back of his neck, his long hair caught in the squeeze. He smelled like cigarettes and sweat. His skin felt grimy and she guessed he hadn't showered in at least a couple of days.

She pulled back against his throat, her gun hand still locked in his grip.

"You fucking—"

She kicked down on the back of his knee and he buckled and dropped to the floor before he could say another word. His voice was loud enough that she knew she had little time.

She pulled her arm back, but he squeezed hard and she had to drop the gun. It fell to the wood floor with a *thud*, not bouncing. She managed to finagle her arm out and lock it against her other one, putting him in a headlock.

He fell to the ground, grasping at her arm. He was wiry, but he had more upper body strength than she did. He threw elbows behind him, nailing her ribs so hard they radiated pain with each blow. Finally, he threw his back hard against the wall, Madds with it.

She released her grip and he fell forward, gasping for air.

"Shit, they ain't here!" the man from the other room yelled. By the volume of his voice, she assumed there was little he could hear of the fight. He could probably barely hear his own voice. But, it was only a matter of time until they realized their friend wasn't around. And it was taking far too long to incapacitate him.

Her opponent climbed to his hands and knees and she saw her angle. She swept her feet around, her bare legs wrapping around his neck.

He went to scream. Tried to yell. But she squeezed her thighs and cut off his air, and ability to vocalize anything.

He rose up slightly, her shoulder blades holding her up on the wooden floor. She squeezed tighter and tighter, his hands slapping at the bare skin exposed on her legs. In the darkness she could see his face go from a light shade of grey to a deep purple. Eventually, his face disappeared into the darkness, matching the background color enough to blend in. If she wasn't squeezing the literal air out of him, she wouldn't know he was even there.

And then the slapping slowed, until it stopped. The struggle stopped. The breathing stopped. His body went limp and the only thing still holding him up was Madds's legs wrapped around his throat. She gave him one more squeeze for good measure and untangled herself from him.

His body slumped over, his head hitting the wall and lay in what looked like a very uncomfortable position. He was either out cold, or dead.

Either one served her purpose.

She panted heavily as she lay on the ground, next to his lifeless body.

"Hey, Tim where the hell are you?" someone yelled from down the hallway.

Madds ran her forearm over her face, smearing the man's blood away from her eyes. Her skin was dotted with perspiration, just on the verge of breaking out into a sweat. There was no time for a break.

She stood, picking up her gun from the floor, out of the dark abyss only a foot away from her face.

Dupray was much darker than where she was from. It was mostly from the lack of streetlights and other buildings. But a little bit of her wondered if it was because there was something darker by nature about Dupray.

And she was facing a bit of it now.

She looked at the door as it opened slightly. If there were light, she was sure she'd see the shadows of the men approaching. She acted quickly and turned, shoving the closet door open. Inside was nothing but junk and the door wouldn't open all the way, catching resistance on whatever was behind it.

But it didn't matter. All she needed was to make them think that's where she was.

She ran to the door to the hallway and pressed her back against the wall.

"Tim, you in there?" the man called out again.

"You think he found the girl?"

"Beats me," the other one said.

"I bet he found her. Thought I heard some ruckus in here earlier. He's probably gettin' his tip wet first," he said.

"I wouldn't know. I can't hear shit after you shooting that rifle right next to my fucking ear," the other snapped.

Madds exhaled slowly and quietly, relieved. They hadn't found Michaela. And they didn't seem to care if they alerted anyone to their presence.

They weren't worried about her. For all she knew, they had no idea she was even there.

And that was going to be their undoing.

CHAPTER FORTY-NINE

THE FIRST MAN ENTERED THE ROOM, HIS BOOTS LOUD AGAINST the wood floor. Not a single care to being inconspicuous. Then again, he assumed his buddy was alive and *getting his tip wet,* so to speak. And from the gunshots that were still ringing in her own ears from the room over, she assumed he couldn't hear his own footsteps.

Madds's heart was already pounding from the fight she'd been in only seconds ago. She was still wired and exhausted, but there was work to be done. She had no time to rest.

As soon as he entered, she pushed harder against the wall, trying to become nothing more than scenery. Like she didn't exist.

And it worked.

He breezed right past her, his own brand of stench wafting by her. A hint of cigarette smoke, though not as strong as his friend, most likely only picking it up by proxy. But more raw tobacco and body odor, mixed with stagnant mud puddles. Thankfully, the tobacco was the most powerful of the scents.

"Tim? You alright?" he asked, hurrying toward the body on the floor. He set his rifle down and knelt beside his dead friend's body.

Madds watched and waited, hoping his friend would follow behind.

"Holy shit, get in here, Herb," he said from the floor.

That was just what she needed. The man from the hallway did as he was requested, except he was much quicker about it.

He set foot inside the room, took two steps forward so that he was just in front of Madds and to the side.

The man kneeling on the floor turned around and locked eyes on Madds.

"Oh, shit," he said.

He didn't reach for his rifle. No, instead, he reached to the side of his hip, pulling a pistol out. It was too dark to tell exactly what it was, other than a deep grey or black.

Madds swept in behind Herb, the man who had just entered the room.

"Drop the weapons," she commanded, this time her voice firm and much louder than a whisper.

But Dan, the man on the floor, did not listen. Instead, his friend that she stood behind dropped his rifle. And that was enough noise to cause it to go down.

Dan yelled, frightened, or at least triggered, by the sudden thud on the wood. He fired his pistol three times, sending a bullet high into the ceiling, and two more into his friend's chest. Madds stood behind his friend, like a live barrier, and fired her own weapon over his shoulder.

She hit Dan once in the shoulder, then a second shot went straight into his head. The bullet blew out the back of his skull and he slumped over his dead friend's body, his back arched backward over his legs. Another uncomfortable position to confirm there was no life left.

The man that had been shot in the chest twice fell to his knees. Madds grabbed him, trying to hold him up. He had his own brand of stink on him, but Madds was far too in the moment to decipher what any of it was.

The blood ran from his chest like a wide-open faucet. She rocked his body back into hers, his head resting on her shoulder as his eyes drifted up to the ceiling. She wrapped her hands around his back and over his chest, trying to keep him from bleeding out.

"Who sent you here? Who did this?" Madds asked.

He opened his mouth, but all that came out was a cough, blood shooting up in the air, raining back down over her face. He gargled a few times and then his body weight no longer held itself up. He slid out of Madds's arms and onto the floor.

The blood pooled around his body, and her left calf was covered in it, running down to her black socks. She stood up slowly, like an elderly person getting up from bed for the first time in the morning.

She sighed and turned around, knowing that there were to be no answers from any of them now.

"Drop the gun, bitch."

Madds froze as she was met with the open end of a rifle barrel five inches from her face. She squeezed the gun in her grip, but it was still pointed down at the floor.

"Now!" he screamed.

Madds let it go. Her heart had either stopped, or was beating so fast that she could no longer feel a rhythm. She had wondered if there was someone else in the house still, and now she had her answer.

"I just wanna know where the girl is," he said.

She looked at him over the rifle. He had long greasy hair, much like his friends. He wasn't filthy, like some of them had smelled, but she wouldn't have described him as clean either.

"It wasn't supposed to be like this," he said. "In and out, easy."

"You can still just leave. I don't know you. I can barely tell who you are. Just walk out right now and nobody will know who to look for," Madds bargained.

"Too late for that. Not after all this. You weren't supposed to be here. It was just the girl who was supposed to die."

"Why was she supposed—"

"Shut up. Where is she?"

Madds shook her head.

"Alright, then," he said. "Guess none of it matters anymore anyway."

He gripped the rifle firmly, with intention. She thought about diving to the side, hitting the barrel, grabbing it, anything that would just give her the illusion of fighting her way out of it. But she knew what was coming and no matter what she did, it would end the same way.

She could feel it in her bones.

"Noooo!" a scream came from the hallway.

The man pulled his attention away from Madds and to Michaela as she charged out of the bathroom. Madds watched the girl run, screaming, nearly frothing at the mouth like a rabid beast. The meek, shy girl was letting out everything she had been through.

And in her hands was the top of the toilet tank. A heavy, porcelain weapon.

The barrel shifted from Madds's face as he spun his weight toward Michaela. If he was trying to live, he had made the wrong decision.

Before he could point his rifle at Michaela, Madds grabbed the barrel and tugged it hard, slamming it against the doorway.

The gun went off, drywall exploding into the hallway. Madds released the barrel as it kicked from her hands, sending throbbing pain from her hands down to her wrists.

Michaela swung the toilet tank lid down and connected with the man's head, breaking the porcelain in half. He let out a shriek and dropped to his knees. He pushed forward, sending Michaela tumbling backward and on her ass.

He shook his head, like he had just taken a baseball to the helmet. Madds wondered how he was still awake from a blow that hard.

But he was.

She grabbed him from behind, wrapping her arm around his neck. With her other hand, she grabbed his wrist and twisted it behind him. He struggled, trying to get out from her grasp, but she was in control now. He was on his knees and she had the leverage she needed.

"Madds?" Elven yelled from downstairs.

Shit. As much as she was grateful he was there, albeit a little late, she needed to get the information out of him first.

"Why did you kill all those people? Who sent you here?" she asked.

He grunted, not talking. She twisted harder and he yelped.

"It was just supposed to be her. We was told not to kill the old guy. Wouldn't get paid until she was dead. Didn't say nothing about some other bitch being here and killing my friends," he said through clenched teeth.

"Four guys to kill one girl?" Madds asked.

"He's alive," Elven said, most likely discovering Driscoll out cold on the floor. "Madds?" Elven yelled from downstairs.

"Who said that? Who paid you?" she demanded.

Madds could hear the footsteps heading up the stairs. Two sets of footsteps were coming up from the sounds of it.

"Some guy I—"

"Madds!" Elven yelled and ran down the hallway toward her. From behind, the large game warden appeared.

She loosened her grip on the man at the sight of them, wishing she had just one more moment with the man alone so she could find out who paid them. And that might have been her mistake.

"Get down," Jesse yelled from behind Elven.

Madds watched the warden draw his revolver up and Elven stepped to the side at the sound of the yell. Madds let go of the guy and fell backward as it looked like Jesse had no problems with shooting directly at a deputy.

The revolver went off three times and from the floor, she watched the attacker take all three of them, center mass.

The last one pierced directly into his heart and he dropped dead in front of her. There were no last words, no sputtering of blood, not even one last exhale.

Just dead.

Jesse grinned as he holstered his revolver. Madds climbed to her feet and watched Elven turn on him.

"You just unloaded your weapon with me in front of you and my deputy at risk of getting shot!" Elven yelled.

She hadn't seen him lose his temper much, but it seemed this whole case had him on edge. She didn't blame him either. She was ready to have her own words with the man next.

Elven stood in his face, looking like he was going to burst a vein.

"What?" Jesse chuckled. "I'd say a thank you might be in order. Maybe not from you, but from her at least."

Elven stared him down a few more seconds before Madds decided it was her turn.

"Me? Thank you?" she asked.

"You're welcome, darlin'," Jesse responded.

"Oh no, that's not fucking happening. You nearly killed Elven and me just to shoot someone I had under control. Are you even legally allowed to fucking do this? A fucking game warden? Why don't you go out in the woods and tell me if a bear shits, alright?"

Jesse chuckled. "The mouth on you. Keep it up darlin' and I might owe you dinner." He gestured with his hand, jerking the air in front of his pelvis.

Madds slapped him across the face, catching his rough beard with her fingers.

He rubbed the spot on his cheek, laughing more. "Oh baby, you take this any further and we might wanna borrow a bedroom. Looks like you're dressed for it already." He looked her up and down, and Madds remembered she was half-naked.

"That's enough," Elven said, stepping between them. Madds backed away, listening to him. The angrier she got, the more Jesse would push. He had already proved himself a real asshole.

"She's not wrong though. What reason did you have to shoot?" Elven demanded.

"Am I the only one with eyes?" Jesse asked. He walked to the body on the floor and kicked at his hand. His wrist flopped over and revealed a knife in his hand.

Jesse looked up and saw Michaela on the floor, huddled in the corner.

"Darlin'," he said, holding his hand out. She hesitated, looking to Madds and Elven, then took it in her hand. He lifted her to her feet.

"I must have missed it," Madds said. "I just—"

"No need to apologize, honey," Jesse said.

"Go fuck yourself," Madds retorted.

Jesse was about to say something, another sly smile on his disgusting pig face, but Elven stepped in again.

"Whatever the reason, our only lead of why he was here or who sent him is gone. You didn't get anything?" he asked Madds.

She shook her head. It was the truth this time. She wished she had gotten something from him. But if she had, she wondered if her answer to Elven would have changed at all.

CHAPTER FIFTY

EVERY LIGHT WAS ON DOWNSTAIRS AND PHIL DRISCOLL WAS awake. Alive, but not so well. He sat on the couch, with his head back. The way he looked, no amount of ibuprofen would make that headache go away.

The lobby was surprisingly much the same way as Phil had left it before heading to bed for the night. Other than a few pieces of moved furniture, and the blood from his head wound, nobody would have known there was a break-in. It was the upstairs that took the brunt of the damage.

Elven had sat Michaela down next to the old guy, and she was surprisingly receptive to taking care of him. She held the icepack against his head as he tried to relax. Groans came out of the doc every so often, like he had woken up from a week-long bender.

"I didn't even see any of them," he moaned, answering Elven. "I just heard something, like a shatter. I came to look. Never even got so far as to see what happened."

"Broken window by the kitchen door," Elven clarified.

"Ah," Phil said. "It was so dark, and then nothing. Hell, I don't even know if I remember anything two minutes ago at this point."

"You've been up for fifteen," Jesse said.

"That's my point," Driscoll said.

Elven smiled. The old guy being short with Jesse was little consolation for everything that had happened. But he'd take what little he could get at that point.

Madds, Jesse, and Elven had carried all the bodies downstairs for the doc to take care of however he saw fit. There was no point in a crime scene, as Madds's statement was all Elven needed. Elven would ID them when he got the chance, though their friend down at the station could do it. Elven was more than sure that the bodies were those of the men he'd met at Frank Dority's farm.

"Hey, look on the bright side," Jesse said. "What better place to have dead bodies than a funeral home. Really saves having to load and unload them. But next time, honey, maybe kill them downstairs."

Elven could see Madds struggle internally with not snapping at the man. And he didn't blame her. He'd had about enough of Jesse Parsons and was ready to contact the Natural Resources Police office himself to tell them to pull their guy out of his county. That if they needed to have someone there, to send someone else.

Something wasn't right with Jesse, and it was more than just being a crass imbecile.

He had to table that idea for the moment. He knew there was someone who had orchestrated that night. A big guy, according to the man at the bar. He'd need to get that man to look at mugshots to confirm, but he was starting to have a feeling he knew who this was all pointing to.

But Michaela was priority. Once news was out that they'd failed, there'd be other attempts, he was sure.

"We're gonna have to get you a better security detail here," Elven said.

"Here?" Madds asked.

"Yeah, here?" Driscoll asked, bringing his head up too fast. The old man groaned and tilted it back again, Michaela reapplying the ice pack.

"Maybe we can have Johnny stay over here, keep an eye out along with you," Elven said.

Madds pursed her lips, obviously unhappy with that answer. And to be honest, he wasn't quite sure he liked it either.

"With Michaela how she is, I think being here with the doc is still the best," Elven said. "No offense, Michaela."

Michaela shrugged, but didn't say a word. She was still meek and shy, but after the night she'd been through, he had to admit that it impressed him to see her doing as well as she was. Maybe Madds taking care of business was enough to calm her nerves.

To say Elven was impressed with Madds would not have done it justice. Madds had taken control of the situation. Incapacitating four men alone was more than Elven was willing to attempt. After a night like that, having to fight for her life, he was going to need to give her a break. Or a raise.

"Elven, if I may," Driscoll began. "In my professional medical opinion, Michaela, as sweet as she is taking care of me right now, seems to be in a fine state of mind. She'll talk when she is ready. But there is no physical damage, so nothing I can do to help her."

"So you're saying—"

"Maybe being here isn't the best idea for everyone," Driscoll said.

Elven tried to hold back a laugh. The old guy was politely kicking them all out.

"Fair enough," Elven said. "Then we'll pack up and head to a safehouse."

Madds looked relieved. Michaela questioned it, her eyes glancing to Madds.

"Madds will come, too," Elven clarified.

That put Michaela at ease.

"Sweet, where to?" Jesse asked.

Elven sneered. "I'll take care of it. I think this is a bit outside of your jurisdiction now, don't you?"

Jesse licked over his teeth. "Whatever you say, Sheriff."

Elven was going to call the head of Jesse's office first thing in the morning. He was done with the man.

CHAPTER FIFTY-ONE

"This is the safehouse?" Madds asked.

She'd been there before, but never overnight. Elven's house, more like his mansion, stood tall in the moonlight. The thick trees surrounded the property on all sides except where the side of the hill dipped down, and the only path to and from the house lay.

Crickets chirped somewhere in the distance, breaking up the silence of the night. It was cold and she was ready to get inside, though a bit of her felt uncomfortable at the thought of sleeping there. It was stupid, she knew. Elven had tons of room at the house, but the thought of waking up in the morning, with him making breakfast for all of them, felt a little bit awkward.

Though no more awkward than her drunkenly inviting him into her motel room just after being hired, she supposed.

"I figured this way I could keep an eye out. And we'd know almost immediately if someone was coming. Any headlights on this road at night is not normal," Elven said, pointing to the long path.

"I don't know," Madds said.

"Would you rather take her back to your place instead?"

Madds bit her lip. "Not a whole lot of room where I'm at."

"You're not still?"

"At the motel," she said.

"Madds, really? You're gonna need to find somewhere else to live. You're gonna get eaten alive by bedbugs at some point. Or go broke paying for that place. I do know what your salary is, after all."

Madds laughed. "Yeah, about that..."

"Let's get this case solved first, alright?"

Michaela shivered on the porch of Elven's house. She had a blanket wrapped around her that she'd taken from Driscoll's, with his permission. But it was obvious she was ready to go inside, and Madds was right there with her, having thrown on a loose pair of sweats before leaving Driscoll's.

"Come on," he said, unlocking the door. He held the door open for them.

The main entry was large, just as it was the last time she was there, but it was different when it was dark. She couldn't see to the end of the room, making it seem like it never ended.

Michaela looked around, mouth open and gawking. Even after everything she had been through, she was able to feel impressed and pull her focus away from the shock.

"Make yourselves at home," Elven said. "I'm gonna set you up in the guest bedroom upstairs."

"Which floor?" Madds smirked.

"Do you have a preference? Second or third?" he asked.

"Second," Madds said. "And only if the windows open. I want to be able to jump out if need be, and not break a leg while doing it."

Elven looked at her like she was crazy.

"Don't pretend that the situation won't come up, 'cause just a few hours ago I was in that very predicament. Except the window wouldn't open."

"Alright then," Elven said, dropping the issue.

Michaela wandered into the kitchen, looking around her as if she'd never been in a place so fancy. And that was probably exactly true. The poor girl had been traveling in a tent, from one shithole town to the next. Elven's house was probably like boarding an alien ship.

Elven stepped in closer to Madds, keeping his voice low.

"She might be coming out of her shell a little, but she's still shaken up pretty bad," he said. "She's taken a liking to you though, and you've really lived up to her expectations, it seems."

Madds's heart dropped, thinking how she should be nobody's mentor or hero. She was just a person trying to survive to the next day, doing whatever it took. Even if it made her hate herself.

"She talk yet?" he asked.

Madds shook her head. "Aside from a yell when she saved my life back at Driscoll's, nothing."

He nodded. "I'm sure it'll take time, but if anyone can get her to, it's gonna be you, Madds. I really believe in you here. You're a good cop, and I'm glad to know you."

"Are you getting all chick flick on me right now?" Madds asked.

Elven shrugged. "Just glad you're okay after all that." He had a little shimmer in his eye, maybe a twinkle, maybe a tear. Either way, she was grateful. And hated herself a little more.

Elven's radio that was on his belt clicked on with static. "Hey, Sheriff," Tank's voice said through it.

Elven clicked it on, raised it to his mouth, and spoke. "Yeah, Tank, what's up?"

"You gotta get down to the station right now," he said. "It's bad."

CHAPTER FIFTY-TWO

Jesse walked into the sheriff's station. It was quiet, but then again, he found that to be true the last time he was there, which was only a few hours ago. He doubted that there would be any more hustle and bustle during the daytime. It seemed to him that Dupray wasn't that kind of place. It wasn't much different in other towns and counties in which he found himself.

Now it was the middle of the night, or maybe the early morning.

He wasn't sure. He hadn't looked at a clock before starting this crazy night, but he knew it was dark and cold out. And he also knew he was exhausted.

On top of all of that, he'd saved the day, shooting down that asshole in the hallway back at the doc's place. Nobody but he saw the knife and what that asshole was gonna try to do with it.

But did anyone thank him?

Of course not. Instead, that sheriff with more looks than sense treated him like *he* was the suspect here. And that side piece deputy of his...well, she needed to learn how to take a compliment.

Tensions were running high. Killing people could do that, he was well aware. He'd been around for some time, exchanging bullets in the woods with all sorts of assholes that were up to no good.

Doing it in the city was a bit different. Though, *city* was a bit of a stretch when talking about anything in Dupray.

But after everything, he'd hoped that Elven, the bizarrely named sheriff, would have been able to calm himself, and see that Jesse wasn't so bad. Sure, he might have a different way of doing things, but overall, Elven could have had it way worse.

He knew some of the other officers in his office, and he liked to think of himself as the most easygoing. Laidback. Sometimes even a little lax on the rules.

So that's why he found himself back at the station. Sheriff Pretty Boy and Deputy Tartlet were going to keep secrets from him, hide the girl in a *safehouse*, and not let him in on any of it. Well, then he was going to do his own investigation.

The lobby of the station was empty, but after a few seconds, he was met by the fat deputy. The guy always seemed to have a dopey grin on his face when meeting with people. That was fine by Jesse. Rather a dopey grin than a stone grimace. He could work with manipulating idiots.

"Warden, what can I do you for?" the deputy asked.

Jesse grinned and didn't feel the need to correct him. That would mean putting him in his place, showing him that he didn't know as much as he thought he did. And Jesse didn't want to make the deputy feel any dumber than he already looked.

"Johnny, right?"

Johnny grinned like his daddy just told him he was proud of him. "Yeah."

"Was wondering if I could talk to the man in lock-up," Jesse asked.

Johnny looked him up and down, assessing the situation Jesse assumed. He didn't give him a stern glance, but more of a look of wanting to understand.

"Oh, I guess Elven didn't radio over," Jesse said. "Don't blame him honestly. After the night we had, well, I'm sure any man wouldn't remember everything."

"I heard what happened," Johnny said, and Jesse worried that maybe Elven had told him not to let Jesse anywhere near the place.

"Oh, yeah?"

"Yeah, heard Madds took out the lot of them and you shot the last guy dead," Johnny said. "Elven didn't get to any more details after that, and said he had to get going somewhere. Didn't seem too happy though."

Jesse grinned. That was good. He hadn't given him any information, and maybe Elven was usually in a less-than-stellar mood.

"Maybe you can radio him over and let him know I'm here. He'll be able to clear it all, though hopefully not too busy like you said," Jesse said.

"Oh, yeah, maybe I can do that," Johnny said, heading to Meredith's desk to pick up the receiver.

"Sorry, didn't realize it was gonna be this big thing. Figured with the man in lock-up, and both of us being officers of the law and all, but I get it. Gotta pass everything through the bossman."

Johnny paused and looked at the receiver, then back to Jesse. Jesse knew he was almost there.

"You know, I was talking to the other deputy...Tank, is it? He around?"

Johnny shook his head. "He stepped out. I told him I'd hold down the fort."

"Too bad, he and I were talking about being a game warden and the benefits we're given."

"Oh, yeah, I bet it's awesome," Johnny said, his eyes lighting up. "Being a deputy is great and all, but out there, being a lone ranger in the woods, I bet there's no greater freedom."

Jesse lifted his eyebrows. Sometimes the ideas of the job that he heard from people were so ridiculous, but then again, it was part of why he took the job in the first place. Turns out, it ain't as adventurous as everyone makes it out to be.

But he didn't need to tell Johnny that.

"Oh, you know it," Jesse said. "I saw you at the crime scene and how you took action. That was great work. You ever thought about being a warden?"

"Me? You think?"

"Well, I mean, it does take a certain type of leadership. Have to make decisions on the fly and not call the office every time something comes up. So maybe you're good here."

Johnny looked at the receiver in his hand again, then set it back on the desk. "You know, we're both law enforcement and you've been working side by side with Elven. I'm sure he meant to call over and have me let you see the perp."

Jesse grinned at Johnny. "I was right about you. Warden material."

CHAPTER FIFTY-THREE

THE CELL BLOCK, IF THAT'S WHAT THEY CALLED IT, WAS SPARSE. It was just a room at the end of the hallway that housed the jail cell. There was enough space on one end of the room to stand far enough away from being within reach of anyone who tried to reach through the bars.

The smell of the room was musty, like there had been a leak at some point and maybe it was fixed, but nobody cleaned up the water, leaving it to mold and rot out whatever it touched.

To Jesse, it smelled like home. The house the state had set him up with was a lot like that. And for a bachelor like himself, it was more than perfect.

Mostly because he found himself living in it less often than in the motels in his region, not to mention the woods themselves.

The man in the jail cell slept on the hard bench against the wall. He was turned on his side, facing the cold brick wall, huddled like a baby. He shivered as he slept.

Johnny cleared his throat, but the man didn't stir.

Johnny looked at Jesse, an unsure smile on his face. Jesse rolled his eyes and picked up the chair from the corner of the room. He smacked it against the bars, rattling the whole place. The chair seemed sturdier than the cell itself.

"Rise and shine, asshole!" Jesse shouted.

The man spurred awake, nearly falling off the bench. His arm hung to the side, and his eyes were open wide.

Johnny didn't seem to approve, but Jesse was done caring about him. He got what he wanted, and now he was going to get what he needed.

"I have a few questions to ask you," Jesse said, plopping the chair back on the floor, but he didn't sit down.

"Now?" the man asked, his voice tired and hoarse. His eyes were red and puffy, like he'd cried himself to sleep.

"Sorry, it's a bit urgent. But I suppose you've had a rough night. Should I wait till you get a good eight hours of rest first? Maybe get you a hot cup of coffee and some eggs over easy in the morning? Would you like a blowjob to go with all that?"

Jesse laughed at his own joke.

"You and your buddies killed a bunch of people out in them woods, so no, I ain't gonna do this on your schedule. You'll do it on mine."

The man sat up, rubbing his eyes. He put both feet on the floor and turned to face Jesse. Strands of hair clung to his stubbled face and ran along the bottom edge of his lip.

"What's your name?" Jesse asked.

"Scotty," he said.

"So, Scotty, what can you tell me?"

Scotty swallowed hard, his eyes darting to Johnny, then back to Jesse. Jesse put his hand on the butt of his revolver, just resting his palm there.

"Don't you worry about him. You and I are talking. And I wanna know what you know. What did you tell the sheriff about this man? The one who commissioned your services."

Scotty shook his head. "I just— I told him it was a big guy. That I didn't know who he was. Nothing else."

Jesse nodded, not happy. "So what can you tell me?"

Scotty stared at him. "What?"

"I wanna know what you can tell me about him. You said a big guy, but what else? Where did you meet him?"

Scotty's eyes went to the revolver on Jesse's hip and lingered a bit too long. He brought his eyes back up to Jesse's, unsure of what to say next. Like he was afraid that Jesse would draw and shoot him. Jesse grinned, enjoying holding the power.

"Sorry, guess it's just a force of habit. The job tends to do that sometimes," Jesse said, fluttering his fingers against the side of his revolver, but not lifting his palm away.

"Well, uh, he was big. Had a beard. A bit like yours?" Scotty said, slowly, like he didn't want to make Jesse mad. Jesse held his smile.

"Where did you meet him?"

"There was some church parking lot. I don't know where exactly it was. Didn't drive myself. I ain't really know much around here as it is, I swear. But the big guy, he seemed to know it well."

"What, like he worked there? A priest or something?" Jesse asked, laughing. He glanced at Johnny who stood in the doorway, shifting his weight like he was uncomfortable.

"No, no, not like that. We didn't go inside, just met out back."

"So how do you know it wasn't the priest?"

"Well, he wasn't wearing the outfit for one."

Jesse cackled. "No shit, asshole. I don't expect a man of the cloth to go around in his robes gunning down people in the woods. I'm just giving you shit about the priest. Why do you think he worked there?"

"The way he walked around. Maybe he frequented it often? But he seemed real comfortable being so close to God and the like."

"That's it? There's nothing else you can tell me?".

He thought for a moment, then shrugged. "I had to take a piss, so I went to the front door. A light was on, so I figured I could just pop in and take a leak. I was nervous anyway, and maybe just being in a place like that would calm me, even if it was just to piss. But the big guy told me not to go in. He seemed almost angry that I even tried. Said I needed to go around back and make water against the wall. I got as far as the window and saw the preacher in there. He was talking to some woman cop. Was sitting in the front row talking."

Jesse nodded.

"Well, Scotty, I gotta say...I'm a bit disappointed."

"I told you everything I know. I even told that sheriff where my friends were headed and what they was planning. Did they find them? Is the girl okay? Are they bringing in my friends? I figured I might get leniency for all the information I gave."

Jesse smiled, still strumming his fingers against his revolver. "Oh, the girl is just fine, don't you worry. Your friends though, not so much."

"What?" Scotty asked, standing up.

Jesse shrugged. "Got themselves dead by that woman cop you say you saw. That's after assaulting an old man in his house."

"No, they ain't dead. You're lying. They would have surrendered. They ain't fighters. Just wanted some extra cash."

He ran to the bars and grabbed onto them, his eyes pleading with Jesse. But there was no other truth to tell.

"Extra cash by murdering people. And since you're the only one left out of the lot, looks like they got no one else to pin all them murders on. Things ain't looking too good for you," Jesse said, unable to hold back a chuckle.

"No, you son of a bitch, no. I helped you. I told you everything I know."

Jesse stepped closer, staring him down, making things even worse.

"Alright, I think we're done here," Johnny said, stepping between Jesse and Scotty even though there were bars to keep Scotty away.

"We're done when I say we are. And this asshole—"

"It's time to leave," Johnny demanded.

"Oh, grow a bit of a backbone in the last five minutes, did ya? What a joke this place is," Jesse said.

Johnny put his hand on Jesse, pointing to the door. That ticked Jesse off just in the wrong kind of way.

Jesse shoved Johnny backward, just enough to get him off of him. But it was enough for even more.

"Get your hands off me," Jesse growled.

Johnny stumbled backward and stepped close enough to be within reach of Scotty. And Scotty didn't let that opportunity slide by.

Scotty grabbed Johnny by the collar, his arms stretched as far as they could go through the bars, and pulled him against the cell. Johnny yelled out as Scotty wrapped one arm around Johnny's throat.

Johnny reached for the gun on his hip, but Scotty was already on it, pulling it from its holster. He put it against Johnny's head. Jesse pulled his own gun, but Johnny's fat ass blocked any shot he might have.

"I didn't want any part of it," Scotty screamed, full-blown tears and snot making a long drip from his nose. "I didn't know what was happening until it was. I swear."

"Drop the gun, asshole!" Jesse yelled. Johnny's face reddened as the oxygen was cut off from his airway.

"I'm sorry," Scotty said, pulling the gun away from Johnny's head, then placing it in his own mouth.

He pulled the trigger before anyone could react, painting the wall with his brains.

Johnny slid down the bars gasping for air, grabbing at his throat where Scotty's arm had been. Jesse stood a moment, shocked at the outcome. He holstered his gun and shook his head.

"You okay?" Jesse asked, being more reactionary than sincere.

Johnny nodded, still gasping, but didn't say a word.

"You shouldn't have gotten so close to the cage," Jesse said, then turned around and walked out of the room.

CHAPTER FIFTY-FOUR

Elven didn't even bother taking his coat off when he charged into the station. The first thing he saw was Johnny sitting in Meredith's chair. Despite being over a decade older than Elven, Johnny looked like a kid who had been brought to his father's business with nothing to do as he looked down at his shoes and spun the chair left and right, back and forth.

"Johnny, what happened?" Elven asked.

Johnny looked up at Elven like he didn't know who he was for a moment. Then it registered and he could only cry.

Getting anything out of Johnny when he was emotional was going to be harder than a virgin on prom night, so he didn't even try. Instead, he left him sobbing alone to find Tank.

As he got closer to the cell at the end of the hallway, he could already smell the iron and sulfur in the air. From what little Tank had told him, he assumed it was bad. But he didn't think it would be this bad.

A gunshot in his station, and not only that, but it was someone in a cell who had gotten hold of a deputy's gun. If it wasn't the middle of the night, the news would have already travelled through the town and to his own ears before he'd seen it himself.

Driscoll was there, crouching down at the body in the cell. The back of his balding head looked nasty, a large goose egg sticking up almost two inches. The skin at the top was split, and Driscoll didn't have a very happy look on his face.

Though looking at a dead man with his brains all over the room wasn't really the most jovial of situations.

"Doc, what in heaven's name are you doing here?" Elven asked.

Driscoll placed his hands on his knees and pushed himself up, his knees popping. "Your two deputies called me out. I am the only one around for this kind of thing, you know."

Elven looked back at the body on the floor. Scotty's hair was like a mullet. The back of his head had the long hair mixed with the blood and gray bits on the floor. But the top of his head was completely gone. Elven spotted a wad of scalp, hair and blood on the wall just above the bench. It slowly peeled away, making a wet sound of pulling duct tape apart until it landed on the bench like someone throwing a soaked towel on the floor.

Johnny's gun was still on the floor next to the body. Elven stepped over the body and between the blood spatter. He picked up the gun, which was surprisingly clean.

"I'd say this looks pretty self-explanatory on cause of death," Elven said. "Go home, Phil."

Driscoll nodded. "Think you can make it the rest of the night without sending me any more bodies?"

Elven stared at him and didn't answer. He wasn't in the mood to exchange quips or banter. And maybe Driscoll wasn't either.

"Tank and Johnny will bring him in. They'll do all the lifting, too. You don't need to overexert yourself in your condition," Elven offered.

"Good night, Elven," Driscoll said, leaving the room.

Elven turned and saw Tank standing in the corner with his arms crossed.

"How?" is all Elven asked.

Tank shrugged. He wasn't ashamed or sad. He was just stone. Which is what Elven would have expected from an ex-marine like him.

"Went out to get some snacks for Johnny and me. Came back and found this. Says the game warden was here asking him a lot of questions."

Elven grit his teeth. Of course, Jesse was here. It only made sense that he would mess things up again for him.

"Where is Jesse?" Elven asked.

Tank shrugged. "Johnny's pretty shaken up about all this, Elven. Just go easy on him, alright? This isn't what he's used to dealing with."

"He let him go?" Elven asked.

Tank sighed. "Jesse just left. Said it's our house, our problem."

Elven was so angry he couldn't see straight. He liked to think of himself as calm and collected, but this was it. He would not let this stand. He turned back to the lobby.

"Elven, I mean it, go easy," Tank said.

"My feud ain't with Johnny," Elven said.

Jesse was right. It was his house, so Elven was going to fix the problem.

CHAPTER FIFTY-FIVE

THERE WAS NO WAY SHE COULD SLEEP. NOT AFTER EVERYTHING she'd been through that night. It probably didn't matter anyway, considering it would be daylight soon enough.

Madds sat up in bed, her back against the tufted headboard of the king-sized frame. It was dark in the room except for the clock on the dresser. The glowing numbers on the face lit up the room enough for her to make out the outline of every piece of furniture that surrounded her.

It was nearly three in the morning.

Elven had plenty of space, and had offered Michaela and Madds rooms that were right next to each other. But Madds knew how Michaela would have reacted to that idea, so she didn't even consider it. Instead, she got in the same bed as the girl and watched over her in the night. The bed was so big, even bigger than a standard king, that no amount of movement disturbed the other side of the mattress.

Thankfully, Michaela could still sleep after everything. Either that, or she could keep her eyes closed and fake it for a long while.

As much as Madds appreciated Elven's hospitality, she didn't feel comfortable in his house. It was much larger than she was used to, and being so far outside the town, it was foreign to her. She was used to suburban life, living in a house that was part of a large neighborhood of houses lined up one after another.

The silence of the night was interrupted with a ringing in the house. She got out of bed immediately, making sure to put pants on before heading out. She didn't need to get into another fight half-dressed on the same night. She grabbed her gun off the nightstand and headed to the door.

She looked back and made sure Michaela was still sleeping, then saw her radio on the nightstand next to where Madds's gun had been. She went back and snatched it in her free hand before she slipped out into the hallway,

The ringing stopped, then started again, and she let out a relieved sigh.

It wasn't an alarm. It was the phone.

She didn't holster her weapon. If she met anyone in the house, she wasn't going to be caught off guard. And with the way she was feeling, she might just shoot on sight.

Hopefully, Elven hadn't made it back without her knowing.

She made her way through the vast house, passing by doorways to a number of rooms that one man had no use for. Even on her best day, if every room had a hobby, there would still be empty space.

She smiled, thinking about Elven having a scrapbooking room somewhere hidden in the house. Maybe on any other day, she could spend her time exploring the place. But right now, she just wanted to get through the night and at some point, if it wasn't too much to ask, maybe get some sleep.

The house was surprisingly warm. The kitchen, with its large tiled flooring and vaulted ceiling, should have been cool. But whatever heater Elven had installed in his home was amazingly efficient. It made Driscoll's place seem like a low-rent motel.

The house phone, which was odd enough to see in the first place, sat at the edge of the counter against the wall. It continued to ring, never being tripped by a voicemail or an answering machine. She smiled at the thought of Elven having a house phone because the cable company convinced him it would be cheaper to bundle it that way. As if he needed the money.

Then she realized that she hadn't yet even seen a television in the house.

She hesitated picking up Elven's phone, but then she thought maybe Elven was calling her with something important. Or even just to tell her he was on his way home. Who else would be calling at such an hour?

She set her radio down before picking up the phone and put it to her ear.

"Elven, you headed back? Everything alright?" she asked.

"Sorry, darlin', but it ain't your boyfriend," the voice said on the other end. The tone was friendly, fatherly even, and she knew immediately it was Hollis Starcher.

"What do you want?" she asked, turning around.

Right behind her, in the dark entrance of the hallway, she saw someone standing, staring right back at her.

"Oh, Jesus," she gasped. Her first thought was to lift her gun, but then the figure stepped out into the moonlit kitchen. It was Michaela.

The poor girl just couldn't be alone.

"You alright there?" Hollis asked, more curious than concerned.

"Yeah, yeah, it's fine. Just in an unfamiliar place," she said, catching her breath. Michaela walked closer and Madds held her hand up and nodded, letting her know she was fine.

"Good to hear. Was just checking to see how you're doing. I heard you had a rough night," Hollis said.

"Was that you? Did you send those men to Driscoll's?" Madds asked.

She could just imagine the smile on Hollis's face, like he knew something, or pretended to know something, that nobody else did while never admitting what it was.

"Why don't you and the girl come on outside?" he asked.

"Outside? You're here?" she asked.

"I'll wait," Hollis said, then hung up.

She set the phone down, then grabbed her radio and clipped it to the edge of her pants. The weight of it made the elastic sag where it hung, but Madds didn't care. She looked at Michaela. She seemed concerned, most likely reflecting the look Madds was giving her.

Madds ran to the girl and spun her around.

"You need to do what I say right now, alright?" she asked.

Michaela let out a little whimper, like a dog being told by its owner to get in a kennel. She turned around and shook her head.

Madds sighed. "Do you trust me?" she asked the girl. She honestly didn't know what to expect. The girl was attached to her, that was for sure, but was it more than just comfort?

Michaela considered, then nodded. She even gave a half smile.

Okay, good.

"Then you need to go back upstairs. Hide under the bed, okay? Can you do that for me?" she asked.

It was obvious Michaela didn't want to, but Madds gripped her hand and squeezed it. That seemed to do the trick.

Michaela ran up the stairs and Madds watched her disappear into the darkness. Once she no longer heard any footsteps, she turned to the front door and stepped outside.

CHAPTER FIFTY-SIX

THE TEMPERATURE OF THE OUTDOOR AIR WAS A STARK contrast to the interior of Elven's house, and Madds immediately wished she was back inside. She also wished that she had put a jacket on over the worn out flannel she wore. But at least she had thought about pants this time.

Hollis leaned against his truck that was parked facing toward the road leading down the hill. It was at least twenty yards from the house. Hollis didn't appear worried about Elven, or anyone else, coming by, but by the positioning of his car, Madds figured that he had taken some precautions.

Her mouth ran dry just looking at the man. But she kept her composure.

"What the hell are you doing here?" Madds asked, keeping her voice just above a whisper.

Hollis chuckled. "I don't see the need to whisper right now, unless you're trying to not wake that girl inside."

"What if Elven comes back?" she asked. "He's gonna know something is up."

Hollis shrugged, standing up from the truck. He walked a few steps forward, his feet crunching in the dirt, but he never set foot on the deck.

"Don't worry yourself none. I got Corbin down the way to keep an eye out, though I don't think he'll be back anytime soon. Passed him coming in while he was going out."

"And you don't think—"

"He just saw another truck driving the roads of Dupray, he didn't know who was in it, and if he did, it ain't like he saw me heading up his private drive. Relax, you're gonna give yourself an ulcer," Hollis said. "I'm not concerned, and I don't even know where he was headed."

"He went to the station."

"Then I guess he'll be a while. Heard there was some commotion down there."

Madds shook her head. "Don't suppose you had anything to do with that?"

"I appreciate the vote of confidence, Maddie, but even I can't pull every string in this town."

"Much to your disappointment I'm sure. So what is it? What are you doing here?"

Hollis started to pace back and forth, seeming to not care about his leg as he limped on it. "I'm sure you heard, but we got ourselves a loose end."

"We? I don't even know what the hell you're into, though at this point, I might be able to take a guess," Madds said.

Hollis grinned again. "Whether you like it or not, *you* is always gonna be a part of the *we*. How much you know or don't will only help you in the long run. Where's that girlie hiding at?"

Madds shook her head. Hollis knew exactly where she was, and after what happened at Driscoll's, she knew what he wanted with her.

"How involved are you then?" she asked. "Were you there the other night, at the revival? Or did you just send those same assholes I met a few hours ago?"

Hollis watched her, his smile still not faltering.

"If you heard about the dust-up, then I'm sure you heard what happened to those boys you sent," she said.

Hollis nodded.

"What does that mean for you and me?" Madds asked.

Hollis's smile shifted from defiant and smug, to...caring? "Maddie, we're family. And if you thinking killing four idiots I hired to do a job is gonna change that, well, maybe I haven't been clear about it. Are you okay?"

She had a hard time trusting him. But he seemed so genuine about it. He was a bad man, doing bad things, but maybe there was something good in him. He had taken her in and given her an escape from her life, after all.

"I'm fine. Nothing more than some bruises. Though maybe next time, a heads-up might cross your mind," she said.

"Glad you're okay," he said. "You being there was a bit of a surprise, but I knew you'd be alright once I heard."

Hollis glanced up and waved his fingers at the second story. Madds looked up and saw Michaela for a brief moment, then the curtain pulled over the window.

"Just send her out. You can make up whatever story you want to tell Elven. He'll get it. I can tell he's got a soft spot for you. Or maybe a hard one, if you catch my drift," Hollis said with a wink.

Madds's appreciation for Hollis's concern quickly dissipated and her disgust returned. She clenched her teeth.

"Come on, step aside," Hollis said, approaching the deck.

Madds stepped forward, getting in his way.

"You set foot on this deck and this will not end the way you want it to," Madds said. She gripped her gun, tapping it against her leg.

Hollis's eyes went to the pistol, then back up to Madds.

"You sure this is how you want to play it?" he asked.

She swallowed hard. No, she wasn't sure this was how she wanted to play it at all. But she knew she wouldn't be able to live with herself if she just let him have the girl. Especially not after she had saved her life.

"You understand that girl seen it all," Hollis said. "I hear she's a bit of a mute right now, but won't be for long. She starts flappin' those lips, Elven starts catching on, starts making arrests. One thing leads to another that leads to another, and that will lead back to you."

He looked her up and down.

"He might have a soft spot for you now, but what do you think he'll do when that happens? We all gotta do things we don't want to, that's what keeps us safe."

As much as Hollis might be right, she just couldn't do it.

"Not this," Madds said.

"And if I insist? You really gonna pull that trigger?" he asked.

Madds grabbed the radio from the waistband of her pants, clicked her radio on and lifted it to her mouth. "Elven, you there? I think I hear someone on the property," she said.

The radio hissed fuzz a moment, then cleared up.

"You okay? I'm headed your way," Elven said from the other end.

"Okay, I'm gonna walk the property and see what I find," she said before clicking the radio off.

She stared Hollis down as he stood in front of her. He nodded, still smiling. Even if he wanted to, she knew Hollis wouldn't be able to get Michaela and get out before Elven came around.

"I mean it, Maddie," he said. "Can't toe the line for long. Sooner or later, you'll have to make a decision about whose side you're really on. His or mine."

"You're making it pretty easy right now," she said.

"Give me your hand," he said.

She narrowed her eyes down on him. He nodded, not giving any sort of hint at what he was getting at. She was suspicious, but she did as he asked, holding her hand out after clipping the radio back on her pants.

"Here," Hollis said, pushing a heavy gun into her hand. It was a small, snub-nosed revolver. It looked old, like it had seen some action in its day.

"What's this?" she asked.

"I'm trying to make it easy on you, but you just keep making it harder on yourself. You find yourself changing your mind, you take care of it. Gun's unregistered. Put one in the girl's head and run into the woods, say the intruder got past you, and you went after him."

Madds looked at her hand, wanting to throw the gun back at Hollis, but part of her wondered if he was right. She hated herself for it, but she kept the revolver.

Hollis turned around and went to the truck. The door groaned with a creak and shifted its weight as he sat down. He started the truck and drove off, leaving a cloud of dust in the air.

She inhaled deep and let out a long relieved sigh. She'd won for the moment, but she knew Hollis wouldn't give up so easily.

Madds lifted the radio back to her mouth.

"Hey, Elven, never mind," she said. "I found a raccoon up here getting into some trash. Never had to deal with these things back in Arizona, you know. Guess I'm a little jumpy," she said, trying to add some truth to the lie.

"Understood," he said through the box. "You gonna be alright for a bit longer if I don't head your way first thing?"

"Yeah, I'll manage," she said.

CHAPTER FIFTY-SEVEN

ELVEN PUT THE RADIO BACK ON THE HOOK IN HIS JEEP. HE flipped the vehicle around, glad that he didn't have to head all the way back up to his place. He didn't blame Madds for being so jumpy, but he knew that she was probably alright. Nobody really went to his place without an invite, unless, of course, they were a little too big for their britches.

And then Elven would put them in their place.

He headed to the other side of town, just to the outskirts. Elven had already checked Jesse's motel room, and that had ended up being a dead end. Sure, he was still checked in, but he wasn't there. Elven had even coaxed the key out of the attendant, some acne-laden college kid Moe Olsen had hired, letting himself into Jesse's room. Nothing but beer bottles, take-out boxes, and used condoms.

A slob, Jesse definitely was. But it also gave Elven an idea of where he was at the moment.

A quick pass by the bar, and it was just as he had assumed it would be. Closed down. Even a crook like Hollis wouldn't operate his business, or anyone else's, after the legal operating hours. At least, not publicly.

Jesse was not at the bar. That left one more place to check.

He left Dupray Proper and took the long stretch of road, passing Starcher Hollow, and went to Birther Hollow instead. That's where Lorraine Whitcomb and the other ladies set up shop.

It had been a minute since he'd been there, but his memory was sharp and he remembered just the way to get in.

The long dirt road wound down, snaking its way back and forth, up and down, until he could see the lights lined up in the distance. He spotted four RVs set up near a large building. The building served as their legal business, though even Elven wasn't sure what that business was supposed to be.

Whatever it was, they probably didn't do any real business to speak of, only funneling their main hustle through it so the tax man didn't come knocking. That was out of Elven's jurisdiction though. Let the IRS figure out how to nail a prostitute.

A wooden cattle fence lined the edge of the property, with only one way in and out. Through the open gate, Elven could see the main building had its lights off. Extension cords ran through the dead grass from the building and to each of the RVs. Strung above them were lights that made it look like Christmas.

Each of the RVs was old, and looked like they hadn't been hitched to the back of a vehicle in some time. He spotted one of them up on blocks instead of wheels. Whatever kept it standing, he supposed.

He parked his Jeep along the side of the building. As much as he wanted to go in there and make his presence well known, he also knew that it wouldn't go over so well in the long run. He didn't really care about scaring the clientele away, but more about the ladies banding together and filing a complaint with the county.

The ladies that ran the place were smart like that, and the last thing that Elven needed was to deal with some legal puckey on his end when in fact, it should be the other way around.

So he kept his Jeep mostly out of sight instead of right dead center.

There were two trailers with the lights on. The one with the blue faded paint was the one he was looking for, and, like he suspected, somebody was home.

He walked over the dead grass, hand on his revolver, keeping it steady so it didn't flap against his thigh. The dead and dying grass stirred up in the air with each step he took. He pounded on the flimsy door with the butt of his fist.

He heard some whispers through the door. He pounded again, and the RV rocked from someone shifting inside.

Elven didn't pound again, and tried the handle. It opened right up and he stepped inside.

He was met with a startled Lorraine Whitcomb, half robed. She was naked underneath, and Elven spotted an areola the size of a dinner plate that seemed to frown before she pulled the robe tight. He could tell by the look on her face that she was not very happy.

"Hey! I paid for the night. Supposed to be uninterrupted. I better get a fuckin' discount for this," Jesse said from the back of the RV.

Inside, the air was warm and thick. It smelled of sweat and incense. Elven was glad he hadn't waited any longer to show up, otherwise the smells might be a little much for him to handle.

"Lorraine," Elven said, tipping his hat.

"You better have a good damn reason for being here. You know you have nothing—"

"Sorry to barge in like this. I ain't here for you," he said.

She considered him for a moment, looking him up and down.

"What is going on?" Jesse said, scrambling to his feet. His shirt was off, and his gut hung low. Thank the Lord for small favors, as his pants were still on, though unbuckled and unzipped. Elven had been cutting it close.

"Elven?" Jesse asked.

"Whoever the hell is stirring up trouble right now ain't too smart," someone said from behind Elven. The voice was far away and getting closer with each word.

The man was spitting a good game, but he wasn't too smart, announcing himself like that.

Elven pulled his revolver out from his holster and spun sideways, pointing it out the door at whoever approached. Elven took a look and saw a big guy, muscular. He was clean-shaven, but his face was scarred from what looked like picking at his skin. A few fresher wounds scabbed underneath his chin.

He held a shotgun in both hands, but it was pointed to the side, nowhere near being ready to fire. It was too dark to see, but Elven thought he heard the sound of piss trickling into the dirt.

"Rufus, you idiot. It's the sheriff!" Lorraine shouted, her accent picking up even more twang as she did.

"Sheriff, I didn't know. I thought you was—"

"You mind setting that popper down?" Elven asked.

Rufus nodded, though still didn't set it down.

"Now?" Elven asked.

"Rufus!" Lorraine shouted.

Rufus threw the shotgun to the ground.

"Good, now why don't you go ahead and sit against the wall until I'm done, over there." Elven pointed with his gun.

Rufus didn't delay that time and did as he was asked. He slid down the wall, putting his knees up and wrapping his arms around them.

"Hire some new help?" Elven asked, turning back to Lorraine.

"Apparently more bark than bite," Lorraine said, irritated.

"That's good. I like that better," Elven said.

"Whatever you see going on here, it's all on the up and up. And if you don't have a warrant, you can't just come in here like you is," Lorraine said. "The weapon is licensed and—"

"Relax. Like I said, I ain't here for you, even if what you're telling me is all lies. But I'll play the game. I'm here for him," Elven said, gesturing to Jesse.

Lorraine rolled her eyes. "Jesus, you're costing me more than you're worth." She tossed Jesse his shirt from where it sat on the counter. Elven smirked as she stepped to the side. "Have at him."

Jesse grabbed his shirt, but hesitated to put it on. He was still confused, and Elven had to make it clear.

"Get dressed," he said. "I ain't gonna drag you out on your backside in your skivvies."

"Drag me out?" Jesse asked, putting his shirt on.

"You and me, we're gonna have some words," Elven said.

Jesse laughed, buttoning his pants and standing up. Elven spotted Jesse's belt, holster and revolver on the floor next to a half-eaten bucket of chicken. Whether the bucket was there before, or Jesse brought it with him for his little...excursion, would have to remain a mystery, though the smear of grease on his bottom lip was evidence enough for Elven to put it together.

"You think you're gonna do that?" Jesse asked.

"Oh, I do," Elven said. "Come on."

Jesse followed Elven out of the RV. Elven walked the steps backward, keeping his eyes and gun on Jesse. In his peripheral vision, he spotted Rufus still balled up against the wall, with no intention of intervening. Elven kicked the shotgun to the side by the RV tire and stopped walking once they were in the center. Like it was their very own arena.

"Kind of unfair advantage you have, ain't it? Your gun being pulled and whatnot," Jesse said. He stood only a few feet away, using his tongue to pick something from his teeth.

Elven holstered his revolver and took his belt off. He folded it up and bent over, setting it on the ground gently.

"After the last time, I figured I'd give you a good show up," Elven said. "Cause I tell you, all this trouble that's come our way, you being here and all, well—"

He stood up and was met with Jesse's fist to his jaw. Elven stumbled backward, his mouth flooded with the metallic taste of blood. He spit out a wad to the side and looked Jesse square in the eye.

He grinned and let out a yell, charging at Jesse.

CHAPTER FIFTY-EIGHT

JESSE CLAIMED THAT ELVEN HAD GOTTEN THE JUMP ON HIM THE first time they met. That if he'd have come at him, face to face, Elven wouldn't have stood a chance. So Elven wanted to make it clear that this was a fair fight. There were no advantages. No surprises.

And what did Jesse do? He sucker-punched Elven.

Elven didn't expect any less. Not from a crooked man like Jesse. They may not be in the same field of law enforcement as each other, but there were still laws they had to uphold and respect. Elven didn't know how deep Jesse's corruption went, but it was far enough.

And that was why Elven had to show him this was his town. This was his county. He wasn't going to let someone come in, taking advantage of it.

Elven charged Jesse, grabbing at his midsection. As soon as he connected, Elven was met with a shockwave from the man's gut, but he pushed on. Jesse tried to stand his ground, but Elven was stronger. Jesse took steps instead of falling over, and eventually slammed his back into the side of the RV with a loud thud.

Jesse swung downward with his elbow, making contact with

Elven's back. Each connection made Elven's ribs ache. But Elven worked his midsection as he held him.

Jesse grabbed at Elven's shoulders, his hands pawing at his collar bone. Elven could smell the eleven herbs and spices on Jesse's fingers, still slick with grease from the chicken. Eventually, Jesse gripped onto Elven's shirt and threw him backward.

Elven spun around until he landed in a dirt patch in the center of the dead grass.

This time, it was Jesse's turn to rush at Elven.

Elven rose to his feet just as Jesse reached him. He sidestepped in time to not take the full force of the hefty slob. He caught his left arm and tumbled backward. Jesse turned and threw a fist, nearly catching Elven before he could plant his feet.

But it didn't work as Jesse planned. Elven lifted his arm and parried the punch. Elven took a swing this time with his free fist. Jesse took it in the bearded chin. He didn't stumble backward like Elven had. He took the punch like a champ, standing his ground, which Elven wasn't ready for.

Jesse threw his own punch, connecting with the side of Elven's face. The world blinked out for a hair of a second, then came rushing back to him. Jesse was a large man, and he hit hard. But he was still slow, even with Elven being dazed.

Jesse tried to swing his giant fist down on Elven again, but he was ready. Jesse put everything he had into that punch, and Elven saw it. Had he taken it to the head, he was sure he would have been down for the count. But he didn't connect—instead, Jesse's weight pulled him forward and he left himself wide open.

Elven interlaced his fingers and swung down on the back of Jesse's neck. Jesse let out a groan and buckled down to the ground. He was on his hands and knees and Elven bent over to make sure Jesse was going to stay down.

As soon as he did, Jesse spun, throwing a fist full of dirt in Elven's eyes. His vision went blurry, his eyes hurt from the grains of sand now scratching and grinding against them. He wiped his eyes with his hands and once he felt like he could see again, he opened his eyes.

Jesse swung again, landing a solid hit against Elven's head. The world blinked again, this time for a bit longer than a hair. Elven raised his hand, trying to block whatever punch might be coming next. But there wasn't one.

Jesse grabbed Elven's arm that was raised and spun him around. He pulled Elven's arm up high, causing Elven to bend over, feeling like his arm was going to pop from its socket. He growled in pain. His eyes watered as he tried to see.

Rufus sat, still against the wall, but no longer balled up. He was watching with curiosity, probably glad that someone was giving Elven a proper beatdown. Lorraine stood in her doorway, smoking a cigarette, watching the fight unfold with indifference.

Jesse pulled hard, and Elven no longer felt like his arm would pop from its socket. He felt like it would be ripped off his body. Jesse's weight shifted, his gut flopping against him.

"I knew a pretty boy like you couldn't fight when it came down to it," Jesse spat, his breath hot and smelled of beer and greasy chicken.

He pulled harder and Elven grit his teeth.

"You ready to give up?" Jesse asked. "Maybe I'll be nice and not tell your department about how I handed their boss's ass to him. Except maybe Deputy Side Piece."

Jesse tugged a little more, increasing the angle to Elven's advantage and Elven knew he had him. The grease on his hands was slick and as painful as the position was, it wasn't impossible to get out of. Elven shifted his own weight, twisting his arm in Jesse's grasp and tucking his arm close to him.

Elven's shoulder went forward, and all of Jesse's weight went with it. Jesse stumbled forward, unable to keep from toppling over. A large, gluttonous Humpty Dumpty.

The two men fell to the ground, but Elven's topple was intentional. He rolled as Jesse face-planted into the dead grass. Elven rose to his knees and grabbed at Jesse from behind. He wrapped his arm around his throat as Jesse tried to get up.

Elven rolled him backward so he lay on the ground, the immense weight of Jesse on top of him. He locked his other arm so he held him in a headlock. Jesse yelled, muffled and gargled, as Elven cut off his air. Jesse swung his arms back, but most of them connected with the ground.

Elven wasn't letting him go.

"I want to know everything," Elven demanded. "Who do you work for?"

"The state," Jesse managed to eke out.

"Funny. You went to see my suspect and he ends up dead."

"Accident," Jesse gargled.

"And you killed the only other suspect and witness back at Driscoll's. What's your angle?" Elven asked.

"No—an—gle," Jesse said. "You—fuck—ing—crazy."

Elven tugged his arms tighter. Jesse stopped swinging at him, trying to pry at his arms instead. But it was useless. Elven was going to get the information he wanted.

"You come in town and I find a drug war in my county. A massacre in my woods. I'm not quite sure whose side you're on, but you know who's dealing, don't you? Who's dealing meth in Dupray? Who are you working for?"

Jesse gargled, but no words came out. Elven tugged tighter and he could feel Jesse's hand slap one last time at his own arms. Feeble, with no purpose behind it. Then it fell against him and slid to the grass.

"Sheriff!" Lorraine shouted from her RV. Elven snapped out of it and realized that any longer and he might kill Jesse. He let him go and rolled him to the side. Elven felt the dead, dry grass poke at his skin, causing it to itch.

The color had faded from Jesse's face, but he inhaled a deep, scratchy breath. It sounded like a death rattle in reverse. The pale white of his skin turned back to a reddish hue, and Elven knew that

Jesse was fine. Maybe just a few brain cells less, which might be a bad thing for someone of Jesse's intelligence.

Jesse had no more fight in him. He lifted himself up to his hands and knees, and started to cough. He hacked up something nasty and spit it out, but there was no pressure behind it. It sort of just hung from his mouth, half of it clinging to his bottom lip.

"You're fucking crazy, you know that? You're nuts," Jesse said, his voice weak.

"Maybe a night in a cell will do you some good," Elven said.

Jesse turned and looked at Elven, mucus and phlegm clinging to his beard.

"I told you, I ain't got nothing to do with it," Jesse shouted. "I came here 'cause of the threats to that damn church in the hills. Spencer Caldwell, the snake. Was told to keep an eye out and make sure nobody did nothing."

"Who sent you?"

"Jesus Christ," Jesse said. "Ain't you get it? The state sent me. The fucking governor's office. Though why they let them have a permit to preach there in the first place is beyond me. I just figured that while I was at it, I might make some cash off the fucker."

"By selling meth?" Elven asked, though he wasn't sure he was following anymore. He felt like he was just throwing out random theories.

"No. I told them I'd keep the hunters away. You know, sort of protection duty or whatever. I ain't have any idea they were running drugs up here, or that they were on some other drug dealer's territory."

Elven considered him a moment. This whole thing was messed up. And he felt so lost.

"What makes more sense?" Jesse asked.

Elven thought a moment. "To be honest, I have no idea what makes sense anymore."

Jesse laughed and pushed himself up, turning around to sit upright.

"You and me both," Jesse said. "Look, I'm a lot of things, alright? I ain't really a good guy, I know that. I drink a lot, I pay for whores—no offense, Lorraine," Jesse said to the woman in the doorway. She waved noncommittally and Elven knew she'd been called worse. "And I might try to make some extra cash on the side in a situation where someone might be having some back luck. But I ain't a murderer. Maybe I'm not a good guy, but I'm not a bad one either."

Elven exhaled and grumbled. He had no evidence of Jesse really being involved. And what he said made a lot more sense than anything else. Elven just didn't like him very much.

"Alright," Elven said.

"You believe me?" he asked.

"You better believe I'm checking in with your office to make sure everything's on the up and up one more time, but yeah," Elven said. "Though you're causing a lot of grief around here, not working with me on things. Giving me the runaround. And now you admitted to squeezing Spencer for money."

"For a job I was doing already," Jesse stated.

"Not very well," Elven added.

"What about you?" Jesse asked. "You found meth up at the revival and you didn't seem interested in keeping me in the loop. If you kept me informed, I wouldn't have gone to talk to that asshole in your jail in the first place and he wouldn't have blown his damn head off."

"I wouldn't have kept it from you if you didn't keep me in the dark about your being here in the first place," Elven shot back. He went to the ground and picked up his belt and gun, strapping it on.

"Alright, so you have both been shitty," Lorraine shouted from her trailer. "Now can you both get the fuck off my property before you scare away any more clients?"

Both men ignored her.

"Shit," Jesse said. "I guess that's my bad then."

"Ya think?"

"Where does that put us then?" Jesse asked.

Elven shrugged. "I guess we're no further than we were a few hours ago."

Jesse's eyes widened, like a lightbulb had just gone off in his head. "That guy, back at the station. Before he blew his head off, he said they met, you know, before shooting all them people in the woods, at some church. Said it was some parking lot and mostly dead."

Elven thought a moment and then had his own lightbulb moment. "You gotta be kidding me," he said.

"You know something?" Jesse asked.

"I'll fill you in on the way," Elven said. "You good?"

Elven held his hand out. Jesse took it and was lifted to his feet.

"I paid for the night," Jesse said.

Elven stared him down. "One, I'm sure Lorraine ain't having you anymore after this. And two, I'm gonna pretend some things here, alright? Instead of making assumptions and arresting you, I'm just gonna go on thinking that it's pretty weird that a man paid for two hotel rooms on the same night. And that there wasn't anything else involved in that payment you made to Lorraine. Definitely nothing that might be frowned upon by the law."

Jesse adjusted himself and nodded. "Fair enough. I'll get my gun."

Elven shook his head as Jesse hobbled his way back into Lorraine's trailer. "You ain't back in thirty seconds, I'm going back in for you."

Lorraine smiled from the doorway and gave him a wink. "Sheriff, you ain't never seen what I can do in thirty seconds."

CHAPTER FIFTY-NINE

ELVEN HAD TO WORK SOME CHARM AT THE NURSES' STATION OF the hospital. Apparently visiting hours, even for law enforcement, was a serious deal around those halls. He wasn't sure it would work, seeing as how Jesse had given him a real beating and his face looked like it had been through the grinder. But he put a spin on it he knew she couldn't resist.

A ruggedly handsome man, in uniform, with some bruises. Nothing was better than a story about having to take down a perp. He told a good story about having to get into it with a dangerous criminal, put his life on the line, guns were drawn and fists were thrown, but in the end, he came out on top. He was pretty sure Jesse found it all too amusing by the stupid grin on his face.

"What's so funny?" Elven asked when the nurse disappeared to get a form.

"Wasn't quite so honest with her, were you?" Jesse asked. "I figured a guy like you wasn't much of a fibber."

Elven shook his head. "Only embellished a little. Didn't really lie to her."

"That so? Dangerous criminal?"

Elven shrugged. "At the time, I did think you were a perp. And with how many bodies I've seen you come up with, I'd say dangerous was the right word. Don't you?"

Jesse considered a moment, then nodded. "Hey, I'll take it. Maybe word will spread and poachers will be shaking in their boots at the story of the dangerous game warden."

Elven watched the nurse come back and place the forms down, which he and Jesse signed hastily.

"You mean, dangerous Natural Resources Police Officer," Elven corrected, then turned down the silent hallway.

The room was silent, only a machine softly beeping in the corner. The lights were off, except the bathroom, the door cracked open about an inch wide. Adam, the meth addict he'd found in the woods all those days ago, slept with his mouth open. Drool dripped down his chin and created a slowly expanding wet spot on his blue gown.

Elven cleared his throat. Adam snorted and turned to the side at the noise. Elven sighed. Jesse turned the first light switch on and the light above the bed kicked on. The rest of the room stayed dark.

Elven knocked on the bed frame and Adam stirred awake. He opened his eyes, disoriented, his head going back and forth. He looked up at the light above his head.

"Oh shit, am I dyin'?" he asked, his voice sleepy and slurred.

"You ain't dead yet, twit," Jesse said.

Adam squinted his eyes down at Jesse, then turned to Elven.

"Oh," is all he said, then fell back into the bed.

Elven took the remote that rested on the edge of the mattress in his hand. He clicked the arrow that pointed up. The bed slowly rose to put Adam in an upright seated position.

"Goddammit, can't you let a guy sleep?" Adam asked, forgetting who he was speaking to. Some people could be a real grouch when being woken up.

"Answer some questions and you can get back to sleep," Elven said. "Remember, this murder is still on you."

Adam grumbled and covered his face in a pillow. He yelled into it and Elven was worried the nurse would come in and make them leave. Luckily, he muffled himself enough to not cause a scene.

He pulled the pillow from his face and threw it at his feet.

"You know what it is like to detox in a shitty hospital like this?"

"Probably a lot better than doing it in some shithole tweaker house," Jesse said.

"Definitely better than being dead in the woods," Elven added.

Adam rolled his eyes. "Alright, ask away," he said.

"We may have misheard some things last we were here," Elven said.

"Yeah? I figured you heard it, but didn't want to listen," he said.

Elven nodded. "Tell it again, then. Where'd you get the drugs?"

"I told you last time. The church," Adam said.

"We know that," Jesse said. "They fuckin' found you in them woods near the revival. Sheriff Pretty—Sheriff Hallie figured it out already. We want to know where you were buying before they rolled into town."

"You ain't listening," Adam said.

Elven knew it when Jesse had told him. He'd been wrong the last time they spoke to Adam. "It wasn't the revival, was it? It was an actual church, right? Like a building in town, not the woods?" Elven asked. He knew he was on the right path now.

"That's right," Adam said. "If I'd have meant the revival, I'd have said the fucking revival."

"Boy, you better tone down that attitude right now," Jesse said.

"I only went to the revival the one time. My friend said they got a good deal on crystal. Said it'll fuck me up so good." He shrugged and looked at his hands. "I don't know about that, but we went. He was buying. I guess he was right in a way."

"This church," Elven said. "Where is it?"

CHAPTER SIXTY

The kitchen was dark and quiet. Madds looked out through the back window as she sipped on a mug of coffee. It was lit up by the moon, though she knew in an hour or so, the sun would be cresting over the hill. It would be a great view when that happened, but it would also be heavily tainted by the night she had been through.

She had watched Hollis's truck drive down the trail from Elven's house. It was long and winding, but she never let her eyes break away from the vehicle. He'd made it to the base of the hill, when another set of headlights had clicked on. Hollis hadn't been lying, not that she thought he was—at least, not about this. It must have been Corbin down there, waiting like Hollis had said.

They stopped for a moment, their headlights crossing paths as the vehicles idled, then they both drove off. She had made sure of it, and didn't let out a breath until they disappeared from sight.

After that, she knew that even trying to sleep would be futile.

So she made her coffee from some exotic beans that Elven had stashed away. The package said each bag was hand-roasted and was from Nicaragua. She didn't expect to find Folgers in his cupboard, but damn, Elven was too much sometimes. Great guy, handsome, intelligent, fair, kind, and lots of money.

But the coffee? She thought the stuff he bought for the station was fancy. But this? Jesus, she was surprised she wasn't going to have to use a French press just to make a cup.

But it wasn't just not being able to sleep that kept her up. She worried about what Hollis might do. She knew it wasn't the end of it. Michaela had witnessed the murders at the revival, and from what she had gathered, Hollis was the one who had come through, executing everyone.

There was no way he was going to let that poor girl live after seeing him kill. And if she decided to talk? Well, it was like Hollis had said—one thing would lead to another, and that would eventually lead back to Madds.

She spun the snub-nosed revolver on the counter as she sipped her coffee.

What was she going to do?

Before having to come up with an answer, the radio static clicked on. She turned and picked up the handheld radio that she'd set on the counter.

"Hey Madds, you there?" Elven asked.

"Yeah, Elven, what's up?"

"I didn't wake you, did I? Wanted to check in. No more raccoons there?"

"No, I'm up. I couldn't sleep if I wanted to. All quiet on my end. You figure anything out?"

"Maybe try getting some sleep. I think we're gonna put this thing to bed soon. I'm gonna need you fresh in the morning. Maybe a few hours."

Technically, it was morning, though she didn't bring it up. She was more curious at what Elven had found, and if it would tie back to her at all.

"Sounds good. What did you find?"

"That meth addict from the woods, the one in the hospital. Says he's been buying at the church."

"Church? No shit, but how does that help us?" Madds asked.

"Not the revival, but the church in town. And the guy from the bar, the one who blew his head off at the station—"

Madds clicked over the radio, having no idea what Elven was talking about. "Blew his head off? What?"

"Oh, right, long story. Anyway, he said he met there with the big guy that did the executing at the revival."

Apparently she wasn't the only one with the long night. There were some pieces that she didn't have, but she got the gist of it from Elven. She was beginning to see where he was going with it. And it was leading to places that she couldn't let it reach.

"Seems to be enough of a connection. But the word of a dead murderer and a meth addict don't go so far," Elven said.

"Agreed," Madds said. "So what does that mean then?"

"Well, I'm not thinking it's the preacher."

"That's probably a good assumption," Madds said.

"They say it's a big guy. Beard, older. Know anyone who fits that description that might also have some not so legal dealings? Maybe wouldn't think twice about killing people who came into his territory?" Elven asked.

Shit.

"Elven, don't go off the deep end here," Madds warned

"I know. I'm not trying to jump to conclusions, but like I said a while back. I could smell the stink of Hollis Starcher on this whole thing. You're right though. I'm gonna do this right. Put the pieces together. Last time I went in on an assumption, I didn't fare too well."

"What?" Madds asked.

"Never mind. I want this done, Madds. In a few hours, we're going to the church. Ask some questions. See if we can get anything. If people are buying meth from the church, then the preacher must know something. Even if he isn't directly involved, he's gotta know someone who is. Maybe someone from the outreach program he has."

"Who's the preacher?"

"Abnel Foster, over in Glover Hollow."

"Got it," Madds said, clenching her teeth. "How soon will you be here?"

"Maybe two hours, max. I mean it, rest up."

And then he clicked off. She took one last sip on her coffee and put the mug on the counter. Two hours meant she didn't have a ton of time. She had to find out for herself what she was looking at.

She knew the exact church they were talking about. She knew that preacher seemed a little off that night, and had been ready to leave so quickly. But she hadn't put it together until now.

She grabbed the revolver and ran upstairs as quietly as she could, stepping into the room. She'd gotten Michaela to sleep after Hollis's visit, though she still didn't know how. She hovered over Michaela, gripping the revolver, watching the girl sleep for a few minutes. Her chest rose and fell in a slow rhythm. Her eyes were closed and she could see the movement beneath the eyelids, back and forth.

Madds hoped she was dreaming of something nice.

CHAPTER SIXTY-ONE

Madds didn't have a vehicle there, having been ushered all over the county after finding Michaela in the outhouse. She wasn't even sure where she last left her vehicle. Maybe at the station? Had she gotten a lift to the revival?

What a long day it had already been. She was exhausted, but there was still more to do. What was that saying again? Oh right...no rest for the wicked.

And she was beginning to realize where her place was within those words.

Thankfully, Elven being the man he was, and with the money he had, and the extra toys lying around his property, she was able to find a vehicle. The keys were next to the door, on a little hook that was drilled into a wooden plaque that said KEYS.

That plaque was a little too cute for a bachelor and she thought how it must have been a gift from a woman. Most likely not his mother. After meeting her, Madds didn't see her as the type to buy kitschy type shit. Or anything under twenty dollars. No, it was probably from an old girlfriend.

But the vehicles on the property were nowhere in sight. She had to open up the detached shed, though shed wasn't the best description of the structure. It made her think of something small, maybe rickety. This thing was the size of some small houses. It was large enough that she could picture four cars fitting inside it, and it was solidly built. Wood and metal together.

She had to move fast, and the first vehicle she saw was an old beat-up truck. Her heart dropped and she wondered if it would even run. She could imagine the exhaust blowing out on her exit, waking Michaela up.

But when she looked at the keys, she saw they weren't old and didn't have the matching emblem of the truck. Further in the dark shed, she saw a large, black shape. It was a vehicle for sure, but it was wrapped by a cover.

She pulled it off and dropped her jaw. "Elven Hallie, you've been holding out on me," she said.

She wasn't much for cars, but even she had taste and knew what she was looking at.

The car was deep blue and immaculate. The fact that it was in the shed next to the pick-up truck was almost an insult. But maybe that was just like how Elven was. Rich among the poor.

In front of her was an Aston Martin DB6. Her father had been a big fan of their vehicles, and had taped pictures of them up in the garage when she grew up. That she was standing in front of one right then, holding the key, almost made her forget about everything she still had to do.

She opened the door and slid into the driver's seat. She placed her hands over the steering wheel. Inside it smelled like old cologne mixed with old leather. Even she had to admit that it was intoxicating to be inside it.

Driving it out into Dupray felt wrong, like a sin that she could never come back from. And that was saying something.

But she did, all the same, and easily pushed the guilt away.

She knew Elven wouldn't be happy about her driving it. There was no way she could get to the church and get back before Elven saw she was gone. A reason for why she'd taken the car and left would be easy to come up with, even if he didn't like it.

At that moment, she really didn't care.

CHAPTER SIXTY-TWO

THE DOOR TO THE CHURCH WAS LOCKED. WHEN SHE PULLED THE Aston Martin into the parking lot, she made note that hers was the only vehicle there. She worried that Abnel Foster, the preacher, wouldn't even show up. That maybe he didn't come in until much later in the day.

It was odd though. The last time she'd been there, he had left in such a hurry, leaving her by herself. Not locking up the building at all. She figured that was just the way the church operated, but here she was, tugging on a locked door. If she didn't already have most of the information, she'd have thought it even more suspicious.

The sun was up by the time she made it there. She paced in front of the door, debating on what to do next. The sidewalk was dusted with sand from the dirt lot that it bordered. Her boots crunched against the grains on the concrete.

She was exhausted and she was sure she looked like a mess. In fact, she was more than sure. It was mostly confirmed by her reflection in the window of the door. Her hair felt matted in places and she hadn't had time to brush it out. Instead, she kept tucking it up into a messy bun with a hair tie. Her skin felt greasy, as it always did when she had no sleep.

Or maybe it was all mental.

Now she had to worry about Elven finding her before she found Abnel. And what if he did? What was her plan then?

She couldn't worry about it and had to believe she would find Abnel first. She had to convince Abnel to leave. Elven was going to figure something out and it wouldn't end well for any of them. She was sure that if she pressed Abnel, the preacher would understand that he was short on time. If he wanted to be free, that is.

Thankfully, the first thing had gone right. A dark green Camry, with a back door that looked like it had taken one hell of a collision, pulled into the lot. She stopped pacing and caught a glimpse of the preacher driving.

Her shoulders relaxed, the tension melting away somewhat. Just because Abnel was here, that didn't mean that Elven wasn't coming. Or that she could convince Abnel to leave.

She still had a big job to do.

He got out from his car and approached her with a smile. There was no robe on him this time, only jeans and a button-up shirt that was tucked somewhere underneath the girth that hung over his belt. He pulled his glasses off and ran a hand over his beard.

"I just need these glasses to drive," he said with a wink. "So you took my offer and decided to come back, did ya?"

"Something like that," Madds said, unsure how to get straight to the point.

"Well, come on in. No sense in standing out here. You look miserable. Too cold for you already?" he asked with a chuckle.

This man didn't seem like a drug dealer mastermind. Part of her wondered if he'd even had anything to do with it or if Hollis had just used his church. Hollis was very convincing with his lies and putting on a face, after all.

"Actually, I don't think there's time," Madds said.

Abnel unlocked the door and opened it anyway. "If you wanna talk, we better go inside. Standing during a sermon is about all the action my legs can take these days. I wanna get settled, if you don't mind. We can talk while we walk."

Madds reluctantly followed him inside. The church was quiet, the chairs undisturbed. It was brighter from the sunlight, but other than that, the room was unchanged from her last visit.

"So what is it that you don't have time for? Is that what's been troubling you this whole time?" Abnel asked. He grabbed his white robe from the coat rack at the end of the first row and slid into it, zipping up the back. It was a smooth transition, presumably from doing it all his life.

"I have had to do some things," Madds said. But that wasn't why she was there.

"The Lord knows we aren't perfect. Sinners we are. We've all done things we aren't proud of," Abnel said, settling down in the front row just like last time.

But Madds didn't sit.

"Like sell drugs out of your church?" she asked, cutting straight to the chase.

Abnel let out a loud chuckle, then saw she wasn't laughing. He narrowed his eyes at her.

"You said it right," she said. "We all do things. But most people don't keep at it if they aren't proud of it, right?"

Abnel stood again, seeming to not mind the act this time. "Maybe it's time for you to go," he said. "I'm not sure what you've got going in your head there, but—"

"No, preacher," she said.

"Pastor," he corrected, his words short.

"Pastor. I know what's going on. I should have noticed the last time I was here. That man you met with when I arrived, he was clearly an addict. He wasn't here for guidance, was he? He was here to score."

Abnel shook his head. "You've got no proof of anything. So either you need to leave or I will."

"That's good," she said. "You should leave. Because soon, the sheriff will be here. And he's got a lot of proof."

He stopped and stared at her, his smile long gone from his face. His mouth was now just a small line surrounded by a beard.

"I'm sure that if anything does happen, I'll be out—"

"Hollis isn't going to get you out of this one," Madds said, playing her card.

"The hell you say?"

"I said that Hollis won't be rescuing you. You sink or swim on your own."

"And what do you have to do with it?" he asked.

"I told you, I've had to do some things, didn't I? I'm trying to help you."

"Jesus. What a messed-up place we find ourselves," Abnel said. He looked at the cross on the wall and swallowed.

"There's no time. If you want your freedom, then you'll get out of here and far from Dupray, you got it?"

"But everything is here. All that I know. How can I just leave that all behind?" he asked, as if Madds had any answers.

"Don't know what to tell you, but it's how it is."

Abnel swallowed hard, but seemed to understand and made a beeline for the door. He was slow and limped, reminding her of Hollis when he walked.

But he didn't get far. Sirens rang out and she could see the flashing blue and red lights through the window of the door.

Elven had figured it out. At least, to some extent.

"No, no, no," Abnel said, spinning around. "You said I had time."

"Can you get out through the back?" she asked.

He shook his head. "And make a break for it? You gotta do something."

She looked at him, no answers coming to her. There was nothing she could do. Even if she went outside to stall, there was no way Abnel could sneak out the back. Maybe he could keep his lips tight when Elven questioned him, but she saw the panic in his eyes.

"I ain't going down. Not after all this. I have a church. I am an upstanding member of the community here in Glover Hollow. Hollis has to fix this." Then he twisted his mouth, and angry scowl forming. "I'll get out of this, alright. If Hollis ain't gonna do something to help me, then I'll have to help myself."

"No, you need to just keep quiet," Madds said. "Just be patient—"

"When the sheriff hears what I have to say, you will all be letting me go. Ain't no secret the sheriff has some issues with the Starcher clan. Hollis and his whole family. Hallie will practically hand me the keys to leave. Everyone ever had dealings with them will go down, I swear," Abnel spat. He just had to keep running his mouth.

Madds sighed, her mouth sagging. She'd never wanted to take any of this on, to be put in this position. But Hollis might have been right.

"Why'd you have to say it?" Madds asked, though it came out more of a statement than a question. Just a moment of disbelief of where she found herself.

The door opened and Elven stepped inside. He didn't have his gun drawn, but his hand was on it and his free hand raised. Jesse came in behind, the same exact way. It was like they weren't sure if they were supposed to be there for questioning or if they were going to step into a fight.

Madds knew Elven didn't suspect it to stop at Abnel, or if Abnel had even been involved at all. She knew she would have to change that.

Abnel spun around, his hands in his robe. Elven and Jesse were at the other end of the building. Madds stood only a few feet from the pastor. Madds watched as Abnel began to pull his hands up, either to show he had no weapon, or to plead his case.

Either way, it was her only chance.

"Gun!" she yelled.

She heard a small *huh* out of Abnel and what looked like he was trying to glance behind him, trying to see what the hell Madds was talking about.

She drew her pistol off her hip and fired three shots. Each of them landed center mass into Abnel's back. The robe blossomed red from the three bullet wounds, the white soaking through and spreading fast.

Abnel dropped to his knees and Madds dropped behind him. She put her hand in her jacket pocket and felt the small revolver that Hollis had given her earlier. She pulled it out and dropped it behind Abnel where Elven and Jesse couldn't see what she was doing.

Elven came running, his revolver pulled. Jesse, once again, followed suit. It was as if they were both on the same page now. Good for them, she thought.

"Madds, you okay?" Elven asked.

"Help me, call Driscoll!" she yelled, grabbing at Abnel. She lay him down on the ground. Elven spotted the revolver on the floor and kicked it away from Abnel's reach.

He could be the one to say that he saw it and kicked it away now, not having anything to do with Madds, other than she had a better line of sight to the weapon.

Jesse holstered his gun and stood over them. Elven let his revolver hang, but didn't holster it.

"What happened?" Madds screamed at Abnel. "Tell me something." She was putting it on thick, knowing that Abnel barely had any life in him to say another word. But she pleaded anyway, playing the part that Elven needed to see.

Abnel choked twice, a spurt of blood firing in the air from his mouth. *Holl—Holl—*and then he was dead. His eyes rolled to the side, directed at nothing in particular.

Elven placed a hand on Madds's shoulder. "He's gone," he said.

Madds slammed her hand on the ground and rolled backward,

sitting on the floor with her back against a chair. She finally let the tears go.

They weren't fake tears either. That wasn't the ending she'd intended. But it was the one that Hollis had predicted. The frustration, the long night of no sleep finally had a chance to come out.

But more than anything, she knew that she was on the wrong path and now there was no way of getting back on the right one.

CHAPTER SIXTY-THREE

DEAD BODIES AND CRIME SCENES WERE BECOMING A REGULAR occurrence with this case, Elven noticed. Though there wasn't much to do at this scene other than take the body to the doc's and search the church. Elven had told Madds to wait in his Jeep while he and Jesse searched the place.

He didn't feel the need to have Tank or Johnny come out. No need in making everyone lose sleep. Johnny was probably still too shaken up, and Tank was having to deal with the mess he'd left. Besides, Jesse had proven himself to not be as bad of a guy as Elven had thought. Maybe not a great guy, or even someone he'd want to work with regularly, but someone who could be useful at least, even if he did admit to extortion.

Madds was reluctant to sit out, but Elven had insisted, saying that if she didn't, he was gonna send her to the hospital to get looked over. It had done the trick and she'd listened. Though he could feel her disapproval from her stare.

The search was quick and extremely fruitful. There was a back office that had a safe in it. At first, the two men thought they were going to find themselves at an impasse, but when they checked the pastor's leather-bound notebook on his desk, the safe combination was written on the first page.

"It's almost like it was handed to us," Jesse said while laughing.

He was right, but Elven didn't think anything of it. A small-town pastor in a dying church probably didn't think he had anything to worry about. Though with addicts around for the supposed outreach program, he would have thought there was plenty to worry about.

Jesse opened the safe and it was full of drugs. It reminded Elven of the tent at the revival. Except this safe was bigger, and the meth was a bit different in color. Elven wasn't up on all the recipes that could be made from it, but he knew crystal when he saw it.

Bags upon bags of the orange-shaded crystals were crammed in the safe. The ones up front were divided into smaller bags, most likely easily sold to someone coming in. But behind the smaller bags were even bigger ones. Gallon-sized plastic zipper bags filled to where the crystals almost burst out through the top of the press seal.

"Jesus Christ," Jesse said. "Oh shit." He covered his mouth when realizing where he stood, then crossed his chest as if he'd committed a cardinal sin.

"I think you might be alright," Elven said. "I'm sure you're a bit lower on the Big Guy's list considering what we're dealing with."

Jesse smiled. "A pastor selling meth? Crazy, ain't it?"

"About as crazy as a preacher in the woods selling. I'd say it's not an everyday thing, or it didn't used to be," Elven said. "But it doesn't put him at the revival."

Jesse nodded and started to go through the entire safe, pulling out all the bags. At the bottom, underneath the larger bags, was a half-filled baggie. On the side was a small spot of blood. Inside the bag, the crystal wasn't an orange hue. Instead, it was a cloudy white.

Just like the bags Elven had found at the revival.

"But that just might," Elven said.

He and Jesse packed up all the evidence, going through every last bit of Abnel's office. There wasn't much else to find, and what they already had was enough.

Something just didn't feel right to Elven and kept eating at him. But as much as he wanted to believe there was more, the evidence said otherwise.

Jesse loaded said evidence into the back of Elven's Jeep as Elven checked on Madds. She sat in the driver's seat, the heater on high.

"So you guys are buddies now?" Madds asked.

"Jesse? I might have been wrong about him."

Jesse came up to the window after loading the last box. "Nah, you weren't wrong. Like I said, I'm not like you. You're a good man, Elven. One of the few I've ever met anyway." He rubbed his hand on his throat. "You also know how to choke the fuck out of a guy."

Elven smiled as Madds looked at him curiously. He shot her a wink.

"So why'd you come up here? Why not wait for us?" Elven asked.

Madds shrugged. "I thought you said we were going. For me to meet you."

"I said I'd come get you. That I needed you rested."

"I don't know. It's been a long night. I must have heard different. Guess I got confused. Lack of sleep, not so quick on the uptake," she said.

"Maybe not on the uptake, but quick enough on the draw. You spotted that gun before anyone else and saved us from taking a bullet," Elven said. "I wonder what his plan was."

"Who knows. Maybe he heard the sirens after a deputy shows up to his church and thought he was caught. Why were the sirens on anyway? I swear you said something about questions."

Elven nodded. "I did. But when my Aston Martin goes missing, you better believe I'm gonna be breaking some laws on the road to get to it."

Madds threw her head against the seat. "So it was my fault this happened."

Elven shook his head. "Don't blame yourself. He was guilty, and we just got lucky he got spooked. Otherwise who knows if he'd have said anything to lead us to him."

"Right," Madds said.

"I just can't shake the feeling that he wasn't alone," Elven said. It was still eating at him and he thought that maybe if he vocalized it, someone would either connect the dots for him or put him at ease to believe it.

"Why not?" Jesse asked.

"I don't know, just a feeling I guess," Elven said.

Jesse shook his head. "Glad I don't go off feelings in my job. I'd be suspicious of everyone any time I ate a bowl of spicy chili."

"Maybe we can get some pictures in front of Michaela. I know she's not talking much, but maybe she can point it out. Think she'd be okay with that?" Elven asked.

Madds looked as if she was going to be sick. Like she'd just gotten the news that her dog had died.

"You alright?" Elven asked.

"Fine. Just a day, like I said. She might be up for it. I should go get her. Maybe talk it out with her and bring her down to the station myself."

Elven shook his head. "Don't bother. She's already there. When I saw you weren't at the house, I took her down there, had Tank keep an eye on her. She wasn't too keen on going with me, but since you and I are friends and we found her together, she came around."

"Oh, that's good," Madds said. "I guess you've got it all taken care of then."

CHAPTER SIXTY-FOUR

MADDS THOUGHT SHE WAS GOING TO PUKE THE ENTIRE WAY back to the station. She'd just killed a man to keep her secret, to keep Hollis's secret, and now Elven was still going to figure it out. The chances of Hollis not being in that line-up of pictures was less than zero. She'd be surprised if there was even anyone else in the line-up. Elven had such a hot nut to bust Hollis that he couldn't accept the evidence.

The problem was, this time he was right.

She had to keep it together. There was no excuse for her to actually throw up. Elven would catch on. But she probably only had a few more moments before he figured it out anyway.

Hollis would be fingered, then the rest of his family. And that meant somewhere down the line, her relation and affiliation would be revealed. Was she going to run, or was she going to deny it and say that there was no proof? And if there was proof, what end would that make for her?

They went inside the station and Meredith sat with Michaela at the desk. She was showing her something on the computer, and

Michaela actually had a small smile on her face. It was surprising to see. Even Elven seemed to pleased about it.

"Glad to see everyone's in good spirits," Elven said, placing his Stetson on the desk.

"Michaela here is actually quite the little artist. She was showing me how to draw some things on the computer, if you can believe that," Meredith said.

"That's great to hear," Elven said. "Michaela, I was wondering if you'd be able to help me out. Maybe take a look at some pictures for me."

Michaela seemed to draw back into her shell. She tucked her hair behind her ears and shrugged her shoulders. She glanced at Meredith, who patted her hand, then she looked to Madds. All Madds could do was swallow.

"Hey, Elven, I don't know if I'm feeling well. Maybe I should head home. I think you've got this handled," Madds said. She had to get out of there. She figured she could pack her things in twenty minutes and get the hell out of West Virginia before they had Hollis in cuffs.

After that, she would figure it out, but at least she'd have a lead on them.

"Nonsense," Elven said. "I need you here. Michaela needs you here. Just sit down, have some water. We'll be done in no time, then you can head home."

Madds had no out now. She followed Elven as he walked Michaela to his office. Madds felt like she was heading to the principal's office, ready to be scolded. She knew that once Michaela identified Hollis as the shooter, she wouldn't be able to make a break for it without being suspicious. Elven would want to arrest Hollis immediately, and that meant all hands on deck.

Michaela sat in the cracked leather chair in front of Elven's desk. He plopped down on his office chair on the other side. Madds didn't feel like she could sit.

Elven pulled out a folder from the cabinet. "I want to let you know, we've made an arrest," Elven started. "I want to make sure we have all our loose ends tied up. That way, nobody can hurt you again, do you understand?"

Michaela looked hopeful. Like she was getting her first chance at real freedom. Madds's heart sank, thinking that identifying Hollis was Michaela's only way of escape. And that was the exact opposite of what Madds wanted.

Michaela nodded, grabbing Madds's hand for support.

Madds wanted to scream. She wanted to tell her *no, don't do it.* But she didn't. Instead, she let Elven continue.

"Good," he said.

He opened the folder and put it in front of Michaela. It was a picture of Hollis. He was a bit younger, a little less gray in the beard and one or two crow's feet still yet to appear, but it was clearly him.

"Is this the man you saw? Is he familiar to you at all?" Elven asked.

Oh, what a question. Of course, Michaela would know him. Not only was he the shooter, but she'd seen him outside of Elven's house just hours ago.

Michaela looked at the picture, her grip on Madds's hand tighter than ever. She felt the bones in her hand pop as Michaela stared down into Hollis's eyes. She looked back up to Elven.

She shook her head.

What? She was saying it wasn't him? But Madds knew it was. And she knew that Michaela knew it was.

Elven frowned in response and took a deep breath, pulling out another folder. He opened it and placed it on top of the image of Hollis. This one was Abnel Foster, and he was on the floor of his church, dead.

Michaela's grip loosened. There was no trauma from him. There was no recognition. She gave a small squeeze to Madds, and in response, Madds squeezed her hand twice.

Michaela took the signal. She nodded and put her finger on the image of Abnel Foster.

"That's him," Michaela said. She spoke for the first time since Madds had found her. "He's the one. He killed them all."

Everyone sat a little shocked at Michaela's words, and a little shocked at the outcome itself. Madds exhaled. It was done. And nobody would be going for Hollis or her.

Elven leaned back, closing the folder. "Okay. Thank you, Michaela. I guess we're done then."

CHAPTER SIXTY-FIVE

"You're disappointed," Madds said.

"That obvious?" Elven asked. He had thought for sure that Hollis had been involved this time. And maybe there still was something. Maybe he wasn't the one who had committed the murders. But there was still no evidence to link him to being involved in any capacity. Not with Michaela saying it wasn't him and with Abnel being dead now.

The only thing he had was the word of a dead man who wouldn't be identifying anyone now.

Nothing but dead ends. Nothing but Elven's hunch. Maybe he was blind when it came to that family. He had to just look at the evidence.

And that's what didn't sit well with him. There was one string that still didn't add up.

"I know you have it in for them, but maybe it just wasn't them this time. You'll get them on the next one," Madds said.

Elven nodded, putting his hands behind his head.

"It's the one statement that doesn't add up," he said.

"Statement?" Madds asked.

Elven nodded. "Something Jesse told me. Scotty, one of the attackers at the revival, the one I picked up at the bar who got himself dead in my cell. He said that it specifically wasn't the pastor. That it wasn't Abnel. That the pastor was inside, and the big guy who did the killing was outside with them."

Madds scrunched her brows and thought for a moment. Elven waited.

"I hate to say it, especially since you guys seem to be getting along alright now, but Jesse isn't really the most reliable person."

Elven laughed. "That's the truth. But Johnny was there, too."

Madds nodded. "A statement we can't verify, secondhand from a man we can't trust, and confirmed by the guy who let his gun get taken away and is too shaken up to talk about it. I love Johnny, don't get me wrong, but—"

"I know," Elven said. "I know."

"Maybe it wasn't Abnel. Maybe it was a different pastor. I mean, he can't be there twenty-four seven, right? Or maybe someone who volunteered at the church who looked like the pastor. You did also say yourself that the word of a dead man isn't worth much. Too bad we can't sit him down like we did Michaela. But as it is, she's the only witness. And the most reliable one."

"Yeah, it is too bad," Elven said. He contemplated a moment, then decided to bring it up. "But, you know, he did also say that he saw a lady cop there."

Madds seemed to tense up for a brief moment, like Elven had outed her. "Is that so?" she asked.

"It is," he said. "As much as I'd like to think of myself as progressive and with the times, hate to say it, but you are the only lady cop around here."

Madds laughed, but it was on the edge of nervous. Was she hiding something from him?

"Sounds like you're grilling me as your next suspect," she said.

He smiled and leaned back, his chair going with him. "Nothing like that. Just, why didn't you tell me?"

"That I went to church?" she asked.

He nodded. "Figured with all this it might have come up."

"I don't normally go in for much religion," she said. "In fact, I was Catholic growing up, which is why I went over there."

Elven cackled. "That placed burned down some years back. Nobody saw fit to build it again after that. Abnel opened up his place not long after that, but I guess the area was burned, literally and figuratively." It made sense. Pastor Luke Magner had said that area was dying for churchgoers. Of course, he didn't also know about the meth-dealing. And then again, maybe it was because he was having a hard time keeping the doors open. Drugs on the side was a good way to fund whatever he wanted.

"Well, someone should really tell Google that," she said. "I guess I just feel a little lost is all. So far from home and all. Maybe I was trying to grasp at old habits to make me feel grounded."

Elven felt bad asking her questions and putting her on the spot. She was in a new place, far away from where she'd grown up. She knew nobody from her past here, and had no family around. She was allowed her privacy, and he was prying too much.

"I can appreciate that," he said.

"I didn't know what Abnel Foster was into, obviously. But I should have known something was off. When I saw him, he was in such a hurry to leave. Didn't figure anything was up. I mean, a preacher selling drugs? Who would have thought?"

Elven let out a long sigh. "Ain't that the truth. Keeping the doors open anywhere is hard enough for anyone in Dupray. But in a place like Dupray, sometimes not even God can help."

"So he made a deal with the devil," Madds remarked.

Elven lifted his eyebrows. There was no disagreement from him on that. But it wasn't what Elven focused on. Madds had said something that didn't add up from what she'd mentioned earlier.

"So you sat with Abnel then, right? The pastor? There was no volunteer like you said might have happened?" he asked.

"Oh, yeah, I did sit with Abnel," she said. "But then he left and, I mean, someone else may have been there. Not who I sat with, but seeing as how he left me sitting alone, I can't imagine someone else wasn't there. Maybe he came in after me and the guy got confused. I don't know honestly what time it was. Was it the same night of the shooting that I was there?"

"That's what the witness said," he said. Elven couldn't help but notice Madds was all over the place with her words. Like she was trying to come up with an answer she didn't have, but there would be no reason for her to try...right?

"Jeez. Two shootings and no sleep. I guess my brain is all scrambled," she said, shaking her head.

"You have definitely been through enough," Elven said with a reassuring smile. He felt a little bad grilling her like he was. He just hated the feeling of not having the whole story. "Sorry for the questions."

She shrugged. "All part of the job, right? Wish I could be more specific, but my memory is shot from all this. I'll be good as new once I sleep for a week."

Elven wasn't fully convinced that everything was connected as neatly as it looked to be, but he let it go. He knew there was no evidence, so no point in continuing to poke at everything. And she was right, she needed sleep and it was too much to ask her to remember everything. He was surprised she was even standing after the couple of days she had.

"What's gonna happen with Michaela?" Madds asked.

"She's free to go," he said. "Though not sure where she has to go. I'm pretty sure Spencer and Betsy were her last of kin. Why else would she have stayed with them?"

"Falling back to family is the easiest thing to do, no matter how awful they are," Madds said. "Maybe I can give her a lift somewhere."

"You sure you're okay to drive? You're running on empty," Elven said.

"Yeah, I'm sure."

"Alright then. I'm sure she'd like you helping out. You did good with that girl," Elven said. "Take a few days off. You've earned it."

"Thanks, Elven," she said, turning to the hallway.

"Oh, and Madds?" Elven asked.

"Yeah?"

"Take your car. It's parked out front. Also, for future reference, you can be sure if I want you to meet me somewhere, I don't mean take my Aston Martin," Elven said.

He winked at her as she left.

CHAPTER SIXTY-SIX

THE LIVING ROOM WAS WARM, BUT THE TONE OF THE ROOM WAS frigid as she spoke. Hollis sat in his chair, like it was another day in retirement. Nothing on his mind troubling him at all. Madds stood, staring him down, but this time, she wasn't afraid.

This time, she was fed up.

The television was running in the background and Madds switched off the soap opera that was on before Hollis could comment on it, as if he didn't give a shit what she was saying. Something about a man crying over the loss of his twin brother who had slept with his girlfriend. She didn't know the specifics. But she needed his full attention if she was going to do this right.

Hollis pulled his attention to Madds. He scrunched his face, but more out of curiosity than anger.

He sat upright, shoving the recliner footstool back into place, like he had something to say, but she didn't let him.

"That was way too close," Madds said. "If you and I are in on this, I need to know more. You understand? I need it all."

Hollis laughed, his throat raspy and his jowls bouncing. "I heard what happened to ol' Abnel at the church. Too bad, he had a good pipeline to those addicts. Was able to go under the radar pretty well, too. Until now, I mean."

"He was a mouth runner," Madds said. "You should have heard the shit he was spouting off about. Saying if you wouldn't get him out of the jam, then he knew enough to get himself out. That Elven would be salivating to know the info he had on you. He would have sold you out in a second if Elven got a hold of him."

Hollis reached for the glass next to the table. It was another iced tea first thing in the morning. She didn't think she'd ever seen Hollis drink coffee.

"I don't doubt it," Hollis said with a grin after taking a sip. His mustache clung to droplets of his beverage, which he wiped clean with his hand. "And if he were to do that, what would that mean?"

Madds pursed her lips, unhappy where the conversation was going. "I'd go down with the whole thing."

"That's right, darlin'. You saved us and yourself along with it. And I guess that means you chose your side," Hollis said. "The right side, I might add."

Hollis was right. But she already knew that. Hollis was a real asshole, but he didn't get as far as he did by not being right most of the time. "I guess so," she said. "Elven's not too happy. He was ready to pin it all on you."

"An elk farts in the woods and that boy wants to blame me," Hollis said.

"He wasn't wrong about this one, though," Madds said.

Hollis shrugged. "Only if the evidence says so."

"And does it?"

He grinned. "Is this that letting-you-in-on-things part? I made sure there were some specific bits of evidence found back at Abnel's office pointing away from me and straight to him."

"So you knew this is how it would end?" she asked.

Hollis shrugged. "You mean, did I think you'd pull the trigger and plant a gun on him? Hell, even I ain't that good. That one was all you. Very clever too, I might add. I just figured if he talked, there'd be no proof of it. You just made things that much easier. No reason to deny something when nobody's blaming you."

"So what now? Abnel is out of the picture, you gonna quit your drug business?" Madds asked.

Hollis chuckled again. "Maddie, we had a good thing with Abnel there. Ain't too often we find someone who can sneak under the radar like a man of the cloth willing to deal drugs to keep the doors open. So we'll probably go quiet for a while, let it seem like Elven got his guy, but sooner or later, we'll be back in business with someone else. And Elven will be none the wiser."

"How much?" Madds asked.

"What's that?" Hollis asked.

"How much did you make from this? Or save? From taking out the Caldwells' operation, I mean?" she asked.

Hollis considered for a moment, truly thinking it over. "Over a month's time, I'd say that was thirty grand we gained back. Ain't it funny? The poor people got no money for this or that, but come drug time, they'll find a way to get it and spend it."

Madds ignored Hollis's commentary. No, she did not find it funny. An addict had a problem, a disease. And Hollis was exploiting that. But if she was gonna be a part of his crimes, then she was going to get paid for it, too.

"I want half," she said.

He stopped laughing. "You done cost me a lot, taking out Abnel. And now you say you want half? Half of what? The money's gonna stop flowing in until we find someone else to distribute."

"I'd say it's fair. You'd have gone down. Maybe not easily, but Elven is a dog with a bone and you know it. If anyone told him you were in on something, he'd never let it go. Hell, I could pay a junkie off the street to point a finger to you right now and he'd start digging."

Hollis stood up, his bouncing jowls turned to stone. "Don't you go threatening—"

"Oh, shove it," Madds said. "I'm not threatening you. I'm just telling you how it is. That money is money you'd have lost to the revival or more if Elven had been in your business. Half is better than nothing. Be grateful I'm not asking for more."

He didn't move. It looked like he was deciding. She stood her ground, knowing she was right.

"Don't get too greedy on me," Hollis said. "But fair is fair and you did save me some anguish with that quick thinking. I'd say you earned it."

He limped over to the credenza across the room. He opened the cabinet and took out a small wooden box. When he opened it, she spotted a lot of green paper inside. Hollis pulled out two bundled stacks, one half the size of the other.

He held it out, the bills just calling out for her to take them. She reached, but he pulled his hand back.

"What about the girl?" Hollis asked. "The one loose end I can't have out there."

She smiled. "By now, I'd say I've proven whose side I'm on. Don't worry about her. I'll take care of it."

He held the bills out and she snatched them out of his hand before he could pull it back.

"Good. I know you will," Hollis said.

CHAPTER SIXTY-SEVEN

MICHAELA'S EYES WENT WIDE AS MADDS STOOD IN FRONT OF her. Madds knew it was for the best, but she still felt sorry for the girl. To have been through everything she had gone through up to that point, just to have to disappear this way.

There was no other way.

It was the only thing Madds could do to keep herself, and Hollis, safe.

Nobody was in sight except for what looked like a homeless man on a bench in the distance. He wouldn't be a problem. He looked half in the bag and it was still morning. He huddled up in a large coat, his back against the stone wall. His head was down, and his chest slowly rose and fell as he dreamt of better times.

Madds made sure nobody had seen her. She was confident that she had accomplished that. Nobody had followed her there.

The only person she'd spoke to since leaving Hollis's was the attendant. And he wasn't connected to this. He'd hardly even lifted his eyes when Madds had approached the kid. He was too busy not caring about his job.

Madds extended her hand toward Michaela, tears welling in her eyes.

"I'm sorry, Michaela. This is the only way," she said.

Madds grabbed Michaela's hand and pulled it forward. She shoved the wad of cash into the girl's hand. Michaela had her own set of tears running down her face, but it seemed like the girl understood.

Madds had only been to a bus station one other time in her life. And it was much larger than the one she stood at now. The bus station in Dupray was a very sad place, but Madds didn't expect anything less. Not from this place.

The attendant paid them no attention from her booth under the ramada. There were two small bathrooms, one for men and one for ladies, which were encased in a stone structure. The very wall that the homeless man in the brown coat was leaning against.

Other than that, it was just sidewalk and pavement. At least it wasn't a dirt walkway or a dirt road. That's the part that surprised her. That it wasn't shittier than it already was. It was funny how low her expectations had become.

Michaela looked at the stack of money that Madds had wrapped in a plastic grocery bag. It's all she had at the time, and she didn't think that handing Michaela fifteen thousand dollars out in the open was safe for the girl. Michaela pulled back the bag opening and dropped her jaw.

"It's fifteen thousand," Madds said. "It's all I could come up with. I wish it was more, but I don't—"

Michaela wrapped her arms around Madds. She felt the warmth of her body against her own. Her arms pulled tight against her neck and Madds wrapped her own arms around Michaela's waist. She could feel her tears drop against her collarbone and her warm breath against her ear.

"Thank you," Michaela said.

Madds squeezed her back and put her hand on the back of her head, holding on tight. She felt like she was saying goodbye to the sister she'd never had.

Michaela pulled back and Madds wiped the tears from Michaela's eyes. "It's gonna be okay, you hear me? Don't be sad."

Michaela smiled. "I'm not. I mean, I am to say goodbye. But nobody's ever done nothing like this for me. I don't know how I'll ever repay you."

Madds shook her head. "By getting out of here. Going to live your life. People here will hurt you, but if you're gone, they'll never know you're out there. Nobody will go looking."

"I know I can't stay. I wish you could come with me."

Madds smiled, and she wished she could go with the girl, too. But she was in too deep now. Whether she liked it or not, Dupray was her home. "I bought you a ticket to Philadelphia. After that, it's up to you," Madds said.

"I've always wanted to go to California," Michaela said, a twinkle in her eye. "Maybe I can take some graphic design classes."

"That sounds like a good plan. Nice place either way. I know you'll be okay," Madds said. "Don't let anyone give you any shit, you understand?"

Michaela nodded and looked back to the money. "I wasn't gonna tell no one, you know? I mean, about your secret. That man who killed my cousins. Whoever he is to you, I ain't saying anything."

Madds started to cry again. The girl really was like a sister to her. "It isn't my secret I'm trying to keep safe. It's you."

A large blue bus pulled up in the parking lot, the brakes letting out a whoosh of air. The door opened and the driver stepped down the stairs.

"Five minutes for boarding to Philadelphia," he shouted. He wore a small jacket that looked about a size too big for him. He walked hastily toward the bathrooms before disappearing inside the one marked with a male stick figure.

"You'd better get going," Madds said. "Just live a great life, okay? Don't come back to this place or anywhere near it."

Michaela nodded and wrapped her arms one last time around her. Madds buried her face in the girl's hair, smelling it one last time, trying to hang on to the feeling of someone appreciating her for doing something good.

Madds knew it would be the last time someone would feel that way about her.

Michaela broke the hug and walked to the bus. She didn't turn around again, which was better, Madds thought. She had nothing to keep her looking back anyway.

CHAPTER SIXTY-EIGHT

ELVEN WALKED BACK INTO HIS OFFICE, TAKING A HUGE BITE from the egg-and-cheese burrito he had picked up from Hank's diner. The long night and morning had left him with a very empty stomach. He didn't realize it until everything seemed to be put to bed. Just like he wished he could be. For someone not obsessed with sleep, it was all he could wish for right then.

As soon as he set foot in his office, he was met with a big grin slapped on Jesse Parsons's face. He sat on the edge of the desk, his leg dangling back and forth. The man had bags under his eyes that looked as big as his cheeks.

"Oh, c'mon," Elven said, his mouth half-full of breakfast burrito. He swallowed his bite, still holding half the foil-wrapped tortilla in his hand. "I'm gonna have to talk to Meredith about letting the riffraff into my office."

"Oh, I ain't that bad am I?" Jesse asked.

Elven nodded to the desk where Jesse sat. "Careful. This desk is old and I don't think it's ever been under such pressure before. The darn thing might just fold in on itself."

Jesse slid off the edge and plopped down in the cracked leather chair. Elven was surprised he didn't try to sit in his office chair.

"Well, Sheriff Pretty Boy, I'd say we didn't make a half-bad team on this thing," Jesse said.

Elven looked up at him in disbelief. "You and I practically beat the tar out of each other and kept running circles around this case having no idea where it began or ended."

"And we closed the case," Jesse added.

Elven couldn't help but laugh. "Alright. I suppose we did."

Jesse stood up and held his hand out to Elven. It caught Elven off guard, but he stood up and took Jesse's hand in his own, giving it a firm shake.

"If you need a Natural Resources Police Officer, give my office a ring and ask for me," Jesse said. "You ain't so bad to work with."

Elven nodded. "I guess I can do that, if they say they don't have anyone else available that is." He grinned back at the man. Elven still wasn't a big fan of Jesse, but Jesse wasn't worth wasting his time on. There was no proof of any crimes he had committed, even if Jesse had admitted to squeezing Spencer Caldwell for money. Mainly, he just wanted the man out of his county.

Jesse and Elven broke their handshake and Jesse reached down onto Elven's desk. He swooped up the burrito and took a giant bite from it.

"Damn, Sheriff. This is delicious. Thanks for the breakfast," Jesse said and walked out.

Elven threw his hands up. There was nothing else to do about it. As much as his stomach told him he was hungry, what he was about to do seemed to curb his appetite.

Elven glanced upward to make sure nobody was coming into the office, then looked down at the paperwork he had on his desk.

He didn't know exactly what he was looking for, but he knew something seemed off. The way Madds had acted when questioned about her being at the church. The idea of there being a different person there. Except she was there and confirmed she spoke to the pastor. Not some volunteer.

And then her racing down there to confront Abnel without him?

She might have been tired when he asked the questions, but she either met with the pastor that night or she didn't. Even if Michaela identified Abnel as the killer, it didn't seem right..

He wanted to ignore it, but the feeling that things weren't adding up, even when the evidence said otherwise, was strong.

Was he crazy?

He sure felt like it. But he couldn't get it out of his head.

Meredith had done a background check on Madds before she was interviewed for the job. And it came back clean, he knew it. But maybe there was more. Maybe she was hiding something else. Something that wouldn't show up on a criminal background check.

Elven picked up Madds's file and opened it up. He hesitated a moment, knowing he could be opening a door he didn't want to open.

He picked the phone up off the desk and dialed, letting it ring.

"Mesa PD," the man said on the other end.

"Hi, this is Sheriff Elven Hallie of Dupray County West Virginia. I was hoping to speak to someone about a previously employed officer," Elven said.

"The name of the officer?"

Elven hesitated, taking a deep breath.

"Maddison Cook," he finally said.

CHAPTER SIXTY-NINE

For the first time in her life, she felt free. There was no worry about what she would mess up and who would hit her or yell at her for whatever they deemed stupid. There was only the fear of the unknown, and it was more exciting than anything she'd ever experienced before.

The bus ride was quick, at least to her. She slept nearly the whole way, not having to worry about what she'd seen or who would be after her.

She was safe. Madds had made sure of it.

Michaela would be forever grateful to her, and she hoped that she could see her again some day. Even though it was unlikely, at the very least, she knew she'd never forget what she had done for her.

Michaela stepped off the bus when it came to a stop in Philadelphia. The station was much busier than the one in Dupray. So many people, rushing back and forth, going about their business that had nothing to do with Michaela.

She liked that she could get lost without anyone giving a second thought to her. She'd never been someone to be in the front of the pack, but she'd always been someone to draw attention. The wrong kind. The kind that was full of pity, that good people would see and feel sorry for her. People that weren't so good only saw someone to take advantage of.

But now, she was just another person. Someone that would be looked at and not given another thought.

As funny as it was, she found it intoxicating.

She was in charge of her own destiny now.

She gripped the grocery bag under her arm. She didn't have a purse to put it in, but she would easily fix that. There had to be a shop nearby where she could purchase something. It didn't even have to be stylish. Just something that could be hers.

She walked through the large building that had vaulted ceilings and made everything echo. The chatter and commotion was more amplified than ever because of it. She walked across the concrete floor to the other side where she saw the bathrooms.

Along the way, she bumped into a man in a suit who held a phone to his ear. She thought it was more that he bumped into her, but from her experience, she knew it was best to apologize first lest she be ridiculed in front of everyone.

As soon as she went to open her mouth, the man turned around, a startled look on his face. He had a bit of stubble on his face and his tie swung over his shoulder, like he'd been in a wind tunnel.

"I'm so sorry," he said, the phone still against his ear. "Are you okay?"

Michaela stopped. He asked if she was ok. She smiled and nodded, eyes wider than ever. "Y-yes," she managed to eke out. The man touched her elbow and smiled, turning away before she could say another word.

Strangers being kind. It was more than her family had ever done for her.

She turned back to the bathroom and entered the room. For the station being as busy as it was, there weren't a lot of people in the bathroom. It was the same concrete floor, two sinks and three stalls. It smelled clean enough, much better than the facilities she had used back at the revival. That was a given.

She headed for the stalls, finding that bottle of water she had drank on the bus finally catching up to her. The door opened to the bathroom and she looked to it, expecting to see another woman.

But it was a man.

"Oh, s-sorry," she said. Immediately, she realized she was in the wrong bathroom. Of course she was. Already out in the real world and she was messing up.

Except, when she looked around, she didn't see any urinals. What sort of men's bathroom had only stalls?

She looked at the man. He was large and seemed very familiar. Like someone she had seen before, but a younger version. She couldn't place where he was from, though. His hair was shaved close to his head, leaving only stubble. His shoulders were large and he was very tall.

"Am I in the wrong place?" she asked.

He grinned. "No, you're right where you're supposed to be," he said, then stomped toward her.

And then she knew that she wasn't in the wrong bathroom. Just the wrong place in general. She realized that he looked a lot like the man who had killed her family. A much younger and stronger version of him.

She felt her excitement of everything new turn to fear. She could smell the sweat coming off of him as his hands wrapped around her throat. She heard the world go quiet around her. She saw the light go dimmer and dimmer. She couldn't breathe anymore and knew that this was the end.

And the last memory, the last experience, that she could hold on to was the stranger smiling to her as he touched her elbow. At the very least, she experienced kindness before she died.

HOLLIS SAT IN HIS CHAIR, watching the television as he sipped on his iced tea. He didn't really give a shit what was on at the moment. He just wanted something to kill the time.

His phone rang, jostling on the table next to him.

"Yeah?" he said after lifting it to his ear.

"It's done," Corbin said on the other line.

"Nobody saw you?" Hollis asked.

"Of course not," he said. "She had all the money, too."

"Good. Make sure and leave a few bills behind on the floor. Make it look like a robbery. Something quick and messy," Hollis said.

"You sure? Don't you want the money?" Corbin asked.

Hollis smiled as he watched the television. Someone had found out their brother had died, only to come back to life. Soap operas were ridiculously entertaining sometimes.

"It ain't about the money," Hollis said. "It's about tying up loose ends."

"Got it," Corbin said, though Hollis wasn't sure he did understand. Corbin was his son, and he loved him as much as any father could, but he was also dimmer than a burned-out bulb in the garage. But he did as he was told and didn't question him.

"Make sure to keep your head down. If there are any video tapes, you need to make sure your face ain't on 'em," Hollis said.

"This ain't my first time, Daddy," Corbin said. "What's this mean for Madds?"

"She's with us, I know that much. But I guess we know where some lines are drawn for her. We'll just keep pushing her. Little by little. She'll cross them eventually," Hollis said. "Just get on back home now."

=GET BOOK 3 in the Sheriff Elven Hallie Mysteries NOW!=

AFTERWORD

Thanks so much for reading Murder in the Mountains, the second book in the Sheriff Elven Hallie Mysteries.

I remember when I started with this book, I wanted to play with the idea of a game warden and a silver-tongued preacher that wasn't quite on the up and up. I'd read an article shortly after about a church being allowed to set up in the national forest... and now, for the life of me, I can't find that article!

So this is the outcome of those little bits and pieces of ideas and information. I hope you enjoyed it!

As always, being an independent author, I don't have a huge publisher's budget, so reviews are very important. If you have the time, please consider popping over to Amazon, or your favorite place to leave reviews, and post one!

To keep up to date and get some fun freebies, join my reader's list: http://drewstricklandbooks.com/readers-list/
   -Drew Strickland
   March 16, 2021

HUNTED IN THE HOLLER

Get Hunted in the Holler, book 3 in the Sheriff Elven Mysteries now!

ALSO BY DREW STRICKLAND

Standalone Thrillers

Last Minute Guest

A Secret Worth Keeping

The Carolina McKay Series

Her Deadly Homecoming (Book 1)

Her Killer Confession (Book 2)

Her Deadly Double Life (Book 3)

Poaching Grounds (Book 4)

Winter's Obsession (Book 5)

The Nameless Graves (Book 6)

Bury Her Twice (Book 7)

The Sheriff Elven Hallie Mysteries

Buried in the Backwater (Book 1)

Murder in the Mountains (Book 2)

Hunted in the Holler (Book 3)

Abducted in Appalachia (Book 4)

Secrets in the Squalor (Book 5)

Vendetta in the Valley (Book 6)

Carnage in the County (Book 7)

The Cannibal Country Series

The Land Darkened (Book 1)

Flesh of the Sons (Book 2)

Valley of Dying Stars (Book 3)

The Soulless Wanderers Series

Tribulation (Book 0)

Soulless Wanderers (Book 1)

Patriarch (Book 2)

Exodus (Book 3)

Resurrection (Book 4)

Coming Soon! (Book 5)

ABOUT THE AUTHOR

Drew Strickland is the author of the Sheriff Elven Hallie Mystery series, Soulless Wanderers: a post-apocalyptic zombie thriller series, and the co-author of the Carolina McKay thriller series and the Cannibal Country series, both written with Tony Urban. When he isn't writing, he enjoys reading, watching horror movies and spending time with his wife and children.

www.drewstricklandbooks.com

Made in United States
Troutdale, OR
11/08/2024

24564995R00210